To Lois -
Thanks for taking
care of me and making
me laugh at physical -
I hope you like this
second book.
Tisha

M000106693

BLOOD WILL TELL

P.L. Doss

PRAISE FOR

ENOUGH ROPE

A JOPLIN/HALLORAN MYSTERY

Winner of the 2014 IPPY Bronze medal for mystery/suspense

"In Doss' debut thriller, a lawyer and a medical investigator both suspect that an accidental death is actually the work of a calculating, meticulous killer . . . As Halloran and Joplin each begin an investigation into the mysterious death, Doss' twisty, curvy plot dishes out the goods: scandalous secrets, including blackmail and extramarital affairs; another death or two that appear to be suicides; and a possible connection to a 20-year-old kidnapping case . . . A murder mystery that sneaks up, takes hold and refuses to let go."

– Kirkus Reviews

"An enthralling murder mystery . . . an exceptional debut that becomes more and more complex as the evidence builds and the tale unfolds . . . intrigues, family secrets, and red herrings aplenty to keep the pages turning . . . characters are wonderfully drawn . . . The author has masterfully woven together a well-crafted tale."

– OnlineBookClub.org

revealed. The characters are well developed, believable and engaging. I look forward to more from this author.

– VixenReindeer22, Amazon

Unexpected twists and turns. Great continuation from previous book. Don't have to read the previous book in order to follow the story line. Awesome characters. Everyone is so unique and brings a different aspect to solving the crime. Can't wait to read the next book to see what Joplin and Halloran get themselves into.

– Erinne Young, Amazon

This book is a worthy successor indeed to Enough Rope. It continues to unfold the relationships between the characters, making them even more real, particularly the friendly sparring between Joplin and Halloran. It was a page-turner from the get-go, drawing me in to Doss' fictional yet very specific Atlanta—as a native, I should know! And the ending truly took me by surprise, although on a second reading I saw all the bread crumbs she dropped to lead the reader on.

– subabysu, Amazon

A good example of a crime thriller, at nearly 500 pages, which lets you get right into the story and gain background information and understand more about the characters too. Leave yourself enough time to sit and read it, as it will take a while due to its length, but you won't want to stop reading.

– Cath, Goodreads

Absolutely engrossed me from page one to the end! The story line while was complex was written and tied together beautifully! The ending was a shock to me ... never saw that one coming at all! Love the characters. I must go and get the first book to get all caught up now!

– Bev, Goodreads

BLOOD WILL TELL

A JOPLIN/HALLORAN MYSTERY

———

P.L. Doss

Mayfair
Press

BLOOD WILL TELL
P. L. Doss

Published in the United States.

Cover design by John Martucci
Author photo by John Martucci
Book design by Morgana Gallaway

Edition ISBNs
Trade Paperback: 978-0-9890934-2-2
Digital: 978-0-9890934-3-9

TO MY PARENTS:

Roy J. Leite: 1922—1995

He introduced me to murder mysteries, logical thinking, and the art of making scrambled eggs. I still talk to him in my head, and he still answers me.

Dorie Leite Aul: 1926—forever.

She read to me from birth, inspired in me a love of humor and Manhattan, and continues to worry about me. I talk to her several times a week, and occasionally I get a word in edgewise.

"Blood will tell, but often it tells too much."

Don Marquis
Archy and Mehitabel

PROLOGUE

The drugs began to take effect. Her eyes, above the thick strip of duct tape over her mouth, crossed as she tried to focus, then the lids fluttered and sank abruptly. He stared down at her: She was a portrait of submission, her wrists and ankles bound tightly. He loved it. Loved it so much he longed for more time to spend with her. But sticking to the plan was of the utmost importance; there was still work to be done. And so he took a deep breath and concentrated on the next step. He smiled, knowing the long-awaited moment had finally arrived. Carefully, he undid the ropes that he'd used to subdue her and repositioned her body. Then, wild with anticipation, he grabbed the mallet and swung it high above his head. Over and over he struck, mesmerized by the gorgeous streams of scarlet that arced above them, spraying the ceiling and the wall and the bed in breathtaking patterns. It was even better than he'd imagined, the desire and fantasy at last becoming reality.

All in all, his best work ever.

He was suddenly tired, and his grip loosened on the mallet. It dropped heavily on the bed, sending another spray of red, a tiny one this time, onto the sheets.

CHAPTER ONE

Hollis Joplin got the call at 9:45 a.m., August 6th, 2012, just as he was leaving the scene of a vehicular death on Northside Drive. That was why he would arrive at the house on Blackland Road, which was less than a mile away, before the detectives even made it there. It was also why he would become involved in a case that would make him regret returning to the Milton County Medical Examiner's Office after only three months recuperating from a knife wound that had almost disemboweled him.

He didn't know that, of course, at the time. All he knew, when Sarah Petersen, the new chief investigator, called him was that a woman had been found dead in her bed by her housekeeper. A uniformed officer was at the scene, she told him, but knew no other details, not even the victim's name.

"Sorry to hit you with back-to-back scenes on your first day, but you're practically around the corner," she said.

"No problem," Joplin replied. "It beats contemplating the navel I don't have anymore."

"Good one, Hollis. I heard you were a funny guy. We need more of that around here," she added, in a tone that implied the contrary. "Come see me when you get in."

There was no need to answer, since Sarah Petersen had clicked off the line. Joplin sighed and pulled away from the curb as two EMTs loaded the body of the teenaged victim into their truck. The boy had been texting when he'd swerved to avoid an oncoming car and then plowed into a telephone pole. This, according to the police officer who had spoken to the driver of the other car and then found the boy's cell phone on the floor of the driver's side as he'd been checking for a pulse. The message on the screen said: *meet me at my locker after homeroom.* It had never been sent. Texting while driving had been illegal in Georgia since 2010, but that didn't seem to be a deterrent. Certainly not for teenagers. Only death—or a very close call—made a lasting impact.

The trip to the house at 445 Blackland Road took five minutes, not quite long enough to cool off his car in the August heat. It was a Tudor-style mansion set high on sloping, well-manicured grounds, a good distance from the iron gate that protected it. This was old Buckhead and old money, Joplin knew. An architect buff, he was certain this was a Neel Reid house, even though he didn't remember seeing it in the book he'd read about Reid by James Grady a few years ago. But Reid had designed several Tudor houses, as well as the East Lake Country Club House. Blackland Road was also on the upper end of what was known as Tuxedo Park, an enclave of mansions developed by Charles Black in the 1920s and built on multi-acre lots by some of Atlanta's wealthiest businessmen. Reid and his partners, Hal Hentz and Philip Schutze, had been the primary architects of the area, which included many of the most well-known residential streets in Atlanta.

Joplin turned into the driveway outside the gate. There was an APD car parked in the circular drive that fronted the house. "Officer Maynard," said a young male voice when he pushed the button on the intercom box to identify himself. A few seconds later the gate slowly opened.

The uniformed cop ushered Joplin into a wide, two-story entry hall with an enormous carved staircase. He looked even younger than his voice, his complexion pink, almost flushed-looking, and his hair neatly combed. A heavy-set woman with long black hair was sitting on a bench to the left of the door, her face in her hands, shoulders heaving. She looked up at Joplin, mascara running down her tear-streaked cheek, then covered her face again.

"Miss Esposito found the body," Maynard said.

"Miss Esposito," Joplin said, nodding deferentially. He turned to Maynard. "Where?"

The cop led Joplin upstairs to a long hallway covered by a very old Persian runner. He turned right, then paused in front of the last door on the left. After glancing quickly at Joplin and nervously licking his lips, he pushed the door open.

The sight that greeted them was one that Joplin had never seen in the four years he had been with the ME's office as a death investigator. Or even when he'd been a homicide detective with the APD. It was a vision straight from Hell, with colors to match. The body on the bed was propped up by two oversized pillows. Blood was spattered on the ceiling over the queen-sized bed and the wall and headboard behind it. It had also saturated the grayish-aqua sheet that concealed everything except her head. That, too, was drenched in blood, the blond hair caked with it.

"Jesus," he said.

"You got that right," said Maynard.

Joplin opened the black bag he always took to death scenes and got out disposable booties to cover his shoes before stepping into the room. Carefully, he skirted the tray, with its broken dishes and food, that he assumed the housekeeper had dropped when she walked through the door. Taking out his digital camera, he shot several preliminary photos for the detective squad. This was sure to be a homicide, and they'd want to see what the scene looked like before he'd begun to examine the body. Officially, he had legal jurisdiction over it until a preliminary cause and manner of death had been determined, but he was usually summoned well after the detectives had already had a chance to look things over.

"The housekeeper said she covered up the body like this," Maynard said. "Shit."

"Yeah, I know. But she said she couldn't let anyone see her like that. I thought it might destroy some evidence if I pulled it off."

"No, you did the right the right thing." Joplin moved over to the right side of the bed, slipping his camera back in the bag. He stared down at the body, momentarily overcome with pity. It was an emotion he rarely allowed himself to feel. He needed to stay as detached as possible to do his job effectively, as well as to keep himself from spiraling into one of his legendary Blue Funks. But this young woman had evidently suffered an agonizing death, a death even more unfair and undeserved than that of the teenage boy he'd examined just a short while ago. With a sigh, Joplin forced himself to focus on the task at hand. It was the only thing he could do for her now.

And then the dead woman began to moan.

CHAPTER TWO

"Christ almighty!" said Joplin. "Didn't you check for a pulse?"

"But she…she wasn't breathing!" Maynard stammered.

"Call an ambulance!" Joplin ordered as he felt for a pulse through the matted hair on the left side of her throat. It was faint and thready, but there nonetheless. Peeling back the sheet, Joplin made a visual search of her body, looking for the source of the blood which covered her. The woman's arms lay outstretched on the bed, as if in beseechment; her white cotton night-gown had been pushed up above her hips, and a pair of beige panties was entwined around her left ankle. He saw a bloody piece of duct tape on her right shoulder and what appeared to be ligature marks on her wrists and ankles, but could find no open wounds, which puzzled him. There didn't seem to be any on her scalp either.

"EMTs on the way," Maynard announced.

Joplin didn't bother to respond. "Help me turn her over," he said. "This blood had to come from somewhere."

Maynard scrambled over to the left side of the bed and grasped the woman's left upper arm as Joplin pushed against her back. There was very little blood on the posterior side of her body, only what had oozed down from her neck and hair. As they repositioned her on the bed, the woman's eyes opened halfway, then closed again.

"You're going to be fine," Joplin said. "An ambulance is on the way. You're safe now," he added as she struggled to open her eyes again. He remembered his own feeble attempts to regain consciousness after coming so close to death himself just a few months ago and searched for the right words to say to her. "Are you in any pain?"

The woman's eyes opened, but she seemed to have trouble focusing. "Who… are you?" she said haltingly, slurring the words.

"My name is Hollis Joplin." He paused, not wanting to scare her to death with his official title, then said, "Your housekeeper found you and called the police."

"The po…lice?" Her face scrunched in apparent bewilderment.

"Yes, ma'am. Can you tell me who did this to you?"

Now the woman's eyes opened a little wider, then sank again. She gave a long sigh.

"Did… wha to me?" she asked.

———

"It's pretty obvious she's been drugged," Joplin said to Ike Simmons as the EMTs skirted the remains of the breakfast tray, one holding up an IV bag, and rolled the victim out of the bedroom. "Probably Rohypnol, since she wasn't able to remember anything. And something that slowed respiration. The uniform should have checked her pulse, but I didn't see her chest move either."

"You think this mighta been a date rape gone real bad?" Simmons, the most senior detective in the Homicide Unit and Joplin's former partner, narrowed his eyes as he looked around the room. "Alfrieda dragged me to a Jackson Pollack show at the High Museum last year, and I'll be damned if this doesn't look like some of the paintings they had."

"Not a Pollack fan, huh?"

Simmons gave him a disgusted look and shook his head, then said, "And I'm not a fan of whoever did this, either. Sweet Jesus!"

"The crazy thing is that I couldn't find a mark on her, except for the rope burns on her wrists and ankles," said Joplin. "But her pulse was very weak, and the EMTs said her blood pressure was 70 over 53. That means she's lost a lot of blood. Not enough to kill her, but a lot, just the same. The house-keeper covered her up when she found her, but the blood on her chest had soaked through the sheet."

"That doesn't make any sense, Hollis."

Before Joplin could respond, Jan MacGregor and Lester Hollinger, two members of the Crime Scene Unit, appeared in the doorway. Simmons nodded, giving them permission to enter the bedroom. They were already wearing coveralls and protective covering on their shoes, but took care not to step on any of the broken crockery and set their photographic equipment down several feet away from the bed.

"Knox told us the victim survived," said Hollinger, referring to Ricky Knox, Simmons' current partner. He shook his head. "Sure is a lot of blood."

"Is Hernandez on his way?" Simmons asked.

Jimmy Hernandez was the bloodstain analyst with CSU and had a national reputation as a "miracle worker" when it came to deciphering the evidence left by blood.

"Naw, he's still tied up with that triple murder in Ellenwood. We'll take some high res photos, but he'll probably want to see this for himself."

"Listen," said Joplin. "There was a piece of duct tape on her right shoulder when I took the sheet off of her. I think it fell off when we turned her over. And when you photograph the sheets, be sure to tell Jimmy those transfer stains are from the victim."

"Will do."

"Thanks for the heads up," said Jan MacGregor as she pulled a video camera out of her bag. "We'll take it from here."

Joplin knew they would. B.J. Reardon, the director of the unit, had very high standards and made sure that everyone under him did, too. Certain there was no more for him to do there, he followed the tall, heavy-set Simmons out of the bedroom.

"Knox is checkin' out all the points of entry and exit," said Simmons as they headed for the stairs. "And I've called in more uniforms to canvas the neighborhood. But if the live-in housekeeper didn't hear or see anything, I don't know how much we'll get."

"Maybe the victim will be able to tell us something when the drugs wear off."

"We can always hope." They reached the entry hall and Simmons turned to look at him, folding his arms across his expansive belly. "You know who she is, don't you?"

"Somebody rich, is all I can tell at this point."

"The lady is Libba Ann Cates Woodridge. Recent widow of Arliss Woodridge, the very old, very wealthy CEO of Phoenix Airways."

"Damn!" Joplin shook his head. "I thought she looked familiar, but with all that blood…" A flurry of images flooded his mind, coming back to him in great detail. He had an eidetic memory, which allowed him to retain what he'd seen in three-dimensional forms. Sometimes he thought of this as a gift, because it helped him be the "eyes and ears" for the pathologists at the ME's office. At other times—when he was forced to re-experience embarrassing or painful things—Joplin felt it was some kind of punishment. Now he saw again all the newspaper and TV images of Libba Ann Woodridge that had been captured by the media since her husband's death.

Several of them included Tom Halloran.

"And guess who her attorney is," said Simmons, as if reading his thoughts.

"Well, at least he won't be dogging my investigation like he did with Elliot Carter," Joplin responded. Halloran was the chief litigator for the trust department at Healey and Caldwell, one of the most prestigious law firms in Atlanta. He had also been the one to find Carter's body hanging from a tree in Piedmont Park. His relentless insistence that his friend hadn't died accidentally as a result of autoerotic asphyxia had forced Joplin to go way outside the scope of his job, first as an attempt to pacify the attorney, but later to flush out a ruthless killer. It had also almost gotten him—and Halloran—killed. And although he'd gotten to know Tom and his wife, Maggie, pretty well during his recuperation, Joplin wouldn't be thrilled at the prospect of working on an investigation with the attorney looking over his shoulder again.

Simmons chuckled and shook his head. "No, the victim's still alive, thank the good Lord, so you're through here. Me, too. I've already called the Sex Crimes Unit. We'll turn over what we've gotten so far, but then it's their case. I'm sure they'll be wantin' to talk to you, though, Hollis. You take any pictures before you examined her?"

Joplin stared at him. "You have to ask me that, Ike?'

"Well, it bein' your first day back on the job, I thought maybe you were a little rusty. How you feelin', by the way? Last time Alfrieda and I stopped by your place, you looked kinda puny. And you don't look much better now. You sure you didn't come back too soon?"

"And miss all this?"

Simmons laughed again. "I hear Dr. Salinger is now a fulltime resident at the ME's office. She the reason you came back?"

Joplin picked up his case. "Let's just leave Carrie out of this, Ike," he said curtly as he headed for the door.

CHAPTER THREE

Carrie Salinger had visited Joplin several times during his month-long stay at Grady Hospital; he was even conscious during some of them. They had still, however, never discussed Jack Tyndall. She had tried to, just before he was finally released, but Joplin had changed the subject. And once he was home, he kept finding excuses not to let her drop by. At first, it was because he was still in pain and trying to deal with the colostomy bag that made his life so miserable. Was *still* making his life miserable, since his doctor hadn't removed it yet. That would involve yet another surgery, on top of the three he'd already had to keep what was left of his intestines in working order.

Not exactly the best time to find out if he still had a chance with her.

Joplin sighed as he left Blackland Road and crossed Roswell, trying to put thoughts of Carrie and any relationship they might have out of his mind. He needed to get through Buckhead before the lunch rush began. Tuxedo Park was smack-dab in the middle of Buckhead, and the ME's office was at the eastern boundary of Milton County. The county, which shared metropolitan Atlanta with Dekalb County to the east and Fulton County to the south, had been created in 2006, when a clever bit of political and socio-economic gerrymandering had resulted in Fulton County being divided into two separate, but unequal counties. Milton encompassed the affluent towns of Roswell, Alpharetta, and Sandy Springs, as well as Buckhead and Midtown, even more affluent areas, which had originally been slated to remain part of

Fulton County. But their moneyed homeowners and influential businesses had mutinied, threatening to sell up and leave in droves. South Fulton had eventually given in and was left with only downtown Atlanta, Hartsfield-Jackson International Airport, and some very affluent black neighborhoods as the only jewels in its tattered crown.

The traffic, however, belonged to everyone, rich and poor alike, in all five metro counties.

As Joplin made his way east on Piedmont, hoping to get through the intersection at Peachtree by noon, thoughts of Carrie crowded his mind again. When *was* a good time to find out if he still had a chance with her? he wondered. And how should he go about it? Jack was dead, but that didn't mean Carrie was over him. Hell, *he* wasn't over Jack's death. Might never be, under the circumstances. And even though she had chucked her lifelong plan to become a pediatric pathologist and accepted a residency at the ME's office, that didn't mean she was ready to jump into a relationship with him.

"Just talk to her," Maggie Halloran had said the week before when she stopped by his apartment to bring him dinner. The phone had rung while she was putting food in the refrigerator, and Joplin had muttered something stupid when Carrie had asked, yet again, if she could visit him. "She cares about you, Hollis. We were all at the hospital together several times, and she was a basket case until you were out of danger. Why won't you see her?"

Somehow, talking to Maggie was so much easier than talking to Carrie. Even in the few months that he'd known her, she'd become the sister Joplin had never had. He could tell her anything, and he did, starting with the few dates he'd had with Carrie, moving on to what he'd thought of as the beginning of a relationship, and then the terrible moment when he'd realized that she and Jack were sleeping together. As he turned left onto Cheshire Bridge, he was blindsided by the memory of Carrie as she'd stammered out an apology to him, conscious, he was sure, of the way her skin and eyes and the very way she stood in front of him, one hip leading, exuded the sex she'd had with his best friend. It had devastated him then and continued to devastate him as he saw again the flush of her cheeks and the way she'd seemed to stop herself from saying something to him. Frustrated, he rewound the memory, softening her stance and making her reach out and take his hand. But it didn't help. His ability to manipulate the three-dimensional memories his mind retained didn't change what had actually happened.

What was it that Carrie had wanted to say? Joplin asked himself as he drove past the Pink Pony and into the parking lot of the ME's office. Would it have made any difference to any of them if he had pressed her to tell him? And even if it wouldn't have, why hadn't he taken Maggie Halloran's advice and simply talked to Carrie a week ago? Why had he waited so long to deal with something that he had known he should confront?

Disgusted with his spectacular cowardice and ability to procrastinate, Joplin slammed out of his car and let himself into the side entrance of the ME's office. He walked past the pathologists' offices, careful not to glance at the one that no longer belonged to Jack Tyndall or wonder which one might be Carrie's. Rounding the corner that led to the Investigative Unit, he paused before knocking on Sarah Petersen's door and took a minute to clear his mind. He had spoken to his new boss several times during his convalescence, but this would be his first time actually meeting her, and he didn't want to screw things up.

"I had to hire someone quickly, Hollis," Lewis Minton had told him while he was still in the hospital. "A new broom, so to speak, to clean up the mess MacKenzie left. So I didn't even consider any of the investigators here. If you hadn't been so severely injured, I would have discounted seniority and made you chief in a heartbeat. And no one would have said a damn thing, I can assure you. But we didn't even know if you were going to live those first few weeks."

"Don't worry about it, Doc," Joplin had told him. "You did what you had to do, and I'm the last person who'd criticize that. I'm not sure I can even handle being an investigator any more, much less chief, when I get back on my feet."

"You're going to be fine, once you get out of here," Minton had replied, giving him a fatherly pat on the knee. "And I think you'll like Sarah, even though she was never in homicide. She was a death investigator in Boston for five years, then chief for another five. They hated to see her go, but she wanted a change of climate, and we're lucky to get her."

"I'm sure you're right," Joplin had said, without really meaning it. He had always liked the paramilitary model that required investigators to have spent seven years working homicide before applying to the ME's office. But MacKenzie's manipulation of that system had convinced Milton County's Chief ME that the culture of the Investigative Unit needed to be changed. Big time, if his choice of Sarah Petersen was any indication.

He'd heard from a few of the other investigators that she was in her office well before the morning shift change and often stayed late. They'd also said she spent the first few weeks after becoming chief observing all aspects of their jobs, asking questions, soliciting opinions, and jotting things down in an ever-present notebook. Then she'd met with them all as a group and announced that she'd be making a few changes, but wanted feedback before making anything permanent.

"She told us she runs a tight ship, but wants everyone to have an oar in the water," Deke Crawford had told him. "Whatever the hell that means. I guess it's a Boston-type saying, like the way she calls everything 'wicked.' 'Wicked hot,' 'wicked crazy.' She's got that accent, by the way. Like the Kennedys."

The voice that responded to his knock on the door did, indeed, have "that accent." And the person who went with it even looked a little like the pictures of the Kennedy women he'd seen over the years: The strong jawlines and angular cheek bones that Caroline Schlossberg and Maria Shriver possessed, as well as the athletic builds of Eunice and Pat. But Sarah Petersen was much taller than any Kennedy woman; she was at least five feet eleven, in what he saw were flat shoes, as she came from behind her desk and offered him her hand. She had a grip that went with everything else and almost made him wince.

"Hello, Hollis," she said, releasing his hand and motioning him to one of the two chairs facing her desk. "I hear our victim wasn't as dead as everyone thought."

"Not so much," he replied. "That's a good thing, of course, but the whole thing bothers me."

"How so?" she asked, planting one hip on the edge of her desk and clasping her hands together. He noticed that her nails were cut short, and that she wore no polish. She was also wearing very little make-up, if any. And yet, she was a very attractive woman in her mid-forties, with sandy, blunt-cut hair and blue eyes that hinted at what might be either a Scandinavian or Germanic heritage, given her last name. Viv Rodriquez had told him that Petersen was quite open about being a member of the Atlanta LBGT community, but was otherwise close-mouthed about her private life. No one in the office knew if she had a partner.

Which suited Joplin fine. Especially if it meant she wouldn't ask him anything about *his* private life.

"Someone went to a lot of trouble to make this lady look and seem dead. There was a lot of blood, but I couldn't find any wounds on her, and I'm pretty sure she was heavily drugged. It was almost like …" Joplin paused, not sure he should finish the sentence.

Petersen's eyebrows rose. "Like…?"

"Like the whole thing was staged," he said finally. "Kind of like a scene in a play, or a set on some television show."

His new boss nodded slowly, as if considering this. "Well, that's very interesting, and you might want to share that observation with the Sex Crimes Unit, but it's really not our case anymore."

"Right," said Joplin. "In fact, I think I'll go shoot them a quick report and the pictures I took before the scene got too messed up." He shrugged. "I mean, unless there's anything else."

"Just one more thing," Petersen said, sounding serious.

"Sure." Joplin had a moment's panic, wondering if she were going to bring up Jack or Carrie or his hot dog actions the night Jack was killed. He still found it hard to believe that he hadn't been fired over that.

"Just want to know how you're feeling," she said. "Physically, I mean," she added, as if concerned that she might sound too touchy-feely. "I've only got you working the day shift for the next month, but Dr. Minton wasn't sure you should even come back before they removed your colostomy bag."

Joplin exhaled, only then aware that he'd been holding his breath. "I'm fine. In fact, I'm really going to miss the old bag when it's gone. It's resolved a lot of my potty-training issues from early childhood."

"Wicked funny, Joplin," Sarah Petersen said, the faintest of smiles on her face.

Joplin gave her a small salute and headed out the door, running straight into Carrie Salinger.

CHAPTER FOUR

"Hollis."

Joplin stared at her, his mouth opening like a guppy. He had almost forgotten how beautiful she was with her long, black hair and wide cheekbones. Almost. He closed his mouth and swallowed, feeling simultaneously overwhelmed by his feelings on seeing her and the wonderful way she smelled. Unlike the other pathologists, she never smelled like formaldehyde, and he wondered how she managed that; he'd always thought it was part of the job. Was the perfume Carrie wore some kind of industrial-strength odor-eater? And was he some kind of idiot for thinking about that the first time he'd seen her in two months? What was wrong with him, for Christ's sake?

"Hey, Carrie," he said finally. Lamely.

"How are you? I mean…it's your first day back." She touched her hair nervously, then shoved her hands into the pockets of her white lab coat.

"I'm fine, really," Joplin said, hoping the fatigue he was beginning to feel after just a few hours on the job wasn't showing. He saw her search his face as if she didn't believe him.

"Are you sure?"

"If he's not, Dr. Salinger, then he just lied to me," Sarah Petersen called out. "And I'm sure he wouldn't do that."

"No, I would not, Chief."

"Good. Now go write that report for the Sex Crimes Unit."

"Right away." Relief flooded through him at the thought that he might escape, yet again, the dreaded conversation he knew he needed to have with Carrie. He wondered how much his new chief knew about the Elliot Carter case and all that went with it. Probably everything there was to know, if his first impression of her was accurate.

"How about lunch?" Carrie asked him. "I'll go get something, so you don't have to go out. Unless you've already eaten?"

"No," said Joplin, inwardly acknowledging defeat. "I mean, I haven't eaten yet."

"I wouldn't make it anything from Tacqueria del Sol just yet," said Sarah Petersen. "Certainly not a bean burrito."

———

Joplin was sitting in his cubicle when Viv Rodriquez returned from a scene. She looked about as stressed out as he felt after dealing with a young teen's vehicular death and the attack on Libba Ann Woodridge. She was a tall, slender woman with dark eyes and long hair that was pulled back into a high ponytail. She also smelled strongly of Eau de Decomposed Body, and he was sure that had something to do with her stress level.

"Caught a ripe one, huh?" he said sympathetically as she sat down at her desk.

"I was hoping you wouldn't notice," she said. "I'm going to type up my report and then head down to the showers," she added, referring to the locker room in the basement that was used by pathologists, investigators and morgue attendants when an especially fragrant body had to be dealt with. They all kept a change of clothes for just such occasions, which was appreciated by family members and significant others. "Unless you'd rather have me do that first."

"Nah, I can handle it," Joplin said. "Just type fast."

Viv grinned at him and said, "I'll try."

"This another one of those prostitute murders?" he asked, referring to a series of homicides that had finally been classified as the work of a serial murderer while he was still in the hospital. The problem had been that the killer hadn't stuck to a definable modus operandi, using a variety of ways to kill the women—strangulation, bludgeoning, knifing—as well as changing the types of sites where he either killed or dumped them. The first body, back in March, had been found under a bridge in Alpharetta by some teenagers; the second, in April, in an abandoned house on DeFoors Ferry. In June and July, two more bodies were found, respectively, in an old warehouse in Midtown and a boarded-up car wash on Piedmont that had gone out of business during the historic drought of 2007, a climatic event that had prompted Governor Sonny Perdue to schedule a prayer meeting at the capital to beg the Almighty for rain. Due to the identification found among the personal effects of the victims, which had been left near the bodies, law enforcement had been able to determine that all of them had records for solicitation and prostitution, among other things.

"Yeah. This one was found in the basement of a church off Windward Parkway. The congregation moved to a new building a few miles away a month ago, and the old one was scheduled to be razed today. The demolition crew found it when they checked to make sure no one was inside."

"Sounds like the killer didn't want the bodies to be discovered right away."

"That's just what the FBI profiler said when the fourth body was found, and everybody was pretty sure we had a serial murderer at work."

"Jesus, did you catch all the scenes, Viv?" Joplin asked.

"All except the third one in July. I was on vacation. The Chief thought it was important to have the same investigator on site when we suspected a serial, back in April."

"Yeah, I remember that one." He sighed in commiseration, then said, "Well, I'll let you get back to it, Viv."

She nodded and turned back to her computer, and Joplin did, too. He had just finished uploading a brief report and the pictures he'd taken at the house on Blackland Road to the Sex Crimes Unit when his office phone rang. "Hollis Joplin," he said, hoping he was being called out on a scene.

"Hollis, it's Tom Halloran," said a familiar voice. "I think you know why I'm calling."

"Not really, Tom, although it's good to hear from you. How's Maggie?"

"She's fine. She told me this morning that she's going to drop by your apartment later with some supplies. Since it's your first day back."

Joplin closed his eyes and took a deep breath. If one more person reminded him that it was his first day back at the ME's Office, he might run screaming down the hall. "She's been wonderful about that all summer, Tom, but it's really not necessary. I can drive now, you know."

"I know, but it makes her feel like she's doing something," Halloran replied. "Actually, though, I'm calling about my client, Libba Ann Woodridge."

"Still don't know why you're calling, Tom. Ms. Woodridge is very much alive, so it's not my case."

"But you were first on the scene this morning, Hollis, and the one who *realized* she was still alive, from what I've heard. I've talked to the EMTs who responded."

Joplin sighed. Halloran was going to be his usual hard-assed self. "And I wrote a report and sent pictures to the Sex Crimes Unit, Tom, so maybe you should talk to *them*. Although I'm not really sure why Ms. Woodridge needs the attorney who's handling her husband's estate to represent her, since she's a sex crime victim. What say we let the detectives handle this?"

"She wants to see you, Hollis. I'm here at Piedmont Hospital, which got in touch with me because I was listed as her contact person when she…when she was a patient here a few months back. She was able to talk to me a little while ago and remembers you. Quite frankly, talking to you this morning is about *all* she remembers. It's obvious she was drugged."

"I put that in my report, Counselor," Joplin replied, wondering what had put Libba Ann Woodridge in the hospital recently. He hadn't read or heard anything about that, but, then again, he'd been in the hospital himself around that time. "I also reported that I couldn't find any wounds that explained all the blood in her bedroom. Did I miss something?"

"Not any wounds, per se, but the ER doctor found bruising and a puncture site on Libba Ann's left arm and another on her left hand when they'd cleaned her up a little. He also determined that her blood volume was considerably below normal, so he ordered the blood still on her body to be tested, and guess what?"

"It matches your client's blood type."

"Type O, to be exact."

Joplin took a minute to process that information, then asked "Did they do a rape kit?"

"I had to talk Libba Ann into it, but she finally agreed. We won't know the results for a few days though."

"A few months or years, more likely," said Joplin. "Do you know how backed up the GBI is on rape kits?"

"I've heard. But I made it clear to the doctor and the detective from the Sex Crimes Unit, who showed up right after I got here, that it needed to be processed immediately. Along with DNA testing on the blood." Halloran paused, then said, "I can be pretty persuasive when necessary."

Joplin chuckled and shook his head. "Oh, I *know* you can, Counselor. My arm is still sore from all the twisting you put me through during the Carter case."

"Help me out on this, Hollis," said Halloran, sounding serious. "I know all the publicity on the Woodridge case has made my client look like a blood-sucking gold-digger, but she's actually a really decent young woman who's been thoroughly traumatized. Seeing and talking to you might help her remember something that could lead us to whoever did this to her."

"There's no 'us' in this, Counselor," Joplin insisted. "Don't even go there. I'll come see her, but I am not going to be involved at any level on this case. My job involves dead people, remember?"

"Understood. When can you get here?"

Joplin looked at his watch; it was 12:30 p.m. Carrie would be there any minute with lunch. He was tempted to use Halloran's request as an excuse to put off talking to her, but decided he'd better man up. "I can't make it for another hour."

"Come to the ER. If she's been assigned a room by then, they'll tell you where. And thanks, Hollis."

"Sure, Tom."

———

"I went to Hong Kong Harbour and got white rice with a little stir-fried chicken," said Carrie, setting the food down on the conference table. "Sticky white rice is supposed to be good for— "

"People who have colostomies," finished Joplin.

"Right," said Carrie, her face flushing. It was one of the endearing things about her. He hadn't known any females who blushed since high school. "I'll just fix a plate for you, okay?"

"That'll be great. Thank you, by the way. This was very nice of you."

"I wish you had let me do more. I mean, after you got out of the hospital," she added, getting paper plates and plastic utensils out of a bag. "I would have been happy to bring food to your apartment...or to cook for you, Hollis."

Joplin took a seat at the table. "I know. And I appreciate that, really. I just...wasn't ready to see you. To talk to you."

"Because of Jack." Carrie busied herself opening cartons and putting rice and chicken on the plates, giving him a little time to decide what to say.

"Yes. Because of Jack. And, Carrie," he said, looking directly into her dark brown eyes, "I still can't talk about him. Can you give me a little more time?"

"Of course." She put a plate in front of him, then sat down across from him. "You don't have to say anything, but *I* need to talk about him. Just a little bit, okay?"

"Okay. I guess."

She took a deep breath. "Whether you believe me or not, I want you to know that I would have broken things off with Jack. Or at least reconsidered the relationship. I was beginning to feel too… rushed by him. I mean, we barely knew each other, and he was talking about marriage."

"I believe you," said Joplin, remembering how Jack had looked as he talked about his plans for his life with Carrie the night he died. The look on his face was forever etched in Joplin's mind. Even if he made Jack change his expression, he'd always remember it.

"Good," said Carrie, tilting her head and staring at him. "Now eat something. Doctor's orders."

"Yes, ma'am," he replied, and dug into his sticky rice.

CHAPTER FIVE

Joplin had never really liked hospitals, even before he'd spent almost a month at Grady. He had too many memories of sitting at death beds or in waiting rooms while relatives or fellow cops were dying, and as soon as he entered the ER, a flood of images assaulted him: his mother's face relaxing as she took fewer and fewer breaths; his Uncle Don rising up off his pillow and grasping his arm before sagging back down; his first partner in Homicide on a gurney, an EMT pumping furiously on his chest as he was being wheeled into the ER. The only happy memory was of rushing into Crawford Long with a newborn baby that he'd found in a dumpster, when he'd been on the job a week. The baby had lived, and Joplin still kept in touch with him. But memories like that were few and far between, and even though Libba Ann Woodridge was alive and no one he knew had ever died in Piedmont Hospital, he wanted to make his visit there as short as possible.

The ER wasn't as large or as packed as the one at Grady Hospital, but it was just as depressing. Joplin bypassed the triage area and pushed through double doors in search of the nurses' station. He held up his badge as he approached it.

"I'm with the ME"s office," he said to the middle-aged nurse who looked up and frowned at him. "Libba Ann Woodridge's attorney asked me to meet with her. Is she still down here?"

The frown didn't disappear, but the nurse flipped through a few papers and said, "She's been moved to the third floor. Room 332."

"Thanks."

After wending his way through the ER, then passing the gift shop to the elevators, Joplin soon found himself at the door of 332. Ignoring the "No Visitors" sign, he knocked quietly.

"Hollis," said Tom Halloran, peering out at him. His six-foot-four frame filled the door as he swung it open. He knew the attorney liked to use his size, as well as his piercing blue eyes and arrogant demeanor, to intimidate people, but his face relaxed into a smile now. "Thanks for coming."

Joplin shook the hand Halloran offered and entered the dimly-lit room. Ushered to one of two chairs at the foot of the bed, he sat down, all the while staring at the narrow form of the most famous widow in Atlanta. Her long blond hair had been washed clean of all the blood, but was still wet, and she lay under at least three blankets. An IV dripped into her right arm.

"After they got her blood volume back up, they gave her something to mitigate the effects of the drugs in her system," Halloran said in a low voice as he sat down. "She's just sleeping right now."

Aside from his horrific encounter with her that morning, Joplin had seen only pictures and TV footage of Libba Ann Woodridge. He would never have been able to recognize her if he hadn't known who she was. The Libba Ann he'd seen before today had seemed larger than life, an almost Marilyn Monroe-like icon of beauty and sexuality. She'd always been photographed wearing extremely high heels, and her well-endowed curves and big hair had contributed to the overall impression of a tall, substantial woman. He knew she'd been a model after becoming Miss Georgia in 2008, and he'd always thought models had to be pretty tall, but the figure on the bed couldn't be more than five-foot-seven. That wasn't short, of course, but Heidi Klum would have towered over her. Without make-up, he decided,

Libba Ann also looked far younger than her reported age of twenty-seven and far less...beautiful? Or maybe just less glamorous?

Joplin cut off that line of thinking. What was he expecting of a woman who'd been through a terrible ordeal and, by rights, shouldn't even be alive? He turned to Halloran and said, "You told me she remembered me. My name? My face?"

"Both. I told her that Rosa—her housekeeper—thought she was dead, and so did the police officer who came to the house, but the investigator from the ME's office had realized she was still alive. And she closed her eyes for a minute, then said, 'Hollis Joplin.' She even remembered that you have blond hair and green eyes."

"The Rohypnol—or whatever she'd been doped with—must have worn off by then, if she could remember all that. Or maybe it was my good looks and charm."

"Definitely the charm," said Halloran dryly. "Anyway, I told her that I knew you, and she insisted on talking to you."

As if on cue, the woman in the hospital bed said, "Tom," her voice just above a hoarse whisper. They both got up and hurried over to her.

"Libba," Halloran said, putting his hand over hers. "This is my friend, Hollis Joplin."

Libba Ann Woodridge stared up at him. "Thank you," she said. "You told me I was...safe. I haven't felt safe in a long time."

"Has someone threatened you?" asked Joplin. "Or harassed you?"

She closed her eyes. "Not really. I just feel people...watching me. The TV cameras are everywhere. And there have been hang-up calls, even though I have an unlisted number."

"Have you been able to remember anything that happened to you last night or early this morning?"

"Just...going to bed last night."

"What time was that?" Halloran asked her

"About ten."

"Did you take anything to help you sleep?" asked Joplin.

"Yes. Half an Ambien. I try not to take any more than that at night, but that's the only thing that helps me sleep since…since Ar—my husband—died."

"I understand," said Joplin. "You've had a big loss."

Libba Ann Woodridge's eyes filled with tears. Joplin found himself almost believing that this beautiful young woman had actually loved the seventy-eight-year-old man she'd married—and not just for his money. Or maybe she was as good at acting as she had been at modeling.

"I think you do understand," she said.

Joplin cleared his throat. "Have you had any workmen in the house recently? New landscape people, maybe?"

She shook her head. "Ar hired the landscape company when we moved into the house on Blackland. Atlanta LawnCare. It's owned by a very nice man named Joseph Feeney. I've only met him once, when he came to the house to give us an estimate. He's a disabled vet, and his wife has lupus, so Jorge, his foreman, pretty much runs the business, and he's had the same crew since we hired the company."

"How long has Rosa worked for you? For the family, I mean."

"About ten years, I think. Ar hired her when Eleanor—his first wife—was so sick."

"Has anyone called you about your security system or been out to the house to fix anything to do with it?"

Libba Ann's brow wrinkled. "No, not that I can remember. I could ask Rosa, though. Is that important?"

"It could be. The police are trying to figure out how the person who did this to you got into the house. But you're safe now, just like I said. And you need to get some rest." He turned to Halloran and said, "I think we should go now and let Mrs. Woodridge sleep."

"Right," said Halloran. He patted Libba Ann's hand again. "I'll call you later today. And you know how to reach me, right?"

"Of course. Thank you, Tom. I appreciate everything you're doing." Her eyes cut to Joplin. "And thank you for coming to see me. And for…this morning."

"You're welcome. Just get better."

Joplin waited until they were both in the corridor and the door was closed, then said, "I think you should spring for an off-duty police officer to guard your client, Counselor."

"I have someone on the way," Halloran assured him. "And I won't leave until he gets here. What's your take on all this?"

"I think somebody went to a lot of trouble to make it look like Mrs. Woodridge had been murdered. Including taking her own blood to throw around the crime scene. I have no idea why, but I wouldn't assume that she's out of danger, Tom."

Halloran nodded. "I think you're right. And the key question is: Why?"

Joplin held out his hand. "I'm sure the Sex Crimes Unit will be looking into that."

"You can bet on it," said Halloran, grasping Joplin's hand.

———

The first thing Halloran did, as he waited for Ed Jenkins, a former GBI agent he used as an investigator and to provide security when necessary, was to place a call to the head of the SCU.

"Captain Mary Martucci speaking."

"This is Tom Halloran, Captain Martucci. I'm the attorney for Libba Ann Woodridge."

"What can I do for you, Mr. Halloran?"

The voice was calm and authoritative. Halloran weighed his possible approaches, then said, "Nothing for me, Captain. But my client needs your help. Someone attacked her in her own home, bound her wrists and ankles, drugged her, and drained a significant amount of blood from her. Then he splashed the blood all over her to make it look like she'd been murdered."

"I've gotten initial reports from Hollis Joplin and the EMTs who responded, Counselor, and it does seem highly probable that the blood on the victim and at the crime scene belonged to her, but we don't know that to be a fact yet."

"But I'm sure that will be your working hypothesis, right?"

"Absolutely. I've got my best people pursuing that angle as we speak."

"I'm relieved to hear that. Really. And I know my client will be, too. Tell me," he continued, deciding to be collegial, "have you ever run across anything like this before, Captain?"

"Never," said Martucci. "But that doesn't mean some other law enforcement agency hasn't. And I mean to find out, if so."

"I feel better already, Captain."

"Anything else we can do for you...or your client?"

"I'd like to go see the crime scene myself sometime this afternoon—Mrs. Woodridge has authorized me to do that. I don't want to interfere with your technicians, but if you could give me an idea of when they might be finished, I'd appreciate it."

"CSU has almost finished processing the scene, Mr. Halloran, but when they do, the bedroom will be sealed to preserve it. That's standard operating procedure."

"I know that. But it's still in the victim's house, and she has legal access to it. You can have a detective or someone from CSU meet me there and make sure I don't compromise the scene."

There was a long pause, and then Captain Martucci said, "I'll see what I can do. Where can I reach you?"

Halloran gave her his office and cell phone numbers and then thanked her for her help.

"You're welcome," she replied, then clicked off.

CHAPTER SIX

Halloran briefed Ed Jenkins, then looked in on Libba Ann. She was sleeping again, so he quietly closed the door and headed for the elevators. He had already called Libba's mother, who lived in Brunswick; she would be there the next morning. The only other "family" his client had were the relatives by blood and marriage that Arliss Woodridge had wanted to cut out of his will shortly after he'd married Libba.

"Except for Julie," Arliss had told him, referring to his only granddaughter, "they're all a bunch of bloodsuckers and ingrates. I've given them a lot of money over the years, and they're just waiting until I die so they can get more. I want Julie's trust to remain in place, but the others get nothing."

"I'll do whatever you want, Arliss, but it would help in the long run if you left them each a nominal sum. They'd have a harder time contesting the will that way."

"Fine. Ten thousand a piece, then. No more."

"How about Emory?" Halloran had asked him. "And Grady Hospital? Any changes to those trusts?"

"Not with regard to the amount designated, but I want Libba named as trustee for all of them. Habitat for Humanity and the Carter Center, too, as well as Julie's trust."

"Have you talked to her about that, Arliss? That's a big job."

"Yes, and at first she wanted no part of it. But I told her I wasn't ready to die yet, and that I'd teach her what she needed to know to handle things. She's a lot smarter than anyone gives her credit for, Tom. Most people seem to forget that before she became Miss Georgia, she graduated from UGA. And, frankly, I don't trust anyone else."

Unfortunately, for him—and Libba Ann, too, in Halloran's mind—Arliss hadn't lived long enough to fulfill that intention. He'd died of a massive heart attack just two months after that meeting. According to Libba, he'd come home from a business dinner, gone into their bedroom where she was reading in bed and stared at her before clutching his chest and falling to the floor. She'd screamed for Rosa to call 911 and started CPR, but by the time the paramedics arrived, he was dead. Since Arliss hadn't been under a doctor's care for heart disease, an autopsy had been performed, but the damage to his heart was clearly visible.

As expected, when Halloran probated the will, the Woodridge heirs had wasted no time in tarring and feathering Libba Ann, painting a picture of her in the media as a gold-digging, unprincipled, low-life hussy who had bewitched their revered father and brother into marrying her and then taking advantage of his "dementia" to manipulate him into changing his will.

Libba Ann, herself, had contributed to the problem by talking to various members of the media in a naive attempt to stem the tide of contempt hurled at her. He'd stopped that, of course, but not before a lot more damage had been done. And, of course, all the footage that could be found of his client, when she became Miss Georgia and was modelling and dating actors with bad reputations, had been paraded before the public. It had been a circus, and although Halloran was an expert at lion-taming, it had been draining for both of them, he admitted to himself as he drove south on Peachtree to his office in the 290 Building.

Halloran's phone rang as he reached the light at West Peachtree.

"It's Joan," his secretary said when he pressed the phone icon on his steering wheel. "I'm sorry to bother you, but Wesley Benning is on the line and insists on talking to you."

Benning was Julie's father and the husband of Arliss Woodridge's daughter, Claudia Woodridge Benning; she always included the "Woodridge" whenever she said her name.

"Shit," said Halloran.

"I think it's already hit the fan," Joan responded. "If you ask me, I don't think he's happy that poor Libba is still alive."

"I'm sure you're right." Halloran grimaced. "Go ahead and put him through, Joan. I'm on my way back to the office. ETA is fifteen minutes."

"Hold for Mr. Benning."

"Wesley, what can I do for you?"

"You can tell me if this latest thing with your client is another one of her stunts," Benning spat at him.

Halloran closed his eyes and took a deep, cleansing breath. "Mrs. Woodridge was viciously attacked, Wesley. I'd hardly classify that as a 'stunt.'"

"It is if the whole thing was made up—just a ploy to get people feeling sorry for her. And please don't call that woman 'Mrs. Woodridge.'"

"That's her legal title, Mr. Benning. Or should I call you by your unofficial title of 'Mr. Woodridge,' since your wife controls the purse strings?" Halloran had been waiting until the trial to make insinuations like that, but he decided it wouldn't hurt to give Wesley Benning a taste of what would happen if he and the rest of Arliss Woodridge's loving family—Claudia Benning and Arliss' widowed sisters, Amelia and Doris—persisted with their plans to vacate the will. Only Chandler Woodridge, Arliss' son, had refused to join the lawsuit, but that was probably because he was still in a residential drug program at Ridgeview following his well-publicized relapse after his father's death.

"You son of a bitch! How dare you say that to me?"

"How did you know about what happened to Libba Ann?" Halloran asked, ignoring Benning's pejorative. "Did you have anything to do with it?"

There was shocked—or so he thought— silence on the line, and then it went dead. Just as well, thought Halloran, as he stopped for a red light at Martin Luther King Avenue. He wished he'd held back until Benning had told him how he knew about Libba, but maybe he'd hit a nerve.

And maybe Wesley Benning would think twice before calling him again.

————

"Mr. Healey asked me to let him know when you got in," said Joan, her heavily-plucked eyebrows arched. "And Mr. Landers called," she added, referring to Carson Landers, the former trustee for the Emory University trust Arliss had set up. Like Wesley Benning, he'd made it a point to call Halloran regularly since the will had been probated.

"Does David know about Libba Woodridge?"

"Seems to. He looked all doom and gloom," she added. "It's been on Channel Two's 'Breaking News' segments. They had cameras in front of the house on Blackland and outside the hospital. I gather a neighbor called it in after seeing the police car and the EMT van."

Halloran frowned. "Give me a few minutes and then let him know I'm here. I'll call Landers back when I get a chance. Oh, and Joan," he added, "that reminds me. Please block out some time for me this afternoon. I want to go to the Woodridge house myself and view the crime scene. Captain Martucci with the Sex Crimes Unit is supposed to let me know when. Just reschedule any appointments after two, okay?"

"I will."

David Healey was the firm's managing partner, and, as such, would be very interested in this turn of events in such a major case. Given the fact that Halloran had suspected—and also accused—Healey of killing Anne and Elliot Carter just before the actual murderer was caught, however, he was sure the man would lose no opportunity to ride him whenever possible. The outcome of the Carter case had resulted in extremely good publicity for Healey and Caldwell—and for Halloran especially. But David had brushed that aside, choosing to focus on the lurid aspects of the case.

Halloran couldn't really blame him. Elliot Carter's name and reputation had been salvaged, but it would be a long time before anyone who read the *Atlanta Journal/Constitution* or watched local TV news would forget that he'd been found dressed in women's clothes and hanging from a tree in Piedmont Park. In fact, it was the only thing that had eclipsed the Libba Ann Woodridge case at the time. Arliss Woodridge had only been dead a month when Elliot's body was found, but for a while at least, she wasn't in—or on—the news every day. The coverage on Libba had re-intensified, however, once all the ink and words spent on the scandal that followed the unmasking of Elliot's killer was used up. She had become a prisoner in her own home, subjected to vicious attacks on her background, her age, her clothes, her lifestyle, and, especially, her reasons for marrying her 78-year-old husband.

And then there was her mother.

Connie Sue Cates could have passed for a somewhat slimmer, less redneck relative of Honey Boo Boo's mother, June. Libba had seemed embarrassed by her, and Arliss had only barely put up with her the few times Halloran had seen them all together. He had urged his client to keep her out of the media's glare, if at all possible, and Arliss had tried, packing Connie Sue off to spas and sending her on an American Express tour to Italy. It didn't work. The woman was outrageous wherever she went, basking in the limelight of her daughter's marriage and thinking she was "helping" her by releasing highly personal information whenever a microphone was held to her mouth.

"Libba Ann could've had any man she wanted," she insisted when the furor over the impending marriage had first erupted. "Why, did you know that she dated Justin Timberlake? She could've had him, too, but she couldn't make up her mind, and he got back with an old girlfriend. And Charlie Sheen was after her a few years ago. Lord, that man wanted her in the worst way! My daughter didn't need to marry Arliss Woodridge. She had prospects!"

Halloran's memories of Connie Sue Cates were cut off when the door suddenly opened, and David Healey walked in, followed closely by Joan. She mouthed the word "sorry" and backed out of the office.

"What in the world is going on with your client now, Tom?"

"Which one do you mean, David? I have several clients."

"You know I'm talking about Libba Ann Woodridge. It's been all over the news."

"I don't know what's been on the news, David, but Mrs. Woodridge was the victim of a particularly vicious attack in her home. She's lucky to be alive."

Uninvited, David Healey took a seat in one of the two chairs in front of Halloran's desk and unbuttoned the jacket of his tan Armani suit. His gray-templed hair and patrician features evoked a gravitas that was wholly unfounded. "Well, I'm certainly sorry to hear that," he said, making an effort to sound empathetic. "But you have to admit there's been a lot of bad publicity surrounding this case."

Halloran stared at him. "None of which is Mrs. Woodridge's fault."

A slight smile, tinged with disbelief, was Healey's response. Flicking an imaginary piece of lint from the right knee of his trousers, he said, "I guess what I'm trying to say is that this case has consumed an inordinate amount of your time in the past few months, Tom."

"Resulting in a lot of billable hours for the firm, David."

"Yes, of course, but to the detriment of other cases, perhaps. Other clients. There've been some complaints."

"I highly doubt that. Unless they were solicited by you."

Healey's mouth tightened, and he stood up. "You might be surprised to know that Alston agrees with me," he said, referring to Alston Caldwell, the only living name partner of the firm.

"I'd be *very* surprised, David. Arliss Woodridge was a long-time client and one of Alston's oldest friends. He asked me to restructure the Woodridge will and trusts as a personal favor to him."

"Yes, but he also thought Arliss would live a little longer than he did." Healey smiled again, then turned and headed for the door. "You know, so his child bride wouldn't seem quite so young," he added, never looking back.

The door slammed behind him.

CHAPTER SEVEN

Jimmy Hernandez stared at the wall in front of him, which was covered with pictures of the crime scene.

When he had seen the ones taken by Hollis Joplin showing the victim covered by a sheet and then the video taken by Jan, he'd been struck by the almost artistic quality of the images that had been captured. The pattern of stains on the wall behind the bed was especially…unreal; he had never seen anything like it. Next, Hernandez had examined the high-resolution photos taken by both Jan and Lester that morning. They had chosen thirty-two stains, drawn plumb lines through them and placed reference scales next to them, then documented their XYZ positions—just as he had trained them. But he could tell, by then, that something was wrong. He'd plugged the digital camera into his computer and entered them into his BackTrack/Images program anyway and, because there were several stains on the ceiling in addition to the wall behind the bed and the bed itself, he'd also applied the Images data to the BackTrack/Win program to obtain a top and side view. Both systems generated virtual strings, which replaced the plastic strings used by bloodstain analysts in the past and made the process of determining the area of convergence and the origin of the bloodstains much faster. Hernandez had originally trained using real strings, as well as tangent trigonometry, to try to reconstruct a crime scene and determine the source of bloodstains and the positions of both victim and perpetrator, but the computer programs cut out a lot of tedious work.

But what they were showing him was…impossible. Or, at the very least, completely bizarre.

Hernandez knew that the victim was alive and didn't seem to have suffered any injuries. He also knew that she'd lost a lot of blood, and that the blood found on her matched her blood type. The DNA of samples taken from her, as well as at the crime scene, hadn't been determined yet, but the working thesis was that it would prove to be hers. Then how, he wondered, did all that blood get spattered everywhere? The photos he was looking at now, on the wall in his office, had captured the gamut of bloodstain patterns: passive stains, impact stains, cast-off stains, transfer stains—almost everything, in fact, but arterial spray. He could also see void patterns on the sheets and pillows and on the headboard where the victim's body had lain, and where the perpetrator had positioned himself. Something he had never seen, however, if the BackTrack analysis was accurate, was that the area of convergence and the origin changed several times.

But not at the same time.

Hernandez was puzzled, but intrigued, as well. He'd had to finish up a report on an earlier case that morning and hadn't been able to get to the crime scene yet. With all he had going on this week, he had even thought he might not need to go there; Jan and Lester were that good at their jobs. But now he needed to see it for himself.

Either the cyber programs were somehow wrong, or something he'd never seen before had happened at 445 Blackland Road.

———

"Carson Landers," said the voice on the other end of the line. It was a quiet, soothing voice, meant to make potential donors to the various departments at Emory University feel relaxed. And special.

That, more than anything.

Before taking on the restructuring of Arliss Woodridge's will and trusts, Halloran had always enjoyed his meetings and conversations with Carson Landers. Unlike Wesley Benning, who was also an attorney, Landers seemed always to look for areas on which he and the person with whom he was dealing could agree. He was a master at the art of negotiation, in Halloran's opinion, and that was fast becoming a lost art. They knew each other socially, as well, both being members of the Driving Club. Landers had been one of the few people to call him during the terrible time after Elliot Carter's body had been found in Piedmont Park and offer his support. And yet, there had been a subtle, but tangible change in their relationship when Halloran had probated Arliss Woodridge's new will. It was almost as if Landers had blamed him for the sweeping changes Arliss had made. As if he'd thought that Halloran had initiated them and influenced his client. That was nonsense, of course, and although he was sure Landers wasn't happy that he was no longer the trustee for the endowment that Arliss had made to Emory, the man had had plenty of experience dealing with wealthy donors and their idiosyncrasies.

"It's Tom Halloran, Carson. Joan said you called earlier."

"Thanks for calling, Tom. I heard about what happened to Mrs. Woodridge and just wanted to express my concern. Is she okay?"

"About as well as can be expected, under the circumstances," Halloran replied. "I can't really go into details, but I'm concerned for her safety."

"I don't blame you. What was reported wasn't much, but it sounded pretty bad. Have you hired security?"

"First thing."

"Good," said Landers. There was silence for a few seconds, and then he said, "I wasn't thrilled when I found out she was replacing me as trustee, Tom, but I want you to know that I wish her well, and I'm so sorry this has happened to her."

"I appreciate that, and I'll tell her."

"Good. Anything I can do?"

"Not at the moment, but thanks for offering."

"Anytime. I mean that."

"I think you do. Thanks, Carson."

"See you at the Club soon, I hope."

"Me, too," said Halloran, clicking off.

Not very likely, though, he thought, staring at the phone. He wasn't really aware of the impact the economy's downturn had had on Emory, but the effects on law firms like Healey and Caldwell were still debilitating. Things were beginning to show an upturn, but the firm's clients had all taken a beating in the stock market—and in the market place as well. Many companies had gone under; most had downsized both their work force and their budgets. Legal retainers were among the first to be affected. He and all the firm's partners were still scrambling to retain clients and find new ones. They'd also—reluctantly—been forced to let a number of young attorneys hired before the recession go.

The domino effect had been felt by everyone in Atlanta, slamming construction, real estate sales, shopping malls, retail businesses, tourism, restaurants, and airlines, of course, like Phoenix. Although considerable, by any measuring stick, Arliss Woodridge's personal fortune had suffered, too, especially with regard to the value of his company's share holdings. Even though the economy was slowly recovering, and Phoenix, like all the other airlines, had recouped losses by charging baggage fees, downsizing passenger space, and cutting back on any amenities, there hadn't been enough time for Arliss to recover his former place among the Forbes 500 company list.

The phone rang, startling Halloran out of his reverie.

"Claudia Woodridge Benning for you," said Joan, with emphasis on the

"Woodridge."

Halloran gritted his teeth. He was about to be punished for his conversation with Wesley Benning. Not for the first time, he wondered how two people like Wesley and Claudia Benning could be the parents of someone like Julie.

"Hello, Claudia."

"Tom," she said, drawing his one-syllable name out until it seemed to make three. "I'm going to have to get after you—you know that. You were very ugly to Wesley."

Halloran closed his eyes. He'd experienced Claudia's "iron fist in a velvet glove" treatment before. He almost preferred her husband's full-on siege.

"I'm sorry you think that, Claudia, but he said some pretty 'ugly' things about my client." "Ugly," he'd learned long ago, was Southern for "mean" or "rude."

"Well," she replied, drawing that word out, too. "We're all getting a little tired of the publicity your…client…has brought upon the family. If you know what I mean."

"I do know what you mean, Claudia, but I assure you she didn't bring this on herself—or you, for that matter. She was the victim of a violent crime."

There was a long pause, and then she said, "Do you really believe that, Tom? I mean, *really*? Think of who she is. *What* she is."

Halloran tried to keep his anger in check this time. "She's a human being, Claudia. And whatever you think of her, she was your father's legal wife."

"As far as I'm concerned, my father's only 'legal wife,' as you put it, was my mother. And I'm fully confident that the court will see it that way, too."

"Your father wasn't coerced into marrying Libba," Halloran said, "nor was he coerced into changing his will. I've told you and all the rest of the family that there's plenty of documentation to withstand any challenge to the will on that basis."

"That's not the only basis for a challenge, Tom, and you know it," she replied coolly.

"The same goes for a challenge of his sanity at the time, Claudia. You'd be well-advised not to go forward with this lawsuit."

"But you're not my lawyer, so you're not in a position to advise me. I guess we'll just have to agree to disagree on this matter. Don't say I didn't warn you," she added, with a low, throaty laugh.

Before he could reply, the line went dead. Halloran replaced the phone in its cradle and stared at it. He had no idea what Claudia Benning thought she had that could possibly affect the outcome of the lawsuit that had been initiated, but her tone and manner seemed to suggest that he should be on his guard.

He picked up the phone again and tapped in his secretary's extension. "Bring me the Woodridge file, please, Joan," he said when she answered.

———

The rest of Joplin's day was, thankfully, relatively unexciting. He was called to one more scene, a drowning at the Chattahoochee River near Sandy Springs, but still had time to finish all his reports. He'd also spent a little time with Lewis Minton, who was anxious to make sure that he hadn't come back to work too soon.

"You're one to talk, Doc," he'd told the older man. "You kept sneaking back here while you were supposed to be recuperating from open-heart surgery. Not a real good example for me."

Minton had chuckled, shaking his head. "You got me there, Hollis. Just don't overdo it, okay? I've asked Sarah to put you on days-only for a while."

"She did just that. And I've decided not to start back to school till the fall quarter." Joplin was almost through the course work for a master's degree in criminal justice at Georgia State. It could wait, at least for a few more months.

"That's fine, son. Fine. You'll be back on track in no time."

Lewis had been like a second father to him, not only since he'd been at the ME's Office, but long before that, during his years in the Homicide Unit, when he'd spent many hours observing autopsies on his cases. Joplin's own father was long dead, a casualty of Vietnam, although it took him five years to drink himself to death after he returned home. He admired and respected the pathologist more than any man he knew, except maybe Ike Simmons.

"I hope so," Joplin said now. "Thanks for believing in me, Doc."

"Couldn't do otherwise, Hollis. Now, go home, before I call Security."

———

Joplin lived in Buckhead, but his apartment building—due to be sold to developers as soon as the economy got a little better—had nothing in common with most of the rest of Buckhead. It was on Mathieson, just half a block from the Wendy's that fronted Peachtree. A two-story red brick building that was ten units long, but short on any kind of architectural appeal. He pulled into a parking spot and immediately saw Maggie Halloran's taupe-colored Lexus SUV parked a few spaces down. He'd given her a key a few months ago when it was difficult for him to answer the door, and had never asked for it to be returned. She'd brought him food, cleaned his house, and, most of all, talked to him about things that were difficult for him to bring up.

Like Jack. Like Carrie. Like what it might have felt like to almost die.

"I just fed Quincy," she said to him as he came into his kitchen.

At the sound of his name, the Siamese cat that was the bane of his existence, as well as the source of great happiness, looked up at him. His clear blue eyes focused a few seconds on Joplin, then he turned back to his bowl. It smelled like fried chicken. Quincy loved fried chicken.

"You're spoiling him," said Joplin. "Me, too."

Maggie smiled at him. She was wearing a pale green tennis dress that showed off her tanned legs and accentuated her short, copper-colored hair. Some coral lipstick and the splash of freckles across her nose and cheeks seemed to be her only make-up. She may have been like a sister to Joplin, but that didn't prevent him from thinking that she was one of the prettiest women he knew, and that Tom Halloran was a very lucky man.

"Quincy was spoiled long before I ever met him," she responded. "And this is the first time I've brought him something from Chick-Fil-A in a long time. As for you, I figured you needed a little TLC. From what I've heard, it's been quite a day." She gestured toward the refrigerator. "I brought you some things from Souper Jenny's that you can just heat up over the next few days. Or freeze, if you can't use them."

"You're a saint, Maggie Halloran."

"I could say the same thing about you, Hollis. Carrie's over the moon that you finally talked to her about…everything."

"Not quite everything," Joplin admitted.

"That'll come in time. You'll see."

"Maybe. But not any time soon."

Maggie shrugged. "Suit yourself. She'll wait for you."

"Don't you need to go pick up Tommy and Megan or something?" Joplin asked, beginning to feel uncomfortable. "Or develop some pictures?"

Maggie Halloran was a nationally acclaimed photographer, famous for capturing the children of rich and famous parents—the Obamas included—in iconic settings. She had also given Joplin the piece of the puzzle—after studying some horrific images of child pornography that came into her husband's possession—that led him to Elliot Carter's murderer.

"I'm leaving, Hollis, don't worry. But first, I need to thank you for going to see Libba Ann at Piedmont today. And for practically saving her life."

He shook his head. "I was just there when whatever drugs she'd been given began to wear off."

Maggie scooped up her Burberry bag from the counter and fished around in it, retrieving her car keys. "Yeah, well, Tom and I both appreciate your going to see her. We care a lot about her."

"So she's not the *femme fatale* the media would have us believe?"

"Not at all." Maggie kissed his cheek and headed for the door. "But I'm hoping you'll find that out for yourself, Hollis."

"Don't you start in on me, too," Joplin pleaded. "I made it clear to Tom that it's not my case anymore."

"Yeah, well, I'm sure he'll take that into consideration," she said as she opened the door. "I brought you some Yuengling, too."

"It's against the law to try to bribe or influence death investigators," he said to her back.

"Call the Attorney General," she replied, without turning around.

———

The Yuengling sure tasted good.

Joplin had almost welcomed the alcohol-free month he'd spent at Grady Hospital, as well as the constraints on drinking while taking pain killers after he'd been released. Things had gotten a little out of control in the weeks leading up to Jack Tyndall's death, when he'd been obsessing about his relationship with Carrie. And her relationship with Jack. But he'd weaned himself off the hydrocodone in the last few weeks, and decided it was time to see if he could handle drinking again. Not Jim Beam anytime soon, but a beer would be okay.

Wouldn't it? he asked himself.

It was so okay that he had another while he was eating some chicken and kale soup and watching the national news. The economy was showing a few weak, but promising signs, especially with regard to the jobless rate, but the angry rhetoric over Obamacare and the total lack of bipartisanship in Congress, now on hiatus, were depressing. And the country was still reeling from the shootings in Aurora in July at the premiere of *The Dark Knight Rises*. Brian Williams turned to coverage of the Summer Olympics in London as quickly as he could, with yet more coverage of

Oscar "Blade Runner" Pistorius' historic run in the 400-meter race two days earlier. He ended on an even higher note with the news that the Mars Science Laboratory's rover, Curiosity, had finally landed on Mars after its nine-month voyage.

"That's our broadcast for August 6th, 2012," said Williams earnestly. "We hope to see you right back here tomorrow."

Joplin watched the Nightly News every night, but Brian Williams' sign-off never failed to irritate him. "You can't *see* us, Brian!" he said to the screen. "We've been over this again and again. Even if we've got our noses pressed up against the TV! We can see *you*, if we choose to, in spite of your lame sign-off, but *you… can't… see… us.* Got it?"

Brian Williams didn't respond; he never did. And Joplin knew he wouldn't, because, not only could he not see Joplin, he couldn't hear him either. He briefly considered having a third Yuengling, but quickly decided against it. There was some Espresso Chip frozen yogurt in the freezer, which would be much better for him. Taking his bowl and the empty beer bottle, Joplin headed for the kitchen. Quincy followed him and headed for his bowl. For some reason, the cat always seemed to think that whenever Joplin went into the kitchen, it was time to be fed again.

"You've got dry food, Quince. It's not morning yet."

Quincy's vivid blue eyes stared up at him in hurt and disbelief. Refusing to be manipulated, Joplin opened the freezer door. His cell phone rang as he was setting the frozen yogurt on the counter.

"Shit!' he said, not wanting to talk to anyone. "Shit!" he said again, when he saw the name of the caller on his phone.

"Hi, Carrie," he said cautiously. "Thanks again for lunch today."

"I was happy to do it," she replied. "How are you feeling?"

"Terrific," he said quickly, hoping to cut off any reference to his "first day back." "I just finished some soup Maggie Halloran brought over and was about to have some frozen yogurt."

"Oh," said Carrie, sounding a little disappointed. "Are you sure you don't need anything else?"

"Not a thing. I'm going to turn in early tonight."

"Okay, I'll see you tomorrow, Hollis."

"Sure thing."

Joplin clicked off and took a deep breath, hoping to slow his racing heart. He stared at the carton of frozen yogurt, then picked it up and put it back in the freezer. Then he opened the refrigerator door and grabbed another Yuengling.

After all, it *was* his first day back on the job.

CHAPTER EIGHT

*Hernandez watched as his team set up the area replicating Libba Ann's bed-*room on Blackland Road. The warrant to remove the rugs and furniture, as well as sections of the floor, wall, and ceiling, had been signed by Judge McAndrews the night before. He'd requested it as soon as he returned from the scene, convinced that even seeing the room himself wouldn't be enough to reconstruct what had happened to Libba Anne Woodridge. Hernandez firmly subscribed to the belief, held by many bloodstain analysts, that their work was just a much an art as it was a science. He needed to study the room and become familiar with every inch of it, letting it seep into his right hemisphere, much as an artist would before painting a picture. Only then could he choose the stains to feed into his computer programs that would help him "see" the actual crime being committed.

When he was finally certain—after running Jan's video a few more times, re-examining the digital photos of the scene, and taking some measure-ments—that the replication was as exact as he could make it, Hernandez thanked everyone .

"Great job, people. I knew I could count on you."

"You need any help, Jimmy?" Lester asked him.

"No, I'm good. Just need to spend some time with it," he added, anxious to be alone. Some memory had pinged in his brain as the crew was setting up the wall that had been behind Libba Woodridge's bed. He tried, without success, to recover it, then gave up.

Lester nodded and walked out with the rest of the group. Even before they were gone, Hernandez had lost himself in the reconstructed bedroom. His focus was such that hours would go by as he took it all in, his mind making calculations that most people could only do with protractors and calculators or strings or lasers. His fourteen years of experience as an analyst had given him the ability to see things immediately that most people—members of his team included—wouldn't. He would never rely on his own first impressions, however. That was for TV characters like Dexter.

Hernandez hated Dexter. He hated people even asking if he *watched* the TV show, much less if he agreed with Dexter's reconstruction of a crime.

At the APD's forensic lab, everything had to be carefully processed and documented according to strict, scientific protocols. When BJ Reardon had become the CSU's director in 1998, he had updated not only the lab's equipment, but the job requirements for the technicians who worked there. After receiving his B.S. in Biology in 1997 from Georgia State University, Hernandez had spent a year completing formal training in blood pattern analysis, which included physics and math courses, followed by competency testing. He'd been certified by the International Association for Identification a few months later. Only then had he applied for a job with the Atlanta PD, after hearing about Reardon from a detective friend. B.J., who had gone through two bloodstain analysts in six months, had implemented the FBI's Scientific Working Group on Bloodstain Pattern Analysis guidelines and wanted only the best. After grilling Hernandez on his education and training, and following up by talking to a few of his professors and trainers, he had hired him on a purely probationary basis and then closely supervised his work.

It had been a match made in heaven.

Hernandez was the son of an American mother and a father who had immigrated from the Dominican Republic to Atlanta in 1970, quickly finding work in construction. Alejandro Hernandez had been one of the lucky ones, able to get a green card with the help of his employer, who valued his work ethic, his ability to master English quickly, and his natural leadership qualities. He'd been made a foreman, overseeing a crew working on a big apartment complex, within six months of being hired. Six months after that, Alejandro had talked Sonya Jenkins, the company's indispensable secretary, into marrying him. Jimmy—christened Jaime—was born two years later and his sister, Christina, three years after that.

Unlike Christina, who knew from an early age that she wanted to be a nurse, Jimmy only knew what he *didn't* want to do, which was to work in construction. He'd spent summer vacations working at his father's various job sites since he was a freshman in high school. And although he enjoyed the easy camaraderie of the work crews and was proud of the way they—and Gary Holbrook, the owner of Southeast Construction—respected his father, it just didn't interest him. His parents had been fine with that, hoping he would be the first on either side of the family to go to college, and would use what his teachers said was a "gifted ability" in science and math to make his family proud. Instead, when he graduated from high school, Hernandez had enlisted in the Army. Sonya and Alejandro, already upset over his decision not to go to college, were devastated when President George H. Bush launched the Persian Gulf War two months later, and their son, who had opted for training as a medic, was sent to Saudi Arabia.

"Why do you want to break their hearts?" his grandmother, Mamie Jenkins, had asked him the week before he shipped out.

"I *don't* want to break their hearts, Momma!" he'd insisted. "I just want to see the world before I settle down. Like Papi did."

"Your father left a poor island with a history of violence and repression to come to a country that offered him hope. He's made a good life for himself and his family—despite being black *and* Latino—and you want to throw that away! Your grandfather died in Vietnam, fighting a war that made fodder of black men, and now you're going to go fight a war in the Middle East that's doing the same thing."

"No, Momma," he'd said, looking into her eyes and touching her hair. "I'm going there to try to *save* men—black, white—whatever color. I'll be a medic there, not a soldier."

"Just save yourself, Jimmy. For us. Come back to us."

"I will," he'd said, as he held her.

And he had. But not for another three years, after he'd seen more of the world than he'd bargained for—the bloody, cruel, unjust, and heartbreaking aspects of it, as well as the brave, selfless, loving ones. He had enrolled in Pre-med at Georgia State University under the G.I. Bill, intending to become a doctor and make his family proud. But even with his parents' help, Hernandez had soon realized that he couldn't put himself through med school and an internship and maybe a residency in some special field. So he had switched his major to Biology, hoping he could at least become a high school teacher. In his senior year, however, he had met with a counselor who asked him if he'd ever thought about looking into the field of forensics.

"Forensics?" Hernandez had asked.

"Yes," the counselor had said. "The discovery of DNA has totally changed what can be accomplished in forensics. And with your math ability, your experience as a medic, and your degree in Biology, you'd be perfect in that field. Do a little research, Jimmy."

A little research was all it had taken to make Hernandez know that he wanted to work in forensics. He'd started out with DNA, learning how it was originally used only to determine paternity, but had then emerged as a criminal investigation tool in 1986 with a case in England that involved two rape murders. The technique had crossed the Atlantic to the U.S. in 1987 when DNA obtained from a rape victim identified Tommy Lee Andrews as the perpetrator in Orange County, Florida. But Hernandez was truly hooked when he stumbled across the Jeffrey MacDonald case, which used not only blood-typing evidence to convict MacDonald of killing his wife and two young daughters, but bloodstain analysis as well.

This is it, he'd told himself. *This is what I want to do.*

With BJ Reardon's help and support, Jimmy Hernandez had built a national reputation in the field, helping detectives reconstruct several high-profile murder cases in Atlanta, contributing to forensic articles and, ultimately, testifying as an expert consultant in cases all over the United States. In return, his expertise had furthered Reardon's ambition to create one of the best crime scene units in the Southeast. Maybe even in the country. Ultimately, the lab had been accredited by the American Society of Crime Laboratory Directors Laboratory Accreditation Board, an internationally recognized program.

Hernandez knew that his parents' pride in him, as well as in his sister, who had become a nurse-anesthetist, was more than words could describe. They were also proud that he was a family man, with three children of his own to add to the two Christina and her husband had. But what drove him these days was not to make his parents proud or to provide for his wife and children, or even to add to his prestige in the world of forensics. It was something that he shared with most homicide detectives and death investigators and his colleagues at the CSU. Something that he and Hollis Joplin had discussed many times over a beer when a case was especially rough.

To speak for the victims.

And as he looked around at Libba Ann Woodridge's reconstructed bedroom, he knew that he would find a way to speak for her. She was alive, but had no memory of what had happened to her.

He would be her memory.

———

By the end of Joplin's first week back at work, he began to feel as if he could handle the job again. Although he wasn't used to working a days-only shift, it was a much more predictable schedule than the usual six-person, three-shift, and twenty-eight-day rotation dubbed the "Menstrual Cycle" years ago. The ME's Office had to be covered twenty-four/seven, which meant that each two-person team had varying eight-hour shifts. This ensured that everyone took turns handling midnight to eight a.m., eight a.m. to four p.m., and four p.m. to midnight. Teams changed every cycle, too, so that each investigator was used to working with every other investigator. Since Joplin was the only stationary member for the next month, he would be paired with all of them: Deke, Viv Rodriguez, Felicia Manson, Glenn Martin, and Jesse Potts. He liked and respected all his colleagues, and although they'd each assured him that they hadn't minded working the extra hours while he was recuperating and wouldn't resent having some back-to-back shifts during this cycle, he still felt guilty.

"Good to have you back, Hollis," said Jesse Potts, rising up from his cubicle in the Investigative Unit on Friday morning. He was a short, wiry black man with a shaved head who had left the APD Homicide Unit to join the Milton ME's Office the year before Joplin did. Jesse was a snappy dresser, with a reputation as a ladies' man. Today, he was wearing a tan suit with a black shirt and a paisley tie. He'd visited Joplin in the hospital several times, but this was the first time Hollis had seen him since getting back to work.

"Good to be here, Jess," Joplin said as he made his way to his own cubicle. The Unit was a large, rectangular room with six work areas lining the two long sides, a conference table with eight chairs in the middle of it, and the Chief Investigator's office at the far end. The blinds that covered Sarah Petersen's windows were open today, and he could see her talking on her phone. "You doing okay?"

Potts gave him a broad smile. "Never better. You?"

"Same here," Joplin lied. Until he got rid of the damned colostomy bag, he wouldn't feel completely healed. "Any calls yet?"

"Nope. So far, so good."

As if the Fates were just waiting for Jesse to say that very thing, the phone on Joplin's desk rang. "Joplin here."

"Good morning, Hollis," said Sarah Petersen. One of the changes she'd instituted was having all calls to the Investigative Unit routed through her during her office hours. "You up for a grisly murder scene?"

"Always," he said.

Petersen gave him the address, which was a Shell station on Roswell Road in Sandy Springs. "A female Hispanic, name unknown, found behind the station by a driver delivering Coke products to the convenience store about a half-hour ago. The uniform who called it in said somebody did a real number on her. Jim Mullins is already at the scene."

"Got it," said Joplin.

"How about taking Dr. Salinger along? Dr. Markowitz says she needs more field time."

Now that Carrie was a full-time resident, she was required to go to crime scenes whenever she wasn't doing an autopsy. Since she, too, worked days only, Joplin had known it was inevitable that she'd be going to a scene with him. So far, either she hadn't been free when he'd gotten called, or there had been no scene when she'd been free. Today, evidently, the planets were all in alignment.

"Happy to oblige, ma'am."

"I've been meaning to tell you to cut the 'ma'am' stuff."

"Happy to oblige, sir."

There was silence on the phone, then she said, "Wicked funny, Joplin. 'Sarah' or 'Chief' is just fine. Your choice."

"'Chief,' it is, then, Sarah."

"You like to go right up to the line, don't you, Joplin?"

"Yeah, but I think you can handle it, Chief. Maybe it's the only fun we'll have on 'grisly murder' days."

He could almost see her smile. "You're on, Joplin."

———

The Shell station was just north of the Fountain Oaks strip mall on Roswell Road. Joplin had worked a pedestrian death scene in the area about a year ago, involving an eighteen-year-old kid. He'd walked a friend to a bus stop, then was hit by a car in the left lane when he'd tried to cross back over Roswell. The memory of his slight form, cordoned off from gawkers in passing cars by a phalanx of uniformed cops, assailed Joplin's mind. He blinked a few times, hoping to erase the video playing in his head.

"I wish Sandy Springs would get going on that crosswalk they've got planned for this area," he said to Carrie as they approached the strip mall.

"What crosswalk?"

"The survey and plans called for one to be put in back there," he replied, jerking his head to the rear. "Just before the mall."

"That's a strange place for a crosswalk. I mean, there's not a light there."

"There's a large Hispanic community living in all those apartment buildings," he told her, gesturing to a warren of brick and stucco complexes to the right. "Most of them are dependent on MARTA, but the buses heading into town are on the other side of the street, as well as a bunch of convenience stores and other shops, and there's a lot of space between intersections. So they gamble that they can make it across Roswell without getting hit, and the city has finally realized that it needs to do something."

"And nobody has complained that this would be encouraging

undocumented Hispanics to flood Atlanta?" Carrie looked at him in mock surprise. "Despite that law passed last year that made us look like yahoos?" she added, referring to an immigration law passed in Georgia in 2011 that required private companies to verify that prospective employees weren't illegal aliens. "Is the city of Sandy Springs soft on crime?"

Joplin shook his head and smiled. He loved the fact that Carrie was almost as liberal as he was. "I guess more compassionate minds are prevailing in this case. And that law hasn't been real popular with construction companies and farmers in the rest of Georgia."

They turned left on West Belle Isle Circle at the light. A Sandy Springs police car was parked near the front doors of the Shell station, but Joplin drove around to the back. The Coke truck was still there, near the delivery entrance, along with another patrol car and several onlookers. Four uniformed cops were keeping them in check. Joplin parked near the truck and got his case from the back seat before he and Carrie approached them. He saw the blood on the beige-colored wall of the building before he saw the body.

"Oh, my God," said Carrie softly, hand to her mouth.

CHAPTER NINE

The woman was half-lying, half-sitting against the wall, legs splayed out in front of her. Her underwear was wrapped around her left ankle, and her short cotton dress was bunched up around her waist. She had been wearing black flip flops, but only one remained on her left foot; the other lay on the ground. She had dark skin and long, dark hair, but even her own mother wouldn't have been able to recognize her. Her face and upper torso were covered in blood. A replay of how Libba Ann Woodridge had looked when he'd pulled back the sheet that covered her filled Joplin's mind, and as he stared down at this victim's body, he manipulated that image so that it was positioned directly over it.

The images fit together perfectly, like a pencil tracing on white paper over a picture beneath it.

When Joplin moved the image of Libba Ann a little to the left, it was as if he were looking at a photograph and its negative, each woman's hair and skin tone in stark contrast. "How many homicide scenes have you been on?" he asked Carrie. Seeing a victim at a death scene had much more of an impact than seeing a body on an autopsy table.

"Two," she answered, her face pale and grave. "But, Jesus, Hollis, they were nothing like this."

"You'll be fine, but it might be better if you let me take the lead."

"I have no problem with that."

Joplin nodded, and after identifying himself to the uniforms, they walked over to where Jim Mullins, a Sandy Springs detective he'd worked with at several other scenes, stood looking down at the victim, hands on his hips. Mullins shook his head, then turned to look at them.

"This is Dr. Salinger, Jim," Joplin said. "She's our newest full-time resident. Carrie, this is Detective Mullins."

"Pleased to meet you," said Mullins, but his hands stayed on his hips. He was a tanned, athletic-looking man in his forties who was rumored to be fond of golf. "You ever see anything like this, Hollis?"

"As a matter of fact, I have," Joplin replied. Out of the corner of his eye, he saw Carrie's head swivel towards him. It was possible she didn't know anything about what had happened to Libba Ann Woodridge; Libba Ann had never made it to an autopsy table. For her benefit, as well as Mullins' he went over the details of the scene at 449 Blackland Road. When he had finished, Carrie was even paler, and Jim Mullins pulled a white handkerchief out of his trouser pocket and mopped his face.

"Any update on the blood or any semen found?" he asked Joplin.

"I haven't talked to anyone at SVU, since it's no longer my case, but according to the victim's attorney, who *did* talk to Martucci a few days ago, no semen was present, and the blood found on the wall and ceiling and on the bed was her own."

Mullin's face clouded. "And, yet, you said there were no wounds on her that would explain the blood spatter evidence." He gestured toward the body. "Not like this, anyway."

"Jimmy Hernandez is working on that. I know you've got a good CSU, Jim, but you might want to let him take a look at this one, too."

Jurisdiction was always an issue among law enforcement agencies, even when they shared certain county and state resources. Mullins didn't answer for several seconds, then nodded and said, "Okay. I guess that'd be a good idea."

"Good. I'll give him a call when I finish up here."

Joplin moved a little closer to the body, then squatted down, set his case on the ground and got out some booties and gloves for himself and Carrie. After they were each properly outfitted, he got his digital camera and carefully studied the corpse and everything around it. Technically, as a representative of the ME's Office, he had jurisdiction only over the body itself until a preliminary manner of death had been established. But old habits die hard, and Joplin's years as a homicide detective had trained him to consider everything when he worked a scene. He was also the "eyes and ears" of the ME who would perform the autopsy, and although it was likely that Carrie would be assigned the case, she was there only as part of her training. Most MEs in the five metro counties that had Medical Examiner systems—Cobb, DeKalb, Fulton, Milton, and Gwinnett—as opposed to those which still had coroner systems, didn't go out to death scenes.

A small canvas purse and a plastic grocery bag lay about two feet away from the victim. Joplin assumed the bag contained items she had purchased in the convenience store. He took several photos of the body, the wall behind it, and the purse and plastic bag. Next, he looked at the area within a five-foot circumference of the body, searching for anything that would suggest whether the woman had met someone behind the store or simply gone there to have a quick smoke before going home to a family that had at least one child in it. There was nothing to indicate the first or last scenarios—no empty beer cans or cigarette butts—but a pattern of shoe prints and scuff marks in the dirt covering the pavement seemed to indicate that she had been forced to come to this place to die.

After photographing this area, Joplin returned the camera to his case. He motioned for Carrie to follow him as he skirted the prints and scuff marks; the CSU would want to make plaster casts of these. Then he squatted down again and opened the plastic bag; in it were a pack of Marlboros, a can of Coke Zero, and a bottle of Children's Advil. The purse held another pack of Marlboros with only two cigarettes in it. There was no wallet, only a five dollar bill and some change, as well as a tissue and a pack of gum. No identification.

"The store cashier says she was a fairly frequent customer," said Mullins, who had followed Joplin, but still stood several feet away from the body. "But he didn't know her name. He thinks she lived in one of the apartments across Roswell. He wasn't working last night, but he ran the security tape for us. It shows she came in at 10:05 p.m. last night, got the Coke out of the cooler on the back wall and the kids' Advil, brought them to the counter, then asked for a pack of Marlboros. She left at 10:10 p.m. Nobody else was in the store when she was, but there were two cars at the pumps. We're checking the camera feed."

"Head wounds," said Carrie, standing over Joplin. "But could they have caused blood spray that far up the wall?"

"I don't know," said Joplin. He peered at a section of the wall above the victim's head. "Based on the color and viscosity, as well as the fact that the clotted blood has separated from the serum, I'd say she's been dead for several hours." He waved away a few blowflies that hadn't been scared off by his approach and felt along the woman's jaw, arms and legs, then palpated her stomach. "Rigor's not quite fixed."

"Want me to do a body temp?" Carrie asked him.

"Sure," he said. He was beginning to feel more comfortable having her on a scene with him, and she was certainly helpful, despite her initial reaction to the body.

Carrie retrieved the necessary tools from his case, then squatted beside him. Scalpel in hand, she made a small incision below the right rib cage and thrust a thermoprobe into the opening. "Eighty-three point four, and the ambient temp is about seventy-five degrees. So maybe ten hours ago," she added, referring to the fact that a dead body loses heat at a rate of 1.5 degrees Fahrenheit an hour until it reaches the temperature around it.

"That's consistent with the fact that she's not in full rigor. Hopefully, we can confirm that estimate with the livor mortis."

Joplin, meanwhile, was studying the head wounds; he wasn't taking anything for granted with this case, even though he knew the victim was very dead. Despite all the blood, he thought she'd sustained at least five blows, two of which he could tell had fractured the skull, since he could see brain matter. The autopsy would tell them more.

"Look at her hands, Hollis," said Carrie. "It looks like she tried to ward off the blows."

Carefully, so that no trace evidence would be lost, Joplin lifted up the victim's bloody right hand where it rested, palm up, on the pavement and gently broke the rigor so he could turn it over. The back of the hand looked even worse; it was obvious that most, if not all, of the metacarpals and phalanges had been broken.

"Defensive wounds on both sides," he said. "She probably held up her hands in front of her initially, then covered her head with them when he started hitting her there." He shook his head and sighed. "Help me turn her over."

Joplin always tried to touch or handle a body as little as necessary at a scene, but Mullins would want to know as much as he could tell him before the body was transported to the morgue. As expected, livor mortis was advanced, and though the signs of pooled blood on the back of the victim's legs and buttocks were less vivid because of the amount of blood she'd lost, they corroborated Carrie's estimation of time of death, as well as his assumption that she'd been murdered where she was found. He relayed this information to the detective as he and Carrie repositioned her. Next, he retrieved paper bags and tape to "bag" the victim's hands and preserve whatever might be under her fingernails. Then he stood up, and after jotting down a few notes in the black book he kept in his coat pocket, turned and looked at Jim Mullins.

"I'll call for transport," he told the detective.

"Thanks," said Mullins, but he continued to stand there, hands on hips as he stared down at the body.

Joplin gathered up his case, but as he and Carrie were walking over to the car, the relative quiet behind the gas station was destroyed by agitated voices that seemed to come from the side of the building. A small group of people, led by a short, but muscular Hispanic male who was pushing against two uniformed cops trying unsuccessfully to keep him from entering the crime scene, came into view. The man seemed enraged, intent only on getting past the human barrier that obstructed him. Abruptly, he looked past them and stopped moving, eyes riveted on the small body lying against the wall like a discarded doll.

"No," he said. "NO!"

And then he sagged against the cops, who turned their barricade into a net for the grieving man.

CHAPTER TEN

One last time, Hernandez went over the information he'd amassed from his exhaustive examination of the recreated crime scene, the images the BackTrack/Win program had generated, and the various tests he'd performed to recreate the bloodstain patterns. He was now confident that what he would put in his report would be an accurate narrative of what had happened on Blackland Road. He still didn't understand the *why* of it; that wasn't his job. But it might help identify *who* had done this to Libba Ann Woodridge, in the long run, and would certainly stand up in court if the perpetrator were arrested and charged. He planned on spending the rest of the day writing up the report. Then maybe, just maybe, he could spend some time with his family over the weekend.

The phone rang before he could even begin. Choosing to ignore it, he let it go to voice mail, determined to get started on the report.

———

Tom Halloran pulled up to the gates at 445 Blackland Road at 11:05 a.m., less than thirty minutes after receiving a frantic, almost hysterical call from Libba Ann. All that he'd been able to make out was that she had gotten something in the mail that had terrified her. He'd rushed out of his office, telling Joan where he was going and asking that she reschedule his next few appointments. Once on I-75, he'd called Ed Jenkins and learned that no mail or deliveries had been made that morning. Jenkins remembered seeing a small package in the mail the day before, but the electronic wand he used to check anything that came to the house had not set off an alarm, and he'd turned it over to Rosa.

The gates swung open after Halloran punched in the code Libba Ann had given him a few months ago, and he drove to the top of the hill, then parked in front of the house. Rosa opened the door before he made it out of the car.

"She want you to go right up, Mr. Tom," the housekeeper told him. Her face showed tension and lack of sleep. "Meesus Cates is with her," she added, eyebrows rising.

For the third time that week, Halloran climbed the stairs to the second floor. He'd insisted on viewing the crime scene on Monday afternoon, but wished that he hadn't when he saw the carnage. Even with the bed stripped of its bloody sheets and pillows, the room had chilled him to the bone, with blood still staining the wall behind the bed, as well as the ceiling above it. Rosa had called him when two technicians from the Crime Scene Unit arrived on Tuesday to cut out those areas and take them to the unit, along with all the furniture and rugs, per instruction of the bloodstain analysis expert. He'd told her to let them do it, knowing he had no control over evidence like that. He was also hopeful that this would help determine what had happened to Libba Ann. But he'd still made sure that Maggie didn't go into that bedroom on Wednesday, when they'd brought Libba home from Piedmont and helped Rosa and Connie Sue get her settled into one of the guestrooms at the front of the house. Now he headed in that direction, wondering what his client had been sent that had so unhinged her.

Not that it would take much, after all she'd been through, thought Halloran, pausing at the door. He'd gotten a report from Captain Martucci the day before that no semen had been found in or on his client's body, according to the GBI's analysis of the rape kit. This had eased Libba's mind somewhat, but then he'd had to tell her that DNA tests performed by technicians at the

APD Crime Scene Unit had confirmed what everyone suspected: the blood covering the sheets and pillows and walls and Libba Ann, herself, was her own. It had been siphoned from her. Siphoned from her and then, somehow, spattered everywhere.

A muffled "come in" responded to his knock, and Halloran pushed the door open. Libba Ann was curled up, almost in the fetal position, on the pale yellow sofa at the foot of the bed. Her hair was pulled back into a messy pony tail, and she wore a long, white bathrobe. She was holding a wad of tissues up to her mouth and nose, her eyes tightly closed, like a frightened child after a bad dream. Connie Sue sat next to her, patting her arm.

"Libba?" Halloran said.

She opened her eyes, then said to her mother, "Mama, I need to talk to Tom alone for a little bit. Why don't you go downstairs? Rosa will fix you some tea or something, okay?"

"But…*honey*! I should be here with *you*! You need me!"

"I'll need you after I talk to Tom, Mama. It's just for a few minutes, I promise."

Reluctantly, Connie Sue pulled away from her daughter and, with no small amount of resentment showing on her face, left the room. Halloran waited until he saw her head down the stairs before closing the door and turning to Libba. A pile of mail, topped by a padded envelope and a disc cover, lay next to an open laptop on the coffee table in front of her. He saw only a blank screen, however, as he sat down beside her.

"Tell me what happened," he said gently.

She shook her head, then turned to look at him. "I got that," she said, nodding toward the lap top. "Play it."

Puzzled, Halloran hunched over the computer and turned it on. The screen indicated that a disc had been inserted, and he tapped the icon to play it. Libba Ann's bedroom—the one down the hall—came into view. It looked as if the person holding the camera was standing just inside the door. The camera panned around the entire room, then moved closer to the bed. Halloran couldn't tell what was illuminating the area, but whatever it was, it didn't wake Libba. She lay on her left side, her hands under the pillow; her hair, looking almost white in the pale light, was splayed across her shoulder. The image abruptly dropped down at that point; within seconds a figure, its back to the camera, came into view. Halloran realized that the person holding the camera had set it down, and since it was still higher than the bed, that it must have been put in a tripod.

The figure, who was wearing some kind of hood, or maybe just a hooded sweatshirt, approached the bed. He was carrying something in each hand, but Halloran couldn't tell what the objects were. Then he stood, looking down at Libba for a few seconds, before laying what was in his left hand on the bed and then holding up what Halloran now saw was a roll of duct tape in the other. In one, swift motion he flipped her over and applied the tape to her mouth. As muted screams sounded, the figure grabbed both of Libba's wrists in his right hand, then circled them with the rope or cord, or whatever it was he had set on the bed. As she began kicking at him, he knotted the rope tightly, then picked up a second one from the bed and grabbed her ankles, repeating what he had done to her wrists.

As Halloran watched, stunned by what he was seeing, the hooded figure grabbed Libba's upper arms and hoisted her up on the bed. With one hand, he shoved the pillows behind her and then let her sink back onto them. Holding his head down so that his face couldn't be seen, the man turned and walked back toward the camera. He disappeared, but several seconds later—which must have seemed like an eternity to Libba—he came back into view, this time carrying a duffel bag. Setting the case on the bed, he opened it and took out what appeared to be IV tubing, three plastic bags, and some other objects Halloran couldn't see.

The man in the hood then pulled Libba's left arm toward him, wrapped a plastic cord around it just above her elbow, and said, "You'd better lie very still, bitch, or this will hurt, and it'll take a long time. Understand?" The words were whispered—maybe in an effort to disguise his voice—and the effect was even more chilling.

Looking terrified, Libba nodded and stared as the man grabbed her left hand and tapped the top of it several times. Then he pulled out something Halloran couldn't see—probably a butterfly needle—and inserted it into her hand, then capped it. Next, he tied some tubing around her upper arm and seemed to be feeling around for a vein, before swabbing her arm and inserting a needle into it. Then he taped the needle to her skin and attached the tubing to it, as well as to one of the plastic bags, which he placed on the floor. He repeated this two more times, until all three bags were filled with blood.

Libba's eyes were still open, but she looked exhausted from all the blood she'd lost. Without saying another word, the man held up a syringe, uncapped it with his teeth, and administered it through the IV in her hand. He then took a sac-like object from the duffel bag, attached some tubing to it and connected this to one of the blood-filled plastic bags. As he pumped blood into the sac, ultimately using all three bags, Libba's eyes began to close. She seemed to be fighting this, jerking herself awake every few seconds. The man, meanwhile, had taken a large mallet out of the bag and placed the blood-filled sac, which now looked like a large ball, on the bed.

When Libba's eyes finally closed for the last time, the figure untied the ropes on her wrists and ankles and then pulled her arms out to the side, hands resting on the mattress. Next, he tugged her underwear down and looped it around one ankle, then jerked her legs open and pulled up her nightgown. This done, he climbed up on the bed and sat on his haunches behind the ball, then raised the mallet high over his head and began pounding the ball, watching as scarlet streams shot out of it. As if he were painting a large canvas, he moved the ball from side to side, watching as the blood sprayed in wide arcs on the wall behind the bed, the ceiling above it, and, of course, Libba herself. This was accompanied by a sound track of groans that turned the whole macabre video into one of the most pornographic scenes Halloran had ever seen.

As if exhausted, the hooded man finally dropped the mallet and fell on his side, lying there for several seconds. Rousing himself with apparent effort, he gathered his equipment from the bed and shoved it all back into the duffel bag. For several seconds, he seemed to be staring at the pitiful figure on the bed, then he let out a long sigh. Nodding, as if very satisfied with what he'd done, the man got off the bed, gently peeled the tape off Libba's mouth, and leaned down to give her what anyone might have thought was a tender kiss on the lips.

Then he walked back toward the camera and disappeared from view.

———

Halloran didn't say anything as he tried to process what he had seen. A dozen questions flooded his mind; he also had no idea what he could possibly say to Libba to comfort her. He wished Maggie were there. She'd developed a rapport with Libba that went beyond a wife/client relationship, although he wasn't really sure why. Maggie was compassionate and intuitive and one of the most "giving" people he knew, but she didn't usually become involved with his clients. Especially the young, trophy wives of his older clients. Libba Ann had been different somehow, and Halloran realized that he'd never asked Maggie why. He'd simply been grateful for the help.

Libba was staring at him when he finally turned to look at her. Her hands were still covering her mouth, but her eyes searched his face, as if trying to gauge the level of repulsion he must be feeling. Halloran cleared his throat, then reached out and grasped her shoulder in an effort to make some kind of reassuring contact with her. "I can't even imagine what seeing that video must have been like for you," he said, still groping for the right words.

She gave a long sigh as tears trickled down her cheeks. But instead of wiping them, she balled up the tissues in her hands and closed her eyes again. "Then I guess you wouldn't be able to imagine what I'd feel like if that video went viral on the internet, would you?"

"What do you mean?"

Out of the pocket of her bathrobe, Libba pulled a crumpled piece of paper and handed it to him. "That was in the package with the disc. I didn't look at any of my mail until this morning. I was about halfway through when I found *that*," she added, nodding toward the padded envelope.

Halloran unfolded the paper and smoothed it out. Typed on it were the words, all in caps:

WIRE $1,000,000 TO THE CAYMAN NATIONAL BANK, ACCCOUNT #00222659, BY MIDNIGHT FRIDAY OR THIS VIDEO WILL RECEIVE GLOBAL DISTRIBUTION.

CHAPTER ELEVEN

"Captain Martucci speaking."

"Hi, Mary. It's Hollis Joplin. Got a minute?"

"For you, always. By the way, thanks for that live one you sent us Monday. Good catch."

"I wish the lady at the scene I worked this morning had been as lucky."

After a few seconds of silence, Martucci said, "You mean the scene is similar to the one at the Woodridge house, but this time the victim is dead?"

"Exactly. Only this one was outside and in Sandy Springs, so you won't get the case. I asked Jim Mullins to let Hernandez look at the scene, but I thought you should get a heads-up, too. The victim's name is Maria Sanchez. Her husband showed up as Carrie and I were leaving. They live in the apartment complex on the other side of Roswell, and she'd evidently gone out around ten the night before to get a few things at the convenience store and never came back."

"Did the husband report her missing?"

"No, but he might not be a legal resident. You know how that goes."

Martucci sighed. "Yeah, I do, Hollis, and I'd appreciate your telling me anything you can about this murder. The Woodridge case is going nowhere fast, and we've got your friend, Tom Halloran, breathing down our necks."

Joplin chuckled. "Better you than me, Mary. Here's what I've got." As succinctly as he could, Joplin outlined the similarities between the two crime scenes, emphasizing the way each victim had been positioned and the copi-ous amounts of blood spatter. "I'm hoping Hernandez can get a handle on it."

"If anyone can, he can," said Martucci. "Jesus, Hollis! I've seen a lot of sick things in the past fifteen years, but this is right up there in the top ten."

"For me, too. Listen, have you gotten a preliminary from Hernandez yet? I called him about the Sandy Springs case, but got voice mail, so I just left a message. But these two cases are really weirding me out."

"I'd tell you if I had anything, Hollis, but you know Hernandez. He's still playing with his strings," she added. Hernandez refused to be rushed in his analysis, frustrating the detectives he worked with, but ultimately amazing them with his reconstructions of the crimes involved.

"Why can't he come up with a suspect by just looking at the blood like that Dexter fellow on TV?"

"I asked him that once, and you know what he told me?"

"Probably what BJ told me when I asked him why he can't get his team to do what the guys on *CSI* do: 'When they pay us as much as the actors on that show, we'll be glad to oblige.'"

"Actually, Jimmy said some very unkind and X-rated things about Dexter in Spanish," said Martucci. "But since I speak Italian fairly well, I got the gist of it. BJ did let us know that they're pretty sure the perp got in through a laundry room window in the basement. They found broken glass inside and some shoe prints outside. The Woodridges had a pretty sophisticated security system, so we're turning it inside-out. He also said that DNA tests of all the blood at the scene showed it to be Mrs. Woodridge's."

"Halloran called me yesterday and told me that. He also said the Piedmont lab confirmed that the blood found on her was her own, but they hadn't been able to determine all the drugs in her system."

"They still haven't. She was positive for Ambien, but we expected that, from what she told the officer doing the rape kit. And they found Ketamine, not trace amounts of Rohypnol, which was a surprise."

"Ketamine? Isn't that a veterinary drug?"

"Yes, but we've also seen it used in so-called 'date rape' cases. The advantage in this case might have been that it can be given intravenously. But whatever he used to depress respiration enough to make her *look* dead, but not actually *kill* her, is still unknown. All the lab can say is that it seems to be some kind of morphine derivative that has, quote, unusual characteristics, unquote. But it's not heroin or hydrocodone or oxycodone. We had what was left of the samples sent over to the GBI; I'm hoping they can find out more. The path lab at Piedmont isn't a forensic lab."

"Well, you sure lit a fire under the GBI to process the rape kit in record time, Mary, so maybe they'll come through."

"That might have been more because of Halloran's reputation as a hardass than anything *I* said to them," Martucci admitted.

"Don't underestimate yourself," Joplin said, although he agreed with her. "Would you call me if they find out anything?"

"You got it, Hollis. Thanks for letting me know about this new case."

"Anything to keep Tom Halloran off my back."

"You and me, both," said Mary Martucci

————

"I need to get this to Captain Martucci at the SVU," said Halloran.

Libba Ann Woodridge shook her head. "That's not going to happen, Tom."

"Bit this will help the police catch the man who did this to you, Libba."

"I doubt that. He was very careful to keep his face hidden."

"There are other ways this can be used to identify him," Halloran insisted.

"Do you honestly think the person who did this left fingerprints or DNA on anything he touched?"

"Maybe not, but the forensics team could get a pretty good idea of his height and weight and do a voice analysis. They could also examine the disc itself, maybe find out where it was purchased or what was used to make the video."

Libba Ann shook her head again. "I can't risk having millions of people seeing this on the slim chance that the police might find out who this... monster is. It was bad enough not really knowing what happened to me. What he...did to me. But seeing that video was a thousand times worse, Tom! Now I know every single disgusting detail, God help me!" She sat up and put her feet on the floor and looked him in the eye. "Whatever public humiliation and notoriety I've experienced since Arliss died can't hold a candle to that, and you know it. Despite what the whole world thinks, I didn't marry him for his money, and there have been times when I just wanted to give it all to his greedy family, but now I'm *glad* I have it! A million dollars is well worth the last little shred of dignity I have."

"As the executor of the estate, I can't authorize an advance that large before it's been probated, Libba."

"You won't have to. Arliss settled two million on me when we married. I can withdraw the funds immediately."

"But this is blackmail, " Halloran insisted. "And it won't stop here. You'll have to *keep* paying. And *paying*."

"Then that's what I'll have to do," she said. "And that's where you can help me."

"Help you? How?"

"I don't know anything about bank accounts in the Cayman Islands or how to wire money." She gave him a weary smile and tucked a stray piece of hair behind her ear. "Arliss never got around to that part of my education. But I'm sure you can arrange that, Tom."

Halloran took her hand in both of his. "More than anyone else, I know what you've been through since Arliss died. Hell, even before that! You've been crucified by the press and hounded by the entire Woodridge family. Julie excepted, of course. I honestly don't know how you've held up as well as you have in the face of all the lies and distortions and accusations you've had to endure. And then to be attacked in your own home by some kind of sick pervert…" He closed his eyes for a moment and shook his head. "It's more than anyone could bear, and I don't blame you for trying to protect yourself. But this video is evidence in an ongoing criminal investigation, Libba. It needs to be turned over to the police. As your attorney, I'm advising you not to pursue this course of action."

"I know you mean well, Tom. And you and Maggie have been a big part of the reason I've been able to keep going. Julie, too. She's come to see me every day since …the attack. And before that, she stood up for me to the family." Libba looked away from him and slowly pulled her hand away from his. "But you have to let me handle this as I see fit. And as my attorney, you also have to keep everything I've told you—and shown you—confidential, don't you?"

"Yes, of course, but—"

"Good. If you don't want to wire the money for me, I understand. But I'll just find someone else to do it. And I'd rather not do that."

He folded the paper again and put it in his inside jacket pocket. "No, I'll do it. Against my better judgment, but I'll do it. May I take the envelope and disc with me? You have my word I'll honor your confidentiality."

"Yes. I don't ever want to see it again."

Halloran was about to caution Libba Ann again about what she wanted done, when there was a discreet knock at the door. It opened slightly, and Rosa's face appeared.

"Miss Libba, Miss Julie just came through the gate," she said. "I told her you wasn't feeling so good, but—"

"It's okay, Rosa. I'm feeling a little better, and Mr. Halloran needs to get back to his office," she added, giving him a quick look. "Send her up when she gets here."

Rosa nodded, and Halloran stood up. "I'll be in touch. Try to get some rest."

"Thanks, Tom."

Halloran followed Rosa out into the hall. "Take care of her," he said. "And call me if anything comes up. Anything."

The housekeeper nodded silently, and they both started down the stairs. Connie Sue Cates rushed into the entry hall, smoothing down her dress.

"Is my baby okay?" she demanded. "Am I to be allowed to be with her now?"

"Of course," Halloran replied calmly. "But she's very tired. I tried to get her to get into bed and rest, but she wouldn't listen to me. Maybe you can convince her, Mrs. Cates. She'll listen to you, I think."

"Why, sure she will," said Connie Sue, in a pleased drawl. "I'm her mother."

She passed them on the stairs, just as the doorbell rang, and Rosa rushed to open the door. Julie Benning, Arliss Woodridge's granddaughter, hurried in. She was wearing jeans and a tank top, but with her long legs and blond good looks, she could have been a model or a beauty queen herself. The money she had inherited from her grandfather would ensure that she'd never need to work a day in her life, but Halloran knew she had no intention of being relegated to a life of charity balls and lunching at fashionable Atlanta restaurants. Julie was in her second year of med school at Emory, with plans to become an orthopedic surgeon.

"Tom!" she said, moving in to give him a quick hug. "Don't tell me you're leaving! Is Maggie here?"

"No, but I think she'll probably be by later. I needed to go over some legal things with Libba, but now I've got to get back to the office."

"Okay, but let's all get together soon. I think it would do Libba good to get out of this house for a few hours, don't you? And I just finished my last exam for summer quarter."

"It's a date. Maggie would love it if you two would come to dinner. Lucas, too, if he's available," he added, referring to Julie's boyfriend.

"Tell her to call me. I'll make sure Libba goes, and I'm sure Lucas would love that, too. "

"I'll tell her."

Hopefully, Connie Sue would be back in Brunswick by the time that happened.

———

As Halloran was getting into his car, he noticed one of the landscape crew driving a rider-mower down the hill to the right of the driveway. He eased down the drive, stopping just in front of the man, and got out, waving. The man cut off the mower's engine and walked over to him.

"Sorry to bother you," he said, offering his hand. "I'm Mrs. Woodridge's attorney, Tom Halloran. Is Jorge around today?"

"No, sir. He stay home today." The man looked away, as if trying to decide what he should say about his boss not being there. Jorge was usually on site whenever the crew was there.

"No problem." Halloran pulled his wallet out of his pants pocket and took out a business card. "Could you ask him to call me when you see him? Or talk to him?"

"Sure. Sure thing."

"Thanks," Halloran said and walked back to his car, an uneasy feeling washing over him. The man had seemed evasive, even though there didn't seem to be a reason. He decided to call Jenkins on his way back to the office and see if he knew anything about Jorge that might bear further scrutiny.

CHAPTER TWELVE

The phone rang as Joplin was finishing up his report on Maria Sanchez.
Hoping it might be Jimmy Hernandez, he snatched it up.

"Hollis Joplin speaking."

"You shilling for Sandy Springs these days, Hollis?"

"Jimmy! I was hoping you'd call. How are you?"

"Working over the weekend, thanks to you."

"Yeah, I know. I feel bad about piling more on you, but you gotta see this scene. It's like a carbon copy of the one on Blackland."

"Sounds like it, but you said on the voice mail I got that this one is dead, right?"

"Yes, but if it's the same perp, that means he's escalating."

There was silence on the line for several seconds, then Hernandez said, "Maybe, but I didn't get that kind of vibe."

"What do you mean?"

"I haven't finished my report yet, but I guess I can share a few things with you. I saw the photos you took before you discovered Mrs. Woodridge was still alive and read in your report that you thought the whole scene looked 'staged.' Is that how this second scene looked to you, too?"

The video his mind had taken of his first sight of Maria Sanchez's body propped up by the blood-spattered concrete wall of the gas station blotted out his surroundings. He let it play for several seconds, then said, "Yes, it did. Not just because the two victims were positioned the same way, but also because of the way the blood looked." Joplin paused, trying to find the words to describe what he meant. "It was like…a painting. Like the perp was using blood as a medium for expressing his feelings. Ike Simmons even mentioned Jackson Pollack when he first saw Libba Ann Woodridge's bedroom. And the blood at the Sandy Springs scene had that same kind of…"

"Artistic quality?" Hernandez offered.

"Exactly."

"Well, I haven't been to the second scene yet, but I trust that eidetic memory of yours, Hollis, and I think you're right. I got the same impression when I was studying the recreated scene at the lab. It reminded me of something. Not Jackson Pollack, exactly, but an artist like that. Anyway, my job isn't to try to figure out this perp's motive in drawing a lot of blood from a victim and spattering it on the walls of Mrs. Woodridge's bedroom, but I do know that what he did was intentional. He *wanted* it to look like a painting. I also know how he did it."

"Don't stop now, Jimmy," Joplin said when the analyst paused. "I don't want to have to wait for the movie to come out, for Christ's sake!"

"Alright, but let me just make sure you know what I'm talking about when I use the terms 'origin' and 'area of convergence.' The origin is the source of the blood spatter—"

"And the area of convergence is the position or positions between the perp and the victim during the crime," Joplin finished.

"Right. But even though Mrs. Woodridge was the victim of what happened in that bedroom, and she was technically its source, because the blood came from her, she wasn't the origin. You still with me?"

"I think so."

"And if she *wasn't* the true origin, then something else had to be. And that was why the area of convergence looked so screwed up when I first ran it through my computer programs. It had no relationship to the victim herself. She was like another object at the scene—a place for the blood spatter to land on—not where it originated."

Joplin thought about this for a moment, again visualizing Libba Ann Woodridge, her head and face and body covered in blood, and nodded in agreement. "So what *was* the origin, Jimmy?"

"It was a partially inflated basketball that the perp filled with Mrs. Woodridge's blood and hit multiple times with a large meat mallet."

"You're shitting me."

"Nope. BJ hasn't seen the expense sheets yet for this particular reconstruction, but I think he'll like the results. I had my team go out and buy every single thing they could think of that would be tough and strong enough not to fall apart when it was struck, as well as porous enough, like skin, to release the blood when struck with a mallet. Footballs didn't hold enough liquid; neither did soccer balls. Basketballs were capable of that volume of blood, but I couldn't get any velocity until I first put some air into them. And then, *voila*, I was Jackson Pollack. Especially when I moved the ball around on the bed and aimed it at the wall."

"You've got a sick mind, Jimmy. Which is probably why you're so good at what you do. Just like—"

"Don't use the D-word, Hollis," said Hernandez, cutting him off. "Don't say his name or I won't ever tell you anything before I turn in an official report again."

Joplin chuckled, then said, "I promise. How'd you figure out the perp used a meat mallet?"

"Well, I knew he had to use something that would penetrate the rubber over a fairly large surface, but I can't really take all the credit. Some of the transfer patterns on the sheets actually showed most of the mallet's spikes. He set it down at some point."

"I still think you're a genius, Jimmy."

"No, the real genius was Dr. Fred Carter, who invented and perfected the

BackTrack programs. I'm only sorry I doubted the results when I uploaded Jan and Lester's photos through them."

"Test and re-test, Jimmy. Isn't that what you science nerds always say?"

"Yeah, that and 'que la fuerza este con usted,' Hollis."

"What does that mean?"

"'May the force be with you.'"

————

Carrie finished the last of the salad she'd brought for lunch and looked at her watch. It was 12:55 p.m. She'd scheduled the autopsy on Maria Sanchez for 1 p.m., but needed to wait for Detective Mullins to arrive before getting started. It was his prerogative to be present, but she hoped he'd be on time. Given the circumstances surrounding this case, she'd asked David Markowitz to assist her, and she knew his schedule was pretty tight today. Carrie had no doubts about her ability to perform a thorough and comprehensive autopsy, but a lot was riding on this particular one. If Hollis were right in thinking that the same person who attacked Libba Ann Woodridge had also murdered Maria Sanchez, it would be important to glean every bit of knowledge she could from the body. Now that she'd been a full-time resident at the ME's for more than three months, David usually just went over everything she'd done, as well as her findings, before signing off on an autopsy. But this time Carrie wanted him to participate. He had far more experience than she did, and her ego could handle having him supervise her closely again. She had a hunch Detective Mullins would appreciate that as well.

As if on cue, Carrie's phone rang and Sherika announced that Mullins was on his way to her office.

"Thanks," she said, cradling the phone on her shoulder as she shoved the plastic container that had held her salad into a bag. With the minute she had left, she applied some fresh lipstick, finishing just as Mullins knocked at the door. "Come in."

"Thanks for getting to this so quickly," the detective said. "I'm sure you've got cases ahead of this one."

"I made it a priority, and I've asked Dr. Markowitz to assist me, since I'm pretty new here."

The relief she saw on Mullins' face told her she'd made the right decision.

"It'll be good to see David," was all he said, however.

Smiling in response, Carrie came out from behind her desk. "We'll pick him up on the way."

Ten minutes later, they were in the autopsy room, suited up and gloved. David had just finished an autopsy on a high school football player who'd collapsed and died during summer training, so they would be working on the one body, rather than two, as was usually done. Tim Meara, the ME's photographer, joined them soon after. Maria Sanchez, wearing what little clothing her murderer had left on her, lay on the stainless steel table closest to the door. As always, before every autopsy, Carrie clicked on the small recorder in her lab coat pocket, then glanced at the sign above the door that read, "Mortui Vivos Docent." Roughly translated, it meant, "This is where the dead teach the living."

Detective Mullins watched as Carrie and David began the post mortem, first taking several x-rays of the body, then examining the clothing and exposed areas with magnifying glasses for any trace evidence. The search revealed several black fibers on the left side of her dress, at mid-torso, as well as what looked like smeared ash residue, probably from a cigarette, on her right foot. Carrie directed Tim to take close-ups of these areas, then had Eddie turn off the lights so they could look for semen stains with a UV lamp. When none was found, she lifted the fibers on the victim's dress and torso with cellophane tape, as David did the same with the ash residue. Both pieces of evidence were placed in bags, which were then sealed, labeled, and initialed. While Tim took full-body photos, Carrie used a very thin-toothed comb to check the pubic hair. This search revealed a one-inch piece of hair that was definitely not pubic. After microscopic examination, she noted that there was no follicle attached, but bagged it anyway. Next they examined the hands, noting the defensive wounds and looking for any hair or fabric that the victim might have torn from the perpetrator, but found nothing. The fingernails were pared and put in an evidence bag, in hopes that there might be skin or other biological evidence under them. David pointed out that the collar of the victim's dress was torn. But it was only when the bloodstained clothing was removed and bagged for further analysis by the CSU that the extent of the injuries on Sanchez's torso could be seen.

"Blunt force trauma to the chest and abdomen," said Carrie as the photographer snapped picture after picture. When he had finished, she grabbed some sterile wipes and began removing the blood. Bending over the body, she said, "I see seven impacts, not counting the head. And they're not as blunt as I'd expected," she added, stepping away so Tim could photograph them.

"What do you mean?" asked Mullins, who had moved closer to the autopsy table.

"It was hard to see with all the blood covering her, but the weapon left a rectangular imprint with indentations in it," Carrie said, frowning in concentration. "Like a mallet. A meat mallet, in fact."

"A meat mallet?"

"I guess you don't cook much," Carrie said to the detective. "You use a meat mallet to tenderize certain cuts of meat before you cook them. And in this case it broke the skin each time she was hit and caused a lot of external bleeding."

Mullins shook his head and looked past Carrie, as if he were trying to figure out what kind of a monster would do something like that. She was sure he'd seen a lot of terrible things during his career, but Maria Sanchez's death seemed to really bother him.

"We need to take measurements of each wound, and then I can try to find a mallet that would fit the dimensions," Carrie said. "Tim, be sure to blow these up to natural proportions, okay?"

"Sure thing."

After the measurements were taken, Carrie said to Mullins, "About all I can add right now is that the killer was right-handed. See how these areas of impact skew to the left?"

"Yes, I can see that."

"Let's turn her over, David."

"Sure," he said, grasping Sanchez's upper left arm.

Carrie noted abrasions on the upper back, and then began checking the posterior side of the victim for any trace evidence. "I also see some dirt on her legs and buttocks, which I'm sure will match samples from the parking area behind the gas station. Can you get pictures of all this, Tim?"

Tim nodded and raised his camera.

"Can you get Carrie the photos your CSU took, Jim?" David asked.

"Sure thing. Speaking of photos, Hernandez called me and said he was pretty busy, but he'd get to our scene this afternoon. Has he turned in a report on the Woodridge case yet?"

"Not that I know of," Carrie replied. "But it would go to Martucci, not us. You might check with her."

"Right," said the detective.

"Livor mortis is confined to the buttocks and legs," Carrie observed, refer- ring to the blood that had pooled there after death. "She was half-sitting, propped up against the wall at the scene when I saw her." When Tim had finished photographing the posterior side of the body, Carrie made a visual examination of the head, then carefully pieced through the matted hair to look at the scalp more clearly. "I can see at least five blows, two of which shattered the skull. Given the blood I saw on the wall behind her at the scene, I think they were dealt last, though. Either one would have been fatal, and the heart would have stopped pumping within seconds."

"We'll know more when we get inside the skull," David said to Mullins.

For a brief moment, Carrie saw Jack Tyndall's face instead of David's. He'd taught her so much in the weeks before his death; she was only now beginning to realize just how much. What David had just said was similar to what Jack would have said. And yet it was…so much less. She shook her head to clear the image of his face.

"You don't agree, Dr. Salinger?" the detective asked.

"No! I mean, yes, I do agree," Carrie added quickly. "I was…I was just thinking that the viciousness of the attack on this woman seems to show a lot of anger."

"And *I* would agree with *that*," said David, glancing at her. "Let's get some swabs, Carrie. Maybe we'll get lucky and have some DNA."

Carrie nodded, but said, "Hollis told me that no semen had been found on Mrs. Woodridge, according to Captain Martucci."

"Maybe that's where the rage came in—he couldn't get it up," suggested Mullins.

"And blamed *her* for that," Carrie said, overwhelmed with pity for the young woman who lay on the autopsy table.

CHAPTER THIRTEEN

As soon as he finished talking to Jimmy Hernandez, Joplin tried Carrie's extension. He wanted to let her know what Hernandez had told him before she started the autopsy on Maria Sanchez, but got her voicemail instead. He left a message and had decided he'd just go downstairs to tell her in person, when his phone rang again. It was BJ Reardon, and he could tell that the director of the CSU wasn't happy with him by the way he said his name.

"I understand why you thought it would be a good idea to have Jimmy consult on that murder in Sandy Springs, Hollis, but you had no business contacting him yourself. He's been swamped this week with two other murders—as well as that crazy case on Blackland Road—and next week he's testifying in the Braverman case. He'll probably be on the stand for two days! You should have gone through me, and you know it."

Joplin was one of the few people who knew that Reardon's initials stood for "Beverley James." He'd discovered this several years ago when he'd gone to the director's office on official business and had seen some correspondence on his desk. Wisely, he'd never mentioned this to BJ. But as he listened to Reardon's slow, Southern drawl as he chewed him out, he was tempted to respond using the man's given name. Instead, he closed his eyes and pictured himself floating on an inner tube on a peaceful lake. It was one of the stress management strategies he'd learned at a training seminar several months back.

One of the few that actually worked for him.

"I realize that now, BJ," he said finally. "And I promise I'll do that next time. I was just hoping he might give me a little information on the Woodridge case, because Tom Halloran's been on my back. Martucci's, too. And while I had him on the line, I told him about the Sandy Springs case."

"And did he update you on the Woodridge case?"

"He did, as a matter of fact."

"Well, I sure hope it was good stuff, because he left his expense sheet with me before he went to Sandy Springs, and he's used up the rest of the budget for this quarter. We're gonna bill Sandy Springs for his services on their case—and then some!"

"I hear you, BJ. Did Mullins send him the particulars?"

"Naw, he said there'd be a detective there to walk him through it when he got there. They're all over that scene like white on rice. Biggest thing to happen in Sandy Springs in years, I imagine."

"Wish we could say that here in Hotlanta, BJ."

"You and me both, Hollis. You and me both."

———

As Eddie, the senior technician at the ME"s office, began prepping the body for the next phase of the autopsy, Carrie made notes on the "body sheet," a two-sided illustration that would show all the external injuries Maria Sanchez had sustained. Examination of the vaginal area determined that sexual activity had taken place within the last twenty-four hours. The vaginal vault and labia had shown minor abrasions, but those could have occurred during normal, but vigorous, sex. She and David had taken oral, vaginal, and anal swabs; semen and sperm remained intact much longer in a dead person than a live one.

Carrie heard the whine of the small, circular saw that Eddie used to open up the ribs and expose the underlying organs. It no longer bothered her, as it had when she first came to the ME's office. She had taught herself to be immune to so many things, she realized now. Not the important ones, she hoped—whatever helped her retain her empathy in the wake of the terrible things that people did to themselves and others. Just what might keep her from doing her job, the job of serving the victims of violent crimes or of their own depression or risk-taking, or the carelessness of their doctors or the drivers of cars that ran into them, or the parents who were supposed to take care of them. Because that was what made her change her field from pediatric pathology to forensic pathology.

It was a way to speak for them.

And so she tuned out the whirring of the saw and concentrated on cataloguing what this victim's perpetrator had done to her.

"Ready for you now, Dr. Salinger," said Eddie.

Carrie and David Markowitz both put on Plexiglas visors and clean latex gloves, then leaned over and looked down into the cavity of Maria Sanchez's body. Carrie noted that two of her ribs on the left side were broken, as well as one on the right. The rib cage had protected the heart and lungs somewhat from the blows the victim had received, but the abdominal organs showed damage. She and David then began the process of examining each internal organ in place.

"The lungs are in pretty good shape, but there's been some cilia damage from her smoking. Still some chyme in the stomach, but most of it's in the duodenum and jejunum, so I'd say she died about three to four hours after her last meal," Carrie observed.

"The husband said he got home about six, and they fed the kids and then had dinner around seven."

"Then I think we can say she died closer to eleven than eleven-thirty. Maybe even a little earlier than that." After drawing fluid from the heart and bladder, Carrie cut each organ free from the body cavity and handed it to David to place in basins. Samples of each were taken and examined under a microscope. Carrie noted that gross examination of the organs, as well as sectioning, revealed no diseases or irregularities, although there was evidence that the victim was a smoker. As she recorded this, Carrie thought of the bottle of Children's Advil that had been in the plastic bag found at the scene. She wondered how old the child was, and if he—or she—knew of the mother's death.

Mullins said, "The husband wants to view the body later today. We couldn't let him get near her at the scene."

"I'll make sure she's presentable," Carrie said, then motioned for Eddie to prep the head.

"Do you consider him a suspect?" asked David, stripping off his gloves and replacing them with clean ones.

"Not at this time. If he was faking his reaction to her death, he deserves an Oscar. Besides, after what Hollis told me about the Woodridge case, I'm inclined to believe the same perp was involved." Detective Mullins frowned, then added, "Of course, there's always the possibility that Jorge Martinez *is* the perp in that case. We'll certainly look for any connection to Libba Ann Woodridge."

———

By 3:30 that afternoon, Joplin was totally spent. After his phone conversation with BJ Reardon, he'd been called to a scene at a community pool in Garden Hills, a popular neighborhood in Buckhead that boasted a duck pond, nearby restaurants, and close proximity to three prominent churches: St. Phillip's Cathedral, the Second Ponce de Leon Baptist Church, and the Cathedral of Christ the King. While he was grateful for the fact that a young child hadn't died, the death of the overweight, middle-aged man who ran the pool's snack bar had traumatized the children and their mothers or caretakers to the point of hysteria by the time he'd arrived.

"Mr. Dan" had eaten a few of his own hot dogs before stepping out behind the fence that surrounded the pool and having a cigarette, according to the teenage boy who had worked for him for the last two summers. When he'd returned, he was clutching his chest and gasping, "Call 911." One of the mothers who knew CPR had tried to revive him when he'd fallen unconscious, just outside the snack bar's screen door, to no avail. By the time the EMTs arrived ten minutes later, everyone able to walk or be carried had gathered around to watch the frantic proceedings. As the uniforms who'd taken the call tried to calm everyone down, while trying to gather as much information as they could, Joplin had examined the victim, talked to the EMTs and the teenage helper, and taken pictures. When he had finished, he'd asked the uniforms to try to disperse the crowd before he ordered transport for the body.

"They don't need to see that," he'd said, thinking of his own "Mr. Dan" at the community pool in the small town of Austell, Georgia where he'd grown up. And then he'd stayed with the body until the van arrived, something he normally didn't do.

Now he sat in his cubicle and waited for 4 p.m. to arrive, something he also normally didn't do. Joplin's years as a homicide detective had made him oblivious to schedules and the hours they imposed. He wondered if maybe he couldn't handle the job anymore and then wondered if it was because of his injuries, or whatever psychological trauma he had suffered during the Carter case, that made him feel the way he did. Or maybe it was the murder scene that morning and its harrowing resemblance to the one at the Woodridge house. The two images of the victims, hovering side-by-side, filled his mind again, and he shook his head, trying to banish them.

Joplin was troubled by the fact that the Piedmont lab hadn't been able to identify the "morphine derivative" found in Libba Ann Woodridge's system. It indicated a level of sophistication that he should have expected, given what he'd observed at the scene.

"Not your job, Hollis," he said out loud.

As if to mock him, two things happened simultaneously: his cell phone rang and flashed Tom Halloran's name on the screen, and Carrie Salinger appeared at his cubicle.

"Let me just take care of this, and I'll be right with you," Joplin said to her. Carrie nodded and sat down in Deke Crawford's chair. "What's up, Tom?"

"Just what I was going to ask you, Hollis. Anything new since we talked on Wednesday?"

"Nothing new here," Joplin replied. He was not going to go down that rabbit hole again and had decided to tell the attorney nothing about the Sanchez case. He was sure Halloran would be all over him once the story hit the evening news, but his plan was to sic him on Jim Mullins when that happened. He also decided not to share what Hernandez had told him about the scene on Blackland Road. Time enough when the official report came out.

Carrie raised her eyebrows and tilted her head, a questioning look on her face.

There was silence on the other end of the phone as, he was sure, Tom Halloran was deciding whether or not to believe him. "Okay," he said finally, "but please keep me posted."

"Will do."

"You doing okay? Maggie said she'd be happy to bring some food over to you this weekend."

Momentarily taken aback by the sincere concern he heard in the attorney's voice, Joplin couldn't answer right away.

"Hollis?"

"I'm fine, really. And I still have food in the freezer from Maggie's last care package," he said, suddenly feeling guilty.

"Good. I'll tell her that. Have a good weekend."

"You, too. And tell Maggie I said hello." Joplin clicked off, then waited for the inevitable.

"You're not going to tell him about the Sanchez case?" Carrie asked.

He shrugged. "He'll find out about it soon enough. And if he makes the connection, I'll put him in touch with Mullins. It's his case. I'm with the ME's office, Carrie, not Halloran's private investigator."

"I thought you two were friends."

"He saved my life; I saved his life. Does that make us friends?"

Carrie stared at him. "Some people would say that it does. Or should, anyway."

"Look, I like Tom. And Maggie, too—especially Maggie. She's been a doll. But when you've spent as much time as I have testifying in murder cases, you'll find out how ruthless attorneys can be. And Tom Halloran's no different."

"Maybe so," she said, eyes flashing. "But if I needed an attorney—or a friend, for that matter—Tom would be a good choice. No one would have known that *his* friend Elliot Carter was murdered if Tom hadn't pushed the envelope. And as Libba Woodridge's attorney, he seems to be doing everything he can to protect her, including pushing the investigation of the attack on her in any way he can." She folded her arms and glared. "Everybody should be so ruthless."

"Okay, okay!" Joplin said, laughing, his hands held up in mock surrender. "I stand corrected: Tom Halloran's a prince of a fellow, and I should be ashamed of myself for thinking otherwise. Just don't forget that we might have been able to solve the Carter case sooner if he hadn't kept so many secrets."

"I'll grant you that," said Carrie, sounding a little mollified.

"And I'll tell him about the Sanchez case, I promise. I've just had a...long day," he added, knowing he was playing the "I'm recovering from gunshot wounds" card. "I'll call him back tomorrow."

Carrie looked stricken, and Joplin felt immediately remorseful.

"Oh, Hollis, I'm so—"

"I'm fine, really," he insisted. "Listen, can you tell me a little about the Sanchez autopsy?"

"Sure." She cleared her throat, then said, "Cause of death was blunt force trauma to the head. Her skull was fractured in two places."

"Was she raped?"

Carrie shrugged. "The UV light didn't show any semen stains on the body or the clothing. There were signs of sexual activity within the past twenty-four hours, but nothing to indicate force. We took swabs, of course."

"How about the weapon?"

"A mallet. A meat tenderizer, to be exact. And a pretty big one, at that."

Joplin stared at her. "That clinches it then."

"What do you mean?"

"Hernandez phoned me just before I was called out to a scene. I tried to get hold of you, but you were already doing the autopsy. He told me the perp in the Woodridge case filled a partially inflated basketball with Libba Ann's blood and then kept hitting it with a meat mallet and moving it around to make the blood spatter all over the wall and ceiling. He found transfer stains from the mallet on the sheet."

"And I found indentation marks made by a meat mallet on Maria Sanchez's skin after we wiped the blood off of her. Hollis, the cases are definitely connected."

"Yes, they are—and not just by the weapon used or the way both women were positioned. Hernandez wanted to know what I meant when I said the Woodridge scene looked 'staged,' and after I thought about it, I told him the whole thing looked like a painting. Like the guy was using the blood to make some kind of hideous piece of art. And he said that was his conclusion, too. His computer program and the experiments he did with a meat mallet and the basketballs showed that the perp kept moving the ball around to make the patterns on the wall and ceiling."

"Detective Mullins said Hernandez was going to visit the scene this afternoon. I sure hope he can make sense of this." Carrie closed her eyes, then opened them and said, "What I mean is—"

"I know what you mean."

———

Halloran sat in his office, dissecting what Hollis Joplin had said to him. He'd had enough experience listening to clients, taking depositions, and cross-examining witnesses in court to know when people weren't telling the truth, and he was certain Joplin was lying to him. Or at the very least, being evasive. He wasn't really surprised; the investigator had made it very clear that he didn't want to be involved in Libba's case. But more than that, he'd sensed that Joplin was deliberately hiding something.

Something important.

This thought reminded Halloran that he, himself, was hiding something important. Something that most certainly would help the police in their investigation of the attack on Libba. And yet, he had a fiduciary responsibility to his client not to reveal anything she'd told him in confidence without her consent. Under the ABA Model Rules of Professional Conduct, he could only reveal such information "to prevent reasonably certain death or substantial bodily harm." There was also a Massachusetts ruling that he might be able to cite as a precedent which bypassed the rule where doing so would prevent "substantial injury to the financial interests or property of another, or prevent the wrongful execution or incarceration of another." Halloran knew them both by heart.

Briefly, he considered whether the video Libba Ann had shown him afforded any recourse. Her attacker hadn't threatened death or even bodily harm, however, and even though the note promised the video would be released if she didn't cough up a million dollars, Halloran doubted that would rise to the level of "substantial injury" to her assets or property. The Woodridge estate was enormous, by any measure. Besides, he'd already wired the money to the account in the Cayman Islands at Libba's insistence.

And yet, Halloran knew that blackmailers usually didn't stop blackmailing their victims, especially when the first attempt was successful. There was also the possibility that even though the money had been sent, Libba's attacker might try to gain access to her again and…Do what? Actually rape her this time? Or even try to kill her? He had hired Ed Jenkins for an indefinite period of time, but even that was no guarantee that she'd be safe. The perpetrator had breached a very expensive security system the first time, and even though all the codes had been changed and more sensors had been added, they were dealing with someone who either had a high level of electronic expertise or had somehow obtained the security code.

Captain Martucci had assured him that everyone at Alderman Security was being interviewed and checked out thoroughly, but now he wondered if he should have told Libba to replace them. Doing that, however, would have allowed even more people access to the house on Blackland Road, which was a risk in itself. It occurred to him that perhaps this very concern over Libba's safety might provide the mitigating circumstance that would allow him to breach confidentiality. He was turning this over in his mind when the phone rang.

"Tom Halloran."

"It's me," said Maggie." I won't keep you, but I went ahead and called Julie after I talked to you and invited her and Libba and Lucas over for dinner this Sunday. She said Connie Sue is going home that morning, so we won't have to have her, too."

"Great. I'll want Ed Jenkins to go along, but that shouldn't be a problem."

"Speaking of going along, what would you think of my inviting Hollis, too? And maybe Carrie?"

Halloran chuckled. "You haven't given up on getting those two together, have you, Maggie?"

"I haven't even begun," she said cryptically.

"Fine with me. I just talked to him. Maybe you can catch him before he leaves his office."

And maybe I can find out what Joplin isn't telling me, if he comes to dinner, thought Halloran after he'd said goodbye to Maggie.

CHAPTER FOURTEEN

Joplin pulled out of the parking lot at the ME's office and turned onto Cheshire Bridge, wondering if he'd done the right thing in accepting Maggie Halloran's invitation to dinner on Sunday. He hadn't been thrilled at the prospect of seeing Libba Ann Woodridge again or meeting Julie Benning, and when Maggie had casually mentioned that she was also going to invite Carrie, he'd started floundering around for excuses. Maggie had nipped that in the bud, of course, pleading "poor Tom's" case at being the only man among four women, since it didn't look like Julie's boyfriend could come.

"I'm sure he'll rise to the occasion, Maggie."

"Please, Hollis—if not for Tom's sake, then mine," she'd said, hitting his obligation nerve big-time. "I'd really like to see you, and I'll even throw in a kitty-bag for Quincy."

Joplin sighed into the phone. He'd learned enough about Maggie Halloran to know that whatever she did came from her heart, but he'd also known that all the creature comforts she supplied him with over the past three months might come with a price tag. Especially if it benefitted Tom, or, perhaps in this case, Libba Woodridge. Or even Carrie. "You drive a hard bargain, Maggie. I'll come, with pleasure, but only if you'll tell me what some of your favorite wines are, so I can contribute to the dinner. You've done far too much for me as it is."

"Done," she answered, laughing. "Let me figure out what I'm cooking, and I'll text you about the wines, okay?"

"Okay," he'd agreed, and they'd parted on a happy note, but now he was second-guessing himself. It wasn't so much the idea of being drawn further into the Woodridge case, as it was being in a social situation with Carrie. Working with her, seeing her almost every day was difficult enough. But this would be almost like a...date. Despite how deep his feelings for her were, things were moving too fast for him.

Everything except the traffic, of course.

Rush hour in Atlanta on a Friday usually started well before four p.m., and today was no exception. Joplin was trying to decide whether it would be better to take Lindbergh to Piedmont rather than Lenox to Peachtree, when his cell phone rang.

"I think I just threw you under the bus, Hollis," said Mary Martucci, her voice tense.

Getting into the left lane to turn onto Lindbergh, he said, "Let me guess— you told Tom Halloran about the Sanchez murder."

"'Fraid so. He called me a few minutes ago, said he wanted an update. I just assumed he was talking about Sanchez, not the Woodridge case, and I told him we were still processing the info from the scene that Jim Mullins sent over, but it looked like a ringer for his client's case. You can guess what happened after that."

Joplin closed his eyes and sighed. "Did it involve shit hitting a fan?"

"Buckets of it. And even though I'm under no directive to give the man information, I ended up stammering out that I thought *you* had told him about the murder. That's when I found out he'd just talked to you, and you never said a word about Sanchez. I owe you big time."

"Forget about it, Mary. It's my problem, not yours. I didn't feel like I needed to let him know as soon as I left the scene, but the autopsy provided strong evidence that the two cases are linked. Halloran had a right to know that, and I stonewalled him. I plan on calling him tomorrow and putting him in touch with Jim Mullins."

Now it was Martucci's turn to sigh. "Yeah, well, you won't need to do that, Hollis. I already gave him Mullins' phone number. I'm just a wealth of information," she added.

"As I said, not your problem. And maybe Halloran will cross me off his list of sources now."

"Anything I can do, you let me know, okay?"

"Sure thing, Mary. Have a good weekend."

———

Quincy was waiting for him by the kitchen door when Joplin let himself into his apartment thirty minutes later. He twined himself in between Joplin's ankles and purred; not quite the raucous, affectionate greeting a dog would give, but welcome nonetheless. Especially after the day Joplin had had. He got a can of Fancy Feast Grilled Chicken out of the cabinet, scooped it into a paper bowl, then put fresh water in one of the plastic bowls that lay on a placemat decorated with green fish. An untouched bowl of Kit 'n Kaboodle was next to it. Quincy only ate that as a last resort. Then Joplin took himself off to the bathroom to empty and change his colostomy bag; it had been about three days since he'd last done it.

Back in the kitchen, Joplin opened the refrigerator door and glanced at the bottles of Yuengling, then slammed it shut and turned to his liquor cabinet.

It was definitely a Jim Beam kind of day.

He knew he'd probably get shit-faced if he didn't make himself eat something. Knew he should call Tom Halloran and explain why he hadn't told him about the Sanchez case. Knew there were better ways to handle his stress.

Didn't care.

He managed to make it through the Nightly News, trying to focus on Brian Williams as he covered the 4x400 meter relay race at the London

Olympics. Williams again featured Oscar Pistorius and the South African team's successful appeal to be allowed to run in the final heat after being disqualified earlier, when Ofentse Mogawane had been unable to finish his lap after being knocked out of his lane by a Kenyan runner. He got up and made himself another drink, tired of all the fuss over Pistorius.

———

Joplin woke up to find Quincy in his lap, a half-empty bottle of Jim Beam on the coffee table, and *Dateline*, its crooning, overly-dramatic narrator talking about murder in a small town in Arizona, on the TV. He looked at his watch; it was 10:35 p.m. He'd had no dinner, but the thought of defrosting something Maggie Halloran had brought him churned up too many guilty feelings. Instead, he patted Quincy and lurched to his feet, carrying the cat, who was complaining loudly; Quincy didn't like being carried, even by Joplin. The distance to his bedroom seemed longer than usual, but he made it without falling down and deposited the cat on the bed. He also managed to strip down to his underwear and then made an attempt to brush his teeth, but the tooth paste was hiding from him. He settled for a quick rinse with mouthwash.

Squinting, Joplin peered at the bedside clock, which told him it was now almost eleven o'clock. He chuckled to himself, sure that it was too late for Tom Halloran to call him. Feeling as if he'd won some kind of victory, he got into bed.

Sleep, however, proved to be somewhat of a mixed bag. At first, it was dreamless, but then the Jim Beam wore off. He had a series of dreams after that, each of which, except for one, jolted him awake and made it difficult to go back to sleep. In the first, Joplin saw a string of alternating black and white paper dolls. Their legs and arms were outstretched, connecting the chain. The only features they had were enormous red mouths stretched out in what he knew were screams, though he couldn't hear them. Then a hand appeared, clutching scissors. It cut the paper dolls into pairs, then began to cut each pair into ribbons. Now he could hear the screams, calling for him to help them. Begging him to stop the pain.

He woke up in a sweat, looking frantically around the room. Quincy was nowhere to be seen. Joplin's heart was racing; he got up and thrust his head under the bathroom faucet, gulping water as fast as he could. It had been a long time since he'd gotten drunk, but he knew the best remedy for it, besides time.

"Hydration," he murmured to himself as he lumbered back to bed.

But hydration could only do so much, especially since he'd had nothing to eat since lunch. When he sank again into sleep, Joplin found himself in an artist's studio. He was surrounded by enormous paintings that showed all kinds of living creatures being attacked by predators: a bird struggling in the mouth of a large cat; a fox being torn apart by hounds; a rhino, one of its forelegs raised in a futile effort to protect itself as human hands were chopping off its horn and most of its face. But the worst was yet to come.

Joplin tried to wake himself up as he turned away from these paintings and saw others that showed human beings. Some of them he recognized from crime scenes over the years, during his time as a beat cop, as well as when he was a detective and then a death investigator: the trembling, mewling baby he'd found in a dumpster his first day as a rookie cop; the teenage boy, lying in a hospital bed, who'd been beaten to a pulp by school bullies for being gay; Elliot Carter, eyes open, tongue blackened, hanging from a tree limb in Piedmont Park; Libba Anne Woodridge, her face contorted by fear as she realized that she couldn't remember what had happened to her. Others were people that he didn't know, but these were the worst. They were all women, and all of them were positioned in the same way Libba and Maria Sanchez had been—arms and legs outstretched—and all were covered in blood. They were the worst, Joplin realized, even as he slept, because they were victims he hadn't been able to save.

"Christ Almighty" he gasped, sitting up in bed. He was covered in sweat and breathing as if he'd been chasing a perp for at least six blocks. He sank back down on the pillow, trying to calm himself and to make sense of what he'd dreamed. He'd long ago learned to believe in intuition, in the feelings and senses that were informed by his subconscious and fueled by his eidetic memory, which was both a gift and a curse. But nothing came, although he lay there for what seemed like hours.

Exhaustion finally overtook him, and he drifted into sleep, despite his fear that he'd have more nightmares. Instead, Joplin found himself on a little boat with Carrie. The sun glinted on her hair, making it look blue-black, and she was laughing as Joplin rowed them out to the middle of a lake.

"Thank you," she said, tilting her head to one side.

"For what?" he answered, smiling back at her.

"For making us safe."

"How am I doing that?"

"You'll see," she said, trailing her hand in the water.

CHAPTER FIFTEEN

The first thing Joplin did on Saturday morning after feeding Quincy, down-ing several cups of coffee and eating a huge plate of scrambled eggs, bacon and toast, was to call Tom Halloran. He fully expected the attorney to be furious with him and was prepared to apologize up and down, but Halloran threw him a curve.

"Don't worry about it," he said pleasantly, when Joplin started explaining. "I know you have certain constraints on what information you can give me and when you can give it."

Joplin couldn't answer right away. Without understanding why, he was certain that Halloran, too, had been keeping something from him.

"Thanks, Tom. I appreciate that. Have you had a chance to talk to Detective Mullins?"

"At length. He agrees that the two cases are very much connected. In fact, he already has a suspect in mind and is getting a warrant for his DNA and fingerprints."

"*What?*" Joplin exploded into the phone. His head immediately felt the effect.

"I think you mean 'who?' Hollis," said Halloran coolly. "And that would be Jorge Martinez."

"Who the hell is Jorge Martinez?"

"He's the foreman of the landscape company that takes care of the Woodridge house. He's also the husband of Maria Sanchez. Or was, anyway."

Joplin rubbed his eyes with the thumb and middle finger of his right hand and swore never to drink again. "Why isn't his name Sanchez, then?"

"Because in many Hispanic countries, a wife doesn't take her husband's name; she retains her mother's family name, as do her own daughters."

Joplin saw a ray of light. "You mean, like the Russians do?"

He heard Halloran sigh. "Not at all. The mother isn't even *considered* in Russia. A woman's last name becomes a feminine version of her father's first name when she's born, and when she marries, she adds a feminine version of her husband's name. Like Anna Karenina."

"I know you're a really smart guy, Tom, and I'm just from the sticks," said Joplin, trying to sound patient. "But did you just pull that out of your butt?"

"Actually, I was a Political Science major at the University of Chicago, but my advisor recommended that I take a Russian Lit course as a sophomore that focused on the political structure of pre-Revolutionary Russia. *Anna Karenina* was one of my favorite novels. So I can tell you that Anna Arkadeyvna, whose father's first name was Arkady, became Anna Ardadyevna Karenina when she married Sergei Karenin."

Joplin felt his brain begin to pour out of his right ear. "No wonder she threw herself under a train." When Halloran didn't respond to this, he switched the subject. "I realize that that's a big connection between the two cases--"

"You mean, besides the fact that the crime scenes were almost identical, Hollis?"

"Again, I'm sorry I didn't tell you about Maria Sanchez. Really. Can we just get past that?"

"Sure," Halloran said, almost too quickly.

He took a deep breath and let it out. "Good. As I said, the fact that Jorge Martinez was employed by the landscape company that took care of the Woodridge grounds and is the husband of the murder victim is pretty damning, but Jim Mullins is a very thorough investigator. Was there anything else that put this Jorge right in his sights?"

"I'm sure that's what the warrant is all about. Semen was found in Maria Sanchez during the autopsy, and the APD Crime Scene Unit found a partial finger print on a piece of glass from the basement window of the Woodridge house where they think Libba's attacker gained entrance. Captain Martucci passed it on to Mullins, and he's looking for a match. But another piece of 'damning' information was also revealed when they interviewed Jorge again yesterday afternoon: He was a medic in Iraq. So he'd certainly have had the ability to extract blood from a victim without killing her and to pump her full of drugs."

Joplin took a minute to digest this and immediately thought of what Jimmy Hernandez had told him about his reconstruction of the crime scene at the Woodridge house, using a meat mallet and a basketball. Halloran would certainly find out about that once Jimmy's report was released, but he decided it wouldn't be right for him to divulge that kind of information until it was. He also wasn't going to put himself on BJ Reardon's shit list again. Instead, he said, "Well, that's certainly true, Tom. And Jim Mullins just gave you all this information because you called him up and said you were Mrs. Woodridge's lawyer?"

"Actually, yes. Especially after I told him that Captain Martucci had given me his name and number and encouraged me to call him."

"And I'm sure you played up your connection to me, right?"

"Of course. What are friends for?"

Joplin laughed, in spite of himself. "You're a piece of work, Tom. Really. Does this mean you're going to come clean about whatever it is you're not telling *me*?"

"I have no idea what you're talking about, Hollis."

Motherfucker! Joplin thought. Aloud, he said, "See you on Sunday."

"Oh, by the way," Halloran said, catching him before he hung up, "I probably won't tell Libba about any of this until Monday, so don't mention it at dinner."

"I wouldn't anyway, but are you sure not letting her know is a good idea?"

"I don't want to talk to her about this until her mother has gone home, which won't happen until tomorrow afternoon. I also want her to enjoy the evening, as much as possible."

"You know your client better than I do, Counselor. What if she asks me about her case, though?"

"Stonewall her," said Halloran. "I think you can handle that."

Joplin laughed again and clicked off his phone without saying goodbye.

————

He took a long shower, and by the time he'd shaved and dressed, Joplin felt almost human again. Resolving to lay off the Jim Beam until he'd recuperated a bit longer, he decided a little housework might be in order. He was separating laundry into piles when his cell phone rang.

"Joplin."

"Hollis, I need to see you. Right away."

"Jimmy?"

"Yes. Can you meet me at the La Fonda on Roswell at Wieuca at noon?"

"Sure, but, what's going on? You sound upset."

"I can't talk about this on the phone. You'll be there?"

"Of course, but—"

Hernandez had already cut the line. Joplin stared at his phone for several seconds, then put it back in his pocket and finished the laundry piles. Jimmy Hernandez had always been one of the calmest, most...contained...

persons he'd ever known. What had happened to make him sound as if his whole world was coming to an end?

———

Joplin was a big believer in the restorative powers of grease after too much alcohol. He usually sought relief at the Varsity—two Glorifieds, onion rings, and French fries—but the cheese dip and an order of pork enchiladas at La Fonda would be just as good, he decided. He looked around for Jimmy before sliding into a booth near the door, but didn't see him. Within seconds, a server had deposited a menu and a bowl of salsa with chips on the table. Briefly, he thought of having a Dos Equis to tide himself over until the cheese dip arrived, but then remembered Jimmy Hernandez's worried tone on the phone and decided to have a Diet Coke instead. The door opened, and he saw Hernandez walk in, looking just as upset as he'd sounded earlier.

"Jimmy," he called, waving.

Several people turned to look at Hernandez as he made his way to Joplin's booth. He was only about five-nine, but his shaved head and lean runner's body made him look more like an athlete than a forensics specialist. He was wearing jeans and a white Tommy Bahama tee shirt, which made his skin seem even darker than it was and the unusual golden color of his eyes more pronounced. As soon as he sat down, a server appeared, pad and pencil in hand, asking if they were ready to order.

"Uno Dos Equis, por favor," said Hernandez quickly.

"Make that two," Joplin said. "And some cheese dip—with jalapenos," he added. "We'll order the rest when you come back."

The server nodded, and when he'd left them, Joplin said, "So what's going on, Jimmy?"

Hernandez shook his head, looked down, then back up at Joplin and said,

"Jorge Martinez is in police custody. I think he's going to be charged with Maria Sanchez's murder."

Puzzled, Joplin said, "Well, I heard from Tom Halloran this morning that he was a person of interest, but why does that upset you so much? Do you know him?"

"Yes, I do. In fact, I got him the job with Joseph Feeney, and that's what's connecting him to the Woodridge case."

Joplin remembered the name from his hospital visit to Libba Woodridge. "He owns the landscape company that services the Woodridge house, right?"

"Yes. After I graduated from GSU, I became part of a support group that was involved with helping Hispanic vets find jobs when they left the military. Giving back, you know?"

"Sure," said Joplin, although he knew of Hernandez' military service in Saudi Arabia and thought that had been "giving back" enough.

"Joseph was a medic in Iraq in 2008 and had lost both his legs from the knees down during a rescue mission. He got blown up by an IED. We helped him get a van outfitted with a lift for his wheel chair and a loan to start his company, which did really well from the get-go. Anyway, I met Jorge about three years ago. He'd been a medic in Iraq, too, and he was so bright, Hollis! I tried to talk him into going to college on the GI bill, like I did, but his wife was pregnant with their first child by then, and he said he needed to work. So I called Joseph, who'd been a good resource in the past, and put him in touch with Jorge. Within a few months, Joseph made him a foreman, he was so hard-working."

"Did you ever meet his wife?"

"No, and I didn't connect the name 'Maria Sanchez' with her when you asked me to process the crime scene. Jorge had talked about her and their two kids whenever we got together, but I only knew her as 'Maria.'"

The server returned with their beers and the cheese dip, then took their lunch orders. Joplin waited until he'd moved away, then said, "So were you the one who told Jim Mullins that Jorge worked for the Woodridges' landscape company?"

"No!" Hernandez insisted. "I didn't even know that myself until Joseph called me this morning and said he was in police custody. Jorge had called him from the police station after they served the warrant on him and took fingerprints and DNA."

"But wasn't his name in the Sanchez file Mullins gave you?"

"Yes, but I didn't know that either. I knew I wouldn't be able to take much from the scene back to the lab, so after talking a little with Detective Mullins, I took my own high-res photos and measurements and some samples, got the file from him and left. I took everything back to the lab, but didn't even look at the file until after Joseph called me this morning. I planned on working on the case this afternoon." Hernandez set his beer down on the table and locked eyes with Joplin. "Hollis, I will never believe that Jorge Martinez had anything to do with killing his wife. Or the attack on Libba Woodridge either! He's a good, decent man who loves his family and works hard to give them what he didn't have growing up. Just like my dad did. And now he's been pulled into some kind of nightmare. I went over the photos taken by the Sandy Springs CSU, and what was done to Maria was the work of…uno psicopata—a crazy person!"

"I agree," said Joplin, remembering his first view of the body. He decided to switch the subject and said, "Have you talked to BJ yet?"

Hernandez shook his head and took another swig of his beer. "You're the only person I've talked to about this since Joseph called me. He wants to hire a lawyer for Jorge and thought I could give him some names. He didn't know I was consulting on the case."

"Jimmy, you know BJ and Mary Martucci are going to see a big problem with this. Jim Mullins, too, for that matter when he finds out. You had already finished your report on Libba Woodridge before you took on

Sanchez, but the fact that you know the person who's probably going to be charged in both cases is too big to ignore. The blood spatter evidence is going to be crucial, and if this goes to trial, whoever defends Jorge Martinez will crucify you."

Their lunch arrived, and they busied themselves with napkins and utensils, but Joplin had lost his appetite. Hernandez evidently had as well, because he put down his fork and shoved his plate aside.

"Not if the forensics back me up," he said. "I may not believe that Jorge is guilty, but my reconstruction of the murder will be based on scientific evidence, not my feelings. You know me well enough to know that about me."

Joplin nodded slowly. "I know that you would do everything in your power to try to ensure that, Jimmy, but I've also heard you say that what you do is as much an art as it is a science. That's where subjectivity can muddy the water, and that's what will open the door for any good defense lawyer."

"No one can do as good a job on this scene as I can," Hernandez said fiercely.

"I believe that, too, Jimmy—that's why I wanted you to work the case. But don't short-change the Sandy Springs CSU. They'll do a good job, and I'm sure Mary Martucci will get a copy of the report. Then you can go over it with a fine-toothed comb and see if there are any problems."

Hernandez nodded, and his shoulders relaxed a little. "I'll talk to BJ when I get back to the lab."

"I'll follow you and pick up the case file. I can call Jim Mullins on my way and explain the situation."

"Thanks, Hollis. I really appreciate this."

"I got you into this, Jimmy. It's the least I can do."

CHAPTER SIXTEEN

Halloran had gone to the office for a few hours after talking to Hollis Joplin, then met Maggie and the kids for lunch at the Park Tavern in Midtown. Despite the rising temperature, they'd decided to sit outside, on a terrace that overlooked Piedmont Park. Tommy and Meghan had been in rare form, telling stories about their first week back at school and competing, he could tell, for his attention, but without their usual snarkiness. He'd made changes in his life in the past three months; the biggest one was spending more time with his family. Almost being killed by the psychopath who'd murdered Elliot Carter had produced a moment of clarity that he'd vowed never to forget. And as he listened to his children's chatter, Halloran tried to be as present in the moment as he could. Yet, something had been nagging at his mind since his phone conversation with Detective Mullins on Friday. Something that lessened his relief that Libba Woodridge's attacker might have been identified.

"Piper Adams is in my class, Daddy!" said Meghan. "And Bridget Maher and Betsy Lowe—just like last year!" She turned to Maggie and said, "Can I have a sleep-over next weekend, Mommy?"

"We'll see," said Maggie, giving the time-honored "maybe" of all mothers.

Tommy gave his sister a disgusted look. "If you do, I'm not gonna be there," he announced. "I mean it. You and your silly friends kept me awake all night the last time they came over."

"So did *your* friends," Meghan insisted. "Playing all those Xbox games!"

Halloran and Maggie looked at each other, and he motioned for the server to bring the check.

Détente was over.

The kids went home with Maggie, and Halloran had time to try to figure out what was bothering him. He'd been remembering the few times he'd seen Jorge Martinez at the Woodridge house and suddenly realized that what he recalled didn't seem to fit the hooded figure in the video that Libba had shown him. Jorge was short and stocky with broad shoulders; the man in the video seemed taller and more slender. Or was that because of the black pants and hoodie he was wearing? Deciding he needed to see it again, especially the first part, where the figure was standing, Halloran turned into off Piedmont onto The Prado, the main street of their Ansley Park neighborhood.

"The kids have play dates," Maggie told him as he walked into the kitchen. "Tommy's having Ryan over here, and Meghan's going to Piper's."

"You mind taking her?" Halloran asked. "I need to check on something?"

"Actually, Susan Adams is picking her up when she's finished running errands. You okay? You seemed a little preoccupied at lunch."

Maggie was very good at reading him. Too good sometimes. "I know. I'm sorry."

"Anything to do with Libba's case?" she asked, head cocked and green eyes staring at him.

Halloran smiled and shook his head. "You're a witch, Maggie Halloran. It does, but I can't talk about it. I *will* promise, however, that I won't let it ruin our Saturday."

Maggie stood up on tiptoes and gave him a quick kiss. "Good, because I have plans for you tonight after we put the hoodlums to bed."

Halloran raised his eyebrows. "Sounds like my favorite type of plans."

"I'll start looking for the Scrabble game," she said, turning and heading for the den.

"Very funny."

She held one hand up and gave him a backward wave, then wiggled her behind.

After twelve years of marriage, she turned him on more than ever.

Pulling his eyes off his wife, Halloran walked quickly to his study and opened the safe hidden behind a lovely Tuscan landscape by Loretta Locanto, a local artist. He retrieved the DVD, locked up the safe and sat down at his desk. After inserting the disc, Libba's bedroom came into view, followed by the hooded figure. Halloran watched again as the figure approached the bed, trying to gauge his height and weight. He paused the video just as the man stood directly next to it and tried to estimate how high the bed was. Unsuccessful, he closed his eyes and pictured it as he had seen it on Monday, before the blood spatter analyst had had everything taken to the lab.

Halloran remembered that when he'd stood next to the bed, the top of it was about level with his left hip. The man in the video must be several inches shorter, he decided, because the bed reached his waist. Granted, he himself was six foot-four, yet the figure seemed to be taller than he remembered Jorge being. And thinner, with narrower shoulders, if his memory were correct. But could that be the result of some distortion by the camera, deliberate or otherwise?

Halloran let the recording play out, hoping to get more information. He was once more struck by the horror of the situation for Libba Woodridge. How having this released to the Internet—or even to the police for that matter—would be devastating for her. But should her feelings take precedence over a possibly innocent man's freedom? he wondered.

Deciding he'd better get an update from Mullins before pursuing this line of thought, Halloran pulled out his cell phone and found the detective's number, then punched the phone icon.

"Detective Mullins."

Halloran identified himself and apologized for bothering him on a Saturday, then said, "Any luck with the warrants on Jorge Martinez yet?"

"Signed last night and executed this morning, as a matter of fact. We asked him to come to the station, and while his prints and DNA were being taken, my partner and some of the folks from our CSU were going over his apartment."

"Were his children there?" Halloran asked, hoping otherwise.

"No, he'd told me when I called him that he'd have to take them to a neighbor's apartment before he could get here. But now that we've charged him with his wife's murder, we'll have to locate a relative or contact Child Protective Services."

"I take it you were able to find enough evidence to support that charge," Halloran said carefully.

"Our expert found eight points of similarity between the partial latent we had from the basement window and the right index fingerprint we took from Mr. Martinez. That's on the low side for two full prints, but pretty damn good for a partial latent and a full. He also admitted having sex with his wife before she left the apartment, so the DNA will match up. Would've been better for our case if he'd denied it, and then we got a match, but we got enough from a canvass of the apartment building and the search warrant to nail him."

"What do you mean?" Halloran held his breath, hoping what had been found would alleviate his concerns about Jorge's guilt.

"Well, two of his neighbors heard what sounded like an argument coming from the apartment around nine-thirty the night she was killed, and a door slamming a little before ten p.m., but that's not the kicker, Mr. Halloran."

"What *is*, Detective Mullins?"

"We found something that belonged to your client hidden in a bureau drawer in his bedroom."

"What was it?"

"Her 2006 Miss Georgia sash."

———

It could have been planted, thought Halloran after he'd thanked Mullins and clicked off his phone. Just as the damning evidence against Elliot Carter had been. Briefly, he thought of calling the Georgia Bar's ethics hotline. On the one hand, he was withholding evidence in a criminal case by not turning the video over to the police; on the other hand, it had been given to him by his client, and he was bound by the attorney/client privilege. He was also loath to do anything that would tip the scales of Libba's already tenuous emotional state. But he couldn't, in conscience, sit by and let Jorge Martinez be charged with a crime he might not have committed.

And then he had an idea.

———

"How'd you like to make a little extra money?"

Maggie looked up from the vegetables she was threading onto a metal skewer and smiled. "What'd you have in mind, sailor?"

Halloran placed a sheet of paper on the kitchen island. "I want to hire you as a consultant on the Woodridge case."

Maggie cocked her head to one side. "A consultant?"

"Remember how you were able to glean a lot of information from those photos Anne Carter claimed to have found in Elliot's bureau drawer at the Highlands house? You said they were 'pictures of pictures?' Hollis was able to figure out who the killer was when I told him about that. So, I'd like you to look at a video that Libba gave me, but I have to hire you so that it can be part of an attorney-client work product and preserve her privilege of confidentiality." He glanced down at the sheet of paper. "This is a contract to engage your services."

"Does she *know* you're hiring me?"

"No," Halloran replied. "But I need your help. It might save an innocent man from being convicted of murder." Seeing the shock on his wife's face, he quickly explained the circumstances, telling her about the video, the million-dollar extortion, Libba's insistence that he not reveal the existence of the video to law enforcement, and the subsequent arrest of Jorge Martinez for the murder of his wife. He had told Maggie about the Sanchez murder the night before, after learning about it from Captain Martucci, but hadn't told her about his conversation with Mullins that morning. He filled her in now, but left out the detail of the Miss Georgia sash, for reasons he wasn't sure about.

Maggie looked down at the kitchen island for several seconds. "I'm still having trouble understanding why you can't take this video to the police. I mean, I can certainly see why Libba doesn't want anyone to see it, but she's allowing herself to be extorted over something she had no control over, and it could help the police catch this guy. She's a *victim*, Tom, not a suspect, and she hasn't been charged with a crime, so why is there an issue of attorney/client privilege?"

"It's just not that simple," Halloran replied. "I said exactly the same things to her after I saw the video, but she invoked the privilege and insisted that I not give it to the police. I can be released from it if I would be preventing a crime, and extortion is certainly a crime, but, again, she's the victim, not the extortionist. And I can't use the excuse that her life is in danger, because the perpetrator threatened her with humiliation, not physical harm. There's also the issue that I'm not only defending Arliss Woodridge's will and trust against a lawsuit brought by his family, I'm also specifically representing Libba as his executrix and major beneficiary. Releasing this tape to the police might somehow negatively impact her in the case."

"How so?"

Halloran shrugged. "Who knows? That's just the point. I wouldn't put anything past that group. The video could be leaked, just as Libba fears, and I wouldn't put it past them to allege that the whole thing was a publicity stunt. Wesley Benning has already suggested that. They could also claim that it was just a sex tape that somehow surfaced, and a jury could be very affected by that."

"Have you discussed this with Alston? I mean, you told me you've consulted with him on the Woodridge case several times in the past six months. Why not about this?"

"Because even though there's a possibility that it might have a connection to the will, it's a very slim one, and I can't justify talking to Alston just yet."

"I still think you should let the police handle this, Tom. If Jorge is innocent, surely they'll come across some evidence that exonerates him."

"In a perfect world, that would happen, of course. But there have been too many men on death row who were later exonerated by DNA evidence to argue against that. On the other hand, he could be guilty as sin. I looked at the video again a little while ago when I heard Jorge had been arrested, and I have trouble believing that it's him. But it could have been…manipulated somehow. Or distorted because of the equipment used. I just don't know enough about videotapes, Maggie."

Maggie stared at him. "And you think I would? I'm a *still* photographer, Tom."

"Yes, but you also use a video camera to get a feel for the families and children you photograph before the actual sitting, right?"

Maggie nodded slowly. "Yes, but that's just a preliminary thing, to sort out backgrounds and interactions between children and the children and their parents. It's research, not what I actually do. It's something the average person can do. What you need is a videographer to advise you."

"What you were able to see in those photos Anne gave me after Elliot died went way beyond what the average person would see. I think you can do the same thing with this video. At the very least, you can tell me if I'm crazy to think that the figure in it isn't Jorge. And if I'm *not* crazy, help me to convince Libba that we have to give it to Captain Martucci or Lt. Mullins."

Maggie turned on the water at the island's sink and slowly washed her hands. Grabbing a towel, she looked up at him and said, "Is this tape going to be as bad as the photos Anne gave you?"

"Worse, in some ways," he said slowly. "But at least there are no children in it."

CHAPTER SEVENTEEN

Julie Benning rode the elevator up to her parents' penthouse apartment at the Park Avenue. The doors opened directly into the black-and-white-tiled foyer, and she braced herself for what probably wouldn't be a pleasant evening. She hadn't wanted to come; it had been over two weeks since she'd seen them, pleading final exams. Now that the summer quarter was over, however, she had no excuses to hide behind and had agreed to come to dinner.

"Bring Lucas, too," her mother had said. "We haven't seen much of him this summer either."

The emphasis placed on the word "either" was meant, of course, to make her feel guilty. Guilty for not visiting or getting together with them often enough. Guilty for not keeping them posted on her relationship with Lucas. And, most of all, guilty for continuing to be friends with Libba and not joining them in their attempt to have her grandfather's will overturned.

That, more than anything.

"I'm changing into something more comfortable," her mother called out to her from the master bedroom. "It's been a long day."

"That's fine," Julie responded.

"Have a glass of Prosecco. It's on the coffee table. Your father will be home any minute."

Julie walked into the huge room, with its ten-foot ceilings, large marble fireplace, Persian rugs and two walls of glass and sat down on one of the enormous over-stuffed sofas. She hadn't grown up here; her parents had "down-sized" from a mansion on Tuxedo Road five years ago, just after she'd started her freshman year at Brown. They still owned the vacation house on Isle of Palms in Charleston that her grandfather had given them as a wedding present, but that might have to be sold in the near future, as her mother had told her several times that summer. It was now heavily mortgaged, Julie knew, from hearing bits and pieces of conversations over the years when her parents thought she was out of ear-shot.

She also knew that her mother had long ago gone through the trust fund that Arliss Woodridge had set up for his only daughter. And although her father was a name partner at his law firm—Gardner, Benning and Stovall— it had suffered the same economic blows that other law firms and businesses in Atlanta had experienced during the recession.

From the day Julie had learned of her grandfather's new will, she had resolved to help her parents—her great-aunts and her uncle, too, if they needed it—with the huge amount of money he had left her. She had told them so, too, hoping it would ease their financial concerns and lessen the vitriol they felt for Libba.

It had been like talking to a wall. A thick, brick one.

"My father would never have bypassed me for my own daughter if that woman hadn't put him up to it," her mother had insisted. "I don't need to take charity from you."

"Much as he loved you, your grandfather wasn't in his right mind," her father had said. "And she took advantage of that. He would *want* us to fight this."

Her great-aunts, both childless widows, had joined the lawsuit and assault on Libba's character, but their financial situations were relatively secure. They contented themselves with updates on upcoming hearings without needing to participate in the frequent meetings with lawyers. Only her Uncle Chandler had refused to join the suit. Or, at least, that was what his psychiatrist at Ridgeview, where he'd been a patient for the past three months, had told her. Her uncle was still not allowed visitors, but she'd been assured that her message and request had been passed on to him and refused. First and foremost, Dr. Langford had told her, Chandler didn't want to jeopardize his sobriety, which the stress of a lawsuit might do.

He was right, and she knew it. She had some vivid memories of her uncle's behavior—and the stress and embarrassment it caused everyone in the family, particularly his latest relapse, just after her grandfather's death. Before that, he'd managed to stay drug-free for three years, after yet another stay at Ridgeview. Arliss Woodridge had paid for it, as usual. Chandler had been forty-three at the time, and it hadn't been his first time in rehab. Or even his fifth.

But while Julie had no desire to jeopardize Chandler's sobriety, she did wish she and Libba had someone else on their side. Even Lucas hadn't been as supportive as she'd hoped. He'd certainly agreed that her grandfather had every right to leave his money to any person and any institution he wished, but he'd urged her to try to convince Libba that they should settle with the family.

"You have no idea how long these things can take, Julie," he'd said to her more than once. "By the time the dust has settled, the family's even more estranged. And the lawyers take away a pile of cash."

Tom Halloran had essentially said the same thing to her and Libba, even the part about the lawyers involved in the process getting rich. And so they'd agreed to let him meet with the opposing attorney, someone named Charles Devereau from Bader, Simpson and Farley, to see if a reasonable settlement were possible. According to Tom, Mr. Devereau had gotten back to him with the "disappointing news"—Devereau's words, accompanied by a sorrowful tone—that the family would accept nothing less than "complete capitulation"—Tom's words, spoken scornfully—and a reinstatement of her grandfather's original will. Devereau had told Tom that he'd urged them to reconsider, but wasn't very optimistic.

"I think the aunts are open to a settlement, from what Charles told me, but not your parents," Tom had said, seeming to search her face for the effect his words might have, when he met with her and Libba. "Your mother, in particular. I think she's very hurt by what seems to be a sort of…rejection or even abandonment by your grandfather."

So the legal process—and the tension between her and her parents—had continued.

Julie picked up one of the flutes on the coffee table and poured herself some Prosecco from the chilled bottle in its silver bucket. "Here's to a fabulous evening," she said softly, raising her glass.

"What did you say, darling?"

Guiltily, she turned around to see her mother standing near the hallway, turning up the sleeves of a long, black-and-white silk shirt she wore over black leggings. Her blonde, feathery hair was perfect, as was her makeup and simple, but expensive, jewelry. Julie had always known that she was a source of disappointment to her mother because of her love of sporty, casual clothes that didn't have designer labels. Likewise, because of her love of sports and outdoor, physical activity. And her height. At five-foot-nine, she towered over her petite mother.

"You must be a throwback to some Viking or Celtic ancestor on your father's side," her mother had told her many times. She had laughed whenever she'd said it, but the implication was clear: Julie didn't fit in with her mother's idea of what a Woodridge woman should look like, what her mother and great-aunts looked like. Neither, of course, did Libba, who was an even greater source of irritation for her mother, with her long legs and "trashy, runway clothes."

Only her father had seemed to accept and even be proud of Julie's looks.

"The Bennings were an important Scottish clan," he would respond whenever he heard her mother talk about her that way. "We *are* descended from Vikings—you're right there, Claudia—but we settled in Scotland in the fourteenth century, and our motto is 'Virtute Doloque,' 'By Valour and Craft.' Don't ever forget that, darlin.'"

And Julie hadn't, but she was never certain whether it was the valor or the craft that her father held in such high esteem, or even what "craft" meant. Did it, she wondered, mean the ability to make something well, or to accomplish some goal through guile or deception?

"Just toasting myself for getting through my last two exams yesterday," she said now to her mother, putting her glass down and standing up. "They were pretty grueling."

"I don't know how you do it," her mother replied, shaking her head. She came up to Julie and gave her a hug, then poured herself a glass of Prosecco. "You should have at least taken the summer off. Is Lucas coming?"

"No. He said to thank you, but he had his last exam today, and he's bushed. He hopes we can all get together for lunch some time before he goes to visit his parents next week."

"Well, that'll be nice. They live in North Carolina, don't they?"

Julie nodded, then quickly switched the subject, hoping to avoid more questions about Lucas's family or her relationship with him. "What kept you so busy today?" she asked.

"Another committee meeting for the Shepherd Center gala," her mother said, taking a long sip of her wine. "It wasn't easy replacing Anne Carter as chair, I can tell you that. And we had to practically start over once we found someone willing to take it on."

Anne Carter's murder three months earlier had been a blow to the movers and shakers of Atlanta's social scene, Julie knew. So had the death of her estranged husband, Elliot Carter. But it had been devastating to Tom Halloran, who had found his body in Piedmont Park and then forced law enforcement agents to investigate the death as a homicide, rather than an accident. She had known Elliot since she was a child and had attended the funeral, even though her parents were conspicuously absent, not wanting to run into Tom. They had gone to Anne's funeral two weeks later, however, knowing they'd have many of their own friends with whom they could congregate.

"Why didn't *you* take it on, Mom?" Julie asked. "I'm sure the committee asked you."

"Yes, but I'd just finished chairing the March of Dimes Dining Out in May, and before that, I was on the Swan Coach House committee for the April Ball. I just couldn't do it." She poured herself another glass of Prosecco and stood up. "Come out to the kitchen with me, darling. Sandra fixed that halibut dish you like so much," she said, referring to the housekeeper the Bennings had had for over a decade. "I need to preheat the oven and find out what she made for appetizers. I'm starving."

They had almost made it to the kitchen when they heard the front door open.

"Where's my favorite daughter?" her father's voice called out.

CHAPTER EIGHTEEN

Joplin sat in a booth at the bar of Horseradish Grill, waiting for Carrie. It was where they'd had their second date, on a warm, breezy Sunday afternoon in May, and he was sure that was why she had chosen it today. They had lingered over brunch, walked around Chastain Park, then ended up back at Horseradish for a drink. Despite the fact that he'd been raised in a small, Southern Baptist town by a family that had only stopped working the land a few decades earlier, and that Carrie came from a wealthy Jewish family that expected her to marry another doctor, or at least an attorney or a CPA, Joplin had begun to believe that they were embarking on something special. Something he hadn't allowed himself to hope for in several years. Two weeks after that, he knew he had lost her to Jack Tyndall, and it had almost killed him.

Literally, as it turned out, as well as figuratively.

The server approached, glanced at the two menus the hostess had placed on the table and asked if he wanted to order a drink or wait for the other person to join him. Knowing the restaurant didn't serve Yuengling, Joplin asked for a Stella Artois and congratulated himself on being so flexible: Yuengling at home; Dos Equis at La Fonda; Stella at Horseradish Grill. The common denominator, of course, was alcohol. And although he'd planned on drinking very little that day, circumstances had conspired against him.

Discussing Jimmy's conflict of interest on the Sanchez case with BJ Reardon, who'd looked back and forth at each of them as Joplin talked, as if trying to decide where he should direct the first diatribe, had been stressful enough. Listening to the ensuing diatribe(s) had certainly added to the stress. And then, although an agreement had finally been reached as to how to deal with the situation—give the Sanchez case back to Sandy Springs and notify Mary Martucci of Jorge Martinez' arrest and the connection between the two cases, then alert the DA's office of the potential problem if either or both cases went to trial—he still had to schlepp the case materials back to Jim Mullins and tell *him* what was going on. BJ had adamantly refused to handle that, reminding Joplin that he hadn't been consulted when Joplin had offered Jimmy's services to Sandy Springs.

All in all, a cluster-fuck of the highest order.

If he'd been allowed to leave Mullins' office, tail between his legs, and nurse his hangover and the stress of dealing with a virtual perfect storm of egos, jurisdictions, angst, and a potential capital murder case, he might have been okay. But then Carrie had called him, ostensibly to find out if he'd let Tom Halloran know about the connections between the Sanchez and Woodridge cases.

Ostensibly.

In the past ten days, they'd spent more time with each other than in the four months that had passed since they'd enjoyed that idyllic—to Joplin, at least—afternoon at this same restaurant. The proximity had certainly gotten to him, despite his efforts to keep Carrie at arms' length. So when she'd found out he was on Roswell Road, returning from Mullins' office, and casually suggested that they meet at Horseradish to discuss the situation, he'd agreed. But he'd begun to realize that Carrie Salinger was not a person who gave up easily, and that realization filled his heart with equal amounts of joy and fear.

His beer arrived at the same moment that Carrie came through the rustic entry hall of the restaurant and approached the hostess' podium. He took a big gulp of it as she was pointed toward his booth, then stood up to greet her. She was wearing the soft pink skirt and sweater she'd worn when he'd taken her to Angelo's in Virginia Highlands on their first date.

It was going to be a full-court press.

"You look pretty," he told her, resisting the impulse to give her a hug.

"You look tired," she said, her doctor face on. "Maybe this wasn't a good idea, after the day you've had."

"It depends upon what you have in mind," he said, ushering her into the booth.

Carrie laughed and shook her head as she scooted into the booth. "I promise I'm not going to lecture you again. Or force myself on you," she added, making him pause as he sat back down. "And from the look on your face, I can tell you were worried about that, Hollis."

"Not worried, really, just…"

"Not ready?" she offered.

He considered this, then said, "Yes, but not in the way you think."

"You don't really *know* what I think, Hollis. I don't think you ever have."

He looked up at her, surprised, then felt himself relax a little. "You're right. I *don't* really know what you think about things, only what I've imagined."

"Then I guess I'd better order a drink and tell you," she said, surprising him again.

"I guess you'd better. What would you like?"

"A Dirty Martini. Stoli, straight up."

Joplin stared at her. "You got it," he said, motioning for the server. "I didn't think you were much of a drinker."

"I'm not, but hard times call for hard liquor. Are you going to stick with beer?"

When the server arrived, Joplin ordered Carrie's Martini and a Jim Beam and water for himself.

"Light on the water," he added.

———

It was as if no time had passed, yet everything had changed. As if, in four months, all that had happened had impacted them each at some deep level, yet they still had an intense connection. Without once referring to Jack Tyndall, Carrie told him of the conflict and turmoil she'd felt in May. She talked of the sheer terror she'd felt as she waited with Maggie and Tom at the hospital while he was in surgery, then the hours she'd spent sitting in a chair by his bed when he was in a coma. She told him about the talks she'd had with Dr. Minton and Ike Simmons and the Hallorans— and even her own parents, who'd known nothing about him until that terrible night. She'd learned things about him from his colleagues and Tom Halloran that had confirmed everything she'd known about him in her heart. And she'd confided things to Maggie and her parents about how important he was to her.

"They want to meet you, by the way."

"Your parents?" he asked, feeling a little panicky again.

"Yes, but that can wait, Hollis. There's no rush."

"Good," he said, taking a big sip of his drink and looking around for the server. "How about another drink?"

"Fine with me, but then we'll order some food and you'll tell me all about Tom and Jimmy Hernandez and BJ. And then we'll go back to your place."

Joplin had taken another big sip of his drink, which he almost spit out. "My place?" he said, his voice a raspy whisper.

"Of course. I have to move out of my place before I can bring you there," she said, still not alluding to Jack Tyndall. "I'm just leasing it, so don't worry."

"I…I wasn't," he said lamely. "It's just that…"

"You don't want things to go any further until your colostomy bag is removed."

His mouth dropped open. "How did you know that?"

"Because I'm very perceptive and analytical. It's a real pain in the ass, but sometimes it's a big help. You're also not that hard to read."

"I'm not?" Joplin said, feeling a little wounded. And exposed.

"That's a good thing, Hollis," she answered, still not alluding to Jack. "And as I said, I'm not going to force myself on you. In fact, I want us to take things very slowly. For myself, as well as you."

He took her hand and brought it up to his mouth. The server appeared just at that moment and coughed discreetly. "Another round," Joplin told him. "We'll order when you get back."

———

Dinner was over, and the kids were in bed, if not asleep. Halloran poured them each a glass of pinot noir and suggested they watch the tape in his office. He didn't want to take any chances that either of the children might wander downstairs and see what was on it. Settling Maggie into the chair at his desk, he pulled another one up next to her and inserted the disc into his computer. Just as with every other time Halloran had viewed it, the first shot showed the bedroom door opening and Libba Anne Woodridge asleep in her bed.

Maggie put a hand up to her mouth, then said, "Jesus, Tom."

He watched her as she watched the video. Her eyes were glued to it, but she closed them from time to time and shook her head. She also sighed at certain points and gasped at others, providing a kind of sound track that made what was happening on screen even worse. What she was expressing were all the things that Halloran himself had felt, but it seemed somehow more disturbing to watch a woman watch what another woman was going through at the hands of a sadist. When the man in the video groaned and let the mallet fall onto the bed and the film went blank, Maggie sagged back on the chair, then sat up and took a deep breath.

"I need to see it again," she said.

———

"I'm sorry for making you watch that," said Halloran. "I wouldn't have done it unless—"

"This is why you're paying me the big bucks, Tom, remember?"

"I hadn't realized we'd ever discussed your fee," he said.

"We didn't, but it's going to be big."

Halloran smiled, despite the circumstances. "What can you tell me?"

Frowning in concentration, Maggie started the video over, then froze it as Libba's bedroom came into view. "A light in the hall is on. I can see shadows reflected on the wall behind the bed, and there must be a light on in the master bath, because there's a faint glow off to the left. He must have entered the room before he turned on the camera because here—" she said, pointing to the right as the image dipped, then settled, "he's putting it into a tripod that's already in place. I use a Benro 3773 when I videotape kids and backgrounds, so that might be what he used. Then the light from the hall disappears, so he must have closed the door, just in case Libba woke up and started screaming. But almost immediately, another source of light, probably from an LED light attached to the camera, focuses on the bed. He could also be speeding up the film to mitigate the lack of light and using a longer lens."

"I'll take your word for that," Halloran said dryly. "Can you tell what kind of camera might have been used? It looks a lot more professional than if he'd used a phone."

"I don't know," Maggie said, shrugging. "Maybe some kind of cad cam. Probably a Panasonic GH 4. I've heard those are good."

"You're speaking in a foreign language, sweetie, remember?"

"It's a type of hybrid camera. A still camera that can also tape things, but only until it runs out of minutes."

"Okay, but why would he use that instead of a regular video camera?"

"Because it's easier to edit content. If he needed to, I mean."

"And did he? I mean, could he edit things like height or weight?"

"Maybe. The question is: Did he? Isn't that what you want to know?"

"Yes."

Maggie frowned again. "There are a few things that show he *might* have. I can see some noise and some hard edges on the hooded figure that could be evidence of editing—of distorting the images. He might also have used a remote filter of some kind to blur the images."

Halloran thought about this and nodded. "Okay. Have you ever seen Jorge Martinez when you've visited Libba?"

"Just once, back in May. At least I'm assuming it was him. He was standing near the company's truck while two men were pruning some bushes."

"He's about five-nine, with a stocky build and broad shoulders." When Maggie nodded, Halloran said, "The figure in this video looks much taller and thinner. Could Jorge—or anyone, for that matter—have been able to edit the video to disguise himself?"

"You're asking two different questions, Counselor. First, I have absolutely no idea if Jorge himself had the ability to do something like that."

Halloran laughed and smiled at her. "Objection sustained, my dear: facts not in evidence. You'd make a good lawyer, Maggie."

"I'm perfectly happy just being the wife of one, thank you. As to whether he or anyone else *could* do that, the answer is, of course."

"What do you mean?"

"Think of any one of the movies in *The Lord of the Ring* trilogy, Tom. The special-effects people made normal-sized actors into hobbits and dwarves."

"Right, but you're talking about professionals. Movie people."

"Yes, but there's software that was created by 'movie people,' as you say, that anyone can buy."

"Like what?"

"Well, Adobe has a program for video cameras called 'After Effects' that can do what you're talking about. I came across that when I briefly considered a client's request to make her overweight young daughter look thinner."

"You're kidding."

"I wish I were. I met with the family, and it was obvious that this little girl felt miserable about herself, especially in comparison to her older, thinner sister. So I went online and found out I could buy a program that would let me edit images like magazines do when they 'air brush' wrinkles and scars from their models and featured actresses, or make them look taller and thinner. But I just couldn't do it. I like to think that my work is about capturing what's…special about a child. Not turning him or her into a cookie-cutter version of what the parent might want to project."

"Good for you."

Maggie shrugged and took a sip of her wine. "Yeah, well, I wish the mother had felt that way. I told her I couldn't do what she asked and suggested that I spend some time with both girls and take a few preliminary shots, see what I could come up with, but she said she'd find somebody else. She was absolutely certain that her daughter would 'lose the baby fat' as she put it, and wouldn't want to see pictures of herself at some later date that captured her in such an 'awkward phase.' Anyway, that's how I know a little about software programs like this. I remember I also came across a program called Fusion that's offered by a site called 'Black Magic,' and you can access the Digital Media Academy for software and tutorials. So, yes, the average person could learn how to manipulate images on a video like this."

"But you can't say for sure that that was actually done, right?"

"Not really. A forensic computer analyst could do it, which is why I think the video should be turned over to the police. Maybe you could relieve Libba's fears by telling her you'd give it directly to this Captain Martucci you've mentioned. And that she would ensure that it would be seen and handled by as few people as possible."

Halloran nodded slowly, wondering if Libba might go for it. "It's a good idea, but something tells me she won't budge. All she wants to do now is forget about the whole thing?"

"Does she know Jorge Martinez has been arrested? Or about the evidence against him?"

"No. She doesn't even know about the Sanchez murder. I'm gambling on the fact that it'll probably take the media a few more days to make a connection between the two cases. I've been assured that no details were given out by the police after Libba's attack."

Maggie gave him a look of disbelief. "What about leaks from the hospital? And now that Jorge has been arrested, won't the media be able to find out that he was a supervisor for the landscape company that worked at the Woodridge estate?"

"Maybe," Halloran said, feeling defensive. "But she's very fragile right now, and I wanted to wait until Connie Sue went back to Brunswick. That woman would probably decide to hold a press conference and demand that Jorge be lynched."

"Well, you're right about that," Maggie admitted. "But there's too much of a risk that she might hear about it from someone else."

"Maybe," Halloran said again. "But if that happens, Ed Jenkins will alert me immediately, and I can get over there to do some damage control. I'm just buying some time, Maggie. I was also hoping this dinner tomorrow night might be a little break for her. In the meantime, would you have a chance to look at the video again? See if you can glean anything else from it? I know you'll be getting ready for the dinner party tomorrow, but maybe Monday?"

"I'd be happy to," Maggie responded, then smiled and said, "Can we discuss my fee now?"

CHAPTER NINETEEN

Joplin awoke to the smell of bacon and coffee. He also heard humming: it sounded like a tune from a Broadway musical, but he couldn't place it. Slowly, he opened his eyes and looked around his bedroom. Quincy was nowhere to be found, but he saw the pink outfit Carrie had been wearing last night draped over the chair on the other side of the room. Groaning, he made himself sit up and then looked down to see what he was wearing: black Jockey boxers and a Braves tee shirt that, fortunately, covered his colostomy bag.

In seconds, images of the night before flooded his brain: Carrie smiling at him from across the booth at Horseradish Grill; her mouth as she opened it to take a bite of the halibut she'd ordered; the hostess as she wished them a great night when they were leaving the restaurant; Quincy's face as he greeted them at the kitchen door; Carrie, looking both beautiful and formidable as she announced that she was going to spend the night and that, no, he wasn't sleeping on the couch.

So they had spent the night together in Joplin's bed. It was the first time since his divorce (not counting the occasional bouts of what the Viagra commercials called "erectile dysfunction") that he had actually slept with a woman and not had sex with her. He'd pulled a Falcons tee shirt out of his bureau for Carrie to change into, and while she was in the bathroom had quickly stripped down to his shorts and thrown on the Braves shirt, the largest one he had. When she'd come out, looking even more beautiful without make-up, the tee shirt reaching to mid-thigh of her long, shapely legs, he'd felt…gobsmacked.

It was the only word Joplin could think of now to describe how he'd felt as he'd stared at her, the light from the bathroom silhouetting her as she'd entered the dimly-lit bedroom. He'd walked over to her and put his arms around her, then kissed her softly and asked, "Are you sure about this?"

"Of course," she'd said and kissed him back. Then she'd cocked her head and said, "Is that a colostomy bag, or are you just glad to see me?"

They'd both exploded into giggles, then crawled, still laughing, into bed. It had been the perfect ice-breaker, and after a little more kissing and snuggling, they'd relaxed, spoon-style, into sleep.

It had been one of the best nights of his life.

"You ready for breakfast?" Carrie asked, suddenly appearing in the door. She was holding Quincy in her arms, and, more amazingly, Quincy seemed to be enjoying it. He was actually purring.

Even cats, Joplin realized, could be gobsmacked.

––––

She had made an amazing frittata, with bacon and cheese and various odds and ends in his refrigerator. She'd also found some cut-up fruit that he'd bought at Publix a few days earlier and had avoided till then. The coffee was strong, just the way he liked it, and he noticed that Carrie, too, drank it black.

"This is delicious," he said between mouthfuls. "You never told me you could cook."

"You never asked."

An image of Jack Tyndall, looking up at him from his desk and asking if Carrie could cook, suddenly flooded his vision, and his fork clattered onto his plate.

"Are you okay, Hollis?"

The alarm in Carrie's voice brought him back to the present. Joplin smiled, retrieved his fork and said, "I'm fine. I just realized that I never briefed Sarah Petersen on the whole Hernandez/Jorge Martinez thing. I talked to BJ, Jim Mullins, and Martucci, but not my own boss. She's gonna be pissed, and I wouldn't blame her." All of this was true, except that it had occurred to him the night before, on the drive home from the restaurant. It was a good cover, however, for his momentary lapse into the past.

"Why don't you call her after we finish breakfast? I need to shower and get home, but maybe we could go to the Hallorans' house together?"

"Of course—I planned on that! Well, I mean, after—"

"I know what you mean."

"Good," he said, smiling. "But, I think I'll clean up the kitchen while you shower, and call Sarah when you've left; it's still a little early to call her on a Sunday morning. Are you sure you have to go though?"

A faint blush spread across Carrie's cheeks, and she ducked her head, then looked back up at him. "I think so. Last night was wonderful, but I may go back on my promise not to jump your bones if I stay here much longer. I really do want to take things slowly, Hollis."

He put down his fork and covered her left hand with his own. "I do, too. But it wouldn't be rushing things if I gave my doctor a call and found out when I can get this damn bag removed, would it?"

She grinned and said, "In my professional opinion, no, it wouldn't be. And if you want a second opinion: No, it wouldn't be."

———

To Joplin's relief, Sarah Petersen kept her cool when he finally called her. He could tell she wasn't thrilled that he hadn't filled her in the day before, but she'd accepted his explanation that he'd been pretty drained by the time he left Mullins' office. And even though he'd rallied by the time Carrie got to the restaurant, it was the God's honest truth.

Pretty much anyway.

The actual truth was that he'd simply forgotten that he should report to her. MacKenzie wouldn't have wanted to be bothered, especially on a Saturday. His former chief, now spending his days in disgrace in the small town of Dublin, Georgia and running his aging father-in-law's funeral parlor, hadn't even bothered to feign interest in the people he supervised, much less the deaths they were investigating. He'd simply been biding his time, waiting for an early retirement to a cabin in north Georgia. Now he'd been stripped of his pension as a result of his failure to do his job—as well as his duty—as a law enforcement officer. And although the powers that be had finally agreed not to charge him with obstruction in the Carter case, the cabin had been sold to pay the lawyer who'd negotiated that particular deal. MacKenzie would be wearing black suits and solemn expressions and shaking hands with grieving family members till he died himself.

"What's your gut saying about this case, Hollis?" There was a pause, and then his boss said, "Bad choice of words. Sorry."

"No offense taken, Ma'am."

Petersen sighed. "We've talked about this, Hollis."

"Sorry…Sarah. Listen, can I just call you 'Chief?' The title fits you far better than your predecessor."

"I'd be honored."

"Great," Joplin replied, relieved. "As far as my 'gut' is concerned, I don't trust it these days. It didn't help me much during the Carter case."

"I disagree. What we call 'gut' in law enforcement is based on observation, analysis and experience, and from what I've heard, this office would have had several more bodies to deal with and a serial killer still on the loose, if you hadn't used yours."

"If you say so, Chief."

"I do. So tell me what you think at this point."

Joplin sighed as he thought of the past few weeks. "It's complicated, for one thing. And more is going on than meets the eye. There are a lot of similarities between the two cases, and a lot of connections—too many, as far as I'm concerned."

"What do you mean?"

"I'm not sure, really. But it still seems…staged, somehow. And Jorge Martinez doesn't seem like the kind of person who could stage all this. But if he did, he sure made a stupid mistake."

"How so?"

"Jimmy didn't know this when I met him for lunch—Mullins told me—but the search warrant for Martinez' apartment turned up some pretty damning evidence—they found a sash Libba Woodridge won when she was crowned 'Miss Georgia.' Not the kind of thing a mastermind would hide in his bureau drawer."

After several seconds, Sarah Petersen said, "Sounds like your gut is doing a fine job, Hollis."

"I'll tell my doctor that when I talk to him tomorrow, Chief."

"Wicked funny," she said dryly. "The thing that occurs to me is that all roads lead back to you, so to speak."

"I'm not quite sure what you mean."

"Well, you handled what we first thought was a death investigation on the Woodridge case, but it was handed over to SVU because the victim wasn't dead. Then you did the investigation on the Sanchez murder, but Sandy Springs has that case. You got Detective Mullins to request that Jimmy Hernandez, who did the analysis on the Woodridge case, also handle the Sanchez scene, but because he knows the suspect, he's now off that case. Dr. Salinger did the autopsy on Maria Sanchez, but she has no connection to the Woodridge case. And both Captain Martucci and Tom Halloran are linked to the Woodridge case, but not to Sanchez. I mean, I'm glad everybody is sharing information, but you're the only one who has an *official* involvement with both cases."

Joplin thought about this for a minute, then said, "I see what you mean, Chief, but what are you actually *saying*?"

Sarah Petersen sighed. "Just that, like you said earlier, it's a complicated situation. I'll try to run interference for you as much as possible, Hollis, but you're fast becoming everybody's football."

"Unfortunately, that's a pretty good analogy. You like football, Chief?"

"The Patriots were the only thing keeping me in Boston after the last few winters we had. Tom Brady's my boy, Hollis. Even my partner understands that."

"Smart woman. I haven't given up on the Falcons yet, but the Patriots are top on my list."

"Good to hear. Only thing that's really disappointed me about Atlanta—and the South in general, for that matter—is that the people here aren't into pro football as much as the college teams. Why do you think that is?"

Joplin chuckled. "Don't ever quote me on this, but I think it's part of the whole Civil War thing. A lot of people in the South—even very educated people—still call it 'The War of Northern Aggression.' Which is why the SEC *rules* here; it's almost like another form of secession from the Union, in a way."

His boss didn't respond to this right away, then said, "I'm not always sure when you're being serious and when you're pulling my leg, Hollis."

"A little bit of both this time. And although I wouldn't trade being Southern for all the tea in Boston Harbor, I think you'll see what I'm talking about when you've lived here a little longer."

"If that's true, how come you're not wrapped in the Confederate flag, so to speak?"

"I guess because I come from a long line of people who didn't grow up on plantations or believe in a fairy-tale South where all the masters were kind, and the slaves were happy. My ancestors were dirt-poor sharecroppers. They worked the land side-by-side with the freed slaves who thought the Emancipation Proclamation was going to change things, and most of them tried to help each other out when they could. I was raised mostly by my grandmother, and *her* grandmother told her stories about winters so bad they would have starved if the black family on the farm next to them hadn't shared what food they had with them. They returned the favor whenever they could."

Joplin closed his eyes, wondering how the conversation had taken such a turn and feeling like an idiot for talking to his boss about something that was far more complicated than the messy case—cases—in which he found himself. He also felt like a traitor, because he believed there were more people in the South who were *not* racist than the ones who were. It was just that those who were seemed to make all the headlines, both for their violent acts, as well as the way they wielded the political power they possessed.

"Sorry," he said. "Didn't mean to get on my soapbox."

"Actually, I've got pictures of myself at some early gay pride demonstrations that would put that little speech to shame, Hollis."

"Love to see them."

"Just keep me posted on the Woodridge and Sanchez cases, and I'll crack out the album when we have something to celebrate," she said, then clicked off.

CHAPTER TWENTY

Hollis had insisted on picking Carrie up at her condominium on Lenox Road, despite her protests that it was in the opposite direction of the Hallorans' house in Ansley Park. She had offered to pick *him* up or even just meet him there, but both suggestions had met with firm refusals.

"If you don't want me to come inside or even go to the door, I'll pretend we're both sixteen and just honk for you when I get there," he'd told her. "My grandmother will spin in her grave, but, if that's what you want, fine."

He hadn't pressed her as to why she didn't want him in her apartment, but Carrie was sure he suspected; there were just too many memories of Jack permeating the atmosphere, even though they'd only been intimate a short time. In the past, she had considered simply abandoning the place and moving somewhere else—anywhere else—but a lot of time had been taken up with the paperwork necessary to change her medical residency and then apply for a fellowship in forensic pathology at the ME's office. Dr. Minton had fast-tracked her application, but it had still taken several weeks. And then, of course, she'd had to deal with her parents' bewilderment over the changes she was making in her career, perhaps even in her personal life.

Carrie had talked to them about Hollis not long after he'd been shot, after a particularly bad day when she'd visited him at Grady. They had known he was a co-worker from the newspaper articles that filled the *Atlanta Journal/ Constitution* for several days, but hadn't known how she felt about him until she broke down that night at their house. The crisis—when Hollis had almost died during the surgery to remove a long section of his intestines—had passed, but, as usual, it had taken a few days for Carrie to acknowledge the depth of her feelings: fear and love, in equal measure. To her parents' credit, despite all the issues of religious and socio-economic differences—as well as Hollis' previous marriage—their only concern seemed to be the happiness of their one, remaining child. It had been an extraordinary revelation to her, one she wouldn't forget for a very long time. Judiciously, Carrie had chosen not to tell them about her involvement with Jack Tyndall. That could wait—maybe forever—as could her move from the condominium her parents had leased for her. Luckily, with everything going on, she'd spent very little time there, and had practically moved into the guest bedroom in an effort to escape the most intense memories of Jack.

Resolving to look up some available properties online the next day, Carrie shoved a lipstick and compact into the purse she was taking that night and headed into the living room to wait for Hollis. She heard three short honks by the time she got to the entry hall.

———

Joplin had jumped out of the driver's seat and was opening Carrie's door when she made it to the car. "My dates never held the door open for me when I was sixteen," she said, lowering herself into the car.

"My dates never looked like you, when I was sixteen," he shot back, closing the door and going back to the driver's side.

"No Jewish girls in Austell, Georgia?" she asked as he started the car.

"No drop-dead gorgeous girls like you, Jewish or not." He said, grinning at her. "But my grandmother worked for a man she called, 'Mr. Sy,' who owned an upscale discount clothing store in the area. She was one of the ladies who put the clothes back on the floor after the women had tried them on. Anyway, his full name was Simon Herschel, and he had a family, but they didn't live in Austell. And his children certainly didn't go to Austell High, if that's what you mean."

Carrie smiled. "I know the family you're talking about, and you're right. They lived in Atlanta, and the daughters—Lauren and Dana—went to Westminster."

"Just like you did, I guess."

"Yes, but a few years later."

"Do you know all the Jewish families in Atlanta, then?"

"Pretty much," she replied, laughing. "And even when I don't, I can always play 'Jewish Geography.'"

"Say what?"

"It's sort of like a Jewish version of 'Six Degrees of Separation.' You keep trying to find people you might know in common, and once you do, the number grows exponentially. It's, I don't know…comforting when you're a member of a minority group. There's a pretty big Jewish community in Atlanta, but it's still pretty small compared to—"

"The Bible Belt, that comprises most of the South?"

She laughed again and said, "Yeah, I guess you could say that."

Joplin glanced over at her as he turned right onto Buford Highway. "Did you experience much anti-Semitism growing up?"

"That's a complicated question," she said, frowning a little. "Or maybe it's the answer that's complicated. I guess the best way I can frame it is by telling you that my great-great-grandfather was one of the founders of the Standard Club."

"Oh, right," he said, nodding. "The Jewish country club here in Atlanta. I mean, that's what I've always heard it called," he added quickly, hoping he hadn't offended her.

She smiled, as if she'd heard that before and wasn't offended. "It was actually a reorganization of an older club founded during the Reconstruction years, called the Concordia Association, but in 1905, my great-grandfather and several other members relocated it and renamed it. Anyway, as you probably know, Jews were excluded from most country clubs—and not just in the South. Hence, the Standard Club. So, the fact that my ancestors were wealthy and had a certain prestige in Atlanta means that I was lucky enough to grow up here in a kind of 'bubble' that insulated me from what a lot of Jews experience."

Joplin glanced at her and said, "How come you don't look like you feel very lucky, then?"

She shook her head and turned to look out her window before answering. "Probably classic Jewish guilt. I haven't had to endure being called a 'kike' or a 'Christ-killer,' but money and position don't always protect people from bigotry, as history has shown us. Anti-Semitism is still alive and well, especially in the Middle East and parts of Europe. Even in Atlanta," she added, looking back at him.

"Yes," he said, thinking of his earlier conversation with Sarah Petersen. And yet he felt conflicted, even disloyal, in a way only another Southerner could understand. This thought was immediately contradicted by the realization that Carrie was just as "Southern" as he was, and had been for several generations, according to what he'd just learned. Deciding he would ponder what, exactly, the term "Southerner" meant another time, Joplin went up the ramp to a part of I-85 that would let them out on Peachtree near Ansley Park, then turned to Carrie and said, "I remember your telling me about going to your parents' house for a 'Shabbat dinner' back in May. They're Orthodox Jews, right?

"Right. I join them on Fridays sometimes, but even though I'll always consider myself to be Jewish, I'm not a practicing Jew anymore."

"That's okay with me," Joplin said, grinning. "I'm not a practicing Baptist anymore."

———

Although invited several times, Joplin had only been to the Hallorans' house on 17th Street once, a few days after his release from the hospital. On the steps of City Hall, Mayor Reed had presented Atlanta's Civilian of the Year award to Tom Halloran for his help in capturing the murderer of Elliot Carter, Ben Mashburn, and Anne Carter; Joplin had received the law enforcement version of the same award, as well as one for valor and bravery for preventing what might have been a blood bath at One Atlantic Center. He had remained in his wheel chair during the ceremony, unable to stand up that long, much less during the picture-taking afterwards. Although he'd tried to beg off, Maggie and Tom had both insisted that he go back to their house for a "family celebration" that had seemed to include most of their neighbors and friends, as well as co-workers from Tom's law firm and the ME's office. Including Carrie, of course.

Joplin had sat with Dr. Minton and his wife on an overstuffed couch in the Hallorans' cheerful, sunlit den, trying to relax, but with minimal success. He had enjoyed meeting Tommy and Megan, the Hallorans' children. The little girl had brought him small plates of food, smiling shyly at him each time, while the boy had peppered him with questions about guns and dead bodies; they were mini versions of their parents. The Hallorans themselves had been warm, generous hosts, looking out for his comfort as they introduced him to a few people they thought he might enjoy meeting, while steering others over to the bar or tables laden with food. Carrie, meanwhile had hovered around him, alternately watching him closely to monitor how he might be feeling, then fading out of view when he caught her looking at him.

He had fled at the first available opportunity, pleading exhaustion, first, then pain when Maggie had asked him to stay a little longer. The Mintons, who had brought him, immediately rose from their seats, ready to take him home, and Carrie had rushed over, offering her own services as a driver.

"No problem," Tom Halloran had said, pulling out his cell phone. "I can have Uber here in five minutes. No one else needs to leave."

Joplin had never used Uber, which was still pretty new to Atlanta, and wasn't sure he wanted to now. "I'll just call a cab," he said.

"This is much faster—and easier," Halloran said, pressing an icon on his phone.

"Well, let me pay for it then."

"It's automatically charged to me," the attorney said. "Tip included, by the way."

Just as Halloran had said, a black SUV was in the driveway five minutes later. Joplin had felt like a groom going off on a brideless honeymoon as a swarm of guests had ushered him out the door and down the front steps to the car, where a driver waited to receive him, passenger door open.

The only thing missing was rice being thrown at him.

Now he turned and looked at Carrie as they reached the Halloran's house, wondering if she was thinking about that day, too.

"I wish you had let me drive you home the last time we were here together," she said, answering his unspoken question.

"And deny me the opportunity of experiencing Uber?" he said, smiling. "That was probably my first *and* last time in the so-called 'black car.' I've been reading up on it," he added.

"And how did you like it?"

"I wish I had let you drive me home, too," he said, parking in front of the house. He took her hand and kissed it, their eyes locking. "But, hey," he added, "If I drink too much tonight, you might just get a second chance."

"You're on," she said, laughing.

———

The house was a beautiful, two-story Federalist-style mini-mansion. Not as ornate or historic as Elliot Carter's house was, but striking, nevertheless.

Joplin had meant to ask Maggie when it was built, and by whom, but had never gotten around to it; maybe tonight he'd remember to do that. He parked on the street behind a black Honda Accord and a fairly old Lexus sedan, neither of which he thought would belong to Libba Woodridge, then they walked up the sloping driveway.

Megan and Tommy opened the front door. Megan giggled at them, and Tommy said to Joplin, "I remember you. Did you bring your gun tonight?"

"Tommy!" Maggie said, rushing into the entry hall. "I *told* you not to ask Mr. Hollis about guns the last time he was here."

"It's okay, Maggie. I was the same way at his age. And no," he added, looking down at the boy, "I *didn't* bring my gun. I brought this nice lady instead."

"We know Dr. Carrie," said Megan shyly, reaching out and taking Carrie's hand. "Do you want to go see the new American Doll I got for my birthday? Mr. Jenkins has already seen it."

"Who's Mr. Jenkins?" Joplin asked, wondering if he belonged to one of the cars parked out front.

"Ed Jenkins is Libba's…security person," Maggie told him. "He's in the den," she added, then turned to her daughter and said, "Megan, why don't we let them come in and sit down first. You can show Dr. Carrie the doll in just a little bit, okay, sweetie? After you two finish your pizza."

"Okay," the little girl said and headed for the kitchen.

"And you go with her, please, Tommy. It's adult time."

Reluctantly, he followed his sister, glancing back at Joplin as he did.

"These are for you," Joplin said, handing Maggie two bottles of red wine.

"Brunello! Wow, I'm impressed."

"Don't be too impressed—I got them at Trader Joe's. One of the guys there recommended it when I said you were making a lamb pasta."

"Well, it was a great recommendation, Hollis, and Brunello is Brunello, no matter where you got it. It's also one of my favorite wines. I'm so glad you're both here, tonight," she added, looked from one to the other. "And did you possibly come together?"

"Don't start, Maggie, or I'll take back the wine," Joplin warned her.

"Well, look who's here," Tom Halloran said, appearing at the doorway to the living room.

"Hollis brought Brunello," said his wife, holding up the bottles.

"And Carrie, too, apparently," the attorney said, eying them speculatively.

"I wish I *had* brought my gun," said Joplin under his breath.

CHAPTER TWENTY-ONE

Joplin was surprised to see three people sitting on the taupe-colored couch
in the living room. Libba Woodridge he knew, and the pretty young blond
woman sitting next to her, who looked like her sister—or at least a cousin—
was obviously Arliss Woodridge's granddaughter, Julie Benning. But the
young man next to Julie, who rose as they came into the room, was an
unknown, although Joplin assumed he owned the Lexus parked outside.

"You've met Libba, Hollis, but I don't think she and Carrie have met,"
Halloran said. After "hellos" were exchanged, he then introduced Julie to
both of them. Finally, he turned to the young man and said, "This is Lucas
Frazier, Julie's boyfriend. He's in med school at Emory as well, and was able
to join us at the last minute."

Joplin held out his hand to Frazier, a tall, lanky redhead with artfully
spiked hair made to look like he'd just stepped out of the shower and then
had run his fingers through his hair. He also had one of those maddeningly
affected "two-day-old" beards that were popular and, in Joplin's opinion,
a big mistake. Frazier did have a surprisingly strong grip, but it didn't do
much to change Joplin's first impression of him.

"So tell me what areas of medicine you're thinking of," Carrie said, looking at Julie, then Lucas while Halloran went to fix drinks.

Glancing first at her boyfriend, Julie Benning smiled and said, "Orthopedics
for me. With an emphasis on sports medicine. I've pretty much been a jock

all my life, and I've been amazed at what these docs can do for injuries. And to help prevent them, of course."

Joplin took an immediate liking to her and wondered how she could have fallen for a guy like Lucas Frazier.

"It's a great field, and really cutting-edge, these days," said Carrie. "Good for you," she added, then turned expectantly to Frazier.

"Surgery, of course," he answered, a condescending smile on his face.

"Why, 'of course?'" Joplin asked, before Carrie could respond.

"Because that's where all the action is," he said, shrugging. "It's the only thing I've ever been interested in. No offense," he added, looking at Julie, then back at Carrie, "but I'd be bored by anything else."

Definitely a dickhead, thought Joplin.

———

Dinner was a lively affair, and Joplin was glad to see that Libba Woodridge seemed to relax as the evening went on. He decided Halloran was probably right not to tell her about the Sanchez murder and Jorge's arrest just yet, although Carrie had agreed with him that the attorney was taking a risk. The copious amounts of wine that the Hallorans served—starting with a Santa Margherita Pinot Grigio that went perfectly with, of all things, a Brussels sprouts Caesar salad—loosened everyone's tongues, including the former beauty queen's. She told several amusing stories about her time on the pageant circuit, which also provided ample evidence of a keen and observant wit. Not the bimbo she was made out to be by the media, he decided.

"Then there was Miss California in the 2003 Miss Teen USA contest," Libba went on. "It was my first national contest. Anyway, she aced the swim suit competition and the talent competition—she sang 'The Greatest Love,' of course—but she was a little freaked out by what we call the Big Bullshit Question that all these pageants have—you know, the ones with answers like 'world peace,' or "I'd like to find a cure for cancer"—that sort of thing.

Anyway, while we were changing into our long dresses for the big finale, she must have had a couple of Xanax or something, because by the time we were all lining up on the on the stage before the curtain came up, she was wasted. I mean *wasted!* I really felt sorry for her, because she was a decent person." Libba paused, her eyes shifting to the right, as if she were re-experiencing the moment. And maybe feeling bad about telling this story about poor Miss California.

"And?" said Lucas Frazier, eagerly. Too eagerly for Joplin's taste. "What happened next?"

Libba took a deep breath and said, "Well, it *was* pretty funny. When it was her turn, she was asked the question, 'How would you advise school administrators who were having drug problems at school?' And she got this real serious look on her face and nodded a little and then said, 'I would tell them not to use drugs—at least not at school. I mean, they're supposed to be giving a good example to the students, right? So if they're using drugs and the students know it—well, that's not a good example, is it?'"

Everyone at the table started laughing, Joplin included.

"So what was *your* question?" Frazier asked her, when the laughter had subsided, looking at her with an intensity that bothered Joplin, although he wasn't sure why. He saw Julie touch her boyfriend's arm, a puzzled look on her face, but Frazier didn't back off. "No, really, tell us. I insist."

"Lucas!" said Julie.

"No worries, Jules," Libba said. She tilted her head and stared back at Lucas Frazier, as if sizing him up, then said, "My question came right after hers, if you can believe it. It was 'Who's the person you admire the most?' And I said, 'Mr. Adams, the principal of my high school, because he sets a really good example for all of us. He's kind; he takes an interest in every single student; and he never uses drugs when he's at school. So I would definitely agree with what Miss California said."

The dining room exploded in laughter again, a few people clapping, and

Joplin had the satisfaction of seeing the almost predatory look on Frazier's face disappear.

"Wonderful!" said Carrie, still laughing. "Did you really say that, Libba?"

"I did," she answered, nodding solemnly. "Those pompous asses deserved it."

"So who won the title?" Halloran asked.

"Miss Arizona, as a matter of fact. She was a class act, and I was happy for her. But the judges could tell I was a hit with the audience, so I made First Runner-Up, which helped me in the Miss Georgia contest."

"And Miss California?" asked Lucas Frazier, his face a mask this time.

"She was actually Second Runner-Up, and she left the contest with her dignity intact. She married her college sweetheart, and has two kids. She friended me on Facebook and follows me on Twitter," Libba added, smiling. "At least, she *did*—before you suggested I close those accounts, Tom."

"It won't be forever," said Halloran, standing up. "And now, who's ready for Maggie's Lamb Pappardelle?"

———

The door to the kitchen swung open, and Hollis Joplin, his wide shoulders and unusually large head dominating the passage, said quietly, "May I come in?" His eyes flicked back to the dining room, separated from them only by a butler's pantry.

"Of, course," said Maggie.

"What do you know about this Lucas Frazier?" Joplin asked, as he approached the granite work island that held dinner plates and a huge platter of pasta and sauce.

Halloran, helping Maggie plate the food, paused and stared at him. "What do you mean?"

"Well, he *is* being kind of a jerk tonight, Tom," Maggie said as she scattered basil leaves over two plates.

"Just tonight?" Joplin asked.

Halloran shrugged. "I don't know him that well—I've only met him once before, and he seemed okay then."

"Was he around Libba then?"

Halloran frowned and handed the two plates to Joplin. "Take these out to the table, while I think about it. It'll also give you an excuse to keep coming back in here. Serve from the left," he added.

"Yes, milord," Joplin said, bowing his head.

"What do you think that's all about?" Maggie asked when they were alone again.

"I'm not sure. Just keep putting pasta on the plates while I think, okay?"

"Sure. And by the way, of course Libba was there when we met Lucas. It was at her house. What Hollis wants to know," she added, "was whether Lucas was acting so..."

"Aggressive around her?" Halloran finished.

"Yes," she answered, strewing basil leaves on two more plates of pasta. "But as I recall, he wasn't. He was very friendly and almost...deferential to her. Is that your recollection?"

"Yes, actually. So why is he acting so aggressive with her tonight, and, more importantly, why is Hollis zeroing in on it?" He frowned and added, "The obvious reason, of course, would be that he suspects Lucas of being involved in some way with the attack on Libba."

"Bingo, Counselor," said Joplin as he came back into the kitchen.

Halloran's mind immediately flashed back to the video Libba had given him, and he had to admit that Lucas Frazier's body type was much more similar to the man in it than Jorge Martinez' was. His eyes met Maggie's, and she gave an almost imperceptible nod. "Why would you think that, Hollis?" he asked, turning back to Joplin. "I mean, what would be his motive?"

"Whoever attacked your client wanted to completely humiliate her and scare the shit out of her. Excuse my language, Maggie," Joplin quickly added.

"He didn't kill her, like he did Maria Sanchez a week later, but he wanted to show her that he *could* have, which adds to the terror she must still be experiencing. It also shows that he wants some kind of control over her. What I saw a little while ago was an animal chasing its prey—and not liking it at all when the prey got away."

Halloran nodded slowly in agreement. "You'd better keep taking plates out," he said, handing them to Joplin.

"Right." He headed for the dining room.

"Tom, you've got to tell him about the video," Maggie whispered as they prepared two more plates.

"No, I don't. Hollis hasn't even said what possible motive Lucas Frazier might have to attack Libba. I have to admit, that little scene with her was certainly strange, but that doesn't raise him to the level of a suspect."

"How serious is the relationship between him and Julie Benning?" Joplin asked, the door swinging shut behind him.

"What does that have to do with anything?" Halloran demanded. "Julie is a beneficiary of Arliss Woodridge's will and trust in her own right. She wasn't cut out in the new will like the others."

"But she won't get anything while it's all tied up in litigation, will she, Counselor? And it could be tied up for a long time. Maybe years."

Before Halloran could respond to this, the door swung open again, and Carrie appeared. The evening was making him feel as if he were an actor in a French farce or an English comedy of manners. Except for the seriousness of the dialogue, of course.

"People are starting to wonder if there's another party going on in here," Carrie said pointedly.

"Here, take these in," Joplin said to her, handing her next two plates. "I'll fill you in later. And serve from the left," he added.

———

"There's one other possibility," Joplin said to the Hallorans when the door closed behind Carrie. It had occurred to him as he set plates of pasta in front of Frazier and Libba. He'd noticed that there was more room to maneuver between Julie and Lucas than between Lucas and Libba.

A very slight difference, but there, nonetheless.

"What if," he said, speaking very slowly, "your client planned the whole attack on herself and got young Lucas to carry it out?"

———

"You don't believe there's a possibility that Libba was behind all of this, do you, Tom—the attack, that ghastly video?" Maggie asked him when the last guest had left, and they were sitting at the kitchen table. "I can't even believe Hollis suggested such a thing."

"Actually, he wasn't the only one," said Halloran. He took a sip of the Glenlivet he'd poured himself a few minutes earlier. "Wesley and Claudia Benning lost no time in accusing her of that, and David Healey insinuated it when I got back to the office that day."

"Well, I'd consider the source with each of those snakes, but how can Hollis think such a thing?"

Halloran sighed. "There wasn't any time to ask him, if you recall, Maggie. But if I had to guess, knowing Hollis, it probably had to do with his observation of Lucas and Libba during the evening—and not just that Lucas seemed to be goading her. Hollis approaches things in a very instinctive way, relying on subliminal cues that the average person doesn't even register."

"You mean, because he has that eidetic memory you told me about?"

"It's partly that. He can tap into memories of things he's seen and play them over in his head when he's not sure why he's thinking something about a person or an event. He's talked to me about this before. But it goes beyond that, I think. He's analytical, but in an almost…spatial way, making connections and putting things together like pieces of a puzzle."

"But you're very analytical, too, Tom. And without the benefit of an eidetic memory."

"Actually," he said, smiling at her, "I'm the polar opposite of Hollis Joplin. Whether because of my legal training or my nature, I rely too much on logic and facts and statistics, and although deductive and inductive reasoning are certainly important in building a case or analyzing a situation, I tend to leave out the human factor. Something Hollis never does."

"So do you think he's right about Libba?"

"I don't think even *he*'s decided if that particular hunch is correct. But I'd certainly like to talk to him a little more about it."

"What about the video?"

Halloran took another sip of his drink. "I'd like you to look at it again tomorrow, just as we planned. But, *especially* because of what Hollis suggested tonight, I have no intention of showing that video to him or anyone else in law enforcement. If it could somehow be used to implicate Libba in a crime, there can be no question of my violating her right to confidentiality."

"Even if that would save an innocent man from being convicted? Or maybe even executed?"

Halloran grimaced and finished the rest of his drink in one, long gulp. Setting the glass down, he said, "Let's just hope and pray it doesn't come to that, Maggie."

CHAPTER TWENTY-TWO

Carrie looked down at the body of her first autopsy of the day, a pedestrian killed in a crosswalk in Midtown. A tourist, no less, and a foreign one, which made it even worse. Swiss, from the information in the file. He was a fit, forty-two-year-old engineer from Bern who had probably skied and hiked all his life in the Swiss Alps, and then he'd died crossing a street in Atlanta.

It reminded Carrie of the song "Ironic" by Alanis Morissette, the one about a fly in your chardonnay. She'd always loved that song; it seemed to express her own belief system. What she had come to see as the randomness of the universe—not concepts of good and evil or a God who meted out punishment and reward—had appealed to her rational nature.

The Carter case had thrown a wrench into that particular wheel of fortune.

How, Carrie wondered as she stared at Dieter Lang's lifeless face, did one approach, much less explain, the nature of evil without a religious or even a spiritual context? What had happened to this man could be explained by the theory of randomness, but not what had happened to those murdered children or Elliot Carter and Ben Mashburn. Or even to Jack Tyndall, for that matter.

This thought brought memories of the evening before—and what had happened afterwards. Memories that she'd been trying to avoid all morn-ing. Hollis had been called out to a scene, according to Glenn Martin, when she stopped by the Investigative Unit on her way to her office, so they hadn't had a chance to talk. Carrie still didn't know what to say to him, so it was just as well.

The door to the autopsy room suddenly opened, and Tim Meara, camera equipment in hand, said, "You ready for me, Carrie?"

"Sure, Tim," Carrie said, grabbing a pair of latex gloves. Briefly, she explained to him what photos she needed, then gave her full attention to the job at hand. Various groups of people— the police, prosecutors, the media—would be much more interested in the cause and manner of this man's death than the "why?" of it. Only his family would want to know that.

Fortunately, that *wasn't* her job.

———

Two hours later, Carrie was back in her office, looking at the body sheet she'd filled out on Dieter Lang. Although the driver of the car that had hit Lang was in custody—his blood-alcohol level had measured 1.8 at the scene—no official results could be issued until the tox report came back on the victim. She would need to give David a preliminary report, however, before the body was released to the family; she was still under his supervision. Trying not to wonder if Hollis had returned from the field, Carrie listened to the recording she'd made during the autopsy, making notes as she did, then plowed through the paperwork. By the time she finished, it was past noon, but she didn't feel like going to lunch. Instead, she closed her eyes and steeled herself to go over the events of the night before.

It had been a little awkward, at first, to go to the dinner party together. She'd been glad that after the good-natured winks and arm squeezes from Tom and the knowing looks and smiles from Maggie, the focus had been on Libba Ann Woodridge, Julie, and the very...patronizing? politically incorrect? arrogant? Lucas Frazier. Carrie wasn't quite sure what adjective to use to describe him, but she hadn't disliked him as much as Hollis had. She'd encountered too many male medical students, interns, and residents, as

well as practicing doctors, just like Frazier—especially surgeons—to consider his attitude surprising. What did seem surprising to her was that Julie
Benning was romantically involved with him, the only thing on which she
and Hollis agreed. Julie seemed to have the sort of natural self-confidence
and easy-going manner that wouldn't fit well with a man so…competitive?
Patronizing toward women?

"Dickhead" was what Hollis had called him, when they were back in his
car. And although that fit him as well as any of the words she'd come up
with, Carrie wasn't sure she agreed that Lucas Frazier was capable of the
attack on Libba Woodridge. Even worse, that Libba herself might have
planned the attack and conspired with Frazier to carry it out.

"Why would you think that?" she'd asked when he'd explained what he
and the Hallorans had been discussing in the kitchen. "To go from not liking the man's aggressive attitude toward Libba to suspecting him of tying
her up, drugging her, and staging a death scene is quite a leap, isn't it?"

"Three reasons," Hollis had said, totally unruffled by her reaction. He'd
paused as he turned the car onto Peachtree, then said, "He had the medical
knowledge to drain just the right amount of blood out of her, knew what
drugs to give her, and he's the boyfriend of the only other major beneficiary
of Arliss Woodridge's will. And as I said to Tom Halloran, he might not
want to wait until the litigation's over to get his hands on that money, if he's
thinking of marrying Julie."

Carrie had stared at him, taken aback by the huge jumps Hollis had taken
in coming to such a conclusion. "I can't believe you," she'd said, shaking
her head. "You've got them engaged, married off, and knee-deep in a court
battle in an attempt to give this young man—whom you've known for all
of three hours—a motive for brutally attacking one woman and sadistically
murdering another. Because that's what you're talking about, Hollis; the two
cases are connected. If Lucas Frazier attacked Libba, it follows that he also
murdered Maria Sanchez."

"I guess it does," Hollis had replied, stubbornly looking straight ahead and not at her.

Carrie took a deep breath. "Okay," she had said, several seconds later, "that's one theory. Please explain the other one—that Libba planned the whole thing—that terrible, humiliating, life-threatening attack—and somehow got Lucas to carry it out. Why in the world would she do something like that?"

"It isn't obvious to you?"

"No, Hollis, it isn't obvious to me."

He had shrugged, then, still not looking at her, and had said, "She's gotten a whole lot of bad publicity in the past year. Actually, since she began dating Arliss Woodridge. Maybe this was an attempt to turn that around. To make herself a victim instead of a predatory gold-digger."

Carrie remembered that her jaw had literally dropped when he'd finished talking. "If you actually believe that, Hollis, then you know nothing about women," she had finally said. "But if you *do* believe that's a possibility, then you've got to throw your first theory out the window. If Libba planned the attack on herself and got Lucas to carry it out, then he didn't attack her to somehow get her to cave on the issue of the will. But if either of your theories is true, they don't explain Maria Sanchez' murder."

"Maybe, maybe not," Hollis had said, further infuriating her. "Maybe Lucas Frazier was Libba's attacker, as I said—either to scare her or because she asked him to do it. And maybe the whole scenario was such a high for him that he decided to do it again—for real, this time."

"And you think a man who had done something like that could sit at a dinner table with his girlfriend, Libba, Libba's attorney and his wife, and us—and act completely normal?" Before the words were barely out of her mouth, Carrie had realized, too late, what she had said.

Still not looking at her, Hollis had said, in a calm and quiet voice, "I don't know what 'normal' is for Lucas Frazier, Carrie. As you said, I barely know the man. But you and I have both had some experience with a man who was capable of doing exactly that, haven't we?"

———

They had sat in silence for the rest of the ride back to her condominium. Carrie had racked her brain for something—anything—that she could say to turn the situation around. Ultimately, she had given up, and when Hollis had pulled up to the front door, she had reached out and touched his arm, then let herself out of the car without a word. Now she sat at her desk, not knowing whether to call his extension to see if he were back or wait to see if he would seek her out. She still didn't know what to say to him. Didn't know whether he would listen anyway.

So much for their recent breakthrough, and everything Carrie had hoped it would mean.

Her cell phone rang, and she snatched it up, hoping it would be Hollis. Instead, Maggie Halloran's name appeared. Disappointed and feeling guilty about it, Carrie said, "Maggie, I was just about to call you! Thank you for the wonderful dinner last night!"

"What's wrong," Maggie had shot back at her. "You sound strange."

With the words, "I don't know what you mean," already forming on her lips, Carrie sighed and gave up on pretense. "Things didn't go very well after we left your house."

"Tell me about it."

And so she did, haltingly at first, then in a flood of words and emotions that ground to a halt with her own self-excoriating view of herself. "How could I have been so oblivious to what I was saying?"

"Because you're human. And because I have a feeling you and Hollis haven't really talked about Jack yet. Tom and I were thrilled that the two of you showed up together last night, but, sweetie, it's not going to go much further until you do talk about him. No matter how reluctant Hollis is."

"You're right, of course," Carrie admitted. She went on to tell Maggie about meeting Hollis at Horseradish Grill on Saturday and spending the night at his apartment, leaving out only the most intimate parts. And about her reluctance to let Hollis even come inside her condominium, with its memories of Jack Tyndall, when he'd picked her up the night before.

"He's the elephant that will always be in the room until you *do* talk about him," Maggie said again. "I've said the same thing to Hollis. And I suspect that that has a lot to do with his zeroing in on Lucas Frazier as a possible suspect in Libba's attack. Tom has a lot of respect for Hollis' ability to put things together that nobody else could—I do, too, for that matter—but I think he's going off the deep end with this. Especially thinking that Libba might have engineered the whole thing herself."

"Well, I met her for the first time last night, but I can't see her— *any* woman, for that matter—doing something that extreme, just to get some sympathetic publicity. What does Tom think?"

Maggie didn't answer right away, and Carrie had begun to think her phone had gone dead when she finally said, "Well, naturally, he doesn't want to think that she would do something like that, but he does want to talk to Hollis about it a little more. It just wasn't the right time or place last night."

"I wish I'd realized that sooner."

"Keep your chin up, sweetie. This, too, shall pass, as my grandmother always used to say. Think of it as an opportunity to take the relationship to the next level—and get rid of a very big elephant."

"Okay," said Carrie uncertainly. "Wish me luck."

"Always."

She clicked off her phone and sat there, lost in thought for several minutes. Just as she was reaching for her purse, finally ready to go out and get some lunch, there was a knock on her door.

"Come in," Carrie said, after taking a deep breath.

The door swung open, and Hollis Joplin took a step inside. He looked tired, as if, like her, he hadn't slept very well. There were smudges under the green eyes, and his thick, blond hair looked as if he hadn't bothered to comb it that morning. He stood there, saying nothing for a few seconds as she stared at him, then thrust his hands in his pockets.

"I'm sorry," he said.

CHAPTER TWENTY-THREE

Jorge Martinez shook his head, then looked up at his employer with tears in his eyes. "I'll never be able to repay you," he said into the phone.

"You're not to worry about that, Jorge," said Joseph Feeney, sitting across from him behind the glass partition that separated them. "The important thing is that you've got a lawyer now, and from everything I've heard, he's a good one. He's coming to see you this afternoon."

"Is he going to get me out of here? I can't be in here, Joseph. I need to be with my children!"

"I know that, but you just have to be patient," said Feeney. His broad, high forehead glistened with sweat in the heat of the poorly air-conditioned visiting room of the Sandy Springs jail, and Jorge worried that he might not be feeling well.

In the three years that he'd worked for Feeney, the man had rarely left his house, relying on phone calls and texts to communicate with him. He had a van equipped with a lift for his wheel chair, but the few times he'd used it to visit landscape sites had seemed to drain him. What little strength and energy he had, Jorge knew, was devoted to his wife, who was dying of lupus. It made him feel even worse to know that his own situation was making things more difficult for someone who had always been so good to him.

"The children are fine," Joseph said. "I'm paying your neighbor, Mrs. Rodriguez, to take care of them for a few days until your sister can get here, so don't worry."

"You don't have to do this, Joseph. It's too much."

"No, it's not, Jorge. I learned a long time ago that I can't fix the world, but I can at least try to fix the things I'm able to see personally. That includes you and your family."

The word forced an image of Maria into his mind. It was of the last time he had seen her, back against the cement wall of the gas station, covered in blood. He closed his eyes and shook his head in a futile effort to expel it.

"I didn't do it," he said. "I swear upon my mother's grave I didn't kill her. And I didn't... hurt Mrs. Woodridge, either. You've got to believe me, Joseph!"

"I do believe you, Jorge," said Feeney, reaching out a hand as if to touch his, then drawing it back, as if only then realizing that there was glass between them. "Mr. Alvarez will be here in a little while. Jimmy Hernandez says he's an excellent attorney. Don't give up."

Jorge nodded fiercely. "I won't. Because of my children...and you. Muchas gracias, mi amigo."

Joseph Feeney held his gaze for a moment, then nodded and hung up the phone. As he pulled the wheel chair back, Jorge saw the pitiful stumps of his legs jutting over the seat. Then he turned and moved off to the right.

Jorge silently replaced the phone in its cradle as a corrections officer came up behind him.

————

"Can I come in?" Hollis asked her.

"Of course you can! I went to see you when I got here this morning, but you were in the field. And I'm the one who should be apologizing to *you*, Hollis."

He shook his head, then sat down heavily in one of the chairs in front of her desk. He still had on the navy ME jacket that he wore to death scenes. "No, it was all my fault. I don't know what got into me last night. I just became fixated on this Lucas guy for some reason and went off the deep end."

"Well, he *was* acting a little…intense with Libba, Hollis. You didn't dream that up." She looked down at the pile of paperwork on her desk, trying to decide if she should do what Maggie had suggested. If she *could* do what Maggie had said needed to be done.

"No, but that didn't mean that he…that he was capable of…" His arms rose and flailed in an effort to find the right words, then dropped to his thighs in defeat.

"But he *might* be, Hollis. Anyone might be—even the people we think we know best. Like Jack," she added softly.

Hollis let his breath out slowly, as if he'd been holding it. "Yes. Like Jack."

And so they began to talk, of his friend and Carrie's lover. Of the pain and jealousy Hollis had experienced, of the spell Carrie had felt under and the guilt and regret she'd been left with after becoming involved with Jack. Of the shock and horror each had felt when the truth was known. Of the betrayal both had felt. Mostly, they agreed, they'd simply felt that everything they'd believed about themselves and their ability to know what was real had been destroyed. It had been a paradigm shift of the gravest sort.

"I thought that if I couldn't…bring him down, that he might kill you, too. And I loathed myself for not knowing what he was in time."

"But you did, finally—in enough time to save a lot of people," Carrie said. "And you almost lost your own life in the process."

What she didn't say as she saw his shoulders relax a little, and the anguished expression on his face begin to soften, was that as she had sat in the waiting room at Grady while he was in surgery, she had realized that she loved him. That she'd probably begun to fall in love with him the day they walked around Chastain park together. That she'd saved a piece of her heart for him even as she let herself be swept away by the terrible tide of her infatuation with Jack Tyndall.

What she did say was, "The morning of the day you almost died, when we were in the conference room, and you told me that you wanted me to be happy, even if it meant being with Jack, I wondered if I were making the biggest mistake of my life. And that night, before I found out that you'd been hurt, I realized that I had, and hoped I could fix it. I don't know if you can believe that, Hollis, but—"

Carrie couldn't get any more words out because Hollis had stood up and come around her desk and pulled her to him. He held her so tightly she almost couldn't breathe, then kissed her so fiercely it took the rest of her breath away. When he finally let her go, she fell back down into her chair, dazed.

Hollis sat on the desk next to her, green eyes boring a hole in her, and said, "I *do* believe you, Carrie, because I remember how you looked at me before you walked away that morning. I've played that image of you over and over in my head, and every time, it seems like you want to say something to me, but you don't."

"Well, now you know," she said, still feeling a little breathless.

"Yes," he said, standing up. He gave her a dazzling smile, all traces of fatigue and anguish gone now, and said, "I'm taking you to the bar at Davio's tonight after work. If you love Dirty Martinis, you need to meet my friends, Gerry and Allan."

"Okay," she said, liking this new, take-charge Hollis. "Are they joining us?"

"They're the best bartenders in Atlanta," he said, over his shoulder. "We're joining *them*."

He turned to look back at her, holding her gaze for at least five seconds, then let himself out.

———

What Joplin hadn't said was that he loved her. She'd told him that Jack had frightened her by declaring his love for her only a few days into their affair.

He wouldn't make the same mistake, he told himself as he walked to the Investigative Unit, even though he knew he'd begun to fall in love with her that day they walked around Chastain Park. He would give her time—and space—before he said anything.

It would also be good not to have a colostomy bag under his shirt the next time he held her that tightly, Joplin decided. He wondered if it had ruined the moment, then tossed that thought out of his head. The expression on Carrie's face after he kissed her had told him everything he needed to know.

For now, anyway.

———

Glenn Martin popped up from his cubicle when Joplin came in the room and said, "Chief wants to see you, Hollis."

"She say why?"

Martin adjusted his glasses and shook his head. He had a pasty complexion from working too many night-shifts—his preference—and dark, gray-streaked hair. He also liked to play video games, which kept him indoors even when he was off and contributed to his considerable girth. He did his job well, though, and had been the first one from the unit to visit Joplin in the hospital. He'd also brought him an Xbox game that Joplin couldn't use, because he didn't have an Xbox player. He had never told Glenn this, of course, instead telling him he loved the game every time he saw him.

"No," Glenn answered, adjusting his glasses again. "But she wasn't smiling, Hollis."

"Good to know, Glenn. I'm still enjoying the football game, by the way."

Martin smiled and said, "I could come over sometime, and we could play together."

"That would be great," said Joplin, a smile pasted on his face.

God help him, he might have to get an Xbox player.

CHAPTER TWENTY-FOUR

"Come in," said Sarah Petersen when he knocked.

Just as Glenn had said, she wasn't smiling. "You wanted to see me?" Joplin said.

"Yes. Have a seat."

"I guess you didn't ask me in here to show me your Gay Pride album, huh?"

She did smile at this, then said, "You're not in trouble, Hollis—at least not with me, anyway. But it's that football thing we talked about yesterday. The ADA handling the Woodridge case wants to talk to you, and I think you're in her crosshairs."

"Story of my life, Chief. Who is it?"

"Janice Bernstein. You know her?"

Joplin sighed and closed his eyes. "Unfortunately, yes."

"That bad, huh?"

"Let's just say that I'd rather try to broker peace in the Middle East than be involved in a case with Ms. Bernstein. She makes dotting every i and crossing every t into an art form."

"I kind of got that impression during our brief conversation," said Petersen, nodding. "We had one like that back in Boston. Anthony Cavatelli. Nobody *ever* called him Tony. One of the Homicide detectives hated working with him so much, he threatened to let a suspect go unless another ADA was assigned to the case."

"Must be her Italian cousin." Joplin sighed again and said, "I take it she wants me to call her."

"Yesterday wouldn't be too soon, as a matter of fact. That's why she called me, when she couldn't get hold of you. I think she was offended that you were out in the field doing your job and not available to her."

"That's Janice Bernstein," he said, standing up. "She handling the Sanchez case, too?"

"No final decision's been made on that yet. The DA's Office is waiting for Sandy Springs CSU to complete its analysis on the blood spatter, and Mullins and his team are continuing to gather evidence. They have more on the Woodridge case than Sanchez at this point, so the DA went ahead and assigned it to Bernstein for the time being."

Joplin nodded slowly at this. "Well, thanks for the heads-up, Chief."

"Anytime. Keep me posted."

————

The thought of calling Janice Bernstein was so unappealing, Joplin decided to risk increasing her displeasure with him and write up his report on the traffic fatality scene he'd worked that morning instead. He was halfway through when his cell phone rang. Tom Halloran's name appeared; he was second only to Bernstein in terms of people Joplin didn't want to talk to, after his heart-to-heart with Carrie, but he pressed "Talk" anyway.

"Hello, Tom. Thanks for a wonderful evening last night."

"Thanks for serving, Hollis. I'll have to remember you for future dinner parties."

"I'll keep my weekends free," Joplin said dryly. "By the way, I think all that wine got to me last night, Counselor. Lucas Frazier is probably as innocent as a newborn panda. I just got a wild hair up my ass about him."

"Maybe, maybe not. I did a little checking on him, and it turns out he's got enough debt on student loans for college and med school to sink a battleship. *And*, according to Libba, who called Maggie a little while ago to thank her for dinner, an engagement between him and Julie is imminent."

"Good work, Tom. You ever think about playing a detective on TV?"

"Every day, Hollis. Especially when I have a messy case like this. Can you tell me a little more about why you got that wild hair up your ass?"

"Yeah, but, just keep in mind that I have absolutely no objective evidence to explain it."

"You have my word that I'll be completely skeptical," Halloran assured him.

"Okay, here goes. Give me a few minutes to play it back in my head."

"Take all the time you need."

Joplin closed his eyes and conjured up a series of images from the night before, selecting the ones that featured Lucas Frazier alone or interacting with Julie and Libba. He paused one that contained Frazier's expression as Julie was telling Carrie about her interest in sports medicine, then another that showed him staring intently at Libba, the predatory look that Joplin had seen unmistakable as he zoomed in for a close-up of the med student's face. A few seconds later, Joplin pulled back and focused on the distance between Frazier's chair and Julie's, as well as Frazier's chair and Libba's as he was serving the salads to them. Eidetic memory has a mathematic component to it that had allowed Joplin to see instantly that Frazier had moved his chair 1.3 inches closer to Libba, just as he came up behind them. Frazier had also leaned in toward Libba as she told the story of poor Miss California, and Libba had moved—consciously or unconsciously—away from him

There was a twitching of Frazier's right shoulder as she did this. Next, Joplin examined Julie's face as she said "Lucas!" when he had pressed Libba for the rest of the story, as well as Libba's reaction to both of them. Then he flipped through several mental photos of Frazier's face after Libba had finished her story about Miss California. Finally, he watched Frazier again as Ed Jenkins came into the entry hall to escort Libba to his car for the ride back to her house, as well as the interaction between the med student and Libba as she left. His eyes remained closed for a few more seconds, then he opened them and took in a cleansing breath before saying anything.

"What I saw—or, rather, what I *interpret* that I saw from the various expressions and the interactions between Frazier, Julie, and Libba Ann—is that Frazier feels very proprietary and just a tad *contemptuous* of his soon-to-be fiancée, Julie. He cares for her—probably even loves her, in his own way—but takes her totally for granted. His…feelings, for lack of a better word, toward Libba are a little more complicated. He's dismissive of her at first, as if she were some kind of specimen that he'd observed—" Joplin paused and said, "What's the name for a person who collects butterflies?"

"A lepidopterist, I think."

"Right," said Joplin. "Not only had observed," he continued, "but something he thought he had already captured. At any rate, when he pressed Libba to finish the story about Miss California, both she and Julie caught a whiff of the predator in him, which seemed to surprise them. And when Libba told everyone how she'd stood up for her fellow beauty contestant and made the judges look silly, she gave Frazier a little 'fuck you' look that caused him to react like a lepidopterist who sees his prize butterfly fly right off the mounting board with a pin still stuck in it. Then, when Ed Jenkins joined them in the entry hall to take Libba home, Frazier gave him a very thorough once-over, as if he were a potential competitor, or even a threat. And although Julie and Libba gave each other a hug goodbye, Libba just gave Frazier a little wave. There was definitely a coolness between them. "

Halloran didn't respond for several seconds, and Joplin finally said, "You still there, Tom? Or have I overloaded your circuits?"

"Yes, and yes," he said. "I'm still trying to process everything you just told me."

"Well, as I said, what I saw last night wasn't enough to justify the wild theories I came up with."

"Yes, but there's that famous 'gut' of yours, Hollis, that we have to take into consideration."

"Not necessarily," Joplin said, wishing everyone could just forget about his gut, himself included.

"Maybe not with regard to your suggestion that Libba could have engineered the attack on herself, but I think the things you observed about Lucas were pretty perceptive. Add them to the things that I discovered, and it's a pretty good theory, wouldn't you say?"

"I'm not saying anything more about the guy," said Joplin. "But I'll ask *you* something: Why would you choose Lucas Frazier as a suspect over Jorge Martinez, who has a very solid connection to both crimes, left a partial print on a pane of glass at the break-in site, and had Libba's Miss Georgia sash in his bureau?"

"The physical evidence could have been planted," said Halloran stubbornly.

"That's exactly what you said about the evidence I found in Elliot Carter's closet, and you turned out to be right. What do you know that you're not telling me, Tom?"

"Nothing I can talk about, unfortunately," Halloran said, then broke the connection.

The conversation with Janice Bernstein didn't go well.

Joplin had prepared himself for another reprimand, similar to the one he'd received from BJ Reardon and, to a lesser extent, from Jim Mullins, but the ADA seemed hell-bent on tearing him a new one. He took it for a while, hoping she'd run out of steam, but when that didn't seem likely to happen, Joplin decided he'd finally had enough.

"Ms. Bernstein," he said between clenched teeth, "I had no idea Hernandez knew Jorge Martinez when I suggested to Lt. Mullins that he let Jimmy take on the case. It just seemed like a good idea at the time—you know his reputation. And Jimmy had no idea that the husband of the victim was Jorge Martinez when he agreed. And when he *did* discover that, he came to me, and we both informed the head of CSU. Everything was done in good faith, and I think you know that, so let's move on."

But Janice Bernstein wasn't ready to move on. "How dare you take that tone with me! I'll say when we move on!"

"Well, say it soon, then," he countered, barely able to keep his temper in check. "Because we're getting nowhere fast, *ma'am*." The emphasis placed on this last word made it sound like another word altogether. A word that rhymed with "rich." He was conscious of the fact that he sounded very much like one of the good ole boys he usually despised, but couldn't stop himself. His dislike of lawyers—prosecutors, defense attorneys, even high-profile *celebrities* like Tom Halloran—rolled over him like a wall of fire eating up a dry forest.

"Tell your supervisor to expect another call from me," Bernstein hissed into the phone.

"My pleasure," Joplin spat back and clicked off.

———

Julie's cell phone rang, and when she saw Lucas' number appear, she almost let it go to voice mail. They'd had a huge fight after dropping Libba off the night before, and Julie was still so upset when they reached her apartment in Druid Hills that she'd told Lucas not to come in with her and then slammed out of the car. She still couldn't believe the way he'd acted at the dinner party. Although she'd long ago accepted that he was a little arrogant and chauvinistic, choosing to laugh at him when he went over the line or to bring him back down to earth when he got too full of himself, the way he'd acted toward Libba had pushed the boundaries of that acceptance.

"I saw your expression when you were goading her about Miss California," she'd told him. "You were out to *get* her, Lucas."

"You're making too much out of this," he'd insisted, trying to keep her from leaving the car. "I was just having a little fun."

"Fun? You call that *fun*?"

He'd shrugged. "Well, she got to tell us how she made the judges look like idiots, right?"

"Yes, but it also put *you* in the same category, Lucas. Can't you see that?"

He'd bristled at that, and before he'd been able to respond, she'd been out the door.

Julie had spent the rest of the evening rethinking their relationship. She had thought that the good qualities she'd seen in Lucas—his intelligence and humor and dedication to becoming a surgeon despite his family's lack of education, much less, money—far outweighed the bad. But maybe that wasn't enough to overcome the things he lacked. Like empathy. And compassion. And just an inkling of his own limitations. She had believed that if and when they married that they could complement each other, not compete, and that they could each bring out in the other what was missing, or, at least, underdeveloped.

Now, she wasn't so sure. The look he'd given Libba had revealed a side of Lucas that she'd never seen before. She shivered a little now, just recalling it. It made her remember the many times he'd seemed almost to side with her parents in the lawsuit, and the subtle ways he'd tried to pull her away from Libba. If they'd made plans to meet for lunch or dinner, or had a meeting with Tom Halloran, Lucas had frequently come up with a reason why he needed to see her. Right *then*, not some other time. And he'd always been quick to call attention to the bad press Libba had received, mentioning a news story on TV or an article in the *AJC*.

Maybe it was time to take a break. At least until classes began in September.

"Hello, Lucas," she said now, trying to sound calm. Or at least detached.

"Julie! Honey. I know you're upset with me, but I want to make this right. Please, baby. Please let me come over."

"I don't think so. I'm pretty tired, Lucas. I didn't sleep much last night."

"Neither did I," he said quickly. "Which is why we have to talk about this. Tonight. I have to leave for North Carolina in the morning instead of Wednesday, because tomorrow night is the only time my aunt and uncle can come for dinner. But I can't go without seeing you and straightening things out."

"Oh, I think you'll survive," she told him, surprising both of them. His sharp intake of breath showed her he wasn't expecting that response. And why should he? She'd really never told him no about anything. Ever.

It was high time.

"I don't think you mean that, baby. It'll be our last night together for a few weeks."

"I *do* mean it. And I think that might be a good thing. Not seeing each other for a few weeks. I think we both need to figure out what the priorities in our relationship are—and maybe what they *should* be."

There was what seemed to be a shocked silence for several seconds, then Lucas said, "This doesn't sound like you at all, Julie. Have you been talking to Libba? Did she say something about me that's made you act this way?"

Instead of answering, Julie clicked the "end" button on her cell phone, then took a sip of the red wine she'd poured herself when she'd gotten home from a long workout at the LA Fitness a few blocks from her apartment building. Without really understanding why, she felt as if she'd let go of a burden she hadn't even realized she was carrying.

———

Claudia Woodridge Benning looked up at her husband as he came into the living room. She was holding a large glass of chardonnay; it was her second. "Get yourself a stiff drink, Wes. We need to talk."

He raised his eyebrows, but said nothing as he went to the bar and poured himself three fingers of Jameson's. Without bothering to add either water or ice, he came and sat down beside her on the sofa. "What's going on?"

"I called Julie to see when we'd be getting together with Lucas for lunch before he goes to see his parents," she said, then took a long sip of her wine. "She said we wouldn't be. That Lucas has to leave tomorrow instead of later in the week. Something to do with his aunt and uncle, I think."

"Do you think they're having problems?"

Claudia gave a short laugh and said, "Oh, I *know* so. They're 'taking a break,' as she put it, but I think it's more than that. You know they had dinner at the Hallorans' house last night."

"No, I didn't know," said Wesley. He suddenly looked very tired and began loosening his tie, as if it were choking him. "Did she tell you that?"

Claudia took another long sip of wine, pondering just what to tell him. "Let's just say I managed to get it out of her. That, and the fact that Libba was there, too."

"Well, I'm not surprised by that. Tom is their attorney."

"What *may* surprise you is that there was some kind of…incident at the dinner that involved Lucas and Libba. And from what I gather, that's the reason Julie wants this so-called 'break.'"

"She *told* you that? What was the 'incident?' It must have been something pretty big for Julie to confide in you. I mean, it's like pulling teeth to get her to open up these days," he added, shifting his eyes away from hers.

Sometimes, thought Claudia, *Wes just asks too many questions.* Aloud, she said, "Mothers can read between the lines, darling."

"I guess so," he said, sighing.

"The important thing is that we have to act."

His eyes cut back to hers. "You mean…?"

"Yes," she said firmly. "I do. It's time, Wes."

Instead of answering, he stood up and walked over to the bar. When he turned around, his glass was half-full of whiskey. "You have no pity, do you, Claudia?"

Her chin rose. "Not for that bitch."

CHAPTER TWENTY-FIVE

Joplin and Carrie took separate cars to Phipps Plaza, where Davio's was located. She left the car with valet parking at the side entrance of the mall, which faced the Buckhead Ritz-Carlton. Two beautiful young black women greeted her from behind a high desk as she entered the restaurant, then motioned toward the dark, rectangular bar, where Hollis was smiling and waving at her. Carrie eased herself into the stool next to him and was greeted by a dark-haired bartender with a brush-cut who smiled and took her hand.

"If this is Carrie, you've won the lottery, Hollis," he said.

"Don't I know it. Carrie, this is Allan. Allan, let go of her hand."

"Touchy, are you now?" said another bartender, who had come around the corner. He had a shaved head and blue eyes that danced from Hollis to her in frank appraisal.

"And this," said Hollis, "is Gerry, who's full of blarney and other waste products."

Gerry immediately captured the hand that Allan had relinquished. "And how are you this evening, darlin'? Carrie, is it?"

"Yes," she said, smiling. She was also blushing a little, she knew, but the darkness of the bar covered that. At least, she hoped so.

"And what are you doing with this poor excuse for a man, if I may ask?"

Carrie gave him her most angelic smile. "Having a drink with him, I hope. He promised to pay this time."

Without letting go of her hand, Gerry threw back his head and gave a bray of a laugh that went on for several seconds, accompanied by Allan. Hollis just grinned at her.

"Oh," said Gerry, finally, "you've got a good one there, I must say, Hollis. Do you have any sisters at home?" he added, looking at Carrie.

"None that I would trust with *you*," she said, still smiling.

Gerry gave the bar a resounding slap, which Carrie took as a compliment, and turned away to gather the tools of his craft. "We all know how Hollis likes his martini," he said, "but how about you?"

"*You* like martinis, too?" she asked Hollis.

This question elicited another spate of laughter from Gerry and Allan.

Before he could answer, Allan said, "Hollis has never met any form of alcohol he *doesn't* like. Isn't that so, Hollis."

Hollis sat up straighter on his bar stool and said, affecting a very dignified tone, "Yes, it is, but that's a good thing. Not many people could come in here as often as I do and drink the horse swill you and Gerry charge fourteen dollars a pop for and still be alive." When the laughter had subsided, he added, "The lady likes Stoli, with regular olives."

"Coming right up," said Gerry.

As Allan moved away to greet two new patrons, Carrie turned to Hollis and said, "I like your friends. I take it you've been coming here awhile?"

"Almost since it opened. It's not as far away as Angelo's, and the food's almost as good. But it's not as noisy as Twist, if you just want a drink. Plus, it's halfway between work and my apartment. And despite what I said, they really do make the best martinis in town."

As if on cue, Gerry appeared with two large, chilled martini glasses, then produced two shakers, beaded with condensation. He carefully poured Carrie's drink, then said, "I hope it's to your liking."

"It's perfect," she said after taking a sip. The ice-cold, salty liquid gave an initial burn as it went down her throat, then settled into a pleasant warmth in her stomach. "I can tell I'd better not have more than one of these, though."

"And she's a cheap date, as well!" Gerry said as he poured Hollis' drink, which had blue cheese olives. Wherever did you find her, Hollis?"

"We work together."

Gerry looked at her, clearly surprised. "You don't go around looking at dead bodies, do you?" he asked. "A pretty thing like you?"

"Of course not!" Carrie said, reaching for her drink and taking another sip. "What kind of girl do you think I am, anyway? I just cut them open and examine their insides."

Gerry gave her a baleful look, clearly appalled. Then he took a deep breath. "Well, then, I expect you'll be hungry. Would you like a menu, or should I just have the chef send out whatever's raw?"

Hollis almost choked on the latest sip of his martini, but Carrie merely smiled and said, "A menu, please. I want something cooked tonight."

They ordered splits of both the chopped salad and the Tagliatelle Bolognese, then turned and looked at each other. "How did the rest of your day go?" Carrie asked.

Hollis made a face and picked up his glass, looking as if he might down the whole thing at once. "Oh, splendid. After getting into a fight with Janice Bernstein at the DA's Office, I got called out to a suicide scene. Another vet receiving what passes for care at the VA in Decatur. He'd missed three appointments with the psychiatric team, but nobody bothered to contact the family and see what was going on. How about you?"

"Pretty routine. But what's this about a fight with Janice Bernstein?"

"You know her?"

Carrie shrugged. "I sat in on a meeting David had with her to go over his testimony for a murder case she was prosecuting. She and I know some of the same people."

"Jewish geography?"

"Jewish geography," she said, smiling at him.

"And what's your impression of her, if I may ask."

"She seems to be a very driven person. Very meticulous and...thorough, I guess you'd say. She had a lot of notes, a lot of questions for David, which I assumed was normal. But after a while, he started looking at his watch rather pointedly and said he needed to get back to the ME's. She kept saying, 'I just have a few more questions, Doctor.'"

"That's our Janice. To her credit, she's lost very few cases, and she wants to keep it that way. Word is she wants to be DA when Robert Marsden leaves office. But she's alienated too many people for that to happen."

"Including you, I take it."

"Including me," Hollis said, and took another long sip of his drink.

A server arrived with their salads, and as Carrie dug into hers, she listened as Hollis told her of his meeting with Sarah Petersen and his phone conversation with Bernstein.

"Sounds like Sarah sized up the situation pretty well," she said, frowning. "And being everybody's football isn't much fun, is it? Did Janice call her after your run-in?"

"Oh, yeah. She came out and told me she'd been ordered to deal with my 'insubordination.' She said she told Bernstein she'd be happy to do that if I were ever 'insubordinate' to her or one of the pathologists or Dr. Minton, but as far as she knew, none of us works for the DA's Office. Said we are a 'cooperating agency' by law and expected to testify in court concerning cause and manner of death, but we are not part of law enforcement, as are the police and the DA's office. Then she assured Janice of our 'continuing cooperation' with regard to the Woodridge case and the Sanchez case, if it were assigned to her, and wished her a good day."

Carrie waved her fork in the air. "Good for her!"

"Yeah," said Hollis, grinning. "I almost kissed her, but I thought maybe that *would* be insubordination."

———

Halloran was tired and ready for a drink when he pulled into his driveway. He'd driven out to the Woodridge house after meeting another client for lunch at Watershed, and Libba hadn't taken the news about Maria Sanchez' murder and the subsequent arrest of Jorge Martinez well, to say the least. Her face had gone absolutely white as he'd detailed the similarities between the murder and her own case. Although he was glad he'd let her enjoy dinner the night before, he'd had a lot of explaining to do about his reasons for not telling her sooner. The only one that seemed to placate her was that he hadn't wanted to tell her while Connie Sue was still there, knowing the woman would use it as an excuse to stay longer.

"Okay," she'd said at last. "I get it. I'm not happy, but I understand why you kept it from me."

"I wasn't trying to keep anything from you, Libba—really. I just needed to gather more information and sort through everything before—"

"Right," she'd said, cutting him off. "Do you really think Jorge could have done this? Both things, I mean?"

"I don't know, Libba. He doesn't seem to fit the body type of the man in the video, and unless he's a great actor or a textbook psychopath, he doesn't seem to have the personality or demeanor of someone capable of committing such terrible crimes. What do you think? You know him better than I do."

She hadn't answered right away, and he'd heard her give a long sigh. "I just can't see it. Jorge is such a gentle, self-effacing person. And the few times he spoke about his wife, it was with a lot of love. But you said the police found my Miss Georgia sash in his apartment, right? How would he have gotten hold of it?"

"I don't know. It could have been planted. We just don't know enough at this point. Let me give the video to Captain Martucci, Libba," Halloran had urged her. "She'll make sure it's protected."

"I'll think about it, Tom," Libba had said. "I'll let you know tomorrow."

———

Maggie was in the kitchen and looked up as he came in. Her smile changed to a look of concern when she saw his face. "That bad, huh?"

"That bad," he agreed and headed for the Beaux Arts cabinet that served as a bar.

"I take it you talked to Libba about Jorge Martinez' arrest."

Halloran nodded as he poured himself a healthy slug of Glenlivet. After adding some ice from the freezer, he settled into one of the stools at the kitchen island. "The news of his wife's murder—especially the similarities to her own attack—scared her to death, but I think she's having her own doubts that Jorge could be responsible for either one. She even agreed to think about turning the video over to Captain Martucci."

Maggie opened the oven door and slid a casserole dish into it, looking back over her shoulder at him. "I'm confused," she said. "Just last night you insisted you would never turn over the video to the police after Hollis said Libba might have planned the attack on herself."

"You're right, I did. But I'm more certain than ever that she's a victim, not part of some scheme to get sympathetic publicity. And if Hollis is right about Lukas Frazier, she might be in even more danger right now."

"Do *you* think he's right?" Maggie asked as she loaded mixing bowls and utensils into the dishwasher.

"He walked me through his observations from last night, and I have to say, I'm concerned," said Halloran, then told her about his own investigation of Lucas Frazier. "And his body type is much closer to the figure in the video than Jorge's is. By the way, did you have a chance to look at it again?"

"I did, but I'm afraid nothing really jumps out at me. Whoever made that video certainly knew how to obscure any identifying characteristics." She paused and cocked her head to one side. "Which makes me wonder: If Jorge *isn't* the person in the video, and the real perpetrator is trying to frame him, why didn't he use it as another opportunity to cast suspicion on him? If he used software to manipulate his image on the video, why didn't he make it look more like Jorge?"

Halloran's eyebrows rose as he took a sip of his drink. "Good question. The first thing that comes to mind is that he never expected anyone but Libba to see it."

"Yes, but he couldn't count on that, Tom. She might have decided not to pay the extortion money and to turn it over to the police instead."

"True," said Halloran, nodding slowly. "Another possibility is that he didn't decide to frame Jorge until after Maria Sanchez' murder." Then he frowned and said, "But that doesn't really make sense, because according to Lt. Mullins, the APD Crime Scene Unit lifted prints on the basement window that was broken into at the Woodridge house which later proved to be Jorge's."

"So maybe Jorge *is* guilty of both crimes, and you don't need to worry about turning the video over to the police," Maggie offered.

"Yeah, I guess. Or maybe he touched that window during the course of his work at the Woodbridge house, and his wife was murdered for the sole purpose of framing him for the attack on Libba."

Maggie's mouth opened in disbelief. "You can't be serious! A *murder*, to cover up extortion?"

"A billion-dollar estate is at stake, Maggie. That's serious as hell."

"Yes, but to kill an innocent young woman for it?"

"Life is cheap to some people," Halloran said, picking up his glass again and almost draining it. "Only their own skins are important, in their minds. But whether or not Jorge Martinez is guilty or innocent, I'd still feel better if the police had that video. Besides, Hollis knows I'm keeping something from him. I'm sure he suspects it has to do with attorney/client privilege, but he's not happy about it."

"Wasn't he holding out on you just a few days ago?"

"Indeed, he was. It's a dance we've danced many times before. And I'm sure it won't be our last."

CHAPTER TWENTY-SIX

"You ready for some good news?" Mary Martucci asked him.

"My favorite kind," Joplin said, cradling the phone between his neck and shoulder as he shuffled paperwork on his desk. He'd only managed one cup of coffee before leaving for work that morning and had been about to go get some from the break room when she'd called. "What's up?"

"I just got off the phone with Jim Mullins. Their blood spatter tech spent the last three days working on the Sanchez scene and agreed with Carrie Salinger's opinion that the weapon was a meat mallet. They were careful not to show him pictures from the Woodridge scene or Hernandez' report, but he came to the same conclusion: that the scene was definitely staged, and that a major focus was on the 'detailing,' as he put it, of the spatter."

"In other words, the perp was creating a painting with the blood."

"Exactly," Martucci agreed.

"Has Bernstein read the report?"

"It's been delivered to her boss. Remember, she hasn't been officially assigned to the case yet."

"She will be," Joplin said. "The DA will see the similarities between the cases immediately. And even if they're not tried together, they're linked. Get a conviction on one, the other's a slam dunk."

"Or, Jorge Martinez might plead out. Good for all of us, if that happens."

He didn't say anything right away, then sighed and said, "Not for Jorge."

"You don't think he did it, do you, Hollis?"

"Doesn't matter what I think."

"It does to *me*. If we don't have the right guy, we need to keep looking. I trust your instincts."

"I really don't have anything to go on, Mary, except that, from what Jimmy told me, he doesn't seem to be the kind of person who would—or even *could*—commit two horrible crimes like this."

"Well, I certainly respect Jimmy Hernandez, but he hasn't had that much contact with Martinez in the past few years, right?"

"Right," Joplin admitted. "But it doesn't make any sense that he would establish himself as the prime suspect by killing his wife and staging the scene to look exactly like the Woodridge scene."

"Maybe it was some kind of…compulsion. Or maybe his wife knew he'd been involved in the attack on Libba Woodridge, and he was afraid she'd go to the police."

"I guess," Joplin said reluctantly. "I just wish we knew why Libba was attacked in the first place. It doesn't make sense."

"You come up with anything that would justify keeping that case open, let me know."

Joplin smiled. "Are you asking me to do something that's outside the scope of my job, Mary?"

"Since when has that ever bothered you?" Martucci said dryly.

"Good point. I need to run it past Sarah Petersen, though."

"Fine by me. In the meantime, you want *me* to call Halloran and update him, or you?"

"I'll let you have that pleasure, Mary. As you said on Friday, you owe me."

"Fine, but then we're even, okay?"

"Neck and neck."

Joplin replaced the phone in its cradle, then went to the break room for some coffee. He wanted to go see if Carrie was in her office, but decided he'd better wait till lunch time. They'd seen each other every day for the last three days, and he didn't want her to feel like he was monopolizing her time. Besides, he was still enjoying the memory of their date at Davio's the night before, which had lasted until after ten. Joplin had walked her to her car, and they'd spent another twenty minutes saying good night. He could still smell the rich, floral scent of her perfume on his clothes when he got home.

With a sigh, he put the mug of coffee on his desk and sat down, ready to tackle the unfinished paperwork left over from Friday. By nine-thirty-five, he was contemplating another cup of bad coffee when Sarah Petersen suddenly appeared at his cubicle. The expression on her face was more serious than he'd ever seen before. Grave, even. He wondered if Bernstein had raised such a stink over his "attitude" that the Chief was about to fire him. Then he realized that she would have called him into her office if that were true.

"You okay, Chief?" he asked, not knowing what else to say.

"I am, but Libba Ann Woodridge isn't," she said tersely.

"What do you mean?" He wondered if it had something to do with the information Mary Martucci had given Halloran about the Sandy Springs blood spatter tech's report; she'd had plenty of time to call him. Maybe Halloran had then talked to his client, and she'd gone ballistic for some reason. And maybe Sarah Petersen *was* going to fire him.

"I mean that it's *déjà vu* all over again. Ike Simmons just called me. He's at the Woodridge house. Her housekeeper found her 'unresponsive' about an hour ago and called 911. You need to get over there, Hollis, because this time she's really dead."

CHAPTER TWENTY-SEVEN

Halloran had gotten a call from Ed Jenkins just as the paramedics arrived at the house on Blackland Road; he'd heard the siren as soon as he picked up the phone. Usually a very calm, matter-of-fact person, which was a necessity in his line of work, Jenkins was obviously agitated as he reported what had happened. Or, at least, what he actually knew.

"She was already cold," he'd said, remorse choking his voice. "Rosa called 911, then came and got me. There was nothing I could do."

"Was there an obvious cause of death?" Halloran had asked.

"There was an empty bottle of Ambien on the bedside table and an almost-empty glass that smelled like whiskey. There was also an envelope addressed to you."

"I hope you took possession of it before the paramedics or police got there."

"Of course. I wrapped it in my handkerchief to save any prints."

"Good. Had anyone called or been to see her yesterday or last night?"

"Besides you, no—I would have called you, if so. But she has…had…a cell phone, and I had no control over that. Tom, this is my fault. I should have—"

"No, it's not. There was nothing you could have done. I'll be there in about twenty minutes."

In fact, it had taken him thirty minutes to get to the house. Police cars were already there, as well as the EMT truck and a black sedan with a portable siren on its roof, which meant that someone from Homicide had arrived. Halloran punched in the code and took a deep breath as the iron gates opened.

———

Jenkins met him at the front door, explaining to a uniformed cop Halloran's relationship to the victim, but it didn't seem to impress the officer.

"This is a death scene, sir," he'd said sternly. "Only authorized personnel can be here."

"I think we can let Mr. Halloran in," said Ike Simmons as he came down the staircase.

"Thanks, Ike," Halloran said, moving past the cop. "Is anyone from the ME's Office here yet?"

"No, but Hollis Joplin is on his way."

"Good. Can I see her?"

Simmons shook his head. "'Fraid not. We still don't know what we're dealing with, Tom."

"But Mr. Jenkins told me there was a glass with some alcohol in it and an empty bottle of Ambien on the bedside table." Halloran frowned, mustering a puzzled expression on his face. "You don't think it was suicide?" he added, very conscious of the fact that the letter addressed to him that Jenkins had taken would likely prove it *was* suicide. But he was still Libba's attorney, and he wasn't about to let anything that might incriminate her—in any way—be seen by the police until he had seen it. And maybe not even after that.

"Anne Carter's death was made to look like a suicide, if you recall," Simmons replied. "And it was anything but. Why don't you come on into the living room and tell me why you're so quick to believe your client took her own life."

Reluctantly, Halloran followed the detective, glancing back at Jenkins as he did and hoping he'd get the message.

"When was the last time you talked to Mrs. Woodridge?" Simmons asked him, motioning Halloran into a chair by the fireplace. He took one opposite to it.

"Yesterday afternoon. I came here to see her."

"And how did she seem?"

Halloran didn't reply right away, his mind going over his options as to what to tell the detective. Finally, he said, "I'm assuming you know about the murder of Maria Sanchez and the arrest of her husband, who was the foreman for the Woodridge's landscaping service."

"Oh, yes." Simmons leaned forward and clasped his hands together. "From what I hear, it was a duplicate of your client's attack. Except Mrs. Sanchez was murdered."

"Exactly. But I didn't tell Mrs. Woodridge about it until yesterday. I wanted to wait until I had as much information as I could get before I talked to her. She'd been in a very…fragile state."

"And how did she handle this news?"

Halloran shrugged. "As well as could be expected, under the circumstances. She was upset with me for not telling her sooner, but she seemed to understand."

"Then why are you so certain that she killed herself?"

Simmons was staring pointedly at him, and Halloran held his gaze. "I'm not 'certain' about anything, Detective. But what Ed told me about the pills and the alcohol disturbed me. And when I talked to Libba yesterday, I could tell that she was very shaken by the knowledge that she, too, could have been murdered. Like Maria Sanchez. It seemed to bring her own harrowing experience back to her, as if she were reliving it."

"Like PTSD?"

"Yes. That's a common reaction among victims of violent crimes, isn't it?" Simmons nodded. "What else did you talk about with Mrs. Woodridge?"

"I'm afraid that's privileged information, Ike."

"But your client's dead."

"But not her privilege. Or my fiduciary responsibility to her."

Simmons started to say something, but was interrupted by the sound of the front door opening. Hollis Joplin and Carrie Salinger came through it, and the uniformed cop motioned toward the living room. Joplin's large green eyes focused on them.

"Is this a private party or can we join you?" he asked.

———

Joplin wasn't thrilled at seeing Halloran as soon as he came inside the house. He was sure Ike hadn't let him anywhere near Libba Woodridge, but he knew the attorney would be waiting for him as soon as he and Carrie completed their examination of her. They listened carefully as Ike and Tom briefed them on what they knew of the circumstances of the victim's death. It was very disconcerting to him. Ike had been his partner at the Homicide Unit for seven years; Tom Halloran had been his "wannabe" partner ever since he'd found Elliot Carter's body in Piedmont Park four months ago.

It was almost like being in the same room with your ex-wife and your new girlfriend.

"No," he said as he saw Halloran's mouth open to say something. He was truly sorry about Libba Ann Woodridge's death and knew what a toll it must be taking on Halloran, but he needed to establish some boundaries from the get-go.

Looking startled, the attorney said, "No, what?"

"No, you can't come with us while we're examining the body."

Halloran seemed to consider this, then said, "Okay, but will you and Carrie answer a few questions when you've finished?"

"It depends upon the questions, Counselor."

———

Touché, thought Halloran as he watched the two go up the staircase. From Joplin's point of view, it was probably what he deserved. Ike Simmons excused himself to talk to two techs from CSU who'd just gotten there, and Halloran went off to look for Ed Jenkins. He hoped the man could tell him a little more than he'd been able to on their brief phone conversation. More importantly, he needed to get the letter Libba had left for him.

He found Jenkins in the kitchen, where he'd set up a temporary work-place. From there, he'd been able to use the house's security system to monitor anyone approaching it or calling the land lines. Jenkins quickly reached into his front coat pocket and retrieved the letter, which had been sealed in a plastic bag, then handed it to Halloran, who slid it into his own coat pocket. He wasn't even going to try to read it in a house swarming with cops.

"I figured you're probably not intending to turn this over to the police, so you don't need to worry about steaming it or freezing it open," Jenkins said in a low voice. "But give me a call once you leave, and I'll tell you what to do to preserve any prints or trace evidence, just in case."

Jenkins was a former GBI agent who'd started his own private investigation/security agency more than six years ago. The first time Halloran had hired him, for a case involving an alleged "heir" to one of his wealthiest clients, he'd made sure that Jenkins understood the difference between working in law enforcement and working for a private attorney.

"Anything you find is a product of my work on a client's case. As such, it's privileged. In the event of a trial, *I'm* the one who decides if it falls under the rules of evidence and discovery. And I assure you, I'm a very ethical person. Understood?"

"Understood," he'd replied, but Halloran could tell that he had as much to prove to Jenkins as Jenkins did to him. After the first year, however, neither had questioned the other's ethics, expertise, or devotion to the job.

"Thanks, Ed," Halloran said now. "By the way, you said Libba could have received a call on her cell phone. Was it on the bedside table as well?"

Jenkins frowned and said, "As a matter of fact, it wasn't. And I didn't have a chance to look around, with Rosa there. I don't think she saw me take the letter, though."

"No problem," Halloran said. "Good work, as usual." He shook Jenkins' hand and turned, heading for the door, the letter from Libba burning a hole in his pocket.

Joplin and Carrie had finished their preliminary examination of the body, noting no external wounds, lacerations, or bruising. No petecchiae in the eyes either, which would have pointed to asphyxiation as a cause of death. While Carrie got a body temp, he leaned down and smelled the victim's mouth; there was a pronounced odor of alcohol, similar to the empty glass on the bedside table. He took a picture of the table, then picked up the plastic prescription bottle, which read "Ambien 10 mg" and placed it, and the glass, in evidence bags. Once Carrie had finished, he took several more pictures of the victim and the surrounding area, then bagged the hands.

"It looks like a suicide, but we won't really know until you autopsy her," he said, remembering Anne Carter. The body on the bed looked like a younger version of her, the blonde hair spread out against the pillow, the face in still repose. But Anne Carter had been murdered, her "overdose" meant to look like she had taken her own life.

"There's no note," said Carrie, turning to look at him.

"Maybe, maybe not."

"What do you mean?"

"I think I told you that suicide notes frequently 'disappear'—and not only for sinister reasons. Sometimes it's just a family member or an employee who doesn't want the victim to have the stigma of such a death, or have certain secrets revealed."

"You think Rosa might have taken it?"

Joplin shook his head. "Not necessarily. Ed Jenkins is also an employee. Of Halloran's."

"So you think Tom might have asked him to—"

"I don't think anything, at this point. But I wouldn't put it past him."

Joplin called for transport for the body, then looked back at Libba Ann Woodridge one last time. He had hardly known her, but in the short time he *had* known her, he'd seen a side of her that had been absent from all the news articles and TV reportage and tweets that had flooded the media. She'd become, in his eyes, just a small-town girl from Brunswick who'd made it big, but had managed to retain the core of what she'd always been: honest, intelligent, down-to-earth, but still a little naïve. He wished he'd been able to help her in some way, a way that might have kept her from dying, whether by her own hand or someone else's. Carrie caught his eye as they left the bedroom, then squeezed his arm.

"She was a good person," she said.

"Yes," he agreed.

Downstairs, they found Halloran, still in the living room, but alone. He rose from the sofa, pocketing his cell phone as he did.

"Anything you can tell me?" the attorney asked.

Swallowing the urge to ask if Ed Jenkins had found a suicide note, Joplin said, "First of all, let me tell you that I'm truly sorry, Tom. I should have said that earlier. I know you cared about her, and that you've been through a lot with her this past year."

Halloran seemed to sag a little as he reacted to this, and his usually icy blue eyes took on a warmer color. "Thanks, Hollis. I'm afraid there aren't that many people who will mourn her death, but I'm one of them, and I appreciate your saying that."

"Right." Joplin straightened his shoulders and glanced at Carrie. "We're putting time of death between midnight and two a.m., give or take an hour. She's in full rigor, and the body temp bears that out. No petecchiae or signs of a struggle or any marks on the body that we can see at this point. If Carrie does the autopsy, she'll be able to tell you more."

Halloran's eyes swiveled to Carrie. "Is that likely? That you'll do the autopsy, I mean."

"Yes," she said. "I can ask to be assigned to it, since I did the Sanchez autopsy."

"Do you need me to come to the ME's to make an official identification?"

Carrie glanced at Joplin, who said, "I don't think that will be necessary, under the circumstances."

"Okay," Halloran said. "I plan to call her mother as soon as I get back to the office. Libba stipulated in her will that Julie and I be in charge of her funeral arrangements, so if you could let me know when the body can be released, I'd appreciate it."

"I'll do that," said Carrie.

"Anything more you can tell us about her will, Tom?" Ike Simmons asked as he entered the room.

"Not just yet," Halloran answered, looking past them at Simmons. "I need to go over it again myself. I'll have it ready for probate in a day or two."

"We'll be in touch," Carrie told him.

Halloran nodded, thanking them for talking to him, then turned and walked into the entry hall. Joplin waited until he'd left before briefing Ike on what he and Carrie had observed during their examination of Libba Woodridge's body, giving a preliminary cause and manner of death, as well as their estimate of time of death. All the while, he couldn't help but think about the difference between Halloran's attitude and demeanor the first time he'd met him—as Elliot Carter's body hung from a tree in Piedmont Park—and the way he'd acted today. The attorney had vehemently insisted that Carter had been murdered, despite evidence to the contrary. He'd also been quite forthcoming about Carter's will. Today, however, he'd seemed to accept without question that his client's death was a suicide, and he was unwilling to provide any details of her will.

As if he'd read Joplin's mind, Ike Simmons said, "Has an alien taken over Tom Halloran's body, Hollis? Or does he know something we don't know?"

"Wouldn't be the first time, Ike, would it?"

Simmons grinned and shook his head. "No, it wouldn't, Hollis."

"I think I'll go have a word with Miss Esposito before we go," Joplin said. "Know where she is?"

"She was pretty done in, so I told her she could go to her room. It's up on the third floor. You think maybe there was a suicide note that somehow ended up in Halloran's hands?"

"You have a suspicious mind, Ike."

"Takes one to know one, Hollis."

CHAPTER TWENTY-EIGHT

Rosa Esposito's quarters were small, but very comfortable. Looking worried, she ushered him into a sitting room filled with pictures of what he assumed to be family members, as well as a few religious paintings and a large crucifix. On the right, he saw a door that opened into a bedroom. It occurred to him that with Libba Woodridge dead, Rosa would soon be out of a job.

"Could I ask you a few questions?" he said softly.

"I already tell the other policeman," she said, the worried look intensifying.

"I know, but I work for the Medical Examiner's office, and I need to know about other things. When Mrs. Woodridge ate dinner, when you last saw her—that sort of thing," Joplin added, although Ike had already told him those details. He didn't want to jump right into questions that might put her on the defensive.

"Okay," she said, looking uncertain. "I bring her dinner in the family room around seven o'clock."

"How did she seem then?"

"Fine, fine. Everything was fine. She ate and watched a little TV."

"Did she get any phone calls?"

"I don't know. I mean, she might, but I was in the kitchen. Nothing rang on the house phone."

"So she had a cell phone with her?"

Rosa nodded. "Always," she said, smiling.

"I didn't see one on her bedside table or anywhere else. Did she leave it in the family room?"

"No. No. She take it with her."

"Did you see it when you found her this morning?"

The worried look reappeared, with a little fear attached. "I don't remember. I was so upset."

"Of course you were. And what time did she go up to bed?"

Rosa scrunched up her eyes, as if trying to remember. "About nine, I think. She usually like to go upstairs and read for a while before she go to sleep. I always check on her around ten o'clock, to see if she need anything," she added, then looked on the verge of tears, as if only then realizing that she would no longer have to perform this nightly service.

"She didn't call on you for anything else, though, after that?"

Rosa shook her head silently.

"Did she seem okay when you checked on her at ten?"

"Si. She was…as usual. She was in a night gown, reading her book."

"Was there a drink on the bedside table? Or any pills?"

Rosa looked to her right, as if she were trying to remember. "No. Nothing."

"How about her cell phone. Was that on the table?"

She nodded quickly. "Si."

"But not this morning?"

Rosa's face fell again. "No, I don't see it."

"Don't worry. It'll turn up. How about a note? Or an envelope? Did you see anything like that?"

"I don't remember," she said, then closed her eyes. When she opened them, she said, "Yes, there was one."

"Did Mr. Jenkins take it?"

"No se," she said. "I don't see him take it."

"But there *was* something, right? An envelope?"

"Si," she agreed reluctantly.

"Did it have a name on it?"

"No se," she replied, the tension creeping back into her voice.

"Don't worry," Joplin assured her. "It's not your fault. We'll find it." He gave her one of his cards. "If you remember anything else, give me a call, okay?"

The housekeeper took the card and nodded.

"You were a good employee," Joplin said. "She knew that."

At this, she smiled, but a tear slid down her face.

———

Halloran sat in his home office and looked at the letter Libba had left for him. Per Jenkins' instructions, he had taken the envelope out of its plastic bag with tweezers and laid it on a sheet of computer paper. He hoped it would give him some answers—answers he'd been unable to give Julie Benning when he'd called to tell her of Libba's death as soon as he left the house on Blackland Road. He was certain the news would be leaked to the media in record time, and he didn't want her to hear about it from anyone else. She had been shocked into silence at first, then began crying and asking him questions in an attempt to understand what had happened.

"You think she *killed* herself, Tom? You think Libba would *do* that?"

"Everything indicates that she did, Julie, but only the ME's office can make that determination."

"But, *why?* I know the attack on her was terrible, but she seemed to be handling it. She was just fine on Sunday, for God's sake, and that was two days ago! What happened between then and now?"

It was a question he'd been asking himself, even as he'd gone about the business of protecting Libba's rights. Nothing that he'd observed about her in the past forty-eight hours—or even the past three weeks—had prepared him for her suicide. He couldn't tell Julie about the letter Libba had left him, but he probably should have read it before calling her.

"I wish I knew, Julie," he'd told her, then assured her he'd call as soon as he knew anything else. When he clicked off, he made a quick call to Alston Caldwell to inform him, too. Alston had seemed so shocked, Halloran decided not to tell him about the note Libba had left him until he'd had a chance to look at it.

Now, bracing himself for what might be in the envelope, Halloran put on latex gloves that he'd gotten from Maggie's darkroom and held it by the lower left corner as he slid a letter-opener under the seal. Then he carefully removed the letter, pulling it gently along the crease. There were two pieces of paper, which he slowly unfolded. One was addressed to him, the other had "Last Will and Testament of Libba Ann Cates Woodridge" at the top. Both were handwritten, with dates and signatures at the top and bottom of each. With a long sigh, Halloran picked up the letter.

Dear Tom,

By the time you read this, I'll be dead. I want to assure you that I have not had anything to drink, nor have I taken any mood- or mind-altering drugs—yet. But after I finish this letter and the will that accompanies it, I intend to drink enough Jack Daniels and take enough Ambien to kill me. Knowing you, I'm sure you'll probably blame yourself, but please don't. This is the best thing for everyone involved, including me. I've had a better life than I ever expected, but I want to leave it on my own terms, with whatever dignity I have left.

For many reasons, I do NOT release you from my privilege of confidentiality. I know that it survives my death, and you don't have my permission to release anything—including this letter or its contents—to the police or anyone not already included in this privileged information, like Ed Jenkins. I know you're concerned about Jorge, but, frankly, I can't be sure that he wasn't somehow involved in the attack on me.

There are only two situations that might occur that would release you from keeping my confidences. One would be if the police or the ME believe that I was murdered instead of taking my own life. The other would be if you discover evidence that Jorge is innocent in the attack on me. My intention is that no one should suffer from anything that I have done or simply because of who I am.

Attached to this letter is a holographic will that will legally change the one you drew up for me after Arliss' death. I know you'll be both shocked and disappointed by its contents, but I assure you that it's what I want to do. Even Arliss would want this, for the sake of the family. For Julie's sake, especially, even if she doesn't realize this right away.

Again, thank you for all that you've done—and tried to do—for me. You and Maggie have been better friends than I deserve. Please thank her for me.

Libba Ann Cates Woodridge

Halloran allowed himself only a few minutes to process Libba's letter, his mind still reeling from everything it contained, then hurried on to the will. As Libba had said, it was in holographic form, written entirely by hand, with nothing else on the page, and giving a date and her full signature. The usual disclaimers that she was "of sound body and mind" and that she was not being coerced in any way were also present. He found it hard to believe, however, that Arliss Woodridge would be happy over what it did, in just one paragraph.

Essentially, Libba's new will completely vacated her late husband's will and reinstated his previous will, as well as the trusts he had set up before he had married her. It accomplished everything that Wesley and Claudia Benning and Arliss' sisters had demanded in their lawsuit and added nothing to mitigate the impact on Julie Benning. She would, of course, receive what her grandfather had originally provided for her: a considerable trust fund, but nowhere near the amount Arliss had left her in the will Halloran had drawn up. And none of the money she would have earned from trustees' fees on the trusts he'd set up to be controlled jointly by her and Libba. The only concession Libba had made was to arrange for $300,000 to be left to her mother. He wondered at the amount; it was small enough that the Bennings would hardly object, but specified that if Connie Sue tried to get more, she would lose even that.

All in all, a complete capitulation.

Or was it, really? Halloran, as Simmons had suggested, had been quick to assume that Libba had killed herself. This assumption was based not only on the stress and fear he was sure she'd felt upon hearing about Maria Sanchez's murder, but also the fact that she had left a letter for him. But was the letter really from Libba? he wondered now. Hastily, he unlocked the file cabinet to the right of his desk and located a file with correspondence from Libba. Besides several type-written letters that had written signatures, he also had a few notes she'd written him by hand. Pulling these from their envelopes, he scanned them, then held one next to the letter he'd just read for comparison.

To his untrained eye, the letter certainly looked as if Libba had written it. It also was consistent with her phraseology and writing style, such as the use of dashes to emphasize certain things. He'd have to have it examined by a handwriting expert, of course, but he was pretty sure that Libba had written it. Whether or not she'd been coerced into writing it was another question, one that Halloran simply couldn't answer at the moment. It was something that he'd have to determine, however, if, and when, the case went to court. Because even if Libba *had* written this holographic will, it would be subjected to many tests and maybe at least one lawsuit. He doubted that Connie Sue Cates would be deterred by any caveat against an attempt to get more money. Julie Benning might have an objection as well, perhaps spurred by her boyfriend.

The thought of Libba's mother reminded Halloran that he hadn't called her yet. He quickly picked up the land line next to his PC and found her number on the "Missed Calls" list; Connie Sue tended to call him often. When there was no answer, he tried her cell phone and left a message asking her to call as soon as she got it. As much as he disliked Connie Sue, he certainly didn't want her to hear the news of her daughter's death on TV or the radio. He wondered where she might be; as far as he knew, the woman had no hobbies or close friends and had quit her part-time job at Kohl's as soon as Libba married Arliss Woodridge.

He was interrupted in this speculation by Maggie's abrupt entrance, the door of his study flying open.

"I just heard," she said.

———

Halloran spent the next thirty minutes filling Maggie in on everything that had happened since he'd received Ed Jenkins' call. Tears welled in her eyes as he told her of Ed's description of Libba and the pills and glass smelling of alcohol on her bedside table. She pulled a Kleenex from her purse and dabbed at them while he read Libba's letter out loud.

"Should you be reading this to me?" she asked, when he reached the paragraph dealing with privileged communication. "I mean, you never had a chance to tell Libba that you hired me as a consultant, did you?"

"No, but I *did* hire you, and the fact that she mentions Ed Jenkins means that she understood that the privilege would include certain other people. Like the handwriting expert I'm going to have to hire. And Alston Caldwell, because this *does* relate directly to the existing will. And you," Halloran added. "I'm going to need your help more than ever now that she's dead."

"You mean with the video?"

"Yes. As soon as I read you what we have to assume for the moment is her new will, I'm hoping we can spend some time going over the video again. I don't plan on going back to the office today."

Maggie nodded slowly. "I'll see if my mother can pick the kids up from school. But, Tom, I can only tell you what I'm able to see, and my expertise is limited in terms of what you need."

"I know that. But I want you to give it one last shot before I have to find someone else. Libba was right when she said that the more people who see the video, the bigger the chance of a leak. You're the only person I trust right now. And Libba would trust you, too."

———

Joplin knocked softly on Carrie's door and opened it when she said to come in. She was sitting at her desk, her laptop in front of her. He noticed how tired she looked and knew that it wasn't from lack of sleep. He felt just as tired, weighed down by the death of yet another young woman so soon after Maria Sanchez. And in a sense, it felt as if it were the second time that Libba Ann Woodridge had died, or at least the second time he'd been saddened by her death. The first time shouldn't really count, but it did. During the few minutes he'd stared down at her as she lay covered in blood that day, now almost three weeks ago, Joplin had felt an immense wave of pity wash over him. It had been eclipsed by the rush of realizing that she was still alive, but he saw it again on the screen in his brain, and it seemed to be compounded by her actual death.

He shut the door softly behind him. "Thanks for calling me. I didn't know when you'd be finished with the autopsy, and I didn't want to bother you."

"There's not much to tell, but you're the only person I want to tell it to right now."

Joplin nodded and sat down, then gave her what he hoped was an encouraging look.

Carrie cleared her throat and closed her laptop. "I found absolutely nothing to contradict a finding of suicide. In fact, everything I *did* see supports it. The housekeeper said she'd eaten a light dinner around seven, which is corroborated by the fact that her stomach was empty at autopsy. Her blood/alcohol level was 1.8, and there were no undigested Ambien capsules in her stomach. It's consistent with a person taking a lot of pills and washing them down with a lot of alcohol. Based on that, as well as her body temp and the ambient temp, along with livor mortis and rigor mortis, I'm estimating TOD to be between two and four a.m. this morning."

"Just to be clear," Joplin said, thinking of the autopsy on Ann Carter, "you didn't find any other…avenues of entry for the Ambien or any other cause of death."

"No, Hollis. No needle marks anywhere on the body— believe me, I looked everywhere—and, obviously, no signs of asphyxiation or blunt force trauma or any other form of trauma. I have to wait on the tox report, of course, but, even in the absence of a suicide note, I'm pretty confident that it wasn't accidental or homicidal. Do you want David to check my work?"

Joplin gave a long sigh. "No, of course not. I'm just trying to process this whole thing. It just doesn't make any sense, Carrie. From start to finish. And I don't really think it's finished."

"Neither do I," said Carrie. "I once heard suicide described as 'a permanent solution to a temporary problem.' Whatever it was that Libba thought she was doing when she killed herself—putting an end to the lawsuit over her husband's will and maybe mending the rift in the family—I don't think it's going to happen. She just won't be around to deal with it anymore."

"Maybe that's all she wanted. Just to be out of it. But whatever her reasons, we'll probably never know. According to Rosa, there *was* a note, but if Ed

224 BLOOD WILL TELL

Jenkins removed it from the scene and gave it to Halloran, we'll never see it. And Jenkins isn't going to tell us anything."

Carrie frowned, then said, "Maybe not, but you could at least tell Tom the housekeeper saw it."

"I think I'll do just that. But I probably won't get anything out of him."

"I'm beginning to see why you don't trust him."

"Actually, he's just doing his job," Joplin said. When he saw the look on Carrie's face, he added, "But don't ever quote me on that."

CHAPTER TWENTY-NINE

While watching the third run-through, Maggie said, "Stop it right there, Tom."

Halloran hit the "pause" button and looked at her, puzzled.

"Now go back a few seconds. Okay, stop right there. Now fast-forward until I tell you to stop. There!" she added triumphantly.

Halloran had no idea what she was seeing. It looked the same to him as the first time he'd viewed the video.

"Now do that again," Maggie ordered.

He did, two more times. The second time, he finally saw what she had seen. Or thought he did.

"It jumps," he said slowly.

"Yes, it does," Maggie agreed. "But not forward. Not horizontally. It makes vertical movements. Do you see that? It's right after he puts the camera into some kind of stand."

Halloran regressed, then fast-forwarded the video again, and it was exactly as she said. "But, why?" he asked her. "What's going on?"

"I'm not sure, but I don't think that's the only time it happens. Run it again, Tom. All the way to the end."

———

They found one more instance where the image jumped; the second occurred after the hooded figure got off of Libba's bed, kissed her and backed away from it, careful not to show his face. Halloran played that section several times, but neither of them could figure out what was happening. Or why. As they were brainstorming the "why," Halloran's cell phone rang. It was Libba's mother.

Reluctantly, knowing the terrible news he would have to give her, Halloran answered it. "Hello, Connie Sue. I've been trying to get hold of you."

"I was out shopping," she said, sounding relaxed. At first, Halloran was glad that she hadn't heard the news of her daughter's death from anyone else. That feeling lasted until he began to try to tell her what had happened. He heard a gasp when he told her that he had bad news to give her, then panic in her voice when he asked if there were anyone with her, or anyone she could call to be with her.

"What is it, for God's sake!" she screamed. "Is it Libba? Did something happen to my baby?"

"Yes," he said softly, then told her that Libba was dead. The screaming began again, intensifying as the seconds, then minutes, passed. Halloran didn't try to stop her for what seemed like ages. "Let me call somebody to be with you," he finally said, repeating this several times, in different ways. "You need someone to be with you," he insisted.

There was one long, harsh sob, and then she said, "There isn't anybody, don't you understand? There is nobody in my life except my daughter, and now she's gone. Nobody!" she added, her voice rising to a pitch that caused Halloran to hold the phone a foot away from his ear.

Maggie took the phone from him and put it in speaker mode, then waited until the screaming had stopped and said, "Connie Sue, it's Maggie. Please let us help you. We'll send a car to drive you to Atlanta. All you have to do is put a few things in a suitcase. We'll take care of you. Of everything. Do you hear what I'm saying? Please, just answer me. We want to help."

There was no answer for another minute, only more sobbing. But then that began to subside, and Maggie just kept repeating what she'd said until Connie Sue finally responded.

"Okay," she said with a long sigh. "But I can't get myself together today. Have the driver here tomorrow morning."

"We'll arrange it and let you know who's picking you up and what time," Maggie told her. "Try to get some rest if you can."

"Thanks," said Halloran when Maggie had clicked off. "I'll see if Ed Jenkins can head down to Brunswick later today. Connie Sue knows him."

"I hope that was okay. I just didn't think she was in any shape to get on a plane, even if we made all the arrangements."

Halloran nodded, envisioning Libba's mother drunk, making a scene at the airport or, worse, calling a press conference and making a scene on the air.

"Funny," said Maggie, frowning. "She never asked how Libba had died."

————

Before calling Halloran, Joplin spent some time on the phone filling Ike Simmons in on Carrie's preliminary autopsy report. He'd told him about his conversation with Rosa before he left the Woodridge house, and they'd agreed on the likelihood that Halloran was now in possession of any note Libba might have left. What they *hadn't* agreed on was what to do about it.

"How 'bout I threaten to charge him and Jenkins with obstruction?" Ike had asked. "If the envelope was addressed to Halloran, he might argue that he had a right to see it first, but Jenkins had no business taking her cell phone, too."

"Maybe he didn't," Joplin had replied. "Jenkins is a former GBI agent. I don't think he'd stick his neck out that far. The phone may still turn up. I didn't look for it, because I didn't know at the time that she'd brought it up to her bedroom, so maybe CSU will find it. It might be better to hold off until you know one way or another."

But CSU hadn't found Libba's phone, Ike now informed him, and Ed Jenkins had insisted that he hadn't seen, much less confiscated, it. He had refused, however, to answer any questions about a note on the bedside table, telling Ike that he wanted his attorney present.

"And, of course, Tom Halloran is his attorney," Ike added.

Joplin grunted. "That's about what I figured he'd do. I find it interesting that he *did* respond when you asked about the cell phone, though. Makes me think he didn't take it. And yet Rosa said she saw it on the bedside table when she checked on Libba at ten."

"Well, *somebody* must be lying."

"Maybe. But there's a third possibility. Maybe—"

"Maybe Libba hid it or destroyed it," Ike finished up.

"Right. If she did kill herself—and the apparent suicide note and the autopsy support this—it might be because of a call she received on her cell. A call that made her choose to end her life rather than face whatever the caller threatened to do."

"But even if we could find the phone, we'd only be able to subpoena the records. There's no way of knowing the *content* of any conversations—just the phone number of the caller."

"Yes, but that might have ultimately been enough to lead us to the caller and find out what was threatened."

"I guess so," Ike said, not sounding convinced. "You gonna call Halloran? It's still the ME's case at this point. If he has that note, he might know who threatened her, and what it was about."

"I plan to call him, but I doubt if even he knows why his client might have killed herself. If she destroyed her phone, she wouldn't be likely to put devastating information in a note that could have been found by anybody."

"And if she did, Halloran sure isn't gonna tell you, is he?"

———

And, true to form, Halloran didn't tell him a thing.

The attorney hadn't seemed concerned by the fact that Rosa Esposito had seen an envelope on the bedside table that had mysteriously disappeared, nor by the fact that Ed Jenkins had asked that his lawyer be present before answering any questions about how said envelope might have disappeared.

"If there were such an envelope, Hollis—and I'm not saying there *was* one, mind you—it would have been addressed to me and is therefore my property," Halloran had responded calmly. "Further, it would have been incumbent upon me to read what it contained to determine if it contained privileged information."

"Save it for the judge, Tom," Joplin had said. "If we end up charging you with obstruction, you might have a little more trouble explaining why Ed Jenkins also took Libba's cell phone, which Rosa saw on the table when she went up to check on her around ten last night. That *wasn't* your property, and it certainly wasn't Jenkins.'"

Halloran *had* seemed a little disturbed by that information, but whether it was because he hadn't known about Libba's cell phone or because he did, in fact, have it, Joplin couldn't tell. He didn't stay on the phone long enough to find out, choosing instead to politely decline answering any of Halloran's questions.

Actually, he'd said, "Kiss my privileged information, Counselor."

———

Joplin's dreams were all about Libba Ann Woodridge.

In one, he saw her as she appeared the first time she'd died, covered in blood. But this time, her eyes were open as he came into her bedroom. They followed him as he approached her, begging him to find out who had done this to her. Then, just as he reached her, she had said, "Too late," and closed them.

He woke up, his heart pounding, and rubbed his face. Got up and went to the bathroom, then lay back down, not wanting to go back to sleep for fear of seeing Libba's eyes again. Sleep overtook him anyway, and this time he found himself in Rosa Esposito's room. He and Libba were trying to comfort the housekeeper as she sat, sobbing, on her bed.

"It's only for a little while, Rosa," Libba was saying as she patted her on the back. "Tell her, Hollis."

But Joplin didn't know what he was supposed to say, and he stood helplessly by the door as the housekeeper continued to weep, and Libba continued to pat her back.

There was a third dream, but Joplin promised himself, as he lay stunned and sweating afterwards, that he would not remember it the next morning. This one, too, involved Libba, but it was not set in any place he had ever seen her. It was in some kind of cave, with primitive drawings like the ones at Lascaux, in France. He'd seen a show about them on the Discovery channel a few years earlier and recognized them as he trudged through the cave, resin torch in hand. At first, the paintings were of pre-historic animals, their bodies made three-dimensional by the natural bulges and crevices of the cave. But then the forms became human, female, their mouths open in terror in faces that looked behind them at predators that Joplin couldn't make out. One of them was clearly Libba. He tried to turn back, but found his feet rooted to the dank cave floor. Up ahead, another torch appeared and illuminated a sight so gruesome it caused him to lose unconsciousness.

CHAPTER THIRTY

Ed Jenkins phoned Halloran at his office at nine-thirty the next morning to tell him that Connie Sue Cates was dead.

"I went to pick her up at her house at nine, like you told me, but when I got there, she didn't answer the doorbell," he said excitedly, as Halloran was still trying to process the first piece of information. "So I called her. Both lines. Still no response. So I went all around the house, looking into the windows, but at the one I thought was her bedroom window, the curtains were closed. Then I tried all the doors and found the carport door unlocked. I was worried that she might be passed out, since she hadn't answered her phone, so I went in."

"Why didn't you call me at that point, Ed?" Halloran asked.

"I know, I know. I should have. Or I just should have called 911. But I had a bad feeling, you know? And I thought maybe there might be something I could do to help her, or at least find something that you might need to see before the police saw it. Like the letter Libba left for you."

Halloran sighed. He was beginning to regret ever keeping that letter from the police or Hollis Joplin. It wasn't as if Libba Ann had revealed anything confidential in it, just that he wasn't free to talk about it, per her instructions. Or, course, her will. "And did you, Ed? Find anything?"

"No. Just Connie Sue. In the bathtub, which was full of blood. It looked like she cut her wrists. I checked for a pulse, but she was dead. And very cold."

"You said it 'looked like' she had cut her wrists. What did you mean?"

"Well, they were cut, both of them. But laterally, like half a bracelet, you know? If you want to kill yourself, you have to cut deep, from the bottom of your hand, towards the crook of your elbow. Otherwise, you don't cut an artery."

"I didn't know that," said Halloran.

"Most people don't, which is why a lot of people don't die that way."

"But she must have bled out somehow, right, Ed? I mean, she was dead, and the bathtub was full of blood, you said."

"I did, and it was. But I'm thinking that there must have been some other wound on her body to cause all that blood. I didn't want to disturb the scene, though, so after determining she was dead, I didn't look any further."

Halloran tried, unsuccessfully, to get the image of Connie Sue in a tub full of blood out of his head, then said. "Okay, but tell me this: Were there any signs of a struggle? Any evidence that someone had broken into her house or taken anything?"

"No, and I've seen a few homicide scenes in my time. I took a few minutes to look around before I called the police, but I didn't see anything to suggest a break-in or a robbery or any sign of violence. I mean, besides the cuts on her wrists. She looked almost peaceful, but I gotta tell you, I don't like it. If this was suicide, it was one too many in one family in a twenty-four-hour period, you know?"

"I'd have to agree with that, Ed. What do the police think?"

"I don't know. They haven't gotten here yet. Figured I better call you before they did and see if you have any instructions."

"Okay. Hang around for a while, and try to find out as much as you can. Go ahead and give them Joplin's and Simmons' contact numbers. And mine, too, if you haven't already. And, Ed?"

"Yes, sir."

"Did you happen to take any pictures with your phone before you called me?"

"Sure did. I'll send them right now."

———

Jenkins had been right; Connie Sue did look peaceful in the photo he sent. Her eyes were closed, and her head lay back against a rolled-up towel. A drink glass with a clear liquid in it—perhaps the remains of the gin and tonic she loved to guzzle—sat on the side of the tub. Only the dark red water in which all but her head was submerged changed the image from one of relaxation to one of horror. And while it was true that Halloran had never cared for Libba's mother and had seen her as a parasite living off his client, he also would never have wished such a death on her. Even if it turned out she'd done this to herself.

But had she?

The other photos Jenkins had sent showed the suitcase Connie Sue had packed and left open on her bed; the carport door he had found unlocked; some dishes in the kitchen sink. It didn't look like anyone had broken into the house, and there were no signs of a struggle that Halloran could see, but it also didn't look like the person who lived in the house had planned on killing herself.

"Too many suicides in one family in a 24-hour period," Jenkins had said.

But what did that mean? That only one of them had killed herself, and the other had been murdered? Or that both of them had been murdered? But if so, why? For either of the scenarios. He still believed that Libba had killed herself—the letter and holographic will truly seemed to have been written by her—but why would that have led to her mother's suicide? Halloran was sure that Connie Sue had loved her only daughter, in her own way, but he was also sure that after the initial shock and trauma had worn off, she would express her grief by acting out and loudly and pub-licly demanding an investigation into Libba's death. Not by killing herself quietly in her own bathtub.

Was that why someone had silenced her, once and for all? Because she would call too much attention to Libba's death? he wondered. Or was it because she had known something, maybe the same thing that had driven Libba to kill herself? If so, would the Brunswick police not see, as Jenkins had, that Connie Sue's wrists weren't cut the right way and wrongly assume suicide? They might not even insist that an autopsy be performed.

Halloran picked up his cell phone, determined to put an end to such fruit-less speculation. He had no idea, at this point, whether Connie Sue Cates had been murdered. Ed Jenkins was there at the scene, but it was unlikely that the police would reveal much to him. If they did suspect foul play, they might even think Ed had a hand in it.

Just as he was punching in the number, Halloran paused, his right index finger poised over the phone, and processed the thought he'd just had— that the police in Brunswick might suspect Ed Jenkins of being involved in Connie Sue Cates' death. It occurred to him that Jenkins had been in the Woodridge house when Libba had died; had found a suicide note addressed to him; had discovered Connie Sue's body. He had no idea when Jenkins had gotten to Brunswick; it could have been as early as ten or eleven in the evening, since Halloran had called around four the afternoon before to ask him to pick up Libba's mother. He didn't actually know when the investiga-tor had gotten on the road, only that he'd asked him to be at Connie Sue's house by nine a.m. this morning.

But what possible motive could Ed Jenkins have for killing either woman? And he certainly couldn't have been involved in the attack on Libba, could he?

Deciding he would have to give what he was sure was a preposterous idea further thought at another time, Halloran finished punching in the number of Hollis Joplin's cell phone.

————

Jimmy Hernandez stood among the remains of the recreated crime scene from the house on Blackland Road. Everything had been dismantled and packed up, either to be stored in the Evidence Room or, as in the case of the bedroom furniture, returned to the Woodridge house. If, of course, Libba Woodridge had even wanted it back. Hernandez had doubted she would, under the circumstances, but now he would never know.

The news that she was dead, and might have killed herself, had hit him like a blow to the solar plexus. He had been distraught when he'd been taken off the Sanchez case—not just because of the issues involved in his knowing Jorge Martinez, but also because it meant that he wouldn't be able to help Libba Ann Woodridge as much as he wanted to. If a suspect for both crimes were found, he could still testify at a subsequent trial—unless some smartass defense attorney was able to get his work disqualified on the basis of his knowing Jorge—but the possibility of that happening was not good, in his opinion. Hernandez knew other people might think he was guilty of the sin of pride, but he was convinced that he, and he alone, could provide the investigators of both cases with the best tools to catch the monster who had attacked Libba and Maria Sanchez. Now, however, his feelings went beyond that; he felt personally responsible for Libba's death.

He had told himself that he would be her memory, that by recreating the attack he could give back to her what the drugs administered to her had destroyed. And that that recreation—his art—would ultimately capture a sadist. But that hadn't happened, and the despair and fear Libba had felt when Maria Sanchez was murdered must have pushed her over the edge.

With a sigh, Hernandez walked over to his desk and pulled up the

Woodridge case on his computer. He went through all of the crime scene photos he and his team had taken, then went over the raw results from the blood spatter analysis he'd performed using the BackTrack programs. Finally, he slowly and carefully reread his report. Then he repeated the process.

If he couldn't have access to the Sanchez photos and findings, he would just have to make do with what he had, searing every image and equation and word into his brain until he came up with something that would help the investigation. *Investigations,* he reminded himself. The investigation of Libba's attack, the murder of Maria Sanchez and, of course, Libba's death. If what Hollis and Carrie thought was wrong, and Libba *hadn't* killed herself, then maybe he could find some clue in her almost-death. Her faked death. And the scene that had been "artistically" staged.

This thought brought to mind fraudulent "masterpieces" that had been copies of original paintings, and he turned back to the computer screen with a new eye.

CHAPTER THIRTY-ONE

"You got a minute, Doc?"

Lewis Minton looked up from his computer and smiled. "Always, Hollis," he said, motioning to one of the chairs in front of his desk. "But first, tell me. How are you feeling these days? I've meant to come by and check on you, but I've had a lot of catching up to do myself."

Joplin folded himself into the chair and said, "I'm doing fine. In fact, I've got an appointment later this afternoon with my gastro doc, to see about getting the damn bag removed. It's been three months, and I don't mind telling you, it's been the longest three months of my life."

"Then I hope he gives you good news today, son. Just don't be disappointed if you have to wait a little longer. They don't like to have to close you up and then start all over if the bowel hasn't healed. Now what can I do for you?"

"Do you know the Glynn County coroner very well?" Joplin asked, trying not to feel discouraged over what Dr. Minton had just said.

"Billy Darden? Sure, we go way back. Why?"

Joplin explained about Connie Sue Cates and her connection to the Woodridge case, as well as Tom Halloran's concern that her death might not get the attention it should. Glynn County, like most counties outside the metro Atlanta area, still used the coroner system, which required only that anyone running for the position be over twenty-five, a high-school graduate, a resident of the county, and not a convicted felon. Once elected, a new coroner received only forty hours of mandated basic training at the Georgia Public Safety Training Center in Forsyth, Georgia. Fortunately, many were morticians and had a working knowledge of anatomy and the various aspects of death, but investigation wasn't their strong suit. They were required to turn any cases of suspicious deaths over to the Georgia Bureau of Investigation, which had forensic labs and medical examiners in both Atlanta and Savannah, but the determination that a death was "suspicious" was often subjective. Too often, deaths that should have been ruled suicidal—or worse, homicidal—were judged "natural" or "accidental."

Minton listened carefully to what had been reported by Ed Jenkins when he found Connie Sue's body, his hands folded on his desk, his expression serious. He raised both eyebrows when told of the pictures the investigator had taken at the scene, but said nothing until Joplin had finished.

"It's no secret that I think the medical examiner system is far superior to the coroner system, Hollis, but Billy Darden is one of the better coroners in this state. Not only has he done the job for almost twenty years, he's been a funeral director far longer than that. And perhaps more importantly, I was one of his trainers at GPSTC after he was elected."

Joplin held up both hands in surrender. "Didn't mean to step on any toes, Doc. It's just that the Libba Ann Woodridge case is pretty high-profile, and now her mother is dead less than twenty-four hours later, and under suspicious circumstances."

Minton sighed and rubbed his face with one hand. He hadn't been back on the job full-time for very long since his heart attack in the spring, and Joplin began to regret bothering him. Before he could say anything, however, the pathologist reached for his Rolodex and began rifling through it.

"I know Dr. Edward Callahan down at the GBI's coastal lab in Savannah pretty well. He's a good guy. Was in the Navy when he got out of med school and the Chief ME for Cook County in Illinois before he retired and moved down here. He's one of three regional MEs at the lab. I'll give him a call and make sure Jimmy turned the case over to them."

"Could you get a copy of the preliminary autopsy report, too?"

Minton squinted up at him. "You don't ask much, do you, son?"

Joplin tried to look innocent. "I'm not the one who wants it, Chief—it's Carrie. Libba Woodridge's death, on top of Maria Sanchez's, really got to her. She's second-guessing herself on the suicide ruling she made on Libba, given the mother's sudden death."

"Well, we can't have that, can we, Hollis?" Lewis Minton said, grinning.

"No, sir, we can't," Joplin agreed.

"That going okay, son?"

"If I don't screw it up, sir."

Minton sighed again and said, "Then God help you."

———

Halloran spent the next hour lining up a handwriting expert to examine Libba's letter and the holographic will. He had no intention of probating the will until he was certain it had been written by her. But even that would present its own set of challenges. Despite what she'd said in the letter, it was incumbent upon him to establish whether she'd been coerced, and he wasn't yet sure how to do that. The missing cell phone troubled him; it seemed to be an indication that Libba had received a text or call from someone that she didn't want discovered. Someone who had said or done something that pushed her over the edge and made killing herself seem like a solution. Someone whose very identity might, in some way, reveal whatever it was that Libba had been so desperate to hide.

Was it the person who had attacked her and sent the video? he wondered. But if that were true, then why couldn't she be sure that Jorge Martinez wasn't her attacker? Did she think that more than one person was involved, perhaps? Halloran still couldn't believe that Jorge was capable of masterminding the whole thing, but the idea that he had worked with someone else was plausible. He could have provided that person with information about the house and the various ways to get into it. Maybe he had thought he was abetting in a burglary or robbery, but not the attack on Libba. Or the murder of his wife. In fact, as Halloran had told Maggie, maybe Maria Sanchez had been murdered solely to implicate Jorge.

These thoughts were interrupted by a phone call from Joan. But before she could tell him why she had called, his office door opened, and Julie Benning rushed in.

"I know you said you'd call me if you heard anything more about...Libba, but I really needed to see you, Tom," she said, her voice hoarse and stressed at the same time. She was dressed in gray sweats and wore no make-up, her hair in a ponytail. "Has the ME's office made a ruling yet?"

"Please sit down, Julie," Halloran said, standing up and motioning toward the chair in front of his desk. "You look exhausted."

"I haven't slept very much in the past few days," she admitted, pushing a stray piece of hair behind her ear. "I still just can't believe Libba killed herself. Could it possibly have been an accident?"

"No," he said gently. "The amounts of alcohol and Ambien in her system don't support that. But I do have something to tell you about that I just found out this morning, and I was going to call you because I didn't want you to hear it on the news. Connie Sue Cates is dead."

Julie stared at him. "Libba's mother? What do you mean? What happened?"

"Ed Jenkins went to Brunswick to get her and drive her back to Atlanta. He found her in her bathtub this morning when she didn't answer the phone or the doorbell."

Her face lost all color. "Was it a heart attack?"

"No. According to Ed, it looked like she had slit her wrists. But he has his doubts about that."

"You mean she...?"

"She might have been murdered," Halloran finished.

Julie blinked her eyes very quickly and slumped in her chair. "Oh, my God!" she said. "Does that mean Libba was murdered, too?"

Again, the suggestion that Libba might have been murdered. Halloran frowned and said, "I don't know at this point. Really. I've asked Hollis Joplin to try to find out what's going on in Brunswick. He hasn't gotten back to me yet. But, Julie, I can tell this has really upset you. Let me—"

She made a dismissive with her right hand, then stood up. "I'm okay. Will you let me know when he does, Tom?"

"Yes, of course," Halloran said, standing, too. He came around the desk and wrapped an arm around Julie, hoping to comfort her, but she stood rigid as he held her, then broke away and hurried out of the office without saying another word.

Whatever conflicting emotions Julie Benning was feeling, he was certain about one of them.

Fear.

CHAPTER THIRTY-TWO

The door to Alston Caldwell's office was closed when Halloran approached it. He wondered if he should have asked Joan to call ahead and see if he were busy, then knocked, knowing Alston would tell him if it were an inconvenient time. The only living name partner of Healey and Caldwell had become his *de facto* mentor since Elliot Carter's death, urging him to drop by any time he wanted—or needed—to do so. Halloran had taken him at his word, consulting with the older man on a regular basis as the Woodridge case played out. He had gone to see him right after calling Joplin about Connie Sue that morning and had finally told Caldwell about the envelope Libba had left for him. The news had unsettled him almost as much as Libba's death, and they'd spent an hour developing a strategy to deal with it.

Now he needed to discuss Julie Benning's disturbing visit and what it might mean. Alston knew just as much, if not more, about the Woodridge/Benning families as he did, and Halloran was hoping he could give him some perspective on what he thought might be a critical situation. Straightening his shoulders, Halloran knocked on the door. When Caldwell's voice urged him to enter, he did, only to find David Healey sitting in one of the chairs in front of the old gentleman's huge antique desk.

"Come in, Tom," Caldwell said warmly.

"If you're busy—"

"David was just leaving," he said, which caused David Healey to rise, scowling, from his chair.

"I'll be in my office till six, Alston," he said, walking past Halloran without acknowledging him.

Halloran refrained from saying something sarcastic, like, "And good afternoon to you, too, David," and, instead, took the chair next to the one Healey had just vacated.

"So, tell me, Mister Tom," Alston said in his soft Southern drawl, "any new developments since we talked this morning?"

When he'd finished telling Caldwell about Julie's surprise visit and her demeanor, the old gentleman took a few minutes before responding, his hands steepled in front of him, his expression impassive.

"Well, now," he said at last, "the rocks are being turned over, aren't they?"

"I don't know what you mean, Alston."

Caldwell sighed, then leaned back in his chair and looked at a point above and beyond Halloran's head. "When I asked you to take over the Woodridge file, I wasn't doing you any favors, Tom." He waved a hand in the air, the thick blue veins and sunspots standing out in contrast to his relatively unlined face. "I'm not just talking about all the media problems you've had to deal with, although God knows you've had your hands full. It goes beyond that. There's something...wrong in that family, and I'm not really sure what it is, but I handed it over to you without any caveats. And for that, I'm truly sorry. I was thinking more of my friendship with Arliss than what I would be asking you to take on."

Halloran found himself at a loss for words. "Can you be a little more specific, Alston?"

"I'm not sure. I'm not even sure that Arliss knew what he was dealing with, as smart and knowledgeable a man as he was. And that said, he also seemed to be totally unaware of the...incongruence, the unsuitability, if you will, of his marriage to Libba Ann. I tried to talk him out of marrying her, you know," he added, the faded blue eyes suddenly darting to Halloran's.

"No, I didn't know," Halloran said, holding the old man's stare. "I take it he wasn't open to any advice, even from you."

"He was besotted with her." Caldwell looked to his right, as if remembering. "But it seemed to be more than just the stereotypical old man/younger woman scenario. He truly cared about her and seemed to believe that he, and he alone, was put on this earth to care for her. I've never seen anything like it, and I've seen a lot in my long life."

"That goes without saying, Alston. But you were saying something about the Woodridge family. Something...dysfunctional that had bothered you?"

Caldwell frowned, as if trying to remember what he'd said, then looked off to the right again. "I think it had a lot to do with Eleanor, Arliss' first wife. She was an extremely cold woman. Very rigid in her beliefs and what she saw as her place in the world." He gave a long sigh. "I think their families were behind the marriage, because it never seemed to me to be a love match, although Arliss always appeared devoted to her. They both came from prominent, wealthy Atlanta families, but Arliss went on to make his own mark in the world with Phoenix Airlines. That meant that he was away a lot, and Eleanor ruled the roost, so to speak. Arliss deferred to her in every way when it came to their children, perhaps to their detriment."

"In what way?"

"Mind you, these are only my own observations, but the Woodridges were friends as well as clients, and we moved in the same circles. Geneva and I," he added, referring to his wife, "felt that it was our duty as parents to raise children to become independent and self-supporting. But Eleanor Woodridge seemed to do everything she could to keep those children tied to her, dependent on her. As if they were extensions of her."

"Well, that's not healthy, of course, but not all that unusual, is it?"

"No, but it had pretty disastrous results, especially in Chandler's case. He started using drugs at age thirteen. I think it was his way of escaping Eleanor. And despite the family money, he was kicked out of just about every private school in Atlanta—Westminster, Pace, Woodward, you name it."

"Did they ever get him any help?"

"Of course, but nothing ever worked, until his stay at Ridgeview three years ago. Those three years were the longest he'd ever been sober and drug-free. And then he relapsed right after Arliss died," Alston added with a sigh.

"Did the family ever get counseling?" Halloran asked. "That's usually advised with addiction."

"I suggested family counseling a few times, but Arliss said Eleanor wouldn't hear of it. Said she felt she didn't have any problems and wouldn't 'subject' herself to that. That Chandler would eventually 'grow out of it,' in her opinion."

"Too bad."

"For Claudia, too. I watched her turn from a fairly happy little girl into a miserable young woman, doing everything she could to try to please her mother. And never succeeding. She became almost a carbon copy of Eleanor, from clothes, to hairstyles, to the way she walked and talked."

"I noticed that," said Halloran. "When I first met her. I had only seen pictures of Eleanor Woodridge, of course, but I was struck by how much Claudia resembled her."

"And not just in looks, unfortunately. She also embraced all of Eleanor's opinions and attitudes, especially her sense of entitlement. And her snobbery. She'd learned to equate money with love, and she's been hell-bent to get her hands on as much as she could for a long time."

"Again, that sounds like a pretty common situation, Alston, albeit a dysfunctional one. But you seemed to imply something a little more...extreme. I mean, when you mentioned turning over rocks. Or maybe I read too much into that."

Caldwell sighed again. "No. No, you didn't, Tom. It's just that I can't seem to express it. All I can say is that it feels…old. And rotten, somehow. Not just your typical 'dysfunctional family,' if there is such a thing. I wish I could describe it better."

"Well, I've been properly warned, anyway. But, tell me this: How did Julie turn out the way she did? She's never made money a priority, as far as I can tell. And I've never met a more independent, liberal, fair-minded woman—unless it's my own wife."

Seemingly lost in thought, Caldwell didn't answer right away. Instead, he picked up a glass paperweight and palmed it back and forth, as if trying to decide what to say, his gaze turned inward. "Believe it or not, I have to give Wesley Benning some credit for that," he said at last. "He's always supported Julie in anything she wanted to do, even when it went against what Claudia wanted. Despite his posturing, he's not a bad guy, and would have been an even better one if Claudia's attitude towards money, and the way she spent it, hadn't gotten in the way."

"I'm afraid I haven't seen that side of him," Halloran said.

Caldwell gave a dry chuckle. "I don't suppose you have. But maybe that's because you didn't meet him until Arliss passed away. When the storm hit, so to speak."

"He was different before that?"

"I'd say so. And so, of course, was Claudia, in a way. Or maybe she just became a more intensified version of herself after Arliss died. Neither one of them was happy when he married Libba Ann, but Claudia seemed to take it personally. Almost as if she, herself, had actually taken her mother's place, and that Arliss was "cheating" on her. And when her father died and she learned about his new will and trust—well, I don't need to tell you what her reaction was."

"I've never seen anyone quite so upset," Halloran said, remembering the scene in his office, soon after the funeral. "Or venomous. I thought she might actually attack Libba. Physically."

"So did I. The fact that Arliss bypassed his own children as heirs and trustees and placed everything in Julie's and Libba's hands devastated Claudia."

Halloran thought of his phone conversation with Claudia Benning after the attack on Libba and said, "The last time I talked to her, Claudia insisted that her mother had been Arliss Woodridge's only legal wife, and when I assured her that we had ample documentation that no coercion or mental weakness was involved in either his marriage to Libba or his change of will, she hinted that they had some new legal basis for contesting the will."

The faded blue eyes stared at him. "Really?" said Caldwell. "Did you believe her?"

"Yes, to tell you the truth. Or, at least, I thought she believed what she was telling me. Do you have any idea what she could be talking about, Alston? I mean, besides the obvious—that she thinks she has evidence that would prove that Libba and Arliss weren't legally married."

"Could she possibly have anything like that, Tom?"

"I have a certified copy of the marriage certificate, so I doubt it. And I took the precaution of doing some research and making sure Libba had never entered into any civil or religious marriage with anyone before that. Which is why I asked if you knew of anything else."

"No, I don't. Geneva and I were at the wedding, despite my attempt to get Arliss to change his mind, and although Claudia and Wesley didn't attend, they never tried to stop the proceedings because of any legal concerns. Arliss would have told me. But if Claudia says she has something, Tom," Alston Caldwell added, his face hardening, "you'd better try to find out what it is."

"I know, although the whole thing might be moot, now, if the holographic will is valid. I haven't told anyone else about that, by the way. I'm not going to probate until I get some definitive word from a handwriting expert. And the medical examiner, as to the manner of death."

Caldwell steepled his fingers again. "But if it does prove to be her hand-writing, I'd be interested in knowing if Claudia Benning had a hand in get-ting Libba to write it and then kill herself. Did Julie happen to tell you what her mother's reaction was when she found out about Libba 's death?"

"No, it didn't come up," Halloran said, "but she certainly seemed afraid, in some way. Almost unhinged, for want of a better word. But I didn't ask why. Just thought it was due to the cumulative effect of hearing about Connie Sue's death so soon after Libba's. But maybe Julie's worried that Claudia—or even Wesley—is involved somehow. I dropped the ball on that one, I guess."

"Pick it up, then, Mister Tom," said Alston Caldwell. "Pick it up."

CHAPTER THIRTY-THREE

"I discussed this with you after your surgery, Mr. Joplin," said Dr. Mallory, "so forgive me if I repeat myself, but I've found that most of my colostomy patients don't remember much of what I tell them then."

Joplin had been weighed, had his blood pressure and blood taken by a nurse, then been poked and prodded and palpated like a honeydew melon by the good doctor himself. He was sitting on an examining table, covered only by a hospital gown that opened in the front. And was still open. All he wanted was the bottom line now, no puns intended. A slide-show of images featuring Dr. Mallory sitting next to his bed flashed through his mind, but the morphine had blunted his ability to record what had been said. "I would definitely be among that group, Doctor," he said. "Repeat away."

Mallory smiled. He was a tall, slender man in his forties with white-blond hair going gray and slate-colored eyes. "Well, then, as I told you back then, I decided on what we call a loop transverse colostomy in your upper right abdomen in order to give what is left of your large intestine a chance to heal. From the injury you suffered, and the resection that was necessary, due to the peritonitis," he added, unnecessarily.

As if Joplin could ever forget.

He was suddenly back on the fifteenth floor of One Atlantic Center, clutching his abdomen with his left hand and backing away from Paul Woodley's desk, as blood spurted between his fingers. He felt again the searing pain that jolted through him as he sagged into one of the chairs in front of Woodley's desk, felt the gun fall from his other hand, felt the overwhelming despair as it was kicked away from him. And although he remembered only bits and pieces of the days that followed, sounds and images came to him now as they had when he lay helpless in the hospital: Simmons crying and cursing him for being such a hot dog; a doctor peering down at him and telling him where he was; Tom Halloran looking grave and concerned as he thanked him for saving his life.

In the background, he heard Dr. Mallory cheerfully describing how he would make an incision around the stoma and then reattach the upper section of his intestine to the lower one. Heard him say that he'd be in the hospital three to four days, but that the recovery time would be about six weeks, and that he could expect some "inconvenient" but "minor" problems such as flatulence, incontinence, and a sore anus, as well as constipation and/or diarrhea. With great effort, Joplin pulled himself from the past and tried to concentrate on what the doctor was saying.

"Unfortunately, none of these side effects can be completely controlled by diet or medication," said Mallory. "Limiting sugar, as well as gaseous and spicy foods can lessen them. It's also best to drink alcohol sparingly, and beer isn't a good idea at all. Too fizzy. Some people are helped by taking Lomotil or Imodium before meals to slow the bowel; you'll just have to find out what works best for you. Each person is different. I've had some patients experience relatively little discomfort or embarrassing symptoms and others who had to delay going back to work or their normal activities for several more weeks than expected."

"What would you consider 'normal activities,' Doctor?" Joplin asked, hoping he wouldn't have to actually mention the word "sex."

"Oh, the usual," Dr. Mallory said, still cheerful. "You won't be able to go back to work for a few weeks. No heavy lifting, of course, and you should add moderate exercise, like walking, very gradually. You can resume sexual activity when your incision has healed, if you feel up to it, usually around two or three weeks. Same with driving. Stop either activity if you feel pain. Hopefully, you won't be driving and having sex at the same time," he added, then laughed at his own joke.

Joplin gave a weak smile. He had waited impatiently for this day for the last three months, and now the prospect of dealing with the "inconvenient" after-effects of the reversal overwhelmed him. Carrie was a doctor, but how could any woman find a man who was constantly running to the bathroom or farting attractive? Add to that the fact that Yuengling would be a no-no, and any other type of alcohol would have to be kept to a minimum, and Joplin began to wonder if he shouldn't put the reversal surgery off indefinitely.

"The good news is that we can go ahead with this pretty much any time," Mallory went on relentlessly, ratcheting up to an even higher level of cheerfulness. "You were in good physical shape before your injury, and you've kept yourself up, so we just have to look for an opening in both our schedules. I'll have my nurse call to give you some options in a day or two. Sound good?"

"Sounds good," Joplin said, aiming for a level of enthusiasm he hoped Dr. Mallory would find acceptable. "Anything I should be doing—or *not* doing—in the meantime?"

'Oh, they'll tell you all that at your pre-op exam, Mr. Joplin," Mallory said, giving him the distinct impression that it was best not to know such details until the last possible minute. "Have you ever had a colonoscopy?" he asked, then shook his head at his own question. "No, I guess not. You're way too young. Anyway, the prep for this operation is a *little* more involved than that. Just keep up your usual level of physical activity. It'll help with recovery."

Giving him a hearty handshake and a friendly slap on the back, Dr. Mallory left the examining room. Joplin stared at the door, still trying to process everything he'd heard, then slowly got down from the table and gathered his clothes. His cell phone rang as he was buttoning his shirt. Ignoring the sign asking all patients to refrain from using cell phones, he answered it.

"Hope I'm not interrupting, Hollis," said Dr. Minton. "You can call me back, if so."

"No, Doc, I'm all through."

"Good news?"

Joplin swallowed the words on the tip of his tongue and said, "Per Dr. Mallory, I can have the surgery at the next available opening in both our schedules."

"Great, son! That *is* good news. And I have some more for you: I was able to get in touch with Dr. Callahan at the GBI lab in Savannah, and Billy Darden *did* refer the Cates death to them. When I told him about Mrs. Woodridge, he offered to do the mother's autopsy himself and send the preliminary report. Said he could have it to us tomorrow sometime."

"I appreciate that, Doc."

"You okay, Hollis? You don't sound like yourself."

Joplin sighed. "Actually, I wish I were anyone *but* myself just now."

There was a long pause, then Minton said dryly, "I gather Dr. Mallory gave you the 'poop' on what to expect after the reversal."

"I'm gonna forget you said that, Doc. And, yes, he did."

"Don't let it get you down, son. You'll get through this, like you have everything else."

"Sure. I just need to wrap my head around it, that's all."

"Just don't go into one of your Blue Funks," Minton said earnestly.

"Not a chance," said Joplin.

But, of course, he was lying.

———

Jimmy Hernandez had gone through his report twice, and the computer recreation of what had happened at the house on Blackland Road three times, when the faint echo in his brain was turned up to full volume. He'd been reminded of something he'd seen before when he'd begun work on the Woodridge crime scene. Something that he'd later mentioned to Hollis, but which had continued to elude him. Now he sat at his desk for several minutes, trying to pull up the image he'd finally remembered and then, the crime scene pictures that contained it. He didn't have an eidetic memory like Hollis Joplin, but he had an artist's eye for details, and he hoped that this particular detail had the potential to break the case.

It was a scene he'd worked five years ago. The Trenton case. Daniel Trenton had been a forty-five-year-old doctor who lived with his wife and two teenage sons in a house on West Paces Ferry Court in Buckhead. On April 7, 2005, a Friday night, he'd been in bed with the flu. His wife had reluctantly left him to attend a dinner party at the home of friends who lived a few blocks away on Rilman Road; his sons had been out on dates. At ten-thirty p.m., the wife returned and went immediately up to the master bedroom on the second floor to check on her husband. She found him dead in their bed, bludgeoned to death.

A frantic call to 911 brought the police to the house within ten minutes, at which time it was discovered that a French door off the family room had been broken into, and a number of expensive items—lap tops, two flat-screen TVs, a sterling silver tea set, and all of Mrs. Trenton's jewelry, among them—had been stolen. The thieves had evidently been alerted to Daniel Trenton's presence by the sound of a TV in the master bedroom and had dispatched him before ransacking the house. No weapon had been found.

Hernandez had been called in to analyze the blood evidence left on the headboard, wall, sheets and carpeting. A palm print he'd found on the contour sheet had resulted in the positive identification of one of the perpetrators, who'd ultimately confessed and led police to two other suspects. They were all presently incarcerated at Jackson.

But it hadn't been the bloodstain evidence that had stirred in Hernandez's memory. It was what was on the wall opposite the bed where Daniel Trenton had been murdered. He pulled up the case on his computer and paged through the crime scene photos until he found it: a large, framed canvas that held a painting that looked as if it had been created in Hell.

After staring at it for several seconds, Hernandez picked up his cell phone and punched in Hollis Joplin's number.

CHAPTER THIRTY-FOUR

After waiting for a break in the rush-hour traffic that was choking Butler Street in front of Grady Hospital, Joplin was finally able to make it to Edgewood Avenue and get on 1-85 North. He was supposed to be meeting Carrie at the Georgia Grille on Peachtree for drinks and an early dinner. He knew she'd be anxious to hear what the doctor had told him, but decided he just wasn't up to it. He needed to go home, feed his cat, then open up what might be his last bottle of Jim Beam for a long time and wait for the waves of self-pity that were beginning to lap at his feet to knock him down. No matter what he'd told Dr. Minton, the inevitable was going to happen.

A full-fledged Blue Funk was on its way.

Joplin had been prone to bouts of depression since he was a young teenager. These had been fueled by stretches of insomnia that were a result of the eidetic memory he didn't know he had. At the time, he'd thought that everybody was kept awake at night by smells and sounds and images that they'd encountered that day. Or even in the past. When he was a little child, he'd amazed people with his ability to recall events, often in great detail. The attention he'd received as a result had made him uncomfortable, however, so he'd learned to hide this strange ability, and in time, most people forgot he'd ever had it.

But when he hit puberty, his mother, concerned about his constant fatigue, had finally taken him to see the family doctor. After a thorough physical exam, as Joplin sat in uncomfortable expectation on the exam table, Dr. O'Brien had asked him a lot of questions about his problem sleeping. He'd seemed puzzled by Joplin's answers, especially those involving three-dimensional images that would suddenly materialize in his darkened bedroom or entire conversations that were replayed in his head. The doctor had then asked Joplin questions about his other senses: Did colors have smells? Did numbers have colors? Could he "see" time?

Joplin had told Dr. O'Brien that, of course, colors had smells, and that he saw time in the form of his geometry protractor, but it was crazy to think of numbers having colors. Or, for that matter, pieces of music having smells. Dr. O'Brien had simply smiled as he wrote down what Joplin said, then told him to get dressed while he talked to his mother. He would later learn that O'Brien had completed an internship in psychiatry before switching to internal medicine, but had never lost interest in brain processes or the medical articles that kept him up-to-date on topics such as eidetic memory and synesthesia.

"He says you have a special kind of memory, Hollis," his mother had told him proudly. "You can remember things like you're seeing them on a TV screen. And when you hear or smell things, they stay with you for a long time, too. I remember my grandmother telling me that she could see colors when she smelled certain things. Dr. O'Brien said it's pretty unusual, though, for someone your age to have this kind of memory. He calls it 'eyedetic,' I think. But it usually goes away by the time you start school. Unless, maybe, kids who have it just don't want to feel different, so they keep it to themselves. Is that what you did?" She'd taken her eyes off the road and turned to look at him. "Because I remember when you were just a tiny little thing, you used to talk about things that had happened months and even years before. Is that what happened? You just stopped talking about things like that?"

"Sort of," Joplin had said, seeing again, as he drove north on Peachtree, the way his mother's face had softened. It made his heart contract, over twenty years later.

"Well, you don't have to talk about them now, either," she'd said, turning back to look out the windshield. "Unless you want to, that is. Dr. O'Brien thinks that's what keeps you awake at night—all these memories in your head. He says it might help you to talk to someone—another doctor. Someone who can help you cope with it. Would you like that, Hollis?"

Joplin remembered feeling a heavy weight roll off his chest. "I just want to talk to *him*," he had told his mother. "Not another doctor. Just him."

Which was how Joplin and Dr. O'Brien—his first name was Aloysius, Joplin later found out—had begun meeting every Thursday afternoon at five o'clock for the next year. During the course of that year, Dr. O'Brien had administered a few tests to give them both some idea of the special way Joplin's brain was wired, but for the most part, he had treated what Joplin later realized was very much an anomaly as simply a normal inconvenience of adolescence. One that he could manage and even use to his benefit. Like getting good grades in high school, as well as one of the highest SAT scores in his graduating class at Austell High. Which led to a scholarship at Clemson, where Joplin had majored in Criminal Justice.

Around the time he began seeing Dr. O'Brien, a young boy named Bobby Greenleaf had been kidnapped on his way to school in Buckhead, and the media attention given to it had been in such contrast to the lack of attention given to poor black children during what became known as the Atlanta Child Murders, it had inspired him to become a police officer. He remembered telling Dr. O'Brien that he wanted to be able to help children like Edward Hope Smith, the first black child to disappear in 1979.

Joplin had continued to see Dr. O'Brien off and on during high school and college, but not as a patient. Instead, he'd looked upon the doctor as the father he'd lost, going to him for advice rather than counseling as he grew older. If O'Brien had been disappointed about his career choice, he'd never shown it, encouraging him to pursue whatever path he felt would make him happy. He had even attended Joplin's graduation from the Police Academy and seemed every bit as proud as his own father would have been.

A year later, Aloysius O'Brien had been killed in a head-on collision with a drunk driver, and Joplin had his first Blue Funk. His previous bouts of depression, which Dr. O'Brien had called "weltschmerz," explaining that he was at times overwhelmed by the way he thought the world should be and how it actually was, couldn't hold a candle to the dark tunnel he went into for over a month. He had been seven when his real father had died; losing Dr. O'Brien was far worse, in ways he would understand only as time went by.

As Joplin left the expressway at the Peachtree-Pine exit, his cell phone rang. It was the third call he'd received since talking to Lewis Minton, but he didn't answer it when he saw that it was Carrie; he just couldn't talk to her. Instead, he pulled into a BP station a few blocks further on and texted her, pleading fatigue and canceling their date. He didn't bother checking to see if she had made the other two calls.

———

Lucas answered his cell phone after the second ring.

"What have you done?" Julie asked him.

"What do you mean?"

"Libba is dead."

"I know," he said. "I saw it on TV. I tried to call you, but you blocked my call. I'm really sorry, Julie, I—"

"Did you have anything to do with it, Lucas?"

There was a long silence, and then he said, "Are you kidding? Do you mean, did I kill her or something?"

"Yes. That's exactly what I mean."

"But the news reports said it looked like suicide!"

"The ME's office hasn't ruled yet, Lucas, but even if she did commit suicide, maybe you helped her decide to do that. Maybe you were the one who attacked her and made it look like she was dead. And maybe you told her you could do it again."

"You are seriously out of your mind, Julie," he protested, his voice rising. "What possible reason could I have for doing something like that? Attacking her, I mean."

"Maybe several million reasons," she spat out. "You've been telling me over and over that I should convince Libba to settle with my parents and my aunts over my grandfather's will. Maybe you decided you'd have better luck scaring her into settling. Or killing herself."

"I didn't do that, I swear!"

"Connie Sue Cates is dead, too. And even though it was made to look like a suicide, the authorities have their doubts. I hope you were in North Carolina all this time," Julie added, then hung up.

————

Carrie sat at her desk, looking at the text Hollis had sent. She was tempted to call him, but thought better of it. Whatever had happened at the doctor's office to make him cancel their date, he obviously didn't want to talk to about it. Not to her, anyway. She was suddenly discouraged by what seemed to be Hollis' continued inability to trust that she could understand what he was going through. Or maybe he just didn't need her.

And never would.

In the last few weeks, Carrie had gone from the frustration of dealing with Hollis' refusal to talk about Jack Tyndall, to the joy of their first night together—albeit a chaste one—to the anxiety following their argument after the Hallorans' dinner party, and, finally, to what seemed to be a new beginning for them. And even though the word "love" had never been spoken, something vital had changed between them. *For* them. So she'd finally admitted, to herself, if not to him, that she loved him.

But what good would that do, she wondered, if he shut her out every time things got rough? Carrie had no idea if a physical exam had resulted in Dr. Mallory's telling Hollis that it was too soon to attempt the colostomy reversal or if Hollis had simply gotten overwhelmed by what the procedure—and his recovery from it—would involve. She was a doctor, for God's sake! Why didn't he believe that she could help him deal with it? Or at least just tell her what had gone on at Mallory's office?

Angrily, Carrie stood up and shrugged out of her hospital coat, then hung it on the coat rack next to her desk. Grabbing her purse out of a bottom drawer, she left her office, then the building. Once in her car, she had an almost overwhelming need to see him. To drive to his apartment and confront him. To make him understand that he couldn't keep retreating into himself; that she was there for him and wasn't going away.

She sat there in her car, looking out at the traffic on Cheshire Bridge Road, not sure what to do. Then she turned on the ignition and backed out of the parking space.

———

Wesley Benning replaced his office phone in its cradle and sat in stunned silence for several seconds. Then he got up and walked over to the discreet bar contained in an antique armoire that Claudia had bought for him when he'd been made a name partner. His hands found the bottle of Glenmorangie and a thick crystal glass, even as he remained lost in thought. After pouring himself three fingers, he went back to his desk and stared, unseeing, out of his twentieth-story window, which overlooked Piedmont Park.

Connie Sue Cates was dead, according to Julie. She'd hung up abruptly, the tears thick in her voice, but not before telling him that it was unlikely that Libba's mother had committed suicide. That the police were investigating the death as a possible homicide, and that Libba's death, too, was now suspect.

Benning took a healthy sip of his drink and thought of The Plan, as Claudia had called it, and how it would achieve what they wanted. That had been the nature of their relationship from Day One. Long ago, she'd told him that it was the only way she'd marry him, if he'd go along with what she had in mind for their life together. And so, against everything that he'd once seen as his better judgment, he had agreed. Some of it was because he'd known that his position in life, as a member of Arliss Woodridge's family, would be guaranteed by such a marriage. Most of it, however, was because he'd loved Claudia from the day he'd met her. And whenever he'd wavered in that love, or, at least, its cost to his pride and autonomy, there had been Julie to keep him tethered to his wife's determination to control what she saw as their destiny.

But now he was beginning to believe that what Claudia wanted, needed— *insisted upon*— would damn them both. Had already damned them, if he were honest with himself. His conscience was clear about almost everything that had happened in the past few weeks. He hadn't attacked Libba or forced her to kill herself; he had never wanted either of those things to happen, for God's sake! And he hadn't even known that Connie Sue was dead until Julie had called him. No, he decided, after finishing off his drink, what had happened had been completely out of his control.

Everything except setting it all in motion, of course.

CHAPTER THIRTY-FIVE

Joplin stayed home for two days, calling in sick each morning. He began drinking at noon on each of those days, but the pity party had no beginning and no apparent end. Sarah Petersen seemed to take it in stride, telling him to feel better and call when he thought he could come back to work. He had no idea how Carrie was taking his absence, though, since he couldn't bring himself to return her calls.

Just as well, he thought to himself, as he fixed some dinner for Quincy. *Better to make it a quick, clean cut, than let things linger on.*

He had settled down on the couch with Quincy and a generous slug of Jim Beam to watch a little PBS News Hour, when the doorbell buzzed. He tried ignoring it, but whoever was pushing the damned button was very persistent. Joplin gave a large sigh and heaved himself up from the couch. There was no way to tell who was at his front door because he had no peephole.

Note to self: add a peephole to the front door, he thought, when he saw who it was.

"You haven't bothered to return my calls," said Carrie Salinger, looking for all the world like a gorgeous, but very deadly member of a Mossad extraction team, "so I decided to pay you a visit. But don't worry, Hollis, it's strictly business. May I come in?"

His mouth had gone dry, but he managed to say, "Of course."

She marched in, briefcase in hand, and stopped short when she'd gotten a good look at his messy living room. The kitchen was even worse, so Hollis quickly cleared clothes and newspapers off the couch, disturbing Quincy, and motioned for her to sit down. "Please excuse the mess," he said apologetically.

"I guess I'll have to," she said icily, but bent down to rub the cat's head. She was wearing a tan pantsuit over a dark-brown tee-shirt that matched her eyes. Joplin's resolve to make a clean break of it wavered.

"Carrie, I—"

Holding up one hand to ward off his excuses, she said, "You'll tell me what's going on with you when you feel like it. Or not," she added, an ominous tone in her voice. "In the meantime, I thought you should know that I got the results of Connie Sue Cates' autopsy."

"Good," said Hollis, eying his half-finished glass of Jim Beam. He could sure use a little liquid support at the moment. "Would you like a drink?"

"No, thanks," she said, dashing his hopes. "As I said, this is strictly business. But you go ahead. I must have interrupted Happy Hour. Or maybe," she added, her eyes sweeping over the collection of glasses and plates on the coffee table, "it's been Happy Afternoon."

"Something like that," he said, sitting down beside her and picking up his glass with as much dignity as he could muster. "I'm self-medicating."

Carrie stared at him, and her mouth started to form a word, then froze. "Right," she said briskly. Delving into her briefcase, she pulled out a manila folder and opened it. "First off, the manner of death *was* homicide. Given the slight angle of the cuts on her wrists, both were made by a right-handed person. Connie Sue, of course, would have had to make the cut on her right wrist with her left hand. But more importantly, as Ed Jenkins knew at once, because the cuts were lateral, that wasn't what killed her."

"What did?" Joplin asked, taking a big sip of his drink.

"Some type of long, thin instrument was shoved up her vagina. She bled out from that. The pathologist thinks it might have been a skewer, like for kebabs. Glynn County CSU hasn't found anything in her house or backyard that matches it, but the killer could have taken it with him."

"Not a pleasant way to die," Joplin said, taking another big sip of his drink.

"Maybe that was the whole point. Whoever did it was expressing a lot of hatred for Connie Sue Cates, and just slitting her wrists wouldn't have been as satisfying. But he still wanted to make it look like suicide, and maybe he thought a coroner would buy into the staged scene."

"That's assuming that the killer *knew* that Glynn County has a coroner system, Carrie."

"So? Whoever attacked Libba and killed Maria Sanchez and Connie Sue seems to know a lot more than the average person."

"And you think one person is responsible for all three crimes?"

Carrie shrugged. "I don't know at this point. But, obviously, Jorge wasn't responsible for these last two deaths."

"Were there any marks or bruises on her hands or arms or torso to show that she'd been held down while the killer cut her?"

"No, but she had a lot of alcohol in her system, as well as some Ambien. Just like Libba," she added, locking eyes with him.

"So, she was probably unconscious," Joplin responded, taking another sip.

"Yes, but there wasn't enough of either, in combination, that would have suppressed her breathing. She would have been pretty vulnerable, though."

"Any DNA evidence?"

"She wasn't sexually assaulted, if that's what you mean," she said, then paused. "Well, except for being penetrated by a metal instrument."

"I knew what you meant."

"Anyway, the killer was careful enough not to leave any incriminating hairs or saliva or blood. But the report *did* tell me something that may be pertinent to Connie Sue Cates' murder. And Libba's death," Carrie added, staring at him. "If you're interested, I mean."

"Of course I am," Joplin said, setting his glass down and trying to look sincere.

"Connie Sue Cates wasn't Libba's biological mother," said Carrie.

———

Hollis stared at her. "That was in the report?"

"No, of course not. But what *was* in the report was that Connie Sue had type A blood with an AA phenotype. And I remembered that Libba had type O blood with an OO phenotype. Do I need to explain dominance and allelic pairs to you to show how I knew Connie Sue wasn't Libba's mother?"

"No," he said, shaking his head slowly. "I understand that that means both of Libba's parents had to have had type O blood and OO phenotypes, so that rules out Connie Sue."

"Did either Tom or Maggie ever mention that Libba was adopted?"

"No, it never came up. Or maybe they didn't know. Have you told Tom about this?"

"No," Carrie said, "but I talked to Captain Martucci and Ike Simmons before I came over here. I'm sure it's just a matter of time. Of course, you could call him yourself."

"No, thanks. He'll hear soon enough."

Carrie fought the impulse to say something she might regret. Instead, she took a deep breath and said, "Hollis, I haven't released a manner of death for Libba yet, and you were the investigator on the case, so it's still yours. Connie Sue's murder—despite the fact that she wasn't Libba's mother—might very well have some connection to Libba's death. You were also the one who asked Dr. Minton to request a copy of the autopsy. I need you to follow up on this."

His eyes slid away from hers. "I don't know if I can," he said. "I mean, if I have the surgery."

"*If* you have it? Did Dr. Mallory say you weren't ready for it?"

"No, it's just that it's going to be a lot more complicated than I thought."

She felt her heart lurch a little, and her guard came down. "Do you want to talk about it?"

"Not really," he answered, still not looking at her.

Hoping her disappointment didn't show, Carrie slapped the autopsy report on the pile of newspapers covering the coffee table and stood up. "I'll leave this copy with you, in case you feel like going over it."

Hollis stood up, too, and jammed his hands into the pockets of his jeans. "I'm sorry, Carrie."

She searched his face for some small sign that her coming to see him had made any kind of impact, but saw nothing but weariness and regret.

"I know," she said, then walked quickly to the front door before he could see the tears gathering in her eyes.

———

"How come you're not returning my calls, Hollis?" Jimmy Hernandez asked when Joplin opened his front door an hour later.

"I've been sick," he said.

"Yeah, I can see," said Hernandez, eying the glass of Jim Beam. He had a laptop carrier slung over one shoulder. Without waiting for an invitation, he marched past Joplin and strode into the (still) messy living room. "I heard you were in one of those Blue Funks of yours, so I decided to come by."

"Who told you that?"

"Doesn't matter." He sat down and pulled the laptop out of its bag, setting it on the coffee table. "I want to show you something."

Joplin took a sip of his drink and said, "I'm off-duty, Jimmy. I told you— I'm sick."

"You and I are never off-duty, Hollis, even when we're sick. Now sit down and look at this."

Reluctantly, and feeling a certain amount of resentment that the best part of his evening had been interrupted, Joplin sat down next to Hernandez. He watched as the blood spatter analyst typed in some commands and then pulled up a case file.

"I was the analyst for a scene on West Paces Ferry Court about five years ago. A doctor, a hematologist, was murdered in his bed during a robbery. Bludgeoned to death."

"Doesn't ring a bell," Joplin said, draining the last of his drink.

"Doesn't matter. I'm about to show you why it's connected to the attack on Libba Anne Woodridge and the murder of Maria Sanchez."

Joplin set his glass down on the coffee table and folded his arms, determined not to be drawn back into the situation. But as Hernandez clicked through the crime scene photos, he found himself leaning forward, straining to make sense of the graphic collage he was viewing. Then Hernandez pulled up a shot of a painting in an ornate frame that caused him to drop all pretense of disinterest. It was the portrait of a woman, or at least her outline, painted in blood.

CHAPTER THIRTY-SIX

"Jesus!" said Joplin. He set his glass down on the coffee table with a thud.

"I don't think *Jesus* was anywhere in the room when this was painted," Hernandez responded, pronouncing Christ's name in a Latin accent. "What you're looking at is the outline of a woman's head and upper body that, if it were found at a crime scene, would be seen as a 'void pattern,' caused by an *absence* of blood spatter. In other words, the victim's body would have protected the space behind her from being spattered with blood. Now, I don't know if the artist actually painted this, in an effort to mimic what blood spatter would do, or whether he used a model to sit up against a canvas while he threw paint at her, but the result looks pretty authentic."

Joplin nodded slowly. "I'd have to agree."

Hernandez let out a long breath. "Okay, let's move on to the attack on Libba Ann Woodridge. The first crime scene photos I saw showed her propped up against the headboard of her bed. You took those, right?"

"Yes," said Joplin, seeing Libba's matted hair and bloody face again. "I thought she was dead at the time."

"Anybody would have thought the same thing," Hernandez reassured him. "She was *supposed* to look dead, Hollis. Only she wasn't. And when the paramedics removed her from the bed, this is what the first photo of the bed and the wall behind it looked like."

Joplin sat, transfixed, as the image appeared on the screen. It was an outline of Libba Woodridge's head and torso. "It looks just like the painting," he said, after staring at it for several seconds.

"Yes." Hernandez paused, then said, "When I first saw the Woodridge photos that my team took, some memory stirred in my mind, but I couldn't place it until a few days ago. And then I remembered the Trenton case. And the painting in the bedroom where Dr. Trenton died."

"Who's the artist? Do you know?"

Hernandez shook his head. "I can't make out the signature on the painting in the photo, and I never talked to the widow. The case moved very quickly after I found the bloody handprint on the sheet. The perp confessed and named the others, and they all pled out. So I never followed up on it. And now I can't, because I'm not supposed to be involved with either case."

Joplin continued to stare at the outline of Libba's head and torso for several seconds, then said, "Okay, I see the similarities between this and the painting, and between the way both Maria and Libba were posed, but what's the connection between Maria and the painting?"

"If you remember, I told you I took my own high-res photos of the Sanchez scene after the body was removed, and although the wall behind the victim didn't look like the Woodridge scene, it had its own elements of artistic composition. Have you seen the photos the Sandy Springs CSU took?"

"No," said Joplin softly, still trying to process what he was seeing. "I only saw the ones that I took of Maria that morning. And Carrie did the autopsy at one that afternoon."

Hernandez bent over his laptop again, fingers flying over the keys. A photo of Maria Sanchez appeared. "That's the one you took, Hollis," he said, then began typing again. The same scene came up, this time without Maria's body in it. "And this is the one CSU took. As I said, it has its own elements of artistic composition—the sort of 'brush strokes' formed by the blood spatter as the killer beat her. And it also resembles the photo of Libba after the

EMTs removed her. But until I looked at the painting in Dr. Trenton's bedroom again, I didn't realize what else was there. Do you see what looks like a sort of splotch in the lower right-hand corner of the area without blood spatter?"

Joplin moved closer to the screen. "Yes. What's it supposed to be?"

Instead of answering, Hernandez typed and brought up the painting from the Trenton scene. "Does that look familiar?" he asked, pointing to a similar splotch in the same place on the painting.

"I guess," said Joplin, squinting. "What is it?"

"A signature."

"But you said you couldn't make out the signature."

"I couldn't. It's deliberately illegible, in my opinion. But it's in the exact same place as the one on the painting, and it looks identical."

Joplin shook his head. "I think you're reaching, Jimmy."

"Then prove me wrong, Hollis. I can't go interview the widow and find out the artist's name. But I just can't let it go. It's still your case, though, until Carrie rules on the manner of death."

"I need a drink," Joplin said, standing up. "You want one?"

"Sure. You got any beer?"

"Yuengling okay? We don't sell Dos Equis here."

"That's fine."

Hernandez followed him into the kitchen, which was even messier than the living room. Joplin got him a beer from the refrigerator, then filled his own glass with ice and a generous slug of Jim Beam.

"You want me to help you clean up a little, Hollis?"

Joplin waved a hand in the air. "Naw, it'll just get cluttered up again. I usually wait till I've gone through every glass and dish I own before I start cleaning up."

"What do you do when you run out of food?" Hernandez asked, looking concerned.

"There's always pizza or Chinese food. It's delivered right to my door, and they come in their own containers. No plates needed—and I know how to use chopsticks," he added, hoping that would relieve Hernandez. "On the Chinese food, I mean."

"Of course," Hernandez said, nodding agreement. "I guess you've had a lot of practice at this, huh?"

"You could say that," Joplin said, heading back to the living room.

They sat back down, and Hernandez asked, "So how long do these Blue Funks of yours last?"

Joplin shrugged and took a sip of his drink. "Depends."

"Well, do you think you could look into this new lead? I think it's pretty important, Hollis."

"Depends," said Joplin as he stared into his glass.

———

Joplin opened the door and walked into an artist's studio, with various unfinished canvases stuck onto easels, like heads on pikes. Each one bore the face of a woman, imprisoned in a background of blood-red paint. Some had only eyes and others had only mouths; all of them seemed to be accusing him of something. At the front of the studio, he saw the figure of a man, standing before an empty canvas on yet another easel. The man turned his head and looked at Joplin.

"I was expecting you," he said pleasantly. "You've come to watch me work, haven't you?"

"No, I really don't want to," Joplin told him.

"Why not? It's a fascinating process."

"But people get hurt."

The man shrugged. "There's always a price to pay. With anything, wouldn't you say? Ambition? Denial? Vengeance? Even love." He smiled. "Maybe love, most of all."

"But, what possible good can come from what you do?" Joplin asked.

The man smiled again. "Art doesn't have to explain itself. I express what I feel. But you, of all people, should know that there's something to learn from it. It's what you've studied all your life, isn't it? Why people do such terrible things to each other?"

"Why don't you just tell me why *you* do this?" Joplin said. "Forget everybody else. I'm interested in you."

The smile disappeared from the man's face. "Maybe I don't *want* you to know," he said coldly and turned back to the canvas. "I do this for myself."

Joplin felt himself growing angry and started toward the man. Before he could reach him, however, the man flung a handful of the blood-red paint at him. It hit him in the face, blinding him, and Joplin frantically tried to wipe it off. When he could finally see again, the man and the studio had disappeared, and he was sitting up in bed, his heart racing, gasping for air.

Quincy was staring at him, his back arched and hair standing on end, as if he, too, had just seen a demon.

CHAPTER THIRTY-SEVEN

Joplin woke up that Friday morning feeling as if his brain was like Spaghetti Junction during rush hour and his tongue was coated with a layer of Quincy's fur. He opened one eye and saw the cat curled up in a tight circle at the foot of the bed. Mustering up a little saliva, he managed to swallow, then winced as his head filled with the dull thudding of what he was sure would be a Class I hangover. Not a personal best, of course, but up there.

The dream from last night came back to him and, reluctantly, Joplin tried to piece it together. He couldn't conjure up a detailed image of the man he'd seen, however. Dreams were created by his subconscious, and weren't memories of things he'd actually seen or heard. What he was able to recall appeared to him in fragments, an image here, a sensation of movement there. Just like everybody else's dreams. But he had an impression of a shadowy, hooded figure in front of an enormous blank canvas. It was obviously connected to the crime scene photos and the horrible painting Jimmy had shown him the night before, but he didn't have a clue about what it was trying to tell him.

Maybe that's a good thing, he thought, staring up at the ceiling.

―――――

The parking lot at the ME's office was occupied by only three cars when Joplin pulled into it at seven a.m. He hadn't been able to go back into a deep sleep after the first time he'd awakened, around three in the morning; hadn't really wanted to, truth be told. As with other disturbing dreams, he'd been afraid that he might go back to it, as sometimes happened, and had slept fitfully. So when he woke again at six a.m., he'd dragged himself out of bed and lurched into the bathroom. Quincy, usually pretty vocal in the morning, didn't bother to raise his head.

Showering and shaving had revived him a little, and after dressing, he'd gone to the kitchen in search of caffeine and Tylenol. It was his morning ritual these days, despite all the warnings during the past decade about taking acetaminophen after heavy drinking. Once there, squinting his eyes at the bright sunlight pouring through the small window above the sink, he'd fed Quincy, then consumed two cups of coffee and a piece of cold pizza, before hunting down his wallet and keys and heading outside to his car. Before turning on the engine, Joplin had said a silent prayer that enough time had passed for his blood/alcohol level to go down.

Now he sat in his car in the parking lot, reluctant to go into the building. He was sure Carrie hadn't arrived yet; none of the cars he saw was hers. The Buick Regal belonged to Deke Crawford, and the Chevy to Viv Rodriguez. He assumed the Honda was Sarah Petersen's, because Sam, the tech on duty in the morning, took the bus. With a sigh, Joplin pushed the car door open and heaved himself out, the effort causing more pounding in his heard and not a little nausea.

The door to Sarah Petersen's office was open, and the light was on, confirming his hunch about the Honda. She was on her computer, fingers splayed on the keypad, but looked up, her expression mildly surprised, when she saw him.

"Didn't know you were coming in today," she said, smiling. "How do you feel?"

"I didn't know myself till this morning," Joplin replied, ignoring her question. "I'm just in for a few hours, though. I need to work on some things involving the Woodridge case so we can close it. That okay with you?"

She shrugged. "Fine with me. The schedule's covered, if that's what you mean."

Joplin nodded, debating whether to tell his boss about Jimmy Hernandez's visit to him. He finally decided he'd rather ask forgiveness than permission, if things panned out. "Carrie coming in today?"

Petersen raised her eyebrows at this. "She's here every day, Hollis. And on call every other weekend, as you know. Is that a problem?"

"No," he said quickly. Maybe too quickly. "I may need to go over a few things with her, is all. About the Woodridge case, I mean. She did the autopsy."

Sarah Petersen took her hands off the keyboard and sat back. "Would you like to talk about anything? The Woodridge case? Your health? Your relationship with Dr. Salinger? Maybe the price of tea in China? I've been told I'm a pretty good listener. I'm also pretty discreet."

He smiled at this. "I'm sure you are, Chief, and I appreciate the offer. I just need to…sort out a few things. But I might need to talk to you later today, if that's okay. If a new lead I got turns out to be something," he added.

She stared at him for several seconds, the expression in her eyes seeming to assess the situation. And him. "My door is always open," she said at last. "And so is my mind, Hollis. I'm not MacKenzie."

"Don't I know that," Joplin said. He gave her a small salute, then headed for his cubicle.

———

Deke was heading out to a scene, equipment bag in hand, when Joplin entered the Investigators' room. He did an exaggerated double-take when he saw him, then grinned. "Funk over, Hollis?"

"I'm working on it, Deke. Thought I'd come in for a few hours and tidy up some loose ends. Sorry if I messed up the rotation. Again," he added, feeling guilty.

Deke clapped him on the back. "No problem. Maybe you just came back too soon, buddy. We've got your back."

"Thanks. I appreciate it."

After chatting a few minutes with Viv, who was just as supportive as Deke Crawford, Joplin went to his desk, trying not to feel overcome by the way his colleagues had treated him. Promising himself that he would make it up to them somehow, he Googled Emily Trenton and found her listed in the White Pages at a condominium behind Phipps Plaza. The Park Regency. It was too early in the morning to call her, much less pay her a visit, so he went into the ME's files and pulled up the Trenton case.

Viv had been the investigator who caught the case, but her report had been fairly brief, given that there had been no mystery about the victim's cause or manner of death. She had detailed the appearance, position and place where the body had been found, as well as a description of the wounds, lividity and blood spatter. She'd also noted the liver temp and ambient temp and given a preliminary time of death. The photos she'd taken were of Daniel Trenton and the blood spatter on the sheets and the wall behind him. There were no photos of the painting Hernandez had shown him; those must have been ones he or his team had taken. The autopsy report gave blunt force trauma as the cause of death, with a ruling of homicide.

Joplin looked at his watch. It was only 8:05, still too early to call the widow. Instead, he picked up his phone and called Hernandez.

"Jimmy," he said, without identifying himself. "I'm at the ME's office looking at the Trenton autopsy report, but it doesn't include the shot of the painting in the bedroom that you showed me last night. Can you email it to me?"

There was a long pause, and then he heard Hernandez laugh. "Sure thing, Hollis. You'll get it in a few minutes. And thanks," he said.

Joplin hung up without responding, then sat back in his chair, fingers steepled.

———

"You remember the Trenton case, Viv?" Joplin asked, standing up so he could make eye contact with her. "Daniel Trenton? White male, bludgeoned in 2007 on West Paces Ferry Court? Ring a bell?" When she frowned in concentration, he said, "He was a doctor. Killed during a home robbery while his wife was at a dinner party."

Viv Rodriguez nodded slowly. "Yes, I do. I remember the wife, especially. She was a basket case. Just devastated. Then the teenage sons came home, and she pulled herself together for their sakes. Really sad case." She gazed up at Joplin. "But they caught the perps, didn't they?"

"Yeah. Hernandez found a bloody print on the sheets."

"That's right. I remember now. Why do you ask?"

Joplin picked up his laptop and carried it over to Viv's cubicle. "Do you remember a painting in the victim's bedroom?" he asked, setting the computer down in front of her. "One that looked like it had been painted in blood?"

Viv looked at the photo. "I'm not likely to forget it, Hollis. It was like some kind of nightmare in a frame."

"You happen to remember what the artist's name was?" Joplin pointed to the illegible signature at the bottom right of the painting.

Viv squinted at it, then shook her head. "Fraid not. I really didn't want to look at it that closely. I see enough of the real thing, you know?"

When Joplin nodded in agreement, she said, "Why would anyone want to paint something like that, Hollis?"

"Beats me. Then again, why do people do the things they do to other human beings? Or even themselves?" A fragment of last night's dream flashed before his eyes as he said this.

Viv Rodriguez stood up, paperwork in her hand. "I guess because they can. And a lot of them get away with it."

———

At exactly nine o'clock, Joplin called Emily Trenton. The phone rang five times, then went to voicemail. Deciding that she could be screening her calls, in the shower, or on another line, he closed his laptop, shoved it into its case, and took it with him to Carrie Salinger's office. Her door was closed, but after hesitating a few seconds, he knocked.

After being told to come in, Joplin pushed open the door, feeling his heart begin to pound and his head begin to ache again. She was sitting at her desk, not yet wearing her white lab coat. Her hair was tied back in a sleek pony-tail, and she had on a sleeveless dress—or top, he really couldn't tell—in a sort of bluish-green color. It made her eyes look even darker. And more lovely. She looked tired, though, and he suddenly felt as guilty as he had the night before, when he'd essentially sent her away.

Why was he so stupid? So fucked up? Why couldn't he just thank the gods that someone as wonderful as she was actually cared about him and wanted to be with him?

The look on Carrie's face seemed to ask the same questions, and he cleared his throat and said, "Can I talk to you for a few minutes?"

"Sure."

He practically fell into one of the chairs facing her desk. "I have a new lead on the Woodridge case," he said, not trusting himself to say anything else. He saw a flash of disappointment in her eyes, but forced himself to go on. "I'd like to show you something."

"Okay."

Joplin pulled out his laptop, set it on her desk and turned it around so she could see image of the painting. Her eyes grew wide as she stared at it, and by the time he'd finished telling her where it had been found, and the circumstances, he knew she was in.

"How did you get this?"

"It doesn't really matter," he said, deciding to leave Jimmy Hernandez out of it for the time being. "The point is, I need to follow up on it. I've called the wife—the widow, I mean—but I got voice mail. Will you go with me to see her? She might feel more comfortable talking to me—to us, I mean—if you're there."

Her mouth started to form some words, then she gave up, grabbed her purse from the floor next to her and stood up. "Let's go," she said.

CHAPTER THIRTY-EIGHT

The Park Regency was a contemporary, almost Asian-looking high-rise on Alexander Place. Carrie's parents had several friends who had bought luxury apartments there at top price before the crash of 2008, she informed Joplin as they turned off Phipps Boulevard. Like most of the other condominium owners in Atlanta during the recession, they had been trapped in underwater mortgages that made them difficult to sell or refinance, but at least there had been no by-law against leasing their units, she added. Joplin remembered reading something in the newspaper a few years ago about hundreds of condo owners who were further trapped by that particular by-law. Cash was king in those days, and those who had it were able to scavenge the foreclosures that resulted.

Now, four years later, the economy had gained some ground, and owners were beginning to test the real estate waters and try to recoup at least some of their losses. Daniel Trenton had been murdered in 2007; he wondered if the widow had been one of the losers or winners in the real estate fiasco that followed the year after his death. Maybe she'd been both.

As if reading his thoughts, Carrie said, "I doubt Mrs. Trenton would want to stay in that house very long. After her husband died, I mean."

"Yeah," said Joplin, as they pulled into the visitors' entry of the Park Regency. "Murder has that kind of effect on a house."

———

They were greeted by a dapper, smiling black man somewhere between forty and fifty who'd been alerted by Security that they were with the Milton County ME's office. "I hope nobody in Mrs. Trenton's family has passed," he said, the smile faltering a little. "Nobody else, I mean. She lost her husband a while back, you know."

"We know, and don't worry, nobody else has died…Berlin," Joplin assured him after reading the gold name tag on his jacket.

Berlin smiled again, and Joplin found himself smiling back. Despite his Blue Funk, he found the concierge's beaming face infectious. They waited while he called Mrs. Trenton and received permission to send them up to Unit 1806.

Emily Trenton was a tall, athletic-looking woman with short, curly hair that was mostly gray, despite the fact that she was probably only in her early forties, an age that most women tried to conceal with hair dye. She was wearing a tennis dress and a wary expression, even though the concierge had been careful to tell her that "nobody's passed, Miz Trenton."

They introduced themselves, showing identification, and Emily Trenton ushered them into a living room that looked out onto the Buckhead skyline with all its silvery, glass offices and condominiums. She seated them on a pale gray sofa that faced a baby grand piano and herself in a chair next to them that looked very French to Joplin. Her light-blue eyes, rimmed by a darker shade, bore into them.

"We just need to ask you about a painting that your husband owned," Carrie hastened to say.

The woman's face froze, then she shook her head and said, "I don't have it anymore."

"Maybe you don't know what we're—"

"Sure I do. You're talking about the one that looks like the outline of a woman painted in blood."

"Yes, we are," said Joplin.

"I sold it," she said tersely. "I would have given it away, if I had to. Or burned it if I couldn't do that. I didn't want to keep anything that was in our bedroom the night Daniel was killed. But I especially didn't want that ghastly…thing."

"Do you know who bought it?" Carrie asked.

She shook her head again. "It was with a consignment of furniture and household goods that I put with some professional estate sale people. I had that house on the market as soon as I was up to it. Some good friends helped me get things ready, and they handled all the details. I turned receipts for anything I sold that was part of the estate over to my attorney during probate and threw all that out once the judge signed off on it." She paused and then said, "The estate sale people might still have copies of the receipts, but I doubt it. The company was called Ashby and Manning, LLC."

Joplin wrote the name down, then looked up. "Do you remember the name of the artist?"

She squinted, just like Viv Rodriguez had, and her face looked troubled. "No," she said, "and I don't think I ever did. It was…hard to make out, and I never tried to examine it. And, come to think of it, Jake never mentioned the artist's name either."

"Jake?"

"Jake Pennington." A faint blush appeared on her cheeks, and Joplin wondered if Carrie noticed it, too. "He was a colleague of my husband's. A surgeon at Piedmont. He said he found it at a gallery somewhere in Atlanta and thought Daniel might like it." She grimaced, then said, "Since he was a hematologist, I mean. It was a birthday present," she added, then looked away. "I wouldn't let him hang it anywhere downstairs, and he didn't have a home office, so he hung it in our bedroom. Great place, huh?"

"Well," said Carrie, "it wouldn't be my choice of bedroom décor, but I'm not a hematologist. Did your husband actually like it?"

Emily Trenton gave a short, bitter-sounding laugh. "Oh, yes. He loved it.

Said it was sort of an 'inside joke.' Something only a surgeon or a hematologist would get."

"Do you know what he meant by that, Mrs. Trenton?"

She wrapped her arms around herself, as if she were cold. "No, and I didn't ask. I guess I didn't want to know." She stood up suddenly and said, "I have a tennis game at ten, and I think I've told you everything I know about the painting, so..."

Joplin and Carrie stood, too. "You've been very helpful, Mrs. Trenton," Carrie said, holding out her hand. "I'm sure this hasn't been easy for you."

"Is Dr. Pennington still at Piedmont?" Joplin asked.

"No," she said, and her eyes slid away again. "He moved back to Baltimore, his hometown, not long after Daniel died. I haven't been in touch with him," she added, her chin lifting, as if prepared to be contradicted.

"Thank you for talking to us," Joplin said.

She bowed her head, then ushered them to the door. It closed softly after they left.

Neither of them said anything until they reached the elevators.

"She never asked us why we wanted to know about the painting," said Carrie after pushing the down button.

"I guess she didn't want to know that either," he answered.

———

Halloran had just gotten off his cell phone with Julie, arranging to meet her to make plans for Libba Woodridge's funeral, when it rang again. "Tom Halloran," he said.

"It's your old buddy, Hollis Joplin, Tom."

"Well, well, well," he said, smiling to himself and sitting back in his chair. "This *is* a surprise. I heard you were laid low with some kind of blue flu."

He heard Joplin sigh. "Why do I get the feeling Carrie's been talking to Maggie?"

"Actually, your boss told me," Halloran said quickly, wishing he hadn't brought it up. "When I hadn't heard back from you about Connie Sue's autopsy report and couldn't get hold of you, I called Chief Petersen. She really cares about you, Hollis. So do Maggie and I. And Carrie. How are you doing, anyway?" he asked, hoping to switch the subject.

There was a long pause, then Joplin said, "I'm okay. Trying to dig myself out. Did Sarah give you the results?"

"She did," Halloran said, mentally shifting gears, after realizing Joplin had gone back to the autopsy report. "It was very disturbing to hear about the way Connie Sue died, but I'm glad it wasn't mistaken for suicide. Thanks for getting that report, Hollis."

"Sure thing. Did you talk to Carrie, too? About the report, I mean?"

"I did. She told me about her discovery that Connie Sue wasn't Libba's biological mother. I think that was a bigger shock than finding out how she died."

"Well, I may have a few more shocks for you, Tom."

"What do you mean?"

"How would you and Maggie like to go to an art gallery tomorrow afternoon?"

———

Halloran opened the bottle of Glenlivet sitting on the Beaux Arts sideboard, and poured himsel a very generous slug. It was, after all, Friday night, and he wasn't going back to the office until Sunday afternoon. Maggie was chopping something on the granite island, and a heavenly aroma of marinara sauce smothered in mozzarella and Parmesan came from the oven. He hoped it was lasagna, but would settle for anything else in her repertoire. Over the years, he had assured her that she didn't have to fix dinner every night, given her booming photography business and all the chauffeuring she did with the children's activities, but she'd always told him that cooking relaxed her. When she found herself too busy with work, she called a nearby college student who often babysat for them to pick up the kids from Christ the King Elementary School and/or go to Fresh Market or Trader Joe's for her. The cooking was never delegated.

"Have you and Julie worked out the funeral arrangements?" she asked as he brought his drink over to the island and sat in one of the bar stools. A glass of white wine, half-finished, sat on the island. She was chopping—no, "chiffonading," as she'd told him many times—a generous bunch of basil.

"Yes," he said. "Libba didn't leave any instructions, so Julie decided to hold a small memorial service and reception at the Botanical Gardens, followed by interment at Arlington for the few of us who cared about her."

"I think that sounds lovely," said Maggie, folding the basil up in a paper towel. "And Connie Sue?"

"I haven't been able to locate any other family members so far, and she wasn't close to any of her neighbors, it seemed, so we opted for a small ceremony at a local funeral parlor in Brunswick. She didn't belong to a church. It'll be next Saturday. You don't have to go, Maggie, but I feel like I should. For Libba's sake."

"So do I," said Maggie firmly. She turned and began to pull plates out of cabinets and then piled silverware on top of them. "Libba was my friend, too."

Halloran took a long sip of his drink, then set it down. "Would you feel differently if I told you that Connie Sue wasn't Libba's real mother?"

She stared at him, then reached for her wine glass. "What does that mean?"

He told her everything Hollis Joplin had told him about Carrie's discovery when she read the autopsy report. When they'd finished speculating about whether or not Libba knew or how Connie Sue had come to adopt her—if she actually had—Maggie asked him if that could have an effect on Libba's will. Or Connie Sue's, if she'd made one.

"Good question. It could definitely affect Libba's will, if anyone turns up claiming to be related to her. I've already called Ed Jenkins and asked him to do an internet search, then head back to Brunswick and check out the court records for any adoption proceedings. In the meantime, we've got another little investigation that Hollis has asked us to help him with."

Maggie set her glass of wine down and stared at him. "Now that sounds like fun. What does it involve? Do I get to wear a disguise and pretend to be someone else?"

"Yes, and yes. In a way. Have you ever heard of an artist named Jonathan Demarest?"

CHAPTER THIRTY-NINE

"Jonathan Demarest?" Maggie said, a guarded expression on her face. "How do you know about him?"

"I don't," Halloran responded. "Joplin sent me an image of one of his paintings. He said his latest work is in a gallery on Bennett Street, and he'd like us to go there tomorrow afternoon. It's the Artists' Loft. Is that where we saw the huge videos of the two chefs with the butter noses and the man dancing with three legs?"

Maggie waved a dismissive hand. "No, that was the Contemporary Museum of Art. I should never have taken you there. I realize that now. It's beyond your level of sophistication."

"I've been hurt before, Maggie, but never like this," said Halloran dryly.

"I think you'll get over it." She picked up the stack of plates and silverware and carried them over to the table. "The Artists' Loft is across from the Contemporary Museum," she said as she set the table. "It's innovative like the museum, but a little edgier."

"What could be edgier than a man clomping around with a prosthetic leg in between his real legs? And don't tell me you didn't realize what that meant."

"That's *one* meaning that the artist might have intended, but there are others."

"Like what?"

"Well, like the idea that a disability—or 'challenge' as some people say—could mean that some people have *more* of something, rather than less." she added. "And that can be just as challenging, in a way."

"You mean like…twelve fingers or a vestigial tail?"

Maggie nodded slowly. "Yes, but I was thinking more in terms of qualities or genetic predispositions, rather than parts of the body. I think the third leg was a metaphor."

"I get it," Halloran said, going back to the sideboard to pour himself another drink. "So you're saying that the artist believes that a man with three legs has to work harder to become a good dancer than the man with two legs. Or," he added, holding the Glenlivet aloft, "a person who has a genetic predisposition to, say, alcoholism or drug addiction, has to work harder not to become addicted."

"Yes, I suppose so. But that's an oversimplification. I think it has more to do with the human condition, which is universal. I mean, we're all flawed in some way—some people more than others. And I believe artists are more sensitive to that. To the things most people don't want to admit or to examine in themselves."

"Wow," said Halloran. "Maybe I need to give the Museum of Contemporary Art another chance."

Maggie laughed as she opened the refrigerator and began taking out things to make a salad. "Let's see how you do after we've gone to the Artists' Loft."

"You seem to know something about this artist, Jonathan Demarest. Tell me about him."

"Well," she said, frowning, "I guess what he's all about is shocking people. He'd probably say his intention is to make people more aware about certain issues, but…I don't know, I think he just likes the effect he has on the viewer."

"Can you give me an example?"

"I've only seen his work one time, so I shouldn't really be judging him."

"I trust your judgement. Tell me about it."

She didn't answer right away and began to chop vegetables for the salad. Then she said, "It was two years ago. You were in the middle of a trial, and Miranda Simms asked me if I wanted to go with her to the Artists' Loft for a new exhibition."

"Ted Simms' ex-wife?" Halloran said, his voice rising a little more than he intended. Simms was one of the newest partners at Healey and Caldwell. "The one who left him for another woman?"

Maggie laughed and shook her head as she dumped the vegetables into the salad bowl. "Your hang-ups are showing, Tom. Miranda is a very interesting, charming young woman who realizes she made a big mistake when she married Ted."

"You mean because he's a man or because he's an insufferable bore?" he asked, hoping to regain a little of his view of himself as an open, tolerant individual. And Maggie's, too.

"A little of both. Anyway, we went to see Jonathan Demarest, and I ran smack into some of my own hang-ups when I saw his work. He doesn't just paint; he's also a photographer and a sculptor."

"I take it he had a real effect on *you*."

She took a long sip of her wine and nodded. "The subject or theme of that particular exhibit was the concept of motherhood. Or mothering. Whatever it is that connotes the idea of giving birth to something and nurturing it. Only his...rendering, I guess you'd say, of this concept ran the gamut of natural and heartwarming to the unimaginable. Madness, even."

"How so?" Halloran was intrigued. Maggie wasn't easily shocked, but her eyes held some kind of remembered revulsion that surprised him.

She didn't answer as she took the salad bowl over to the table and set it down. "He had some really beautiful photographs of mothers and children that showed what anyone would see as the positive, transcendent bond between mother and child. It reminded me of my own work, and I thought about going up to him after I'd seen everything and asking him about that. If he'd ever seen any of my photographs, I mean." She turned back to him and shook her head. "But then he had a series of sculptures that became increasingly grotesque."

"Grotesque? I wouldn't have thought that belonged in an exhibit like that."

"Well, that's what I meant when I said he likes to shock people." She opened the refrigerator door and poured herself more wine. "The first few sculptures weren't too bad. Some torsos of women in various stages of pregnancy. Then he added arms and legs and…faces. Not heads, just faces. And they had horrific expressions, varying from anger and pain to—I don't know—malevolence. Or just hatred for the children they were carrying. And the limbs of the women were bent and distorted, as if they were in terrible pain." Maggie took a big gulp of her wine. "But it was the paintings that were the worst. He had depicted Medea slaying her children, then serving them to Jason; a truly ghastly-looking she-wolf suckling Romulus and Remus; Grendel's mother, giving birth to him, along with dozens of hideous snakes."

"God, Maggie, why didn't you just walk out?"

"I wanted to. Miranda told me later that she did, too. But it was like watching the proverbial train wreck: you just couldn't look away. And then we got to the more…modern…depictions of motherhood, like Andrea Martin drowning her kids in a bathtub and Susan Smith driving her car with her two young sons into the lake to kill them."

Halloran held up both hands. "I don't think I want to hear any more, Maggie. I get the picture."

"You don't, actually. Because the really repulsive thing about the paintings was that Demarest portrayed the children themselves as demonic. As if they had *caused* the madness that the mothers possessed, and deserved to be killed."

Halloran stared at her, trying to take in what she had said. "I think I should call Hollis and tell him we can't go to that gallery tomorrow," he said finally.

Maggie looked up at him. "You never told me why he wants us to go there in the first place, Tom What's this all about?"

"I'll show you." Halloran went over to the briefcase he'd stashed next to the bar and pulled out his laptop. After booting it up, he opened the email containing the painting that Joplin had sent him and turned it so Maggie could see it.

She put a hand up to her mouth and stared at it, then said, "Obviously, it's the outline of a woman, painted in what looks like blood. Is it?"

"Hollis doesn't know. It was in the bedroom of a doctor—a hematologist—who was murdered, then it was sold at an estate sale after his death. Hollis was able to contact the man who originally gave it to the victim—another doctor—who identified Jonathan Demarest as the painter. He said he bought it at a gallery in Atlanta about six years ago."

"Where is it now?"

"Nobody knows. The company that held the estate sale is no longer in business, and according to Hollis, the widow disposed of any paperwork once the will was probated. So Hollis googled Demarest and found out some of his work is currently at the Artists' Loft. He doesn't want to go there himself because he thinks either Demarest or the staff there might peg him as law enforcement, and according to the his website, Demarest is usually there on Saturday afternoons when he's in town. If this guy is involved in any way in the attack on Libba or the murder of Maria Sanchez, and thinks Hollis is law enforcement, he'll assume he's under investigation."

"But anyone who watches the news or reads the *AJC* knows you were Libba's lawyer, Tom. How are you any less visible?"

"I guess because we're known as 'patrons of the art world,' in Atlanta, as Hollis put it. He thinks that gives us some cover."

Maggie rubbed the upper part of her arms, as if she were cold and nodded.

"I can see how Hollis thought of Libba when he saw this painting, but does he have anything else to connect it to her attack, or to Maria Sanchez?"

Without answering, Halloran pulled up the images left on Libba Woodridge's headboard and bedroom wall and the wall behind the gas station after Sanchez's body had been removed, as well as Demarest's painting, and positioned them so that they were a vertical row. This time, Maggie made an audible gasp as she looked at them. And when he pointed out what Hollis had told him appeared to be the same "signature" on the image that had been behind Maria Sanchez and on the painting, she grabbed his arm and looked directly into his eyes.

"Tom, you have to turn that video over to Hollis now. This has got to prove to you that Jorge had nothing to do with his wife's murder or the attack on Libba. We can't just let him rot in jail."

Before Halloran could answer, Tommy and Megan burst into the kitchen from the TV room, putting an end—thankfully, in his mind—to any further discussion of blood paintings, a possibly innocent man, and his duty to honor attorney/client privilege.

———

Joplin savored his second—and last, if he could stick to his own self-imposed limit—glass of Jim Beam. It had been a long day, after a fitful night's sleep, and he was both mentally and physically exhausted. But it had also been a good start to what he hoped was the beginning of the end of his most recent Blue Funk. It seemed like this time, unlike others, he'd been able to catch himself before he spiraled down any further. A more objective observer might say that it had been Carrie's or Jimmy Hernandez's visit to him that had provided a toe-hold in the steep cliff he'd been about to topple over, but Joplin preferred to cling to the belief that rescue attempts in the past had never made a dent in his self-pity. Or his resolve to drink himself into recovery during the self-medication phase.

He'd even made an attempt to find his way back to Carrie. At least, he thought he had, telling her that he'd really appreciated her going with him to see Emily Trenton. And then, after he'd spent the next several hours tracking down Dr. Pennington and googling Jonathan Demarest, then writing up his notes and contacting Hernandez and Tom Halloran, he'd stopped by her office and given her an update. He'd also asked if she wanted to go with him the next afternoon to meet with Maggie and Tom after they'd gone to the Artist's Loft.

Carrie's response hadn't been quite what he'd hoped. Or maybe feared, because he still believed he wasn't the person she really deserved, and didn't know if he could ever be that person. But still, he had hoped for a little more enthusiasm on her part. Or at least some pretended enthusiasm. But at least she'd said yes. Finally.

"Okay, then," he'd said, bobbing his head up and down like some kind of bird he'd once seen on *National Geographic*. "We're going to meet up at the Houston's on Peachtree afterwards. I'll pick you up as soon as I hear from Tom, okay?"

"I can just meet the three of you there, Hollis."

"Sure, sure," he'd answered, doing the bobbing thing again. "I'll call you when I hear from him."

He'd trudged back to his cubicle, knowing that Carrie had wanted him to open up, tell her why he'd cut himself off from her and what he was feeling, and knowing that he just couldn't do it.

Joplin's heart had stopped for several minutes after he'd been shot back in the spring. Days later, a young doctor at Grady had asked him if he'd had a "life after death" experience, and Joplin told him he hadn't, but that wasn't really true. He remembered moving down the tunnel that other near-death survivors had written about, and he'd seen an impossibly bright light at the end of that tunnel. He'd also had a glimpse of something he wasn't able to describe, even to himself. Something incredibly beautiful, although the word "beautiful" didn't begin to articulate what he'd seen. But he'd never experienced the loving presence so often mentioned by others, and no one had told him he had unfinished work to do and needed to go back. Instead, he'd simply felt himself go back into the body that lay on the operating table, experiencing an intense regret that he couldn't remain wherever he'd been.

During the ten days he'd been in a coma, he had fought regaining consciousness, as if that would be a ticket back to what he'd seen. But it hadn't, and Joplin had returned to his own world, a world filled with pain and suffering and the torments that human beings inflicted on each other. He hadn't brought with him any new understanding of life or his purpose in it; he knew he would simply do what he had always done, which was to engage in battle with whatever it was that made this world so…misshapen. It was the only word he could think of to describe its comparison to the world he'd glimpsed while he was dead.

Joplin suddenly realized that his Blue Funks—the "weltschmertz" that Dr. O'Brien had told him about—were a sort of moratorium for him, a virtual waiting place that buffered him from that misshapen world for a time, even though he suffered while he was there. Maybe they did some good, in the scheme of things. But did that give him the right to bring someone like Carrie into his own little psychodrama? Inflict his suffering on her by sharing with her what he was going through, even if she asked him to? A few days ago, he had been convinced that the best thing to do would be to get out of her life, and nothing had changed.

Not really, he said to a voice that seemed to contradict him.

Yes, it has, the voice insisted.

Too tired to continue the argument, Joplin struggled up from the couch, startling Quincy, who'd been curled up beside him. "Let's go to bed, Quince," he said. The cat mewed his agreement.

Fifteen minutes later, he fell into a deep and, apparently, dreamless sleep.

CHAPTER FORTY

Jonathan Demarest was a tall, gangly man with a brooding manner and a fringe of brown hair that made him look like a very unhappy monk. He was dressed all in black, which added to the resemblance, and stood near the entrance of the gallery, arms folded, as he nodded absently to a few of the people who waved or smiled at him as they straggled in.

Halloran and Maggie had dressed carefully for their walk-on roles as patrons of the arts on a Saturday afternoon, he in jeans and a black tee shirt under a black blazer and Maggie in some kind of tunic thing over leggings, a scarf encircling her neck. Maggie managed to produce a smile and nod in the artist's direction, but Halloran, who was not supposed to know who the man was, despite a careful examination of Demarest's website and photo, merely glanced at him.

The Artists' Loft was a converted warehouse that tried hard to look like something that might be found in SoHo, but was only mildly successful, despite the high, industrial ceiling and the enormous iron supports that had been used to delineate the various artists' spaces. They made their way around the gallery, stopping to admire some blank canvases with only a series of dots in their centers that had been created—if that could be said—by someone named Jed Thompson, followed by a quick perusal of a small mountain of garbage bags that smelled as if they were filled with actual garbage. This opus magnus was titled "Can You Believe This Crap?"

Halloran thought this was pure genius on the artist's part. It also summed up his feelings thus far about the gallery. He revised them, slightly, after viewing the next exhibit, a video of a tired-looking woman dressed in a business suit and carrying a bulging briefcase as she trudged up a flight of stairs that collapsed once she reached the top and sent her sliding back down to the floor. The sequence then began again. It was titled "Sisyphus Was No Myth," which Halloran thought needed a little work, but he liked the concept.

"Not bad," he said, nudging Maggie. "Would you like me to buy it for you? We could put it in the entry hall to weed out any chauvinists who might drop by."

"That would be most of the senior partners at Healey and Caldwell, darling," she responded, smiling brightly and moving past him.

By the time they reached Jonathan Demarest's space, they had been treated to a grouping of anatomically-correct papier Mache figures involved in what could only be called an orgy, as well as a series of water-colors whose delicate pastels and whimsical style clashed with the objects depicted in each: a road-kill cat, a particularly obscene-looking dildo, dog poop on a sidewalk, and what seemed to be some kind of afterbirth, umbilicus and all.

"I need a drink," he hissed into Maggie's ear.

"So do I!" Maggie chirped, as if she'd just agreed that she, too, loved the water colors. The artist, a young woman with blue eyes and blond dread-locks, smiled and handed her a brochure.

"Let's get this over with," Halloran whispered, leading her over to the back left corner of the gallery, where Demarest's paintings hung. A few others rested on elaborate easels in a circle around his space. Halloran couldn't shake the impression they gave of a spider's web, drawing them in.

"Tom, look," Maggie said quietly, drawing his attention to three paintings that hung on the right-hand wall. They were very similar to the painting that had been hanging in Daniel Trenton's bedroom, but these showed outlines of bodies that were lying down, their limbs in awkward positions. All were female, with shapely contours and long hair.

"The medium couldn't possibly be real blood, couldn't it?" Maggie said.

"Thank you for the compliment," said a deep, contralto voice behind them.

They both whirled around at the same time. Jonathan Demarest had managed to get within two feet of them without their hearing a thing.

"I'm sorry I startled you," he said, smiling. "But I couldn't help overhearing, and I wanted to reassure you that I'm not some kind of…ghoul."

"Not at all," said Maggie, recovering her composure before Halloran did. "I hope I didn't offend you. It's just that it looks so real."

Demarest inclined his head in a small bow. "As I said, it was a compliment that you thought I had used real blood. That was the whole idea, you know. Or at least one of them. But I can assure you that I achieved it by mixing several different pigments. A blend of my own, so to speak, that took quite a while to perfect. Real blood, you know, will turn brown after about three days."

"I didn't know that," Maggie said, eyes wide.

"I'm impressed, too," said Halloran, trying to make sure he looked the part. When Demarest inclined his head again, Halloran said, "You mentioned that was *one* of your intentions—to make the viewer think it was real blood. May I ask what the others were?"

Demarest smiled again. "I think the paintings should speak for themselves. What do *you* see, Mr.….?"

"Halloran," he replied, holding out his hand. "Tom Halloran. And this is my wife, Maggie."

After firmly shaking Halloran's hand, he reached for Maggie's and brought it to his lips. "I've never had the pleasure of actually *meeting* you, but I know I've seen you before. I wonder where."

Maggie stared back at him, and Halloran could sense her unease. "Well," she said, finally, casually disengaging her hand, "I was here two years ago, to see your work involving…mothering, I guess the brochure called it—but, you're right, we didn't meet."

Demarest's eyes suddenly came alive, and he said, "No, but now I realize who you are! The photographer, right?" He clasped her hand again and beamed at her. "I've admired your work for a very long time."

"Thank you," she said, seeming to relax a little, despite her captive hand. "I saw some of the same things that I try to do in the first part of the show."

Demarest let go of her hand and folded his arms, but he was still smiling. "But not, I take it, in the rest of the show."

Maggie smiled, too, and dipped her head to the side. "The rest of the show was very powerful, I must say."

"In what way?"

Demarest was not going to let her off the hook, and Halloran thought about intervening, but he knew his wife could hold her own.

"I think you were trying to show that mothering, or the concept of motherhood, is part of a continuum, like so many things. That it's all a matter of degree, not black and white. A so-called 'good mother' can take that concept to its destructive side, hovering too much, doing too much—keeping a child tied to her instead of learning from his own mistakes." She paused, then added, "And the women we think of as 'bad mothers' can turn out extraordinary human beings or…monsters."

The artist made another small bow and said, "I couldn't have said it better. Thank you for seeing what I hoped the viewer would see."

"There was one disturbing aspect of the work, however," Maggie said. "To me, anyway."

"Tell me."

"Well, in some of the sculptures where birth was depicted, you made the faces of the children demonic, but their mothers just…ordinary-looking, or even loving. And then the next sculpture would show that same mother doing something terrible to the child. Almost as if—"

"As if the child itself were the cause of the mother's cruelty?" Demarest asked.

Maggie nodded. "Yes. As if the child had been born evil. Did you mean to convey that idea? That human beings can be intrinsically evil?"

Demarest gave a small shrug. "If that's what you saw, then I must have intended it. At some level."

Maggie started to say something, but Demarest turned to look at him instead. "Mr. Halloran, are you as perceptive as your wife? You haven't told me what you see in my blood paintings," he added, sweeping a hand toward the paintings on the wall.

Halloran had had some time to consider what he would say to Jonathan Demarest. Not what he wanted to say, but what he *should* say, if, as Joplin thought, the man might be involved in the attack on Libba and Maria Sanchez' murder. He had been studying Demarest—his height and build and the way he carried himself, as well as the motions he made with his arms. There was nothing there to rule out that he could have been the figure in the video sent to Libba. And everything about him seemed to show that he was capable not only of envisioning violence against women, but of actually committing it.

"Some people might be shocked by what they see in these paintings," he said, nodding toward them. "But I think that's integral to them. You want them to be shocked by the fact that women are so often the victims of violence, especially murder. That they've become nothing but outlines at a crime scene. But instead of outlining them in chalk, you've outlined them in blood. It's pure genius," he added solemnly. "Pure genius. And I want to buy one of them."

———

"What the hell were you thinking, Tom?" Maggie asked him once they were headed for their car, painting in hand. "I don't want that painting, for God's sake! And I certainly don't want it in my house."

"Neither do I," he replied calmly. "Especially not at that price," he added, referring to the $3,000 he'd just charged to his American Express card.

"Then *why*? I don't think Hollis intended for you to go *that* far when he asked us to come here this afternoon."

"Because I think—contrary to what Jonathan Demarest says—that he *does* use real blood in these paintings. And I want Hollis to have the so-called 'blend of several different pigments' analyzed. It was the only way I could think of to get a sample of it."

CHAPTER FORTY-ONE

Maggie and Halloran were already seated in a booth in the bar at Houston's, drinks in hand, by the time Hollis Joplin walked in a little after four. Maggie had called him as they were pulling out of the gallery's parking lot.

"I'm glad you didn't wait for me," he said, grinning as he slid into the booth.

Halloran raised his Scotch and water and said, "Thank God for alcohol. You wouldn't have wanted us to wait if you knew what that exhibition was like."

"I had a pretty good idea after I looked at the website," Joplin said. "In fact, the drinks are on me."

"I won't turn you down," said Halloran. "Is Carrie coming? You mentioned you might see if she wanted to."

"Yeah, she should be here soon." Joplin turned and motioned for the server, hoping the distraction would keep the Hallorans from asking about the current state of his and Carrie's relationship. "I'll have a Stella on draft," he said when the server, a pretty woman in her late twenties came up to them. He knew from past experience that they only had bottled Yuengling.

"How *is* Carrie?" Maggie asked, her voice a little too casual.

"Fine!" Joplin said, eyes wide open in what he hoped was his best sincere expression.

"Gooood," Maggie responded, dragging the word out and obviously not believing him. He would never understand why women needed to talk to each other about their relationships, but it was clear that Maggie and Carrie had discussed him. And his current Blue Funk. His beer arrived, but before he could take a sip, so did Carrie. She looked gorgeous in a pair of white jeans with some kind of filmy blue poncho—that's what he'd been told those things were—over them, and his heart lurched at the sight of her. He stood up abruptly, almost knocking his chair over, and Halloran did the same, but more smoothly, of course. He frequently envied the attorney his poise, even when he came off as arrogant, although Halloran was presently showing his warm and personable side.

God damn him! Joplin thought, but he smiled at Carrie and pulled out her chair as she sat down. "Would you like something to drink?"

"Yes," she said. "A glass of Kendall Jackson chardonnay."

He turned to motion for the server again, but she was already there, and after nodding to show that she knew Carrie's order, moved swiftly away, a small, mocking smile on her lips. Or so Joplin thought.

"I'm really anxious to hear what you found out—if anything, I mean—at the art gallery," Carrie said, looking directly at the Hallorans. "Hollis showed me the painting from the Trenton scene, and I was blown away by the similarities to the attack on Libba and Maria Sanchez's murder."

They both listened intently as Maggie and Halloran described what they'd observed at the Artists' Loft, laughing at their descriptions of the other artists' showings, their expressions turning serious as the talk turned to Jonathan Demarest's current exhibit.

"This guy sounds like he's really got a screw loose," Joplin said, shaking his head.

"Maybe several," said Maggie. "The thing that really disturbs me about him is that he seems to have an obsession with women—in a negative, violent way." She went on to describe the showing of his paintings she'd seen two years before.

Carrie seemed riveted, and when Maggie had finished, said, "I can't help but think of Connie Sue Cates and the way she was murdered—her womb was essentially 'skewered' by something long and thin, and she bled out."

"I'd say that's pretty anti-mother, wouldn't you?" said Joplin.

"I certainly would," Halloran said, and Maggie nodded in agreement.

"Given the fact that Connie Sue couldn't be Libba's biological mother based on their blood types, are you suggesting that she might have been the mother of the person who killed her?" Joplin asked.

"And that that person might be Jonathan Demarest?" Maggie added.

Carrie held up one hand and said, "Whoa, people! I'm not saying that at all, because the autopsy report also showed that Connie Sue Cates had never given birth. Not to Libba, not to anybody."

"How could the pathologist know that?" asked Halloran.

"Because of the absence of certain 'notches' found on the pelvic bones made as a baby's head passes through the birth canal. A pathologist usually can't tell how many children a woman has had, but it will be obvious is she's had at least one."

"Well, I guess we can scratch the mother theory," Joplin said.

"Not necessarily," Carrie responded.

Whatever she was about to say had to wait, as their attention was drawn to a man's voice calling out Halloran's name.

———

Halloran turned and saw Carson Landers standing a few feet behind him, a teenage boy next to him. The attorney, dressed in khaki shorts and a polo shirt that did nothing to hide his expanding waistline, held out his hand and smiled.

"Carson," Halloran said, standing up. He quickly introduced the attorney to Hollis and Carrie. "And Maggie you already know, of course."

"Nice to see you, Carson," she said. "Is this your son?"

"Yes, this is Matthew, my oldest. He started at UGA a few weeks ago, and he's back in town to pick up some things. He's been missing Houston's hamburgers, though, so I brought him here before he went back to Athens."

Matthew, a taller, thinner version of his father, dutifully shook hands with Halloran and awkwardly nodded at the others.

"So you decided against going to Emory, like your dad?" Halloran asked, then immediately regretted it. The boy might not have been able to get in.

"His grades were so good, he was able to get into UGA on the Hope scholarship," Landers said proudly. We couldn't pass that up, and he can always go to Emory for law school. If he *wants* to go to law school, I mean," he added quickly.

"How do you like UGA so far?" Maggie asked, relieving the somewhat awkward atmosphere.

"It's pretty big and all, but I'm starting rush next week, so I'll get to know some more people, I guess. Besides my high school friends," he added, shrugging.

"Listen, Tom, I was sure sorry to hear about Libba Ann Woodridge," Carson Landers said, his expression turning serious. "I meant to call, but…"

"No worries. You called a few weeks ago, and I appreciated it."

"Yeah, well, I still feel bad. Please let me know the funeral details, okay? Jenna and I would like to be there. Out of respect for Arliss, if nothing else, but Libba was always very gracious to me."

"It's going to be next week, Carson. I'll email you the details."

"Thanks." Landers nodded to Hollis and Carrie and said, "Nice to meet you folks. Good to see you, Maggie."

"Tell Jenna hello for me."

"Will do."

———

When Landers and his son had walked away, Joplin said, "He seems like a nice guy. Is he a part of the lawsuit?"

"No," said Halloran. "He was certainly disappointed that Libba replaced him as trustee; he really didn't believe she had the experience to handle it, but he was graceful about having to bow out. And the bottom line for him is that Emory still gets the money Arliss placed in the trust. Carson got his law degree there and has been involved with fundraising for the university and the hospital and law school for over twenty years. But, Carrie, before Carson came over to the table, you were about to say why we shouldn't necessarily discard the 'mother theory' with regard to Connie Sue's murder."

Carrie nodded slowly. "I was, but I don't want you to put too much stock in what I'm about to say. I've only been with the ME's Office a few months, and I'm certainly not any kind of profiler, but the…savagery that was inflicted on Maria Sanchez and the specific way in which Connie Sue was killed seem to show such anger and hatred toward women. He might not have known that Maria was a mother, but what he did to Connie Sue seems…personal somehow. I don't know if that makes sense, though."

"You mean that he might have known her?" Joplin asked. "It's obvious that Libba's and Connie Sue's deaths are connected somehow, even if Libba *did* commit suicide, but it could have been just *because* she was Libba's adoptive mother that she had to be killed. Because she knew something that he wanted to keep secret. Or because she might have contested Libba's new will."

"Yes, but why kill her so brutally, if she were just some obstacle in his path?" Carrie insisted. "No, this was very personal for the killer."

"What if she represented, or *reminded* the killer of his own mother in some way?" Halloran suggested.

"That's certainly a possibility," Carrie responded.

"But you don't buy it," said Maggie.

"It's just that we're…missing something. Something crucial. But I don't know what it is."

Joplin saw Maggie's eyes slide over to her husband's, and a questioning look flashed on her face for just a second. But it was long enough for him to be certain that his suspicions about Halloran's hiding something from him were on the money.

Halloran's own face was impassive. "Well, why don't we order another drink, and then I'll tell you what I have in my car that might shed a little more light on Jonathan Demarest, even if it doesn't give us a clue about the killer's reasons for murdering Connie Sue Cates the way he did."

CHAPTER FORTY-TWO

"If the forensics unit determines that Demarest used real blood as paint, are you going to turn over the video to Hollis?" Maggie demanded as they headed south on Peachtree.

"Not necessarily," Halloran said. "But it will make me *consider* it."

"Do you really think Libba would want you to go to these lengths, if an innocent man is in jail?"

"Libba herself was concerned that Jorge could still have been involved in some way in what happened to her. Remember, her Miss Georgia sash was found in his apartment. And she specifically mentioned the confidentiality clause in the letter she left for me, refusing permission for me to show it to law enforcement."

"Unless it could be determined that someone other than Jorge was involved in the attack on her and killed his wife," Maggie said.

"That wasn't all. She also said that if the ME's Office ruled her death a homicide, I could turn over the letter and the video. And it's pretty obvious that both Carrie and Hollis believe that since Connie Sue was murdered, Libba might have been as well."

"But you don't believe that, do you?"

He gripped the steering wheel a little more tightly as he said, "No, I don't. But I do believe that someone *drove* her to her death, and I intend to find out why."

Yet even as he said this, Halloran's mind went over other parts of Libba's letter and made him uneasy. He felt sure she had said he could be released from the attorney/client privilege if her death were ruled a homicide because she had, in fact, committed suicide and didn't want anyone falsely accused of murder. Hence, the fear that someone would "...suffer from anything that I have done..." But the rest of that sentence read "...or simply because of who I am." What could that possibly mean? She had also assured him that Arliss would *want* her to change the will and trust he'd made after they'd been married, "...for the sake of the family." Did that simply mean that she felt the lawsuit was tearing the family apart or was there something in Libba's background—or even her very identity—that would hurt the Woodridge family? And Julie, especially? He decided to call Ed Jenkins as soon as they got home.

"Tom, you're a million miles away," he heard Maggie say.

"I'm sorry, sweetie. Did you say something?"

"I asked you how you thought Hollis and Carrie seemed. She's been very upset over the way he's handling this whole surgery thing. It's sent him into some kind of tailspin."

"Well, he *has* been through a lot in the past three months. I don't blame him for not wanting to spend more time in a hospital."

"I think it's a little more than that. So does Carrie."

Halloran shook his head and smiled. "Have you been meddling, Maggie?"

"Absolutely not," she answered solemnly. "I just listen when people tell me things."

"Well, then, listen to this," he said, just as solemnly. "Hollis and Carrie need to figure this out for themselves. I know you've been like a sister to Hollis all summer, but he's a big boy. And she's a very intelligent, independent woman who can take care of herself."

When she didn't answer, he stole a sideways glance and knew from her stern profile that he'd said the wrong thing. "What?" he asked cautiously. "You don't agree with that?"

She turned to face him, eyes blazing. "Not only do I not agree with it, you wouldn't either, if you remembered everything *we* went through before you finally proposed to me. And how your best friend had to slap some sense into you when you decided you couldn't inflict your 'family situation' on me. Does that ring a bell, Tom? "

Pulling his eyes back onto the road, he acknowledged to himself that it did, indeed, ring a bell. The summer before Halloran's third year of law school at Notre Dame, his father had been convicted of embezzlement and begun serving a five-year sentence at the federal penitentiary in Marion, Illinois. His family had known nothing about the predicament Richard Halloran was in until the day he'd been arrested at his office, and very little even after the arrest. He'd pled guilty almost immediately, against the advice of the attorney his wife had hired, and had steadfastly refused to discuss what had happened, not to any of them, saying only that he'd "made mistakes."

Tom had been dating Maggie, who was in her junior year at St. Mary's, the Catholic girls' college nearby, for almost a year by that summer. They'd talked about getting married when he graduated, but the subsequent scandal had brought things to a screeching halt. At least on Halloran's part. Although his mother had insisted that he return to Notre Dame and finish law school, he had broken up with Maggie by the time they'd both gotten back to South Bend.

His resolve had begun to weaken after numerous phone calls from her and a few impromptu visits to the studio apartment he was renting in nearby Mishawaka, but his father's suicide, in late September, had sounded the death knell to any chance that they might get back together. It was only when Dan Kirkpatrick, his life-long friend, who was also a third-year law student at Notre Dame, had intervened that Halloran had finally seen the light at the proverbial end of the tunnel.

"The girl is crazy about you, Thomas," Dan had said, pouring him another glass of Scotch after he'd gotten Halloran to talk about the situation. "I have no idea why a beautiful Southern belle would be interested in your mangy, uptight ass, but she *is*, goddammit. And I think if you agree to have a vasectomy so you'll never pollute her immaculate family lineage with your spawn, she might consider marrying you."

"Can't do it," Halloran had answered, managing to slur even that short sentence. "Wouldn't be fair."

"What? The vasectomy or marrying her?" Dan had said. "Actually, if you mean the vasectomy, don't worry about it. Maggie told me she has several corrupt judges and two members of Sinn Fein on her family tree, so you're okay there. There's just as much dark stuff on her side of the family as yours. Genetically, you'll have an equal chance of creating a child who ends up in either the White House or the Big House."

In the end, Halloran had agreed to meet with Maggie—just to let her down easy, he'd promised himself. But all his resolve had deserted him when he saw her, resulting in a somewhat stilted proposal, due to the turbulent feelings he was trying to suppress. Despite this, Maggie had said yes immediately, seeming to know him better than he knew himself.

"Okay," said Halloran, holding the wheel with his left hand as he reached out for hers. "I stand corrected. Meddle all you want."

"I planned to, with or without your permission," said his wife.

―――――

Their parting was awkward, to say the least. Joplin and Carrie had followed the Hallorans out to their car to see the painting Tom had bought from the gallery and agreed it would be a good idea to have CSU examine it. But after seeing them off, Joplin had stood there in the parking lot, holding the painting and wondering what to say to Carrie. He'd finally asked if she'd like to go back into the restaurant and have dinner, then suggested that they go somewhere else when she declined. She had declined again, not surprising him, even though she hadn't seemed angry. And then he'd wished that she *had* acted angry, so that they might have been able to get things out in the open. It had somehow been beyond his ability to do that himself, even though he'd searched his memory for something—*anything*—that would get him jump-started. But what had popped into his mind was the strange way she had looked at him that morning over three months ago, as if she had wanted to tell him something, but couldn't bring herself to do it. He'd seen again the almost wistful expression on her face as they'd stood in the break room at the ME's Office, and had wondered if his own face looked like that now as he'd reluctantly said goodbye and walked to his car.

By the time he'd pulled into the APD parking lot twenty minutes later, Joplin had come to the conclusion that maybe he and Carrie had more in common with regard to communicating their true feelings than he'd thought. She had needed to tell him about her relationship with Jack just a few weeks ago. No, not *tell*, he corrected himself. *Confess.* Confess to him her reasons for falling for Jack, but also her reluctance to break away entirely from Joplin himself. But that confession had evidently cost her more, emotionally, than she'd realized, and in the face of his current struggle with his medical problems and the Blue Funk that had resulted, Carrie had shut down. He remembered the inner voice that had insisted the night before that something *had* changed in his world and resolved to follow that voice, as scary as it might seem to him.

Satisfied that he had gotten to the bottom of the latest obstacle to their relationship and hopeful that he could at least try to overcome it, Joplin got out of his car, retrieved the painting from the back seat, and headed toward the APD building. It was abuzz with officers bringing in cuffed perps for booking, family and friends of already-booked perps, and several bondsmen he knew who had arrived to negotiate bail with the family and friends of those who'd been allowed to make bail. He waived to the desk sergeant and headed downstairs to the CSU, confident that it would be open, and just as busy.

This was, after all, Atlanta on a Saturday night.

CHAPTER FORTY-THREE

Joplin slept better Saturday night than he had in over a week, and whatever dreams he'd had must have been fairly mediocre, because he couldn't remember them. It might have had something to do with the fact that he'd had very little to drink once he got home. Or, it might have been a result of his decision to try to repair things with Carrie; it didn't matter. He almost jumped out of bed the next morning, scaring Quincy in the process, and after making coffee and feeding the cat, put on work clothes and started cleaning up the apartment.

By noon, with breaks for coffee and a breakfast of eggs and bacon, Joplin was satisfied that he had successfully dealt with the destruction caused by his latest Blue Funk. After much thought, involving what he would say and how he would say it, he called Carrie.

She answered after three rings, and at first, Joplin was struck dumb, despite all his preparation.

"Hollis?" she said finally, and he realized he'd been outed by caller ID.

"Yes," he croaked, then cleared his throat and said, "I'm calling to see if you'll let me cook dinner for you tonight. I cleaned up my apartment," he added, hoping that would be an incentive, rather than the lamest thing he'd ever said in his life while trying to ask a woman to have dinner with him. "I mean, the last time you were here…"

"I knew what you meant," Carrie said. "But what does that *mean?*" After a pause, she said, "No, wait, that doesn't make sense."

"Yes, it does. You want to know *why* I want to have you over. If I'm finally going to talk to you about what's going on with me. Right?"

"Well, yes, I guess so."

"And the answer is yes. I *am* going to talk, and I just hope it's not too late. Is it too late, Carrie?"

There was a longish pause, and then she said, "What are you fixing for dinner?"

"My famous shrimp and grits," he said, barely breathing.

"Why are they famous?"

"Because that's the only thing I know how to make when I have people over for dinner."

"Okay," she said. "Lucky for you, I happen to like shrimp and grits."

———

He left nothing to chance. The lights were low; the candles were lit on both the small dining table and the coffee table. Soft music played in the background, and what he hoped was a wonderful aroma coming from the garlic and cheese he'd added to the grits had wafted into the living room. A bottle of wine stood in a cooler on the coffee table, next to a plate of cheese and olives and two fluted glasses. It was Prosecco, something Maggie Halloran had served him once at their house in Ansley.

Carrie arrived promptly at six. She was wearing a white sun dress that made her skin look bronzed and her eyes enormous. Her hair was in a loose knot that rested on the back of her neck. She smelled of lavender and some other fragrance he couldn't name, but which he remembered from somewhere.

"I'm so glad you came, Carrie," Joplin said, ushering her in.

"I'm just here for the shrimp and grits," she said, but the corners of her wide mouth turned up.

"How about a glass of Prosecco first?"

"Love one."

He led her to the couch and poured them each some wine when she'd settled in.

She took a sip, then looked around. "I almost don't recognize this room. Have you redecorated?"

"Yes," he said. "I had my personal stylists come in. They said pizza boxes, Chinese food cartons and dirty glasses were passé, so everything had to go. I was somewhat attached to my empty beer bottle collection, but they stood firm. Do you like the new look?"

She nodded solemnly and raised her glass. "It's fabulous. Out with the old, in with the new."

"Exactly," Joplin said and moved closer to her.

———

He had told her all about his insomnia and his years of being mentored and cared for by Dr. O'Brian by the time they each had a second glass of Prosecco. When they moved to the kitchen, she perched on a stool as he manned the stove. Joplin forced himself to talk about his visit to Dr. Mallory and his fear that inflicting his physical and medical problems on her would ruin their relationship. When she started to speak, he put a finger to her lips and asked her to let him talk while he felt he could. While he finished fixing the shrimp and grits, then plated that and their salads, he didn't look at her as he told her about feeling something break loose in him. Something that signaled that he could trust himself to move on now. That he could also trust her to tell him what she could handle and what she couldn't. That he didn't have to handle everything by himself.

Joplin set their plates on the table and pulled out Carrie's chair. When they were both sitting, he poured some Sonoma Cutrer Chardonnay—another of Maggie's favorites—and raised his glass to her. "To new beginnings," he said.

Carrie smiled and said, "Didn't we already have one of those a few weeks ago?"

"To second beginnings," he said, not missing a beat as their glasses clinked.

———

"Stay with me tonight, Carrie," Joplin said, when they'd finished dessert. He reached out and put his hand over hers.

She stared at him for several seconds. "What about your rule that you weren't going to have sex until after the operation? You haven't even told me if you're *going* to have the operation."

"I *am* going to have it. And the rule about no sex is still in effect, but I decided to amend it a little."

Her mouth twitched. "You mean there's a sexual discrimination amendment?"

Joplin nodded solemnly. "Exactly. I've decided that outlawing all forms of sexual expression is downright unconstitutional." He held her eyes with his and took a deep breath. "As you've certainly discovered, I'm not very good at expressing my feelings. Not the deepest and most important ones, anyway. But I want to show you how I feel about you. If you'll let me," he added.

———

They left the table without clearing it and didn't bother to put up any leftovers in the kitchen. Once they were in his bedroom, Hollis asked if he could undress her, and she found herself shivering while he did, but not from the air conditioning. After he'd tucked her under the sheets, he disappeared into the bathroom. He was wearing a Braves tee shirt and nothing else when he came out, but she could still see the outline of the colostomy bag. He didn't seem self-conscious about it, though—at least, not like the last time they'd spent the night together. His attention was focused completely on her. And even though he never actually *told* her that he loved her, Carrie felt that love with every kiss, his tongue probing, gently at first, and then more and more insistent. The kisses moved from her mouth to her neck, then down to her breasts, giving each one equal attention. His mouth engulfed first one nipple, then the other, teasing and gently nipping at them. After this came some full-out sucking, with accompanying noises that would have made her laugh if she weren't quite so stimulated. And then, just when she thought she couldn't take it anymore, his mouth moved to her abdomen, spreading the kisses from left to right, then up and down. They ended in the "down" direction and continued to follow it until they nestled in her pubic hair, his lips moving at first from side-to-side in a playful manner.

The real loving began after that, and Carrie almost lost consciousness when she finally surrendered, wave after wave of pleasure pounding her body like some kind of orgasmic tsunami.

CHAPTER FORTY-FOUR

Joplin had barely gotten to his office cubicle Monday morning when his cell phone rang.

"Hollis Joplin."

"Hollis, it's Ike. I need to come by and see you. Right away."

"Sure, Ike. What's this about?"

"The painting you brought to CSU Saturday night. I'll tell you about when I get there."

Simmons had disconnected before Joplin could say anything more. He sat back in his chair and wondered what it was that CSU had discovered in the thirty-six hours since he'd dropped off the painting. Was it that the "pigments" Jonathan Demarest used did, in fact, include real blood, as Halloran suspected? And if so, could the blood belong to either Libba Ann Woodridge or Maria Sanchez? Or both? That would certainly tie the two cases together in the way that Jimmy Hernandez suspected. It would also mean that Demarest was involved in both Libba's attack and Maria's murder, and that perhaps Jorge was an innocent man.

He was still weighing the implications of this when Ike Simmons walked into the investigators' room, a manila envelope in his hand. It hadn't even been ten minutes since they'd spoken, which meant something really big was up. But the first thing that came out of Ike's mouth surprised him.

"Is Viv here?" he asked, eyes darting around the room.

Joplin shook his head. "No, she was called out on a scene before I even got here. I saw her in the parking lot."

"Then we need to go talk to your boss."

"Sarah?"

"Yes, and Dr. Minton, too, if he's here today."

"You're really freaking me out, Ike."

"Then that makes two of us."

After discovering that Lewis Minton wasn't in his office yet, they went directly to Sarah Petersen's. Her eyebrows arched when she saw Simmons, but she quickly gestured toward the two chairs that faced her desk.

"What's going on?" was all she said.

Simmons took a breath and said, "Viv Rodriquez was the investigator called to the scene of four out of five homicides involving prostitutes in the past six months. Some were in Atlanta—two in Midtown and one in Buckhead—and two in Alpharetta. The one in Buckhead was handled by Deke Crawford because Viv was on vacation. That's when we finally determined that all of them were the work of a serial killer and called in the FBI."

Sarah's expression was puzzled. "Was there any problem with Viv's investigations?"

"None at all," Simmons said. "I just want to go over some things with her since she examined the bodies before anyone else."

"But you told me on the phone that this had something to do with the painting I took to CSI on Saturday night, Ike," Joplin said.

"What painting?" Sarah Petersen asked.

Joplin quickly explained about the Hallorans, the art gallery, and the painting they'd brought to him at Houston's, leaving out only the parts about Hernandez and his and Carrie's visit to Emily Trenton. "I planned to tell you all about it first thing this morning, but Ike called," he added, hoping she and Ike wouldn't notice the glaring omissions.

"I don't think that's going to fly, Hollis," Petersen said coolly.

"Not even with jet thrusters," Simmons added, shaking his head.

So Joplin took a deep breath and started over, filling them in on Hernandez' visit to his apartment on Thursday night, the meeting with Emily Trenton and his subsequent phone call to Dr. Jake Pennington, his request that the Hallorans drop by the Artists' Loft, and the meeting at Houston's.

"You couldn't call my cell phone, Hollis, when all this was going on?" Simmons protested.

"Or tell me about this Friday afternoon, after you checked out that 'new lead' you told me about?" Petersen demanded, frowning. "You said you'd get back to me if anything came of it."

Joplin held up his hands in surrender. "Guilty on both counts. I should have let you know about the painting, Ike, when I was on my way to CSU." He turned to Petersen. "And I should have let you know what Carrie and I found out when we visited the former owner of the painting."

Joplin quickly moved on to explain his reluctance to let anyone know Jimmy Hernandez' part in bringing this latest lead to his attention when he didn't even know if it meant anything. They both nodded, seeming to understand, even if they didn't agree. But when Joplin got to the part about asking Tom and Maggie to scope out Jonathan Demarest at the Artist's Loft, Simmons exploded.

"Why in hell would you involve Tom Halloran in this, much less his wife?"

"Because I couldn't go there myself, Ike. My face was plastered all over the papers just a few months ago, if you recall, and I didn't want to give Demarest a head's up that we were looking at him."

Simmons scrubbed his hand over his face. "*We* were not looking at him, Hollis, until you took the painting to CSU. And *we* didn't even know who he was, except for the signature on it."

"So what *did* you find out about the painting? CSU, I mean."

"Good diversion tactic, Hollis," Petersen said dryly.

"And don't think I don't know it, Chief," said Simmons heatedly. "We are *not*—I repeat, *not*—through discussing what you did, Hollis, just so you know."

"I know," Joplin said, trying to sound penitent. This was where the asking for forgiveness came in after failing to get permission. "I take full responsibility."

Sarah Petersen smiled knowingly. In the future, he'd have to remember that she seemed to know adages just as well as he did.

Simmons didn't seem to be buying it either, but he said, "You specifically asked that the pigments used to paint the picture be tested for the presence of blood. And they did."

"Test positive for blood, you mean?" Joplin asked, somewhat shocked that Halloran had been right.

"Yes, human blood. And, CSU also found a match: Tiffany Jones, the first victim found that can be connected to the serial killer in the prostitute murders."

———

Halloran ended the call from Hollis Joplin, still overwhelmed by what he'd told him about the Demarest painting. Especially its connection to the prostitute murders. He didn't remember hearing about any of them; he'd been consumed by Elliot Carter's death in the spring and everything that had gone on with the Woodridge case since then. Frankly, all that he'd hoped—or, rather, suspected—was that a scientific test could prove that Jonathan Demarest was actually using human blood in his so-called "special blend of pigments."

Deep down, without really acknowledging it to himself, he'd wondered if Demarest had used Libba's blood. If so, it might have freed him to turn over the video she had given him and perhaps get Jorge Martinez released from jail. But to know that the artist might be involved in a series of brutal murders boggled his mind. The man was certainly sinister enough, and his paintings and sculptures were extremely violent, especially towards women. Halloran also remembered noting that the man's physique was similar to the man on the video. But was that enough to release him from the attorney/client privilege that Libba had invoked in her letter to him?

His cell phone rang again as he was still mulling this over. It was Ed Jenkins, who had told him it would be Monday morning before he could get any records on adoption proceedings in Glynn County. "Were you able to find out anything, Ed?"

"Yes, but not much, at this point. There's a public record that Connie Sue Cates, married at the time to a Herbert Cates, adopted an infant girl in 1985. But the child's original birth certificate, in keeping with state law, was sealed, along with any other particulars about her or the biological parents. The amended birth certificate, which was attached to the record, just shows the names of the adoptive parents and the new name of the child, which was Libba Ann Cates. You can petition the court for access to the original certificate, but that won't be easy. Access is pretty much limited to the parties concerned—the adoptive and biological parents, adoptees over eighteen, and biological siblings. You'd have to come up with a pretty good reason to get the court to agree to grant access."

Halloran thought about this, then said, "I think I can petition on the basis of determining any potential heirs to her estate, now that I know she was adopted. In the meantime, can you nose around some more and see if Connie Sue has family or friends who might have some information?"

"Sure thing. I'll be in touch."

"I appreciate that," Halloran said. "Just see what you can do."

———

Dr. Minton was in his office by the time Joplin got off the phone with Tom

Halloran, so they gathered there while he and Simmons briefed him on the serial murders and the new evidence furnished by the Demarest painting. Although Ike had gone through the copies of the original files, now in the hands of the FBI, Dr. Minton made a quick call to order the ME autopsy files to be brought to them.

"I got hold of Viv," Sarah Petersen said. "She's wrapping things up at a vehicular scene and will be here in about fifteen minutes. I told her what was going on, but I didn't go into detail."

"I understand how the painting is connected to the serial murders, but how is it connected to the Sanchez murder and to the Woodridge case?" Dr. Minton asked.

Ike and Sarah turned to look at Joplin. He took a deep breath and explained about the call from Jimmy Hernandez, describing the painting at the Trenton house and the similarities to the silhouettes made by blood spatter at the Sanchez and Woodridge crime scenes. If Minton knew that Jimmy had been suspended from the case and shouldn't have contacted Joplin, he didn't acknowledge it.

"Who performed the autopsies on the serial victims?" he asked, turning to Simmons.

"I did two of them."

They all turned to look at Carrie, who was standing in the doorway. Joplin had had no time to talk to her that morning since they had come to the office in separate cars, and now felt as if he had let her down. Again.

"Come in, Dr. Salinger," said Lewis Minton. "We're going to need your help." He waited until she'd pulled up one of the chairs and taken a seat, then caught her up on what had been discovered by CSU's analysis of the Demarest painting.

She seemed stunned by the revelation. "What was used to keep the iron in the blood from oxidizing on the canvas and turning brown?" she asked.

"Potassium lactate," Simmons said. "According to the lab, it can revive an enzyme system found in blood that will constantly regenerate enough myoglobin to keep blood oxygenated. At least, that's what they told me," he added, "and I'll take their word for it."

"Of course," said Carrie, nodding slowly. "Myoglobin is a molecule in blood that stores oxygen. When blood leaves the body or is exposed to air, the myoglobin is depleted and the iron in blood oxidizes, creating rust. But how would Jonathan Demarest know about potassium lactate?"

"We don't know the answer to that yet," said Simmons. "Or if he has a connection to any of the other victims."

"By 'connection,' you mean their blood," said Carrie.

"To begin with, anyway. The fact that Tiffany Jones' blood was used to paint the picture Hollis took to CSU means that we can get a warrant to get the other paintings at the gallery that look like crime scene outlines. And any others he has like the one at the Trenton crime scene. At least I hope so. I have a call into the DA's Office. After that, we'll need to try to connect him to the women in other ways. To establish how he knew them, or at least made contact with them."

"What were the names of the victims you autopsied, Dr. Salinger?" Lewis Minton asked.

She took a deep breath, then said, "The first was Amber Pittman in April. I was doing my thirty-day rotation then, so I actually just assisted… Dr. Tyndall." She looked down at her lap, then raised her head. "But I remember it well," she continued, her voice breaking a little, "because it was my first decomposed body. She was found in a boarded-up house on Juniper. She'd been strangled. Her hyoid bone was broken."

"So there wasn't any blood at that scene, was there?" Joplin asked, hoping she knew that he was trying to give her a little moral support.

"No," she said, looking at him for the first time since she'd come into the room. "Not that I know of, anyway."

"I'm guessing you didn't go to the scene because of your rotation status, correct?" he suggested.

"That's correct, but we...I... reviewed the crime scene photos very carefully. And Viv's report."

"I'm sure you did," Dr. Minton said, nodding. "What was the second autopsy you handled?"

"Her name was Jenna Clark. Cause of death was blunt force trauma, probably with a hammer, so there was plenty of blood. In the crime scene photos and on her body."

"Head trauma?" Joplin asked.

"Yes, but that wasn't what killed her. The murder weapon shattered her right collar bone and severed the subclavian artery."

"That one was in July, right?" said Simmons. "The body was discovered in a carwash that had gone bankrupt a few months earlier."

"Yes," Carrie said. "Both bodies were in advanced states of decomposition, so the interval between death and discovery was hard to pinpoint because both sites had been unoccupied for a while. But due to insect activity, we were able to determine that Britney had been dead at least five weeks, and Jenna around three."

"Dr. Salinger," said Ike Simmons, "it was after Jenna Clark's death that we were able to determine that these two deaths were the work of a serial killer and connected them to the bodies found in March and April. Did you observe anything then—or even now, looking back—that was similar?"

"I've asked myself that several times since the FBI became involved. And the only thing I can come up with, besides the fact that they were prostitutes, is that the killer chose sites that wouldn't be discovered for a while."

"That's what I thought, too, when Viv and I discussed the murders a few weeks ago," said Joplin, pulling up a visual memory of his first day back at the office, when Viv had come into the investigators' room reeking of decomposed body. "She had just gotten back from the latest scene, the basement of a church off Windward Parkway that was scheduled for demolition."

"The FBI profiler thinks the killer may be going back to the crime scenes after the murders," Ike Simmons said. "Either to relive them for some kind of sexual thrill or just to spend more time with them. So he chooses places to kill them, or at least dump the bodies, that are off the beaten track. Which means he'd have to have a pretty good sense of where places like that would be. The profiler says it fits the description of a blue collar worker who makes deliveries or services businesses or homes that take him all over the county."

"You mean like Jorge Martinez?" Sarah Petersen suggested.

Simmons nodded. "Exactly like Jorge Martinez."

"And Jorge was a medic in the military, right?" said Carrie, frowning. When Simmons nodded, she said, "Medics and EMTs use Ringer's Lactate, which contains potassium lactate, for resuscitation when victims of trauma have lost a lot of blood or other fluids."

"And most doctors would know that, too, not just medics, right?" Joplin said. "But, Jorge is Hispanic, and from what I can tell, the victims were all white, blonde females. Don't serial killers choose victims from their own race or ethnic background?"

"Usually, but not always. Most of Jeffrey Dahmer's victims were young, black males."

"Not all of the women were blonde," Carrie said. "Britney Grady was wearing a long, blonde wig. She had brown hair. So did Maria Sanchez, if we're including her."

"And, don't forget," said Simmons, "except for Maria, and Libba, of course, they were all prostitutes—maybe chosen for their vulnerability, as well as the fact that they wouldn't be missed right away. And a lot of prostitutes dye their hair blonde or wear blonde wigs."

"But what's the connection between Jorge and Jonathan Demarest?" Carrie asked. "Demarest would have to get the victim's blood from him, right?"

"Or maybe," Joplin said, frowning, "We can take Jorge out of the equation entirely. Maybe the killer isn't a blue collar worker with a job that takes him all over the city. Maybe he's a person without a nine-to-five job, and that allows him to explore the city for the perfect places to kill women and have access to their bodies for weeks and even months. And maybe he's not reliving the murders when he visits the sites."

"Then what is he doing?" asked Simmons.

"Maybe he's sketching them for his paintings," Joplin said.

CHAPTER FORTY-FIVE

Viv Rodriguez joined the group gathered in Lewis Minton's office as they were looking through the autopsy files on the serial killer's victims. Once more, Minton detailed the latest developments on the case, after ushering her to a chair. She was clearly taken aback by the news.

"I get that there's a connection between this Jonathan Demarest and the serial killings," she said finally, "but how are you connecting him to the Sanchez murder or the attack on Libba Woodridge?"

"So far, the only connection is something Jimmy Hernandez showed me," said Joplin, opening his laptop and pulling up the image of the painting found at the Trenton crime scene. When she had had a chance to examine it, he quickly changed the screen to the photos Hernandez had taken of the concrete wall behind the gas station after Maria Sanchez's body had been removed, then the headboard and wall in Libba's bedroom.

Viv stared at them, then put her hand up to her mouth. "This is fucking crazy," she said, then looked up at Lewis Minton and added, "Excuse me, sir."

"Not necessary," Minton said. "I feel the same way. But, tell me something. You and maybe Detective Simmons were at the scenes soon after the bodies were discovered." He turned to Simmons and said, "Is that right, Ike? Were you there for any of the scenes?"

"I was. I caught the Tiffany Jones case and the Britney Grady case."

"From what I read in the files, Jones was stabbed and Grady was beaten to death. The photos don't really show the blood spatter in detail. Viv, you handled the Jones case as well as Pittman, Grady and Sandra Harris in August. Did either of you see anything like the two paintings of Jonathan Demarest that you've seen today or the crime scenes Hollis just showed us?"

Rodriguez thought for a minute then said, "Who's got the file on Tiffany Jones?"

"I do," said Carrie, handing it to Viv.

She took out the stack of crime scene photos she'd taken, thumbed through them, then pulled out one and showed it to them. "This is the first picture I took, right after I examined the body. You can't really tell from this because I took it fairly close up, but the body was in a sitting position, with her buttocks and legs on the compacted dirt under the bridge and her back against the concrete support behind her. She was in an advanced state of decomposition, and the blood spatter was totally degraded, so it didn't look anything like the Trenton painting, but the position of the head and shoulders is similar, now that I can compare them. And Amber Pittman was in a sitting position up against a bedroom wall in that house on Juniper."

Simmons, who had that file, rifled through the photos and pulled out one showing what Viv had described. "Except for the lack of blood spatter, it looks like the Sanchez scene. I never saw that one until today, because Jim Mullins handled that case. And I never saw Libba Ann Woodridge until after you worked on her, Hollis, so I didn't make the connection to Tiffany Jones." He looked around the room and said, "Who has the Britney Grady file?"

"Right here," said Sarah Petersen. She handed the crime scene photos to Simmons, then said, "But there's no similarity there. She's clearly on her back on the floor of the warehouse in Midtown where she was found."

"Yes," Simmons agreed, taking the file. "She was beaten to death." He stared down at the photo Petersen had focused on, then thumbed through the others. Pulling out one that was taken from a greater distance from the body than the others, he turned to Joplin and said, "This look familiar?"

Joplin took the photo and nodded slowly, then looked up at Ike. "The body's in the same position as the silhouette made in blood in the Demarest painting that I took to CSU."

———

The noise level in Lewis Minton's office ratcheted up as everyone tried to process this information. When Janice Bernstein called Simmons a few minutes later, he held up his hand to request silence and told her about what they believed to be the latest connections to the serial murder case. After a brief silence, she let him know the warrant to confiscate Demarest's paintings still at the Artist's Loft had been signed, but also said she'd request a search warrant for his house as well, listing any paint, blood, other paintings, and items that might have been taken from or used at the murder scenes and the attack on Libba as objects of the search. She then advised him to bring the artist in for questioning while both warrants were being executed.

"Hopefully, that will be later today," said Simmons after telling them everything Bernstein had said. He shook his head, clearly bowled over by her reaction. "Man, I've never heard her revved up like this! We usually have to jump through our asses before she'll work with us." He turned quickly to Lewis Minton and added, "Pardon my French, Doc."

"Why," Lewis Minton asked, looking slowly around the room, "does everyone think my ears are so delicate?"

"Because you're like a father to all of us," Joplin said, hoping he wasn't crossing the line.

"Well, then," said Minton, placing both hands on his desk, palms down, "as your father figure, I'm ordering you all to get out of my office and see if you can help Detective Simmons figure out how to question this fucking bastard."

———

They regrouped in the investigators' room, but after ten minutes, Simmons stood up and said he was going back to his own office. "I think I know what to ask Demarest. And if I don't, there are plenty of FBI agents who will. They're not gonna like the fact that he doesn't fit their profile."

"You mean, like Jorge Martinez does?" Joplin asked.

"Yep," said Simmons.

"Any chance he could be released if you get more evidence on Demarest?"

Simmons chuckled. "I'll take it up with Bernstein, but I think she's shot her wad, as far as being flexible for the day, don't you?"

"And then some."

"You gonna let Halloran know the latest?"

Joplin sighed. "I guess I better."

———

To Joplin's surprise, Tom Halloran seemed a little subdued after he'd filled him in, especially when he said it was unlikely that Bernstein would authorize Jorge Martinez' release.

"What do you expect, Tom? We still don't even know if there's more evidence on the paintings or at Demarest's house."

"I know. It's just that I don't see Jorge for any of this. It was hard enough to believe he was capable of attacking Libba—more so when it came to murdering his wife. But to imagine that he's a serial killer who gathers blood from his victims and mixes it into an artist's paints? It just doesn't make any sense."

"Several serial killers have worked in pairs, Tom. Leonard Lake and Charles Ng in the Eighties; Angelo Buono and Kenneth Bianchi in the Seventies; and Paul Bernardo and Karla Homolka in Canada in the Nineties. I could go on."

"Yes, but I just don't see the two of them together. You haven't met Jonathan Demarest. I have. The two men have nothing in common."

"That you know of, anyway," Joplin insisted. "And in each of the pairs of killers I mentioned, one dominated the other, pretty much calling the shots. I can see Demarest playing that role. And it would support the FBI profiler's description of the killer as a delivery man or someone who services homes or businesses in the Atlanta area, meaning Jorge, but connects him with the type of mastermind you think Demarest is."

Halloran gave a long sigh. "Maybe," he said, clearly not convinced. "Will you let me know when the search warrant is executed?"

"Whatever I can pass on to you, I will," said Joplin.

———

Carrie sat at her desk going over Deke Crawford's report on a gunshot victim who'd been found behind a liquor store on Monroe Drive the day before. She had scheduled the autopsy for earlier in the morning, but was only now beginning to prepare for it. She had trouble focusing on the report, however; her mind kept going back to the serial murders and their connections to Jonathan Demarest. Like Hollis, she had thought it was possible that the artist had used human blood in his paintings, and that there might be a connection to the Sanchez murder and Libba Woodridge. But the possibility—even probability—that he could have also killed at least five women in the Atlanta area blew her mind.

She didn't really fault herself for not seeing the similarities between Annie Pittman, Jenna Clark, Maria Sanchez, and Libba Woodridge—like everyone involved, she had seen only parts of the whole. They were all like the six blind men in India asked to describe an elephant by touching different parts of it. And it wasn't until Jimmy Hernandez brought Hollis a crime scene photo from a 2007 murder that they were able to see the whole elephant.

Her thoughts were interrupted by Hollis, suddenly standing in her doorway.

"Can I come in?"

"Of course. Did you get hold of Tom?"

He nodded as he sat in one of the chairs in front of her desk. "He's as shocked by the connection to the serial murders as the rest of us are. I also think he was hoping the blood might be Libba's, and that this would prove Jorge Martinez' innocence."

"I'm sure Jimmy was, too. Have you let him know about all this?"

"I called him right after I talked to Tom, and he feels totally vindicated. Of course, he's pushing to get Jorge released. But I don't think that's going to happen unless Demarest breaks down and confesses, which is highly unlikely, from what I've heard about the man."

Carrie gave a little shudder. "Just listening to Tom and Maggie describe him and his showing at that gallery gave me the creeps. He'd certainly fit the bill for the type of woman-hater who could shove a barbeque skewer into a woman's uterus. His whole show seemed to be about terrible mothers and what they did to their children."

"I agree," Hollis said. "Listen, why don't we get out of here for a while and go have some lunch. This is the first chance I've had to talk to you alone since…last night."

Carrie felt herself turning red and cursed whatever gene she'd inherited that made her betray her emotions so blatantly. As Hollis grinned at her, apparently enjoying her embarrassment, the phone rang. "Dr. Salinger," she said, grateful for the distraction.

"Mr. Halloran is here to see Hollis," Sherika said. "I thought maybe you knew where he was," she added, her voice full of insinuation.

"Have you tried his cell phone?"

"Does that mean he's not in your office?"

"What do you think?"

"Is it okay if I just send Mr. Halloran to your office, Dr. Salinger?"

"Sure," said Carrie, giving in. What right to privacy did she have, anyway? Any red-blooded American office staff always knew exactly what was going on. And with whom. She hung up and turned to Hollis. "Tom Halloran is here to see you. Sherika, our very own NSA agent, figured you were here. Why am I not surprised?"

"Because you're a very intelligent woman," Hollis said, still grinning. "And so is Sherika."

"I agree," said Tom Halloran, walking into the room. He carefully closed the door, then said, "And I'm glad you're here together, because I need to talk to both of you."

CHAPTER FORTY-SIX

When the video Tom Halloran had played on his laptop was finished, Joplin was too stunned to say anything at first. He looked at Carrie, who seemed just as stunned, then at Halloran, who was sitting next to him and said, finally, "How long have you been sitting on this, Tom?"

Halloran cleared his throat, "Libba received it on Friday, August 10th. Actually, it had come in the mail the day before, but she didn't open it until Friday."

"That was the same day Maria Sanchez was found, wasn't it?"

"Yes. I got a call from her around eleven that morning. She was crying, almost hysterical. When I got to her house, she had me play the video."

"Captain Martucci must have forgotten to tell me that you brought it right over to her, I guess."

"Obviously, I didn't do that, Hollis. I couldn't. Libba held me to the attorney/client privilege."

"But, why?" Carrie asked. "It could have helped the police find out who did this to her."

Halloran nodded slowly. "I told her that, of course. And I begged her to let me turn the video over to them, but she was adamant. This note was sent with the video," Halloran said, reaching into his briefcase and offering him a baggie that held a piece of paper. "It instructed Libba to wire one million dollars to a bank in the Cayman Islands or the video would be sent out to the media. I advised her not to pay it, but her mind was made up. I warned her that blackmailers never quit blackmailing, but she told me she'd just get someone else to wire the money if I wouldn't help her."

Joplin glanced briefly at the note, then said, "And did you?"

"Yes, Hollis, I did. She was my client, and she'd been horribly trauma-tized. She told me she couldn't handle the police looking at that video, much less members of the media and their various audiences. Even if most broadcasters refused to show it, she knew it would probably be leaked and aired on social media. Even without her celebrity, it would have gone viral within an hour, and you know it. I was afraid she'd kill herself if that happened."

Joplin stared at him and shook his head. "She *did* kill herself, Tom. At least, that's what you've been insisting this past week. Did it ever occur to you that the guy who did this to her decided to go back to the well again for more money and that *that's* what pushed her over the edge?"

"Hollis!" said Carrie, putting her hand on his arm. "Don't you think you—"

"No, he's right," Halloran interrupted. "It did occur to me. Every day since she died, in fact."

"Then, why wait till now to turn this over? Libba died over a week ago. Why didn't you give this to me or Simmons then?"

"Because the privilege remained in effect even after her death. Libba knew that, but she left this for me to make sure I knew she hadn't released me from it." Again Halloran reached into his briefcase, this time retrieving a flat paper bag. "There's a letter from her in here."

"Well, I'm glad you at least kept this one in a paper bag so we could try to get prints," he said, hearing the sarcasm in his voice.

"I didn't know at the time that putting a document in plastic might destroy any prints."

"Let me guess: Ed Jenkins recovered this from the death scene and told you what to do."

"I'm not at liberty to say who advised me."

"Yeah, right," Joplin spat out. "Did he also find her cell phone?"

"No, and that's the truth."

Without responding to this, Joplin carefully tugged the document out of the bag by one corner and began to read it. When he was finished, he looked up at Halloran and said, "You truly believe this is Libba Ann Woodridge's handwriting?"

"I do," Halloran said, nodding. "I've hired an expert to examine it, but I haven't gotten his report yet. Yet even without his confirmation, I'm convinced she wrote it, because I'm very familiar with her handwriting, as well as her style of writing. An argument could be made that she was coerced into writing it, but, I don't think so. I think she knew exactly what she was doing when she killed herself."

"And what was that?" Carrie asked, leaning in, as if to hear him better.

"I think she was protecting Arliss Woodridge. And his family."

"From what?"

"That I don't know. Yet. But I think it has something to do with Libba's identity. I'm having my paralegal draw up a petition to get her adoption records unsealed, but it'll take a while." Halloran explained about the confidentiality surrounding this issue.

"That's something we might have been able to green-light, you know, in connection with a homicide," said Joplin.

"Yes, but her death hasn't been *ruled* a homicide. And you didn't know that Libba wasn't Connie Sue's biological child until Carrie got the results of Connie Sue's autopsy, remember?"

Joplin exhaled. Loudly. "Okay, but before I call Simmons and Mary Martucci, is there anything else about this video I need to know?"

"Well, just that Maggie saw something unusual when she viewed it."

"*Maggie* saw this video?" Joplin exploded. "You showed it to Maggie, but not to us? What about the attorney/client privilege, Tom?"

"I got around that by hiring her as a consultant. Remember how she helped us with the photos Anne Carter gave me?"

Joplin covered his face with his hands and then rubbed his temples. "Yes, I remember," he said between clenched teeth. "So what did Maggie see that was so unusual?"

Halloran swiveled the laptop toward himself and reversed the video to a point near the beginning, then clicked the "play" button. The hooded figure advanced toward Libba from where he had set up the tripod and camera. Halloran waited until he had reached the bed, then stopped the action. "Did you see that?" he asked them.

Joplin turned to look at him. "See what?"

"I'll play it again."

The third time Halloran played that segment of the video, Carrie said, "I see it!"

This time, Joplin nodded. "I do, too. The image of the man dips and goes back up a tiny, tiny bit."

"Twice," added Carrie.

Something flashed in Joplin's brain, then disappeared. "But why?" he asked, deciding to pull that thread later. "Did Maggie have any idea?"

"No," said Halloran. "And neither do I."

Ten minutes later, Halloran was gone, leaving Joplin with a mixture of conflicting emotions—shock, resentment, pity for Libba Woodridge, and some hope that they might now be able to find out who had attacked her. Maybe even find a serial murderer. He looked at his watch and said to Carrie, "Ike should be at the FBI field office by now. I'd better call him."

After telling Simmons he had even more evidence to show them, he stood up, holding the disc and an evidence bag containing the two notes Halloran had left with him. "I'm going to stop by Sarah's office to let her know about this, then head out, we'll have to forget about lunch. Don't know what the rest of the day will be like, but I'd love to see you later."

"I'll be here," she said.

———

On the way to his office, Halloran called Maggie and told her about giving the video to Joplin.

"Thank God," she said. "I haven't felt good about keeping that from the police since the first time I saw it. But why now, Tom? What's changed?"

When he told her about the CSI's analysis of the Demarest painting and its connection to the serial murders that neither one of them had known much about, she sounded even more relieved that he'd turned in the video. And horrified that someone she knew, even as peripherally as Jonathan Demarest, might have committed them.

"Jesus, Tom! He kissed my hand!"

Halloran started to laugh, then thought better of it. "Nobody knows anything for sure yet, Maggie. They're getting a warrant for the other paintings and a search warrant for his house, but he's not under arrest yet."

"Yes, but doesn't this clear Jorge Martinez?"

"Not at this point. But he might be released if the warrants turn up further evidence. We just have to wait and see."

"I guess," she said, clearly not happy about that. "By the way, did Hollis see what I saw on the video?"

"He did, on the third run-through. It's not obvious to the average person. But he trusts your eye, sweetie. As I do."

"I hope it means something. Something that helps."

"So do I, believe me. Listen, I've got to go. See you tonight. Maybe I'll know more by then."

Halloran had barely clicked off when his phone rang again. It was Ed Jenkins.

"I was able to track down an elderly relative of Connie Sue Cates. An aunt, named Mildred Liddell, who still lives in Brunswick. And she told me something interesting. Said there was another child, an older sibling of the baby girl Connie Sue adopted. But that her niece only wanted the baby."

"Another child?" said Halloran, stunned. "I mean, ostensibly, that was the reason I gave the court for wanting the adoption records unsealed, but I wasn't expecting it. Boy or girl?"

"A boy. Which is why Mrs. Liddell thinks Connie Sue didn't want him. She was really into the beauty pageant scene even then—had won a few local contests herself. And according to the aunt, Libba was beautiful even as a baby, so Connie Sue had high hopes. But a boy wouldn't fit into that world. The aunt tried to talk her into taking him anyway, so she wouldn't be splitting up a brother and a sister— so did the county adoption agency—but Connie Sue had her mind made up. Mrs. Liddell told me she always felt bad for the little boy."

"So do I," Halloran agreed. "Except having Connie Sue Cates for a mother wasn't exactly a blessing for Libba. Did the aunt know what happened to the child? Or anything about the circumstances surrounding their being put up for adoption?"

"No, but I'm looking through the local newspaper's archives and the county birth and death records, hoping to find a connection to the kids. If they were placed in a county adoption agency, it must mean they'd lived in Glynn County."

"Thanks, Ed. Keep up the good work."

As Halloran drove to his office, all he could think about was the little boy who'd lost his parents and his sister and then been rejected by a woman who just couldn't be bothered with him. Had he ever tried to find his sister? Or the parents who'd abandoned him or caused him to be taken away from them? He thought again about how Libba seemed to think that it was *who* she was that would somehow harm the Woodridge family name. He still didn't know what that meant or if it had anything to do with her adoption or a long-lost brother, though. Had she even known she was adopted and, if so, had she obtained access to the records herself? If she had, maybe she thought it was the brother who might bring shame to the Woodridge family. Deciding it was best if he kept Joplin in the loop, he tapped in the number on his cell phone and left him a message when he got voice mail.

———

As Joplin was going over the video Halloran had brought him with Ike and two special agents at the Atlanta FBI field office on Century Parkway in Dekalb County, he got called to a vehicular homicide scene. Since he'd almost finished briefing them, he was urged by Simmons to wrap things up and take off. He did so, making sure the agents saw the vertical dips that Halloran had shown him. Joplin also made sure they understood how crucial Maggie Halloran's input had been in analyzing the photos involved in the Carter case.

He called Sarah Petersen to tell her he was on his way to the scene, which was on 400, near the Haynes Bridge exit. When he'd stopped by her office to brief her about the video, she'd been as bowled over as everyone else by this latest twist in an already convoluted and horrific case. And now perhaps part of an even more horrific series of murders. He'd asked her to let Mary Martucci know about the video and explain that he would answer any questions she might have when he returned from his meeting with the FBI.

"I was hoping you'd call, Hollis," she said now. "How'd things go at the meeting?"

"Well, they're happy to have the new evidence, but they haven't even had a chance to process the evidence connecting Jonathan Demarest to the murders. And I just listened to a message from Tom Halloran letting me know that his investigator found out that Libba Woodridge has a brother out there somewhere, who *wasn't* adopted by Connie Sue Cates. Which is one more twist in this effing case."

"You're kidding."

"Nope. Anything new on the search warrant for Demarest's house?"

"Janice Bernstein fast-tracked it to the presiding judge, according to Captain Barrow. Barrow called right after you left, trying to get hold of Simmons. He agrees with Bernstein that Demarest needs to be brought in for questioning while it's being executed, and he wants a swat team along. He's probably talking to Ike and the FBI team now."

"Even more evidence to process once that's done. Things are moving pretty fast."

"Wicked fast, Hollis. But the serial murders aren't on our plate anymore. Manner of death for Libba Woodridge *is*. You said Tom Halloran is convinced the note she left for him is genuine, and that he believes she committed suicide. How does Dr. Salinger see it?"

"I'm just rolling up to the scene right now, but I'll be seeing her later, and I'll ask her."

CHAPTER FORTY-SEVEN

The search warrant for Jonathan Demarest's house and the warrant to con-fiscate his paintings at the Artist's Loft were executed at six p.m., just as the art gallery was closing for the day. The owner of the gallery was alarmed by the warrant, but didn't try to stop the officers from taking the paintings. Demarest himself wasn't there, which seemed to relieve her, given the situation. He was found having a drink on the terrace behind his house by two members of the SWAT team sent to cover the back entrance. When Ike Simmons showed him the search warrant, he seemed dumbstruck, then demanded to know what was going on. Simmons told him that they would explain everything at the police station, and the artist agreed to go so that he could "clear things up." He was left alone in an interrogation room until samples of the red pigment used on the paintings from the gallery, as well as those in his home studio, tested positive for human blood.

After a brief discussion with Captain Barrow and the two FBI agents, Dan Ringel and Joe Delano, a decision was made to read Demarest his Miranda rights. He was no longer just a "person of interest," which had granted them the right to question him without an attorney present. They had enough evidence to arrest him and had no intention of letting him leave the police station. Legally, that meant he was in custody, and needed to be informed of his rights. Simmons was hoping that the arrogance and air of superiority he'd exhibited would make him feel capable of controlling the interrogation.

He was right. Jonathon Demarest waved away any suggestion that he might need an attorney, especially when Simmons told him there was evidence to show that he was connected to a series of prostitute murders.

"You've got to be kidding," he said, and even managed to laugh. "Me? With prostitutes? I'm gay, for God's sake! And, no, I don't use male prostitutes, either."

Demarest vehemently denied killing anyone and insisted that it was "absolutely impossible" that his paintings contained real blood on them. When Simmons asked him to come up with a possible explanation for the blood, he shook his head and said that someone had framed him, a scenario that everyone in the interrogation room, including the two FBI agents, had heard before. Many times, in fact, along with the ever-popular, "wrong place at the wrong time."

"But, Mr. Demarest, you have to admit that it seems like more than a coincidence that many of your paintings resemble outlines of bodies at crime scenes," said Simmons. "And then there's this one." He turned the laptop he'd brought into the interrogation room with him around, so the artist could see it. It showed the painting found at the Trenton crime scene.

For the first time, Demarest looked spooked. He opened his mouth to say something, then closed it. "I want to call my attorney now," he said. "And I don't want to answer any more questions."

"That's your constitutional right," Simmons said, standing up.

———

On Wednesday, Simmons reported that expedited DNA testing of the paint samples connected them to the four other serial victims. DNA of dried blood on a towel in Demarest's home studio also proved to be Maria Sanchez's, and a deflated basketball found in his basement had two ounces of Libba Woodridge's blood in it. Joplin was happy to hear that the District

Attorney agreed with ADA Bernstein that there no longer remained much of a case against Jorge Martinez and ordered his release, although he was still troubled by the fact that Libba's Miss Georgia sash had been found in Jorge's apartment.

"Demarest planted it," said Simmons.

"But, how?" Joplin asked. "How would he get into the apartment? Or Libba Ann Woodridge's house, for that matter? I can see why Libba would appeal to him, with her long, blonde hair. And he probably considered her as much of a prostitute as the others, given her marriage to a rich, elderly man. But why just make her *look* like she was dead? And why would he kill Maria Sanchez? I think we're missing something here, Ike."

"He killed Maria to implicate Jorge, since he had access to the Woodridge house. Then he planted the sash, to seal the deal. I don't know why he did it, Hollis, but there's plenty of evidence to support that he did. We don't have to show intent or motive. You're overthinking this, partner."

"You're probably right," Joplin said, sighing.

"Go take that pretty doctor out for a drink and celebrate, Hollis. You deserve it."

"Okay, Ike, you convinced me."

Instead, Joplin's plans for the evening took a different turn. A jubilant Jimmy Hernandez called him just before his shift ended to say that Jorge was out and had been reunited with his children earlier that afternoon, although the kids and his sister, who had traveled from Alabama to take care of them, would continue to stay with friends. The family had been evicted from their apartment during Jorge's incarceration. Joseph Feeney, however, who offered Jorge a temporary place to stay, had managed to save most of the furniture when a neighbor had alerted him to the fact that all of the family's possessions had been put out on the curb. Joplin and Carrie were invited to a celebration dinner at the Hernandez house that night and were toasted, along with Feeney, for everything they had done to help the Martinez family.

———

Libba Ann Cates Woodridge's memorial service was held the next day. Joplin and Carrie, Rosa Esposito, Ike Simmons and his wife, Mary Martucci and Sarah Petersen, Carson Landers, a few attorneys from Healey and Caldwell, including Alston and his wife, and two former beauty pageant contestants who'd kept in touch with Libba over the years, were in attendance. Lucas Graham was conspicuously absent, as well as the other members of the Woodridge family.

The atmosphere in the private room at the Atlanta Botanical Gardens that Julie had reserved was both sad and somber, befitting the death of someone so young. Halloran couldn't help but remember Elliot Carter's funeral, held just three months earlier, and even more devastating to him. He looked over at Julie Benning, her head bowed in grief, and thought of Trip Carter, who'd lost both of his parents within a two-week period. Trip was living with Elliot's mother, Olivia, in Charleston and doing well, but Halloran knew he was still traumatized. He planned on visiting the boy in the near future, now that Jonathan Demarest had been charged with Libba's attack, as well as Maria Sanchez' murder and five others. The lawsuit brought by the Bennings and Arliss' sisters hadn't gone away, but he would deal with it. The handwriting expert had confirmed that the note left by Libba was, indeed, written by her, and he would vigorously fight the suit.

After a prayer led by a minister from Peachtree Road Methodist Church, which Libba and Arliss had attended, Julie stood and asked if anyone would like to say a few words about Libba.

"Do you want to say anything" Halloran said quietly to Maggie.

"I don't think I can, Tom," she said, tearing up.

He turned to look at Joplin, but noticed him whispering something in Carrie's ear. He was happy that the couple seemed to have resolved whatever problem they were having. Turning away from them, Halloran rose and cleared his throat. Heads turned to look at him, and he took a deep breath. "I would," he said, his voice sounding husky to him.

———

On Friday, Joplin got a phone call from Dr. Mallory's nurse, who managed to pin him down on a date for his resection surgery. He'd pretty much forgotten about the surgery with everything that was going on and, at a very deep level, had hoped that Dr. Mallory had as well.

"I was thinking two weeks from now would be good," the nurse prattled on as he tried to clear his head. "Doctor has surgery on Mondays, Wednesdays, and Thursdays, and he has slot available at ten a.m. September 13th. Would that work for you, Mr. Joplin?"

He was tempted to tell her that it would absolutely *not* work for him, for a number of reasons, when an image of Carrie from the night before, her hair splayed out on the pillow next to his, popped into his head. He also remembered his recent realization that things had changed for him, and that he needed to keep moving forward because of that. Because of Carrie, really.

"I think so, yes," he said finally.

"Do you need to check your schedule, Mr. Joplin? You don't sound very sure."

"No, that'll be fine. I'll make sure I can take the time off."

"Okay. Expect to hear from Admissions in the next few days about pre-registration and any restrictions on diet and medication before the surgery."

"Will do," Joplin assured her, then clicked off. He sat at his desk and contemplated his navel and the future for several minutes, then sighed and turned back to his computer to finish a report.

He hoped he was stepping into a brave, new world.

————

That night at 7:30, Joplin pulled up in front of Carrie's condominium on Lenox Road and parked. He was eager to tell her about his upcoming surgery, but he also just wanted to be with her. They hadn't really seen much of each other since the party at the Hernandez house on Wednesday, what with all the media attention about the Demarest case. The ME's office had had to deal with almost as much of it as the Atlanta police and the FBI field office. There wasn't much that could be reported, however, because Demarest had clammed up since asking for his attorney, and the forensic evidence wasn't being released. Except through leaked channels, of course, which wasn't surprising.

As Joplin got out of the car, he *was* surprised to note that there were no lights on in the condominium, not even in Carrie's bedroom. Reflexively, he looked at his watch, although he knew he hadn't mistaken the time. Just as he thought, he was there at the right time; it was 7:31p.m by then. Puzzled, but not yet alarmed, he went quickly up the front steps and rang the doorbell. When there was no response, he reached for the doorknob and was then properly alarmed, because it turned in his hand. Knowing that Carrie would never have left her door unlocked, he rushed into the entry hall, calling her name. He'd only taken three or four steps when his head exploded in pain and he fell, unconscious, to the floor.

CHAPTER FORTY-EIGHT

When Joplin opened his eyes, he had no idea where he was or how much time had passed. His wrists and ankles were bound behind him, and his eyes were covered with some kind of cloth. He was lying on his side. The pungent, acrid smell of vomit assaulted his nostrils, and since it smelled like it was on him or very near him, he figured it was his. He also felt dizzy, which was odd, because he had no way of seeing anything spinning in front of him, then decided it had something to do with the throbbing coming from the back of his head. He took a deep breath and tried to gather his thoughts, but the sudden realization that the person who had knocked him unconscious had either killed or kidnapped Carrie made this impossible, and he began to hyperventilate.

Willing himself to focus on what he should do next, Joplin slowed his breathing and his heart rate. He made a concerted effort to listen to the sounds around him and heard a faint buzz of traffic, then a clock ticking nearby. Relief flooded through him as he realized he was still in Carrie's condominium, probably still in the entry hall, because he recognized the sound of the grandfather clock he'd seen the few times she'd allowed him to pick her up there. This spurred him to turn his head from side to side, and he managed to work the blindfold off of it.

Blinking, Joplin saw that he was, indeed, in Carrie's entry hall. Weak light filtered in through the half-moon transom above the door and the windows in the living room to the left of the hall; he knew that not too much time had passed since he'd gotten there. It didn't get dark in Atlanta in that time of year until around eight p.m. There didn't seem to be any lights on in the condominium, though, so he needed to try to get free before darkness fell.

He straightened his legs, then lurched to a sitting position. Slowly, laboriously digging his heels into the wood floor, he rump-scooted into the hall next to the stairs. A few minutes later he had made it to the work island in the kitchen's center. Knowing he wouldn't be able to stand unless he could free either his wrists or his ankles, Joplin positioned his head under one of the island's drawers and bumped against the handle until he could feel it pulling away enough so that he could thud against the underside of the drawer. He did this until it was loosened from its track and crashed down beside him, praying all the while that it contained utensils—preferably knives—and not dish towel or pot holders.

The sound of clashing metal thrilled him beyond words, and he was soon able to grasp a paring knife from behind and begin the agonizingly slow process of cutting through the duct tape around his wrists. Once this was accomplished, he made short work of the tape around his ankles. Still dizzy, he clutched the island counter and pulled himself up. When he was fairly certain that he could remain standing, Joplin felt for his phone in his blazer pocket and was relieved to find it. He was about to call Ike Simmons and let him know what had happened, when he felt something warm and wet trickling down his neck.

He reached up and felt an egg-sized lump on the back of his heard, and his hand came away smeared with blood. "Goddammit!" he said loudly, then winced as the back of his head throbbed in complaint. He couldn't worry about that now, he decided, and although he was convinced that neither Carrie nor the person who had assaulted and tied him up was still there, Joplin made a search of the condominium, pausing every now and then to stop his head from spinning.

He found Carrie's purse upstairs in the master bedroom on a chair next to the window, as well as signs that she'd changed out of her work clothes and into whatever she intended to wear that night. The pair of black flats he'd seen her in at the ME's office now lay on the floor of her walk-in closet, as well as the black slacks and blue blouse she'd worn under her lab coat, in a heap next to the shoes. He had no idea what she might have changed into, but he noticed a small red Fendi purse that sat next to a cloth storage bag on the floor as well. For some reason, though, Carrie had evidently stopped what she was doing because…because she'd heard something downstairs? Because someone had come into the bedroom and surprised her? He had no idea; there were no signs of a struggle, so he assumed that the first scenario was more likely, but it was only an assumption.

Joplin left the closet and walked back to where the other purse was. A quick check showed that her keys, wallet and cell phone were still in it, which meant that she probably hadn't been attacked in her bedroom. It seemed more likely that she'd heard a noise and gone back downstairs to check it out. Hastily, he checked out the second bedroom and bath down the hall. When those, too, proved to be empty, he hurried back downstairs and walked into the living room, looking for anything that might tell him what had happened.

It had now grown darker, so Joplin turned on an overhead light. Again, there were no signs of a struggle, but he noticed some marks on the wood floor not covered by the thick Persian rug that almost filled the room. They were more like scuffs, really, but they had scratched the wood's veneer. Joplin got down on his hands and knees—slowly, so as not to aggravate his head wound—and looked at the marks more closely. This time he saw more than just scuff marks. There appeared to be small indentations in the wood, like from cleats of some kind.

Golf shoes? he wondered, trying to think of someone in the crowd of suspects who was an avid golfer. Wesley Benning came to mind; most attorneys, in his experience were golfers. Maybe even Claudia Benning, although the idea that a woman could have cold-cocked him and taped him up was humiliating. He didn't see Jorge as a golfer, but maybe he wore cleated shoes when he aerated lawns. It was a possibility, anyway.

Julie's boyfriend was a possibility, as well; doctors often spent a lot of time on the golf course, if his memory of early office hours on Wednesday for most of his own doctors, specifically for that purpose, served him well. But Lucas Graham was still a resident, which didn't fit the whole golfing thing. Julie was very athletic, of course, but his mind immediately rejected her as a suspect. Then, of course, there was Jake Pennington, the doctor who'd given his friend a portrait of a woman painted in blood. He'd never met the man, but there was still something fishy about the whole story. And as he'd pointed out to Carrie, doctors knew about Ringer's Lactate just as medics did.

Frustrated, Joplin took out his phone to call Ike, but realized that all he could tell him was that Carrie had been abducted by someone, and that he'd been assaulted and tied up. He still had no idea about the *who* and the *where,* and both were crucial. Simmons could bring a CSU team over to search for evidence, but his gut told him that Carrie would probably be dead before they came up with anything, and he couldn't let that happen.

Think, he said to himself, trying not to lose control. Yet the only connections he could make between the events of the past week and Carrie's abduction were that Jonathan Demarest had been arrested, and Jorge had been released.

Jorge had been released.

Joplin stood stock-still in the living room. Did that mean that Jorge had been Libba's attacker and his wife's killer all along? Was he also the serial killer? But, if so, how had blood from the victims been mixed in with Jonathan Demarest's paintings? Were they partners in all the murders, like the ones he'd described to Tom Halloran? And as his mind considered this possibility, images began to flood his brain without any rhyme or reason: news coverage of the London Olympics; the gas station on Roswell where Maria Sanchez had been murdered; Halloran pointing out the vertical jumps on the video made of Libba's attack; Carrie asking how Jonathan Demarest would know about potassium lactate.

A mind-boggling scenario emerged that could explain most, if not all, of the terrible events that had happened in the past month, maybe well before that. Even the marks on the floor in Carrie's living room. He still didn't understand the part that Libba had played in all of this; she was the only anomaly in the case. But the scenario meant that Maria Sanchez' murder must have been one of necessity, not compulsion, he decided. Once again, he was about to call Ike Simmons when it occurred to him that he still had no idea where Carrie was. And time was running out, especially if what he believed was true.

And if what he believed was true, Carrie's body was one that would be found very quickly.

———

"Jimmy, do you know where Jorge is right now?" Joplin asked as he pulled out of Carrie's condominium complex onto Lenox Road.

"Why are you asking?" Hernandez said, sounding suspicious.

"Just tell me. Do you know?"

"No, Hollis. I don't. He was over here this afternoon with his kids. We're trying to get them another apartment, you know? They stayed for dinner, then Jorge said he was going to take them back to the neighbors' house, where they're staying. What's going on?"

"He's got a car, then?"

"Yes. I helped him get it out of the police impound on Wednesday."

"What's the make and color, Jimmy?"

"Why do you want to know, Hollis? Is Jorge in trouble again?"

"He might be," said Joplin. "And that's all I can tell you right now. You'll just have to trust me."

Without hesitation, Hernandez said, "His car is a blue Toyota Corolla. A 2009."

"Does he have a cell phone?"

"Yes," said Hernandez, still sounding irritated, but he gave him the number.

"What's Feeney's address? In case I can't get hold of Jorge?"

Ignoring Hernandez's questions after getting the address, Joplin hung up and tried Jorge's cell phone. It went immediately to voice mail. He left a message, but without much hope that it would be answered. Trying not to panic, he tapped in Ike's number and also got voice mail. Cursing, he called 911 and identified himself, requesting that Detective Simmons be contacted immediately and giving Joseph Feeney's address in Dunwoody.

———

Simmons called as Joplin was getting off 400 at the Abernathy exit. He'd made good time, despite the Saturday night traffic, since he'd used his portable siren and light. Quickly, he filled the detective in on what had happened, brushing off Ike's obvious reluctance to believe what he was hearing.

"This is crazy, Hollis! What the hell makes you think that—"

"I don't have time to explain, Ike. I'm turning onto Spaulding now, and I need to shut off my siren and light. Just get here as soon as you can, okay? And see if your FBI buddies will join us. But tell them we need to surprise the guy, or he might kill Carrie sooner rather than later." Joplin clicked off without waiting for Simmons' response, then turned onto Franklin Lane. Feeney's house, an older ranch set back on a sloping lot, had lights on in the living room. There was a prominent ADT Security sign next to the mail box, and Jorge's blue Toyota Corolla sat in the driveway. Next to it was a white van with Atlanta LawnCare printed on it.

He drove past the house and parked a few hundred yards down the street. Before getting out of the car, he pulled his service weapon out from under the driver's seat and stuck it into his waistband. Then he headed towards Feeney's house, silently praying that Carrie was still alive.

Remembering what had happened the last time he'd decided to take matters into his own hands without waiting for back-up, Joplin managed to keep himself from storming the house. It was barely three months ago that he'd hidden in Dr. Paul Woodley's office in the IBM Tower in a desperate attempt to catch the murderer of three people and almost gotten himself killed. But he couldn't just stand there with his thumb up his ass until Ike and the FBI arrived. He decided that scoping out the perimeter of the house wouldn't hurt, though, especially since the sun had finally set and he'd have the cover of darkness. Cautiously, he walked between Feeney's house and the one next to it, being careful to stay on the neighbor's lot. As he passed the Corolla, he looked to see if anyone was in it, but saw only a child's hoodie. Resisting the urge to try to open the trunk, he kept going.

The patio at the back of the house was lit only by a light from the inside, probably the one he'd seen in the living room. Another ADT sign had been pasted onto the back door. Joplin could detect no movement inside the house, but he did hear a faint sound of music coming from somewhere. He pulled his weapon from his waistband and walked around to the far side of the house. Two double windows were there, but no light came from them, and there were no smaller windows lower down to indicate a basement. Puzzled, Joplin was debating whether to go back and try the patio door, when he heard a car turn onto Franklin Lane. Then another. Holding his gun at the side of his leg, he quietly retraced his footsteps and went to meet what he hoped was his backup.

———

After a brief conference, in which Joplin outlined his theory and listed the reasons why he thought Carrie was being held captive inside Feeney's house, and the phrases "exigent circumstances," "imminent danger," and "hot pursuit" were thrown around, it was decided that they had the right to enter the house without a warrant. Joplin, who claimed to be the best at breaking and entering, led the way with a set of lock picks he always kept in his trunk. He'd warned the group about the security system, but they'd decided that even if it were on, the element of surprise would give them enough time to swarm the house and get to Carrie in time. Leaving her in there any longer wasn't an option if they were dealing with someone who'd killed at least six women. Joplin had also told them that he was pretty sure there was a basement in the house, and that he believed that was where she was being kept. He was also concerned for the safety of Mrs. Feeney, who, he'd been told by Jimmy Hernandez, was confined to the house because of lupus.

They approached the back door quietly and cautiously, all weapons drawn. Joplin worked the locks, and nobody breathed when he opened the door. Their luck seemed to be holding; the alarm hadn't been turned on. Once they were in, each man was responsible for checking and clearing a room. A bedroom at the back of the house, which Joplin checked, was furnished with a hospital bed and an IV stand; there were prescription drug bottles on the bedside table and women's clothes in the closet, but the woman herself was nowhere to be seen, which alarmed him. He headed for the kitchen, where he found the others; each man shook his head to show that no one had been found in the house. Silently, they gathered in front of a door which seemed to lead to a basement or downstairs den. The music Joplin had heard from outside the house seeped through the door.

Danny Ringel, one of the FBI agents, gave a series of hand signals indicating that they would deploy the offensive they'd discussed in the event there was a basement, as Joplin had speculated. Accordingly, they waited for his count of three, then followed him as he rushed down the stairs, yelling, "FBI! Throw down your weapons! Hands in the air!"

Gunfire erupted from below almost immediately. Joplin heard a woman scream, then the guttural sound of someone in pain. He saw Ringel fall from midway on the stairs, Joe Delano, his partner, diving after him. He and Simmons were behind the partial wall that covered half of the stairs, but Joplin returned fire, shooting straight ahead as he threw himself down the stairs in a desperate effort to protect the two agents, yet avoid hitting Carrie.

He dove for the floor, then quickly swiveled, his hands instinctively bringing his weapon up to a firing position. Joe Delano did the same, and as they stared straight ahead into the basement, they were each hit by the sight of Joseph Feeney towering above them as he leveled his own weapon at them. He was wearing the same Ossur Flex-Foot Cheetah legs that Oscar Pistorius had worn at the London Olympics. Except the race they were all running was about survival, and no medals would be given out.

Joplin's eyes remained locked on Feeney's, which showed a calculated madness that he had seen before, especially in his dreams. But his peripheral vision allowed him to see Carrie, propped up against a wall to his right. Her ankles were bound, straight out in front of her, and her arms were secured behind her. He saw Jorge next to her, also tied up, but on his side and seemingly unconscious. Straight ahead, just to the right of Feeney's head, he could see a large painting lit from below, as if it were in an art gallery. In a place of honor. It was the painting he'd seen in the crime scene photos Hernandez had shown him.

The woman outlined in blood.

CHAPTER FORTY-NINE

Ike Simmons crouched on the stairs, sweat pouring down his face despite the coolness wafting up from the basement.

"Drop your weapon, Feeney!" he heard Joe Delano yell and knew that Hollis had been right. He'd been skeptical, right up to the end, even after he'd heard all the reasons his former partner had given for believing that a paraplegic who was a decorated veteran was also a serial killer.

"I don't think so," he heard Feeney say. "I really don't mind dying today. Especially since I can take out one of you guys before I do. Won't be as much fun as what I had planned for the doctor, here, but a kill's a kill, right?"

"Why didn't you kill Libba Woodridge then?" he heard Hollis ask. "What was that all about?"

"I guess that's for me to know, and you to find out, isn't it?" Simmons could almost see the smirk on Feeney's face. "She was special, and that's all I'm going to say."

"And Maria Sanchez wasn't?" Hollis asked.

"Actually, she was just an accident. I was on my way to meet a prostitute in Midtown, but I had to stop for gas. She saw me get out of my van wearing my special legs, so I had to get rid of her."

"Yeah, but you made her look just like Libba," Hollis said. "The way you left her, I mean. Just like some of the prostitutes you killed. Like the women in Jonathan Demarest's paintings. You have one of his paintings over there. Is he your partner?"

Simmons heard a derisive snort, followed by laughter. "You're kidding me! Jonathan? He's just a wannabe. I found that painting at an estate sale about two years ago. My wife liked to go to them when she could still get out. And when I saw the artist's name, I realized that I knew him—from when we were kids. So I found out where he lived, and I put a flyer in his mailbox, advertising my services. When he called, he said he recognized my name, but I played dumb and acted like it was an amazing coincidence that we'd reconnected. Anyway, he signed with us. After that, we got together on a pretty regular basis, and I gave him some ideas—for some other paintings. I used to go by his house, ask him how my guys were doing, talk to him about his work, that kind of thing. I just used the wheel chair around him though. Then, when he started painting those outlines, like I'd suggested to him a few times, saying it would be cool, I began mixing in some of my ladies' blood into his red paint. I'd made a paraffin copy of his house key by swiping his keys one time when I got him talking about art and all that. It was easy; artists are such bottomless pits of ego-stroking, you know? They need a lot of props and kudos."

"You mixed the blood with Ringers Lactate, right?" said Joplin. "Something you would have used a lot when you were a medic during the war."

"You bet. Worked like a charm. And it was my little secret until that attorney bought one of Jonathan's paintings and had it analyzed."

"How did you know about that?" Joplin asked.

Feeney gave a big laugh. "The lawyer I bought for Jorge told me all about the connection to the serial murders. So I had to come up with a new plan."

"To implicate Jorge again," said Hollis.

"You got it," said Feeney, sounding smug.

"Why not just kill another prostitute? Why Dr. Salinger?"

"Because it had to be someone the police would look for and find right away. Not like…the others. And when I met her at Jimmy Hernandez's house the other night, I thought she was pretty sexy, if you know what I mean." Feeney gave a sick chuckle that put ice in Simmons' veins. "And I think you do, right? You two looked pretty tight. What I don't really get is how you figured out where she was. And that it was me who took her, not Jorge."

"I saw the marks on the floor in Carrie's living room," said Hollis. "And I remembered the up-and-down motion of the camera taking the video of Libba Woodridge's attack. Then I saw a replay in my head of all the Olympic coverage of Oscar Pistorius in London and his 'special legs,' as you call them. I remembered Carrie saying that Ringer's Lactate would contain potassium lactate, and that a medic, like Jorge, would use Ringer's Lactate. Then I finally remembered that you'd been a medic, too."

Joseph Feeney didn't respond for several seconds, and Simmons tensed again, ready to act.

"Where is your wife, by the way, Feeney?" Delano asked suddenly, as if to diffuse the almost palpable tension.

There was a pause, then Feeney said, "Amy? She died about a year ago."

"Natural causes?" the agent asked.

"I really think lupus is a pretty *unnatural* way to die, but, yeah, she died on her own, if that's what you mean. I don't think she trusted me too much at the end, but what could she do about it, really? She couldn't get out of bed by then, you know?"

"Connie Sue Cates didn't die of natural causes, though," Hollis said, and Simmons held his breath, knowing the tension would rev up again. "And her death wasn't a suicide either. It was a pretty sick way to kill someone, wasn't it, Feeney? A meat skewer shoved up her vagina? Sounds like something you'd do."

"I don't have anything to say about that bitch, except that she deserved to die," Feeney spat out. "Now, either you lay your weapons down or I'm gonna shoot one of you."

Simmons' hand tensed around his weapon, wondering what he should do. If he rushed down the stairs and started firing, he risked shooting either Carrie or Jorge Martinez, and Feeney might have time to get off a round aimed at Hollis or Delano. His knees and quads ached as he continued to crouch, hoping to hear or see some kind of sign from Hollis telling him what to do. He couldn't see Delano, but he had a clear sight on his former partner, and he sent him mental messages asking him to give him a heads up.

As if he were receiving those messages, Hollis jerked his head to the right, then looked down. "You okay, Carrie?" he asked. "I know you can't talk, but just nod your head." There were a few seconds of silence, then Hollis said, "Okay, Joseph, I don't really have a choice, do I? If you promise not to shoot us, Joe and I will drop our weapons, and you can hop up the stairs on your special legs and make a clean getaway. We'll give you a ten-minute start. That sound good?"

The response was more laughter from Feeney. "You think I'm stupid? You'd have cops on me before I got to 400."

Simmons heard Hollis sigh, then say, "You got me, Joseph. I was just trying to distract you."

It was the cue Ike Simmons was waiting for. He sprang into action, hollering "Feeney!" as loudly as he could as he bounded down the stairs. He was able to catch sight of the killer's shocked face before the basement exploded into gunfire. By the time he made it to the bottom, Joseph Feeney was sprawled on the floor, blood streaming from several wounds, with Hollis and Joe Delano still pointing their weapons at him. He heard Carrie screaming from the other side of the room and rushed toward her, his shoes slipping in the blood on the concrete floor.

Halloran was fixing his third Friday-night Glenlivet when Maggie cried out, "Tom, you've got to see this!" He made his way to the family room, where she sat staring at the flat-screen TV encased in a mahogany armoire.

He heard the anchor say that there was 'breaking news on a hostage situation taking place in Dunwoody, with reports that a suspect and a law enforcement officer have been shot.' He stood, riveted by the screen, as the reporter mentioned the name Jorge Martinez and referred to the serial murders that had been featured on previous broadcasts, unable to sit or contain the guilt and stress that engulfed him.

The guilt was because he felt responsible for whatever carnage had taken place. He was certain that giving the video of Libba's attack had precipitated the release of Jorge Martinez and whatever "hostage situation" had occurred. The almost overwhelming stress was because he had no idea who the "law enforcement officer" who had been shot was. It could have been anyone involved with the case, but, God help him, all he hoped was that it wasn't Ike Simmons or the man he'd come to think of as one of the best friends he had in this life. Even if the feeling wasn't reciprocated.

As if reading his mind, Maggie said, "It might not be Hollis, Tom. Or Ike Simmons."

"I know," he said, but his hand gripped his glass even more tightly.

———

Halloran tried Joplin's cell, then Simmons' when it went to voice mail.

"Ike," he said quickly, when the detective answered. "You're alive."

"Damned straight I'm alive!" said the detective. "And so are Carrie and Hollis."

"Carrie?" Halloran said, then let out a long breath, not realizing till then that he'd been holding it. "You mean, she was the hostage? I just saw it on the news."

"One of them. The other was Jorge Martinez."

Whether it was the alcohol or the magnitude of what had just happened,

Halloran just couldn't process what Ike was saying. "Jorge? I thought he was the suspect."

He listened as Ike Simmons explained what had been going on, sitting down at last next to Maggie, dumbfounded, as he heard about Hollis and Simmons and the FBI agents storming Joseph Feeney's house. And that Feeney himself was the serial murderer who had killed the prostitutes and Maria Sanchez, and had also admitted to attacking Libba Woodridge.

"None of this makes sense, Ike," he said when Simmons paused. "Feeney's a paraplegic, and he's been *helping* Jorge."

"Not helping Jorge—he was framing him, using him as the fall guy for the attack on Libba and the murder of Jorge's wife, as well as the serial killings. Only he was also roping Jonathan Demarest into those murders. Listen, Tom, things are still pretty crazy around here, and I've gotta go. Why don't you give Hollis a call tomorrow, and he'll lay the whole thing out."

"Just tell me who was shot first, Ike."

"It was Danny Ringel, one of the FBI agents. Looks like he's gonna make it, though. He and Carrie have been taken to Grady."

Alarmed, he said, "What happened to Carrie?"

"She was roughed up some, and she's in shock, so the EMTs thought she should be checked out. Hollis went in the ambulance with her, which was a good thing, because in the ER they determined he had a mild concussion. Feeney knocked him out with a hammer when Hollis went to pick Carrie up at her apartment. Jorge was roughed up, too, but he refused go to the hospital. Said he just wanted to go be with his kids. I don't blame the guy, actually."

"Please tell me what's going on, Tom," Maggie interrupted. "I'm going crazy."

Halloran raised a hand, then thanked Ike Simmons and said goodbye. He looked over at Maggie and said, "I don't even know where to begin."

"Then just jump in and give it your best shot, because otherwise I'm going to hit you," she said. "What the hell is going on?"

"Hell doesn't even begin to describe it," Halloran said.

CHAPTER FIFTY

Carrie was staying with her parents for a while, Halloran learned when he called Joplin the next morning. The Salingers had rushed to Grady as soon as they'd heard what had happened, then insisted she go home with them. According to Joplin, she hadn't protested too much, not wanting to return to her condominium, and he hadn't blamed her.

"Simmons told me she got roughed up some, but I'm sure that doesn't hold a candle to the emotional and psychological trauma she went through. For you either."

He heard Joplin sigh. "Her parents thanked me for getting to her in time, but I could tell that they think she would never have been kidnapped and almost killed if she weren't working at the ME's office. Or if she weren't involved with me."

"Don't beat yourself up over this, Hollis," said Halloran, although he knew that if his work ever put Maggie or his children in danger, he'd never forgive himself. "Carrie's decision to switch fields was her's, and I'm sure she doesn't blame you."

"Yeah, well, we'll see. This is the second time she's had to deal with a psychopath in the past six months, you know? Listen, I'm sure you want to hear about what went down, but I really don't want to leave this apartment. The media's circling my building, and Quincy's on high alert. He won't get off my lap. How 'bout if I order some pizzas tonight, and you and Maggie come over here? I cleaned up last Sunday, so it's not as bad as it usually is. And Papa John's voted me 'Customer of the Month' a few weeks ago."

"We'd love to," said Halloran, although he knew Maggie wouldn't be very enthusiastic about a Papa John's pizza. "But only if we can bring the liquid refreshments. And maybe a salad," he added quickly.

"You're on," said Joplin.

———

"I just feel like we're missing something," said Halloran as they sat in Joplin's living room eating pizza and the healthy antipasto salad Maggie had made. She had also given Quincy some Chick-fil-a nuggets they'd bought on the way. The cat had scarfed them down and was now parked at her side, his blue eyes filled with adoration, as well as hope that she would share whatever she was eating. Joplin had told them everything that had happened the night before, as well as what had been discovered since.

"That's what I said to Ike when he liked Demarest for the all the murders and the attack on Libba," Joplin said as he helped himself to another slice of the 'Ultimate Meats Pizza.' "I just couldn't see it, though. And now we know that it was Joseph Feeney all along, manipulating Demarest and framing both him and Jorge. Demarest wouldn't have had access to Libba's beauty pageant sash, but Feeney evidently figured out how to bypass the security code so he could get into the house and attack Libba. He took the sash that night, maybe as a souvenir. And the other things I told you about: some pictures of her from the pageants and with Julie, for some reason." He turned to Maggie and said, "And what you saw in the video—the vertical movements—correspond with someone wearing those Cheetah prostheses, Maggie. That was amazing, kiddo."

Maggie raised her glass. "Thank you, Hollis. But I still don't understand why he attacked her in the first place. I mean, he extorted a million dollars from her, but it seems more…personal than that. Like Connie Sue's murder."

"That's because it was, in my opinion. I can't prove it yet, because Demarest still hasn't talked to us, and Feeney wouldn't tell me, but he did say that he and Demarest knew each other when they were kids. I think they met when they were in a foster home. I think Joseph Feeney was Libba Ann's biological brother. Which means Connie Sue was the woman who wouldn't adopt him."

There was a long silence after this, during which both Hallorans seemed to be considering this latest twist in an already twisted case. Finally, Tom Halloran said, "I think you're right, Hollis, although I still believe there's more to the case than Feeney would admit to you. Demarest could still have been involved somehow. But we might not need to wait for him to start talking. I'm hoping to get a response this week from Judge Stephens in Glynn County regarding my petition to get Libba's adoption records unsealed. It might answer a lot of questions."

———

On Monday, Carrie moved in with Joplin. She had thanked her parents for their support, she told Joplin, but didn't want to stay with them any longer. She also didn't want to go back to her condominium. After contacting a real estate agent, she'd come into the ME's office and announced her intention of moving in with Joplin.

"It's just temporary," she said, as they talked in her office. "Your place is too small, and mine has too many bad memories. I just can't go back there, Hollis."

"I don't want you to," he said quickly. "What did you have in mind?"

She lowered her eyes, then looked up at him. "Well, I could get another place or…we could find one that accommodates both of us."

"Which I couldn't afford, on my salary," said Joplin. "Of course, I've always wanted to be a kept man."

"Have you?" she asked, hopefully.

"Not on your life."

"Well, then," she said, rearranging some pens on her desk. "I guess I better look around for another apartment."

Joplin cleared his throat. "We could make my apartment more…Jewish-American princess-friendly," he offered, smiling.

"I am *not* a JAP," she said, eyes flaring.

"Forget I said that," said Joplin quickly. "What I mean is that I could move some of my furniture out—probably most of it—and you could move some of your furniture in. Does that sound like a plan?"

"Yes," she said, drawing the word out so that it sounded like, "no."

"Do you have a better idea?"

"Well, there are some loft condominiums right up the street that are renting for way below the normal rate, due to the economy and the fact that nobody can sell them. I think I could negotiate a rent that we could share. Sound interesting?"

"Living with *you* sounds interesting, Carrie," said Joplin, staring at her with a tenderness he hoped she could see. He had known he loved her for a long time, but when he'd almost lost her—again—he also knew he wanted to be with her for the rest of his life. "I love those lofts, even though they're pretty contemporary."

She cocked her head. "And your apartment is…what? Sixties Dilapidated?"

"Point taken. Negotiate away," he added, waving his hand. "Just let me bring two things: my leather Barcalounger and Quincy."

She stood up and came around her desk. Leaning down, she gave him a long, slow kiss with tongue.

"Quincy is always welcome."

———

On Tuesday, Halloran received a call from Judge Mark Stephens' clerk at the Glynn County Family Court notifying him that the judge would see him in his chambers, to respond to his petition, that Thursday if he could make it down to Brunswick. It was an unexpected concession, especially since the petition had only been filed the week before.

"I really appreciate the judge offering to do that," Halloran said. "I'm pretty sure I can get a flight to Brunswick sometime tomorrow. What time would the judge want to see me on Thursday?"

"Preferably before court," said the clerk, who'd identified herself as Ginny Parsons. "Eight a.m., if you can make it. The information contained in your petition has been kept strictly confidential, and that's really why he suggested a hearing in chambers. You're pretty well-known, Mr. Halloran, and he doesn't want this matter turned into a circus like they've done in Atlanta. We've all been following the ongoing lawsuit down here. And what happened to Libba Ann. She was one of ours, so to speak."

"She'd appreciate that," he said softly.

"Unless I hear back from you by five today, we'll expect you then," said Parsons.

"Thanks again."

Halloran sat at his desk for several minutes, going over the phone call. From what he could tell, it seemed like the judge viewed the hearing as something he needed to hold simply for the record. Whether that meant he intended to deny the petition, but wanted to explain his reasons in private, given all the media attention the Woodridge case had attracted, or that he intended to turn over the unsealed records directly to him, Halloran had no idea. He certainly hoped it was the latter, especially since he'd be out of the office for two days. But if it would shed more light on the reason for Libba's ending her life, as well the connection to Joseph Feeney, it would be worth it. After looking at his schedule for Wednesday and Thursday, he got Joan on the phone to make plane reservations for him to fly to Golden Isles Airport in Brunswick the next day and to reschedule his appointments.

———

Carrie leased a two-bedroom unit at the Mathieson Exchange Lofts on Wednesday. Only her name was on the lease, but, as agreed, after swallowing hard when he saw the monthly rent, Joplin insisted on paying half of it. Despite her apparent resilience after Feeney had kidnapped and almost killed her, he knew the desire to move immediately from her condominium reflected an inner panic and fear that he understood completely. He had felt the same way during his stay at Grady. But instead of moving on, as Carrie seemed to be doing, he had simply been running in place. Joplin had taken steps to change that, by scheduling his surgery and committing himself to their relationship; now he wanted to move ahead *with* her.

Even if it meant giving up his beloved Barcalounger.

Her voice full of excitement, Carrie asked him to meet her at the apartment during his lunch break. When he got there, she was standing near the tall Palladian windows that overlooked Peachtree. She turned to look at him, her face glowing, and swept an arm around the high-ceilinged room.

"Don't you love the brick walls and the hardwood floors, Hollis?" she asked.

"I do," he said, smiling. "This is more than I expected. I mean, architecturally," he added. "I really like the details."

She walked over to him and took his hand, pulling him into the kitchen to admire the granite countertops and white cabinets; the silver appliances and gas stove; the wine rack and cooler. Next came the master bedroom and bath on one side, then the guest room and bath on the other side of the entry hall.

"It'll be just ours," she said, after telling him about the fitness center and the concierge, and the rooftop terrace. "Just ours," she repeated, this time with a little more emphasis.

"I can't wait," he said, and found himself meaning it.

CHAPTER FIFTY-ONE

Halloran was in Brunswick by five p.m. the next day. Ed Jenkins picked him up at the airport and drove him to the nearby Marriott Courtyard. They met in the bar thirty minutes later and discussed the judge's somewhat unusual request to hold the hearing in his chambers. Both of them thought the decision on unsealing the records could go either way. Jenkins had nothing new to report and had actually been planning to return to Atlanta when he got Halloran's call about the hearing. When they'd finished their drinks, he suggested going to the Indigo Coastal Shanty in downtown Brunswick for dinner.

"It's a little noisy, but it's a cut above most of the other restaurants here."

"Sounds good," said Halloran. "I want to make it an early night, though. I plan on going right to the airport after I meet with the judge. If you want to ditch your rental car, you can fly back with me, Ed. No sense in your staying here if all the leads have dried up."

"Suits me fine, unless the judge unseals the records and you need me to look into anything else," Jenkins said as they left the bar.

"Well, I can call you as soon as I leave his chambers and let you know. I have an open return to Atlanta, so if nothing else comes up, we can both go sit and wait at the airport."

"I'd love to get home and remind my wife she's still married, Tom, but we really need a break on this case. I don't feel like I've earned my fees."

"Oh, yes, you have, Ed," Halloran said as they walked towards the rental car. "Brunswick's not a bad little town for a few days—or if you're passing through on your way to St. Simon's or Sea Island. But you've been down here almost ten days. Plus, you should get combat pay for finding Connie Sue's body and dealing with all that involved. What's the most expensive thing on this restaurant's menu?"

Jenkins thought about it a minute, then said, "Probably whatever the Daily Catch is. I never checked."

"The Daily Catch it is, then," said Halloran, as he headed to the passenger side of the car. "And maybe their most expensive vodka in a martini with blue cheese olives."

"Damn!" said Jenkins, his usually serious face breaking into a wide smile. "Can I get Hush Puppies, too?"

———

Joplin, Carrie, and Quincy (who now preferred to curl up against Carrie's leg) had gone to bed at nine p.m. At ten, the landline on the table next to Joplin woke him just as he was falling asleep.

"Mister Joplin," said a voice, and he knew at once that it was Libba Woodridge's former housekeeper. Actually, not quite former, since Tom Halloran, as executor, had asked her to stay on until he finished probating the will and doing an inventory of the house and its contents.

"Rosa?" he said, sleepily.

"I am so sorry to call you now. So late, I mean. But you told me to. If I find anything. And I did."

"No, no, that's okay," he said, sitting up in bed. He heard Carrie turn over murmur something. "I'm glad you called. What did you find?"

"Her phone. The cell—you know? You couldn't find it when she...died."

Joplin heard her break into tears, and he said, "It's okay, Rosa. I know how upset you are," when she began apologizing. "Where did you find it?" he asked when the crying subsided a little.

"In my closet," she got out between sobs. "In a purse she give me for Christmas. There was a note, too. She ask me to throw the phone in a creek near the house. Not show it to anybody. But I cannot, Mister Joplin. I think it would be wrong," she added, then broke down completely.

"You did the right thing, Rosa," Joplin said soothingly, then noticed that Carrie was sitting up in bed, too. She turned the lamp on next to her and gave him a questioning look. He held up a finger and waited for the house-keeper to calm down a little. When she finally did, he said, "I can be over there in twenty minutes, Rosa. Just hang on. And don't tell anyone else about this, okay?

"Who am I gonna tell?" she asked plaintively.

———

After telling Carrie about Libba's phone and refusing her offer to go with him, Joplin threw on the clothes he'd piled on the chair in the corner. "I'll be back as soon as I can," he told her as he gathered his wallet, car keys, and evidence bag. "But I need to take the phone to CSU. There must be something pretty important on it, if she wanted Rosa to get rid of it, and I don't want to compromise the chain of custody. Try to go back to sleep, okay? You, too, Quincy," he said to the cat, who was sitting up straight with a reproachful look in his eyes.

"I doubt that's possible, but I'll try. Wake me when you come back, though, if I *am* asleep," she added, stifling a yawn.

Joplin gave her a quick kiss, then was out the door.

———

Rosa met him at the front door, her face still tear-streaked. She was holding a black purse with a long strap. Joplin pulled on latex gloves, then took the purse from her. He ushered her into the living room, which was lit up, then motioned to the large camelback sofa.

"Did you touch the phone, Rosa?" Joplin asked when they were sitting down. He didn't want to just put the purse and the phone into an evidence bag and leave. She was obviously traumatized; not just from finding the phone and the note, but because she had not done what her employer had instructed her to do.

She shook her head. "I was packing it in my suitcase, when I see the note she left. After I read it and saw the phone, I call you. Right away."

"Like I told you when you called, you did the right thing. Even if it doesn't feel like it right now. But this might tell us what happened to Mrs. Woodridge, and that's important."

Rosa nodded. "Si, I know. But she was so good to me, and I couldn't do this for her."

"Is there anyone I can call for you? Someone to come stay with you?"

"I'm going to go to my sister's tonight. I'll come back tomorrow to finish going through things for Mr. Halloran."

"I'm sure he'll be fine with that."

A few minutes later, after putting the purse in an evidence bag and making sure Rosa locked the door behind him, Joplin left. He was sure Tom Halloran would understand why the housekeeper needed to get out of the house that night, but he was also sure the attorney would be very unhappy that she'd turned over the phone to him.

CHAPTER FIFTY-TWO

Halloran was ushered into the judge's chambers at exactly eight a.m. on Thursday morning. Judge Stephens, a lanky tow-head who was almost as tall as he was and appeared to be in his late forties, rose from his chair and reached out to shake his hand.

"Thanks for coming, Mr. Halloran," the judge said, sitting back down. He motioned Halloran to one of the chairs in front of his desk.

Puzzled, Halloran smiled and said, "This was a hearing I petitioned for, Your Honor. I wouldn't have missed it. And, again, I appreciate your holding it in chambers." He glanced around the room. "Are we waiting on the court reporter?"

Judge Stephens, who had also been smiling, now looked somber and said, "No. We don't need a court reporter, because there won't be a hearing."

"I don't understand. Was there something wrong with my petition, Judge?"

"Not at all. And I intend to turn over the records to you, because I agree with your reasons for wanting them. But because of the sensitive nature of what's in them, I don't want any record of our conversation." The judge paused and steepled his fingers. "You have a fiduciary responsibility to your clients— Arliss Woodridge, as well as Libba Ann Woodridge. But the information contained in the records might also be pertinent to an ongoing criminal case."

"You mean, the serial murders in Atlanta and the attack on Libba Woodridge?"

"Yes. The police have a suspect still in custody, according to the news, but it appears that one Joseph Feeney may have been responsible for some or even all of those crimes."

"And the adoption records show that Feeney was Libba Woodridge's brother. Right?"

The judge's eyebrows shot up. "You knew that?"

Halloran nodded. "Not for certain, but we thought so." He explained about Ed Jenkins' interview with Connie Sue Cates' aunt, and Joplin's deduction after his violent encounter with Feeney. "We also think he murdered Connie Sue Cates because she wouldn't adopt him when she adopted Libba."

"Well, it's certainly no excuse for murder, but she left him to suffer a pretty harrowing childhood. I've had his records pulled as well, and it doesn't make us look very good here in Glynn County. The Family and Children's Services has been completely overhauled since Joseph Feeney was in foster care, but it was a mess back in the Eighties. He went through ten different foster homes between the age of four and when he maxed out of the system at age eighteen. And three of them were prosecuted for abuse during that time. Joseph was victimized several times, both physically and sexually."

Halloran took a minute to process this, then said, "Was Jonathan Demarest in any of those homes with him?"

Judge Stephens gave a long sigh and said, "Yes. He was. I requested his records as well, when I saw his name on the list of victims from those abuse cases."

"We thought that might have been how they met—as children in state custody."

"Jonathan's mother was a prostitute who would lock him in a closet from a very young age when she had 'clients' visiting. She also beat him on a regular basis, which is why he became a ward of the court. And then we made his life even worse."

"I think the press published some of the paintings in his gallery showings," said Halloran. "Did you see them?"

"I did. They were horrifying."

"Joseph Feeney told Investigator Joplin that Demarest was just a patsy. That he manipulated him and gave him the ideas for his paintings, but I'm not so sure. Was there anything in his background that would explain the kind of art he produced?" Halloran asked.

Stephens didn't answer right away. Then he said, "The suffering he experienced at the hands of his own mother could certainly have caused him to view mothers in the extremely…negative way he portrayed them in his art, in my opinion. And maybe even to harm women. But I think Feeney was telling the truth when he said that he had influenced Jonathan." He shuffled through the paperwork on his desk and handed Halloran some photographs. "These were also in Joseph Feeney's file. They were taken by the police when the children were found, and given to the counselor in charge of his case. Libba Ann, or Jean Marie Feeney, as she was originally named, was about a year old and extremely malnourished. Joseph was four. He went to a neighbor's house when he found his mother dead and got help."

Halloran looked down at the stack of photos, not sure what he was about to see, but knowing it wouldn't be pleasant. The top one showed a young woman with long blonde hair that was streaked with blood sitting on a floor, her hands out at her sides, her back against a wall. Blood had also spilled down her face and onto a short nightgown. Her legs were splayed out in front of her.

"This photo could have been the model for one of Jonathan Demarest's painting," he said after staring at it a while. "It's also the way Libba Woodridge and Maria Sanchez, another victim, were posed."

"That's Belinda Feeney, the children's mother. She was a known drug addict, and the family was under the so-called "care" of Family Services. When the baby was born with cocaine and heroin in her system, both children were taken away from her, but she entered a program and managed to stay clean for a few months. Just long enough to get the children back." Judge Stephens gave a long sigh. "Why she wanted them back, I have no idea, because evidence after the fact shows she went right back to the drugs within a month."

"This looks like a violent death," Halloran said.

"It was. Her dealer was charged with her murder, according to police and court records I've read. He later admitted it, in exchange for a lighter sentence. His excuse was that she owed him a lot of money and threatened to go to the cops when he wouldn't give her more drugs. He claimed he didn't know the children were in the house that night. That she'd told him they were at a friend's house when she invited him to 'party' with her. He also said he didn't know he'd killed her. Said he just hit her a few times then threw her against the wall in the bedroom to 'get her off me,' in his words."

Halloran pulled his eyes from the photo and said, "And Family Services never knew she was back on drugs?"

The judge shook his head. "As I said, Family and Children's Services has been completely overhauled since the Feeney family was in our care, but they were 'understaffed and overwhelmed,' in their words, back then. Something Atlanta's DFACS system has also claimed in the past ten years."

Halloran nodded at this, then shuffled through the other photos. They showed the living conditions the two children had endured, as well some of the children themselves. Libba, though a beautiful baby, was obviously undernourished, and Joseph looked very small for his age. And very sad. It was difficult to believe that he was the same big-shouldered, jovial man Halloran had met on the grounds of the Woodridge estate. It was also hard to believe this same young child had grown up to be a serial killer.

"I've included some of the newspaper articles about the murder and the children in what I'm giving you," said Judge Stephens. Then he handed Halloran the adoption records. "The original birth certificate is in there, which is one of the main reasons I wanted this meeting to be completely confidential."

Halloran looked up, puzzled, then flipped through to the birth certificate. When he saw the name given for the child's father, he slumped back against his chair. "I can't believe this," he said softly. "No wonder she hoped this information would die with her."

————

Halloran and Ed Jenkins took the noon shuttle back to Atlanta. On the ride to the airport, he'd shared what he'd learned in the judge's chambers with the former GBI agent, who was all for turning the information over to law enforcement. Halloran, however, was still pondering what to do during the flight. He'd discussed the situation further with the judge before leaving his chambers, but Stephens had made it clear that the decision would have to be his.

"Your fiduciary duty to your clients is clear," the judge had said. "But a man's life and liberty are at stake. Then again, you can't really be certain that Joseph Feeney acted alone, can you?"

That was the problem, of course. And yet, despite all the evidence found in Jonathan Demarest's house, Halloran just wasn't convinced that the artist had collaborated with Feeney. As with the evidence found at Jorge's apartment, it might have been planted. Even Feeney himself had discounted Demarest as a killer, telling Hollis Joplin that he had manipulated the artist into creating the paintings that were made to look like crimes scenes. He had also probably told Demarest about the way his mother looked when he'd found her when they'd met as children in some foster home, which would explain the painting of the woman outlined in blood.

The fact that they had both been abused made more of a case for their being partners in crime, but Halloran couldn't get rid of a nagging feeling that someone other than Demarest might be involved, especially where Libba was concerned. Was the attack on her simply revenge because she'd been adopted, and Feeney had been left in foster care? Or was it a scheme to extort a million dollars from her? It could have been both, of course, but then why had she killed herself? He was convinced that she'd somehow found out who her father was, and that had made her decide to commit suicide. But how had she found out? Had Feeney contacted her again somehow? This time to threaten to go public with the information?

Libba's phone had never been found, Halloran remembered. It would have been easy enough to destroy, he supposed. But maybe she wasn't sure the information itself would be destroyed. Like a picture of the birth certificate. Or a telephone number from the person who might have called or texted her. Had she been threatened with exposure unless she changed her will? But why would Joseph Feeney care about that? He couldn't very well turn up as her long-lost brother and make a claim against the estate without bringing a whole lot of attention to himself.

The judge had told Halloran that Feeney had requested the adoption records about a year ago, around the same time his landscape company had been hired by Arliss Woodridge. Had he known Libba was his sister then and put a flier in the mailbox, as he'd done with Jonathan Demarest? The publicity surrounding Arliss and Libba's engagement was at fever pitch then; he must have seen it and known she was his half-sister. But if Feeney had already found out who Libba's real father was, why didn't he just try to blackmail her? Or Arliss? Obviously, he hadn't done that; the couple had gotten married, and Arliss had changed his will and trust to make his young wife and his granddaughter the prime beneficiaries.

And a few months later, he'd died.

Something tugged at Halloran's brain as he thought of Arliss Woodridge's death, but he let it go when he couldn't figure out what was bothering him. His mind returned to Joseph Feeney and the terrible power he had gained when he'd gotten Libba's adoption records unsealed. Who stood to gain— or lose—the most from the identification of her biological father? In terms of loss, the obvious answer was the father himself, but it was highly doubtful that he could have paid much to cover it up. What little he actually knew of the man-made Halloran think that he also might not have wanted to, might have believed he had a moral obligation to tell Arliss and Libba himself, and Feeney would have lost his meal ticket. Besides, he'd been pretty much out of commission for the past few months. Then there were the family members who'd initiated the lawsuit to vacate the new will Arliss Woodridge had drawn up when he'd married Feeney's sister. Half-sister, actually. Feeney's own birth certificate had left the space for the father's name blank.

Another abandonment for the child who would grow up to become a serial killer.

But the identification of the biological father was a double-edged sword. It could be used to overturn Arliss's will, but it would also have brought the kind of shame and public humiliation on the family that Libba had killed herself to prevent. Unless, of course, it could be kept quiet in some way. Halloran remembered Claudia Woodridge telling him that neither insanity nor coercion was the only basis for successfully challenging a will. She'd also said that her mother, Eleanor Woodridge, was her father's only "legal" wife. He now believed he knew what she meant, and that knowledge made the odds that she was the person Joseph Feeney had approached with the terrible secret of Libba's birth very likely.

Judge Stephens' words came back to him as he was trying to decide on his next move. He still had a fiduciary responsibility to his clients—first, Arliss, then Libba—and before he went to the police or even Hollis Joplin with what he now believed had happened, he needed to be sure.

————

Simmons called him at two p.m., just as Joplin was writing up a report on a pedestrian death on Roswell Road. Another young Hispanic trying to cross the road without a crosswalk.

"What's up?" he asked, hoping they'd gotten some information from Libba's phone.

"Just thought I'd let you know that Ricky and I are on our way to interview Libba's biological father. At least, we hope so."

Joplin took a deep, cleansing breath. "You're kidding me. Is that what was on the phone?"

"Yes," said Simmons. "The person who sent her a copy of her birth certificate used a burner phone, so we don't know who that was, but we know what the text message said."

"And what was that? More importantly, who was her father?"

"Her father was Chandler Woodridge," Simmons said.

"Jesus H. Christ! Do you mean to tell me Arliss Woodridge married his biological granddaughter?"

There was a long sigh, then Simmons said, "We've talked about you takin' the Lord's name in vain, Hollis. You know how I feel about that."

"Sorry, Ike, but you gotta admit that's pretty mind-boggling, to say the least." When Simmons didn't respond to this, Joplin said, "I guess we know now what pushed Libba Woodridge over the edge."

"It looks like that. The text informed her that unless she agreed to the terms and conditions brought by the Woodridge family's lawsuit challenging Arliss Woodridge's will and trust, her father's identity would be made public. But the question is: Who did the pushing? We're going to start by assuming Chandler Woodridge might know something about that."

"Isn't he still at Ridgeview?"

"Yes, which is why I said we're hoping to interview the man. I contacted his psychiatrist, and we have a meeting set up for this afternoon, but just to lay out our reasons for needing to talk to Chandler. We might have to get a court order if the doc doesn't grant an interview."

"Good luck with that, Ike. Psychiatrists are on my shit list, too. At least the ones who testify in court. Right behind attorneys."

"I know that's right, Hollis," Simmons chuckled.

CHAPTER FIFTY-THREE

After calling Wesley Benning's office and learning that he'd left early for the day and gone home, Halloran had picked up his car from the North Economy parking lot at the airport and headed for the Park Avenue condominiums in Buckhead. He spent the drive there formulating what he would say to the Bennings when he saw them. If he saw them. There was no guarantee that they would agree to see him, although he was hoping curiosity would overcome caution.

Although the graphologist had verified that Libba had written the note she'd left for him, as well as the holographic will, Halloran had delayed probating the new will. No one, not even Julie, knew that Libba had wanted to nullify the terms of her late husband's will. He now believed that decision had been coerced and, if so, he would do everything he could to keep it out of probate court. Neither Wesley nor Claudia had contacted him since Libba's death, but he was sure they were anxious to know how they were impacted by it. Probably more than just anxious. Arliss had told him that the Bennings had an "underwater" mortgage on their unit as a result of the 2008 housing debacle, and Ed Jenkins had uncovered even more debt after they'd filed the lawsuit.

Halloran turned his car over to the valet at the Park Avenue and entered the lobby. After a brief phone call, during which he seemed to be waiting for a response, the concierge nodded and told him to take the elevator to the penthouse floor. He rode it up thirty stories and was surprised when the doors opened directly into a fairly large entry hall. Black and white tiles and an elegant table graced by a tall flower arrangement greeted him, as did Wesley Benning, drink in hand.

"Come on in," he said cheerfully, raising his glass. "To what do we owe this honor, Tom?"

"I'd rather explain it to both of you, Wesley," said Halloran. "Is Claudia here?"

"Of course," Benning responded, still smiling benignly. "Can I get you a drink first?"

"I'm fine."

"Okay, then, follow me."

———

Claudia Benning was sitting on an extremely large, pale yellow sofa that flanked a marble fireplace. Like her husband, she held a large glass of something, but her expression wasn't friendly or welcoming. Not that Halloran believed the façade that Benning had put on.

"I think you have a lot of nerve asking to see us," she said as they came into the spacious, high-ceilinged living room.

"Claudia, honey, why don't we just hear what Tom has to say?" Wesley Benning intervened. He gestured for Halloran to sit on the equally enormous sofa that flanked the other side of the fireplace, then went to sit down beside his wife.

Halloran again saw the resemblance between Claudia and her mother, but found it hard to believe that Julie was her daughter. Her face had a hard, frozen quality to it, so unlike Julie's warm countenance. Their coloring was similar, though; she and Julie both had blue eyes and blond hair. Just as Libba had, Halloran thought and remembered seeing the two young women together at the little dinner party he and Maggie had given. He recalled thinking that they'd looked like sisters and was surprised to realize how close he'd been to their real relationship at the time. Now, the thought that Julie's mother was also Libba's biological aunt and might have engineered everything that had happened in the past month almost staggered him.

"Well, Tom?" Claudia said pointedly. "We're all ears."

"I just got back from Brunswick," he said, just as pointedly. "I went there to meet with a judge who'd agreed to unseal Libba's adoption records."

He thought her color faded a bit, but she didn't crack. "I had no idea she was adopted," was all she said.

"But you heard that Connie Sue was dead, didn't you? It was in the news."

"Of course," Wesley broke in. "It was in the paper and on TV. Like everything else that had to do with Libba. But there was no report about... about that."

"Dr. Salinger, who performed the autopsy on Libba, requested the autopsy report on Connie Sue and discovered from the blood types listed that she couldn't have been Libba's biological mother."

"How fascinating," said Claudia. "But what does that have to do with us?"

"Do we really have to go through this charade, Claudia?" Halloran asked.

"I have no idea what you're talking about," she said, lifting her jaw, daring him to contradict her.

For a brief moment, Halloran wondered if he'd gotten it all wrong, and Claudia had no idea what he was going to say. Out of the corner of his eye, he noticed that Wesley had turned his whole body to face his wife and was staring at her, a stricken look on his face.

"Your brother, Chandler, was Libba's biological father."

"I don't believe you," Claudia said and looked straight at him.

"Claudia," Wesley said, putting his hand on her arm.

She shook it off, then said, "If you're not man enough to throw him out, Wesley, I'll call Security."

Halloran stared at Wesley Benning. "She didn't know, did she?"

Claudia slammed her glass down on the coffee table between the sofas. "I can't *know* something that isn't true, Tom! You're crazy if you think I'll believe that Chandler fathered that...that girl. Or that my father would have married his own..."

"Granddaughter," Halloran finished, and he pitied her in that moment.

Claudia Woodridge Benning lost all color then and sat back heavily against the sofa cushions.

"Tell her," Halloran said to Wesley.

Wesley cleared his throat, and his wife roused herself to turn and look at him.

"You told me that you'd found out she'd been married before, Wesley," she said slowly. "That she'd never told my father about it, and never divorced the man. Somebody she met in Las Vegas and married in one of those quickie ceremonies. You told me that," she repeated, as if that would make it true.

"I did," he agreed. "Because I didn't want you to know. It would have killed you, Claudia. Honey, I just couldn't tell you something so...sordid. You can understand that, can't you?"

When she didn't answer him, just stared, open-mouthed, Halloran said, "How did you find out, Wesley? From Chandler?"

"Chandler? No. Why would you think that? Chandler's been in rehab since Arliss died. No one's even seen him, as far as I know."

"Then it was Joseph Feeney. He didn't know how to contact your wife directly, so he called you at your office. He also didn't know you and Claudia are almost completely bankrupt, did he? No blackmail money there, and you couldn't even pay him to provide the proof of Libba's birth. So the two of you collaborated on that sick video he made of Libba when he attacked her."

"No!" Wesley Benning insisted. "I had no idea that he was going to do that to her! He was just supposed to scare her into changing the will! I didn't even know he was going to tie her up and do all that stuff to her, I swear!"

"But you found out, didn't you? I'm sure he told you every perverted detail, Wesley. Or maybe he just showed you the video."

"I never saw that," he said, but he looked away, and Halloran was sure he was lying.

"But you helped him blackmail Libba over it, didn't you? You made all the arrangements for the bank in the Cayman Islands. That was his payment for the adoption records. Did Feeney tell you that Libba was his half-sister? That that was how he'd managed to get hold of the records?"

Benning suddenly looked queasy and slowly shook his head. Claudia continued to stare at him as if he were someone she'd never met. "I didn't know about that till later, I swear it. I also had no idea he was involved in all those...murders. I was totally shocked when I saw that on the news. I swear it, Tom!"

"And yet you became a murderer yourself, Wesley. Only your weapon was a cell phone."

"What are you talking about?" he said indignantly. "I've never killed any-one in my life."

"Feeney turned over the adoption papers to you when Libba paid the extortion money. The night she killed herself, you sent pictures of her original birth certificate and threatened to make the fact that she'd married her own grandfather public if she didn't comply with the lawsuit's terms. I can only imagine how completely devastated she was. How humiliated and guilty she felt, even though none of it was her fault. But it worked. For Arliss' sake—and the sake of the family name—she wrote a holographic will changing everything he'd tried to do. Then she left a letter for me telling me she was in her right mind when she did it. And *then* she took her terrible secret with her to her grave. Or thought she did. She was actually a better Woodridge than the whole lot of you put together, except for Julie."

Claudia Benning began to weep, holding her head in her hands. Her hus-band stood up and walked over to the small bar near the entry to the dining room and began to mix himself another drink. But when he turned around, he was holding a gun instead of a glass in his right hand.

———

After talking to Carrie, Joplin reluctantly decided to call Tom Halloran and tell him what forensics had found on Libba's phone. He doubted the attorney would have done the same, given the nature of what was on it. He would probably have convinced himself that he'd be "protecting" his clients or some other legal nonsense. But Carrie had reminded him that Halloran had been extremely forthcoming in the past week, and it was likely that he'd find out that Chandler Woodridge was Libba's father anyway, if the judge in Brunswick unsealed the adoption record.

When Halloran's cell phone went to voice mail, Joplin tried his office, only to be told by his secretary that her boss was out of town. When she wouldn't say where he'd gone, Joplin clicked off and called the Halloran's landline. Maggie answered and told him what he'd already guessed—that Halloran had gotten a call from a judge in Brunswick concerning the adoption records.

"He called from the airport about an hour ago to tell me he was back, but said he needed to make a stop before he went to the office," she said. "Have you tried his cell?"

"I did, but got voice mail. Did he happen to say where he was going?"

"You sound strange, Hollis. Is something wrong?"

"No, of course not," Joplin said, but his voice sounded strange to him, too. Without even understanding why, he was suddenly convinced that Tom Halloran not only knew the identity of Libba's father, he'd decided to confront whoever it was who might have used that information to blackmail her. And cause her to take her own life.

His gut was acting up big time.

"You're scaring me, Hollis. Tell me what's going on. Please."

Joplin sighed. "Probably nothing, Maggie. Really."

"Tell me anyway."

———

"I don't think you want to use that, Wesley," said Halloran carefully.

Claudia Benning turned to look at her husband and put a hand up to her mouth.

"I don't," said Benning. "But I can't let you ruin everything. You said it, yourself: Libba wrote out a new will and left you a letter telling you that's what she wanted to do. That's all I wanted from her, Tom, even if you don't believe me. Just simple justice. She had no right to all that money. Claudia did."

Claudia stood up slowly. "No, Wesley. I didn't. At least, not this way. I was wrong, sweetheart. Are you listening to me? My father had every right to leave his money the way he wanted to, and I shouldn't have tried to fight that. He gave us—me—more than enough while he was alive." She swallowed and said, "I know that now. I just wish I'd realized it sooner. Before I drove you to do these things. It was all my fault, Wesley. My fault that you thought you had to do all this for me. My fault that I was so wrapped up in my own misery that I couldn't see what was happening. If only you'd come to me, told me what you were involved in. I would never have wanted you to do it."

The devastated look on Wesley Benning's face touched even Halloran, drawing him into a family drama that was both a tragedy and a heart-sickening, cold-blooded scheme. Claudia must have been affected by it, too, because she went over to her husband and reached out her right hand.

"Give me the gun, Wesley," she said softly. "I love you. Give me the gun."

Instead, Wesley Benning put the gun to his temple and pulled the trigger.

CHAPTER FIFTY-FOUR

Joplin arrived at the Park Avenue just as an EMT van was leaving. Two APD cars were parked in the valet area. He hurried into the lobby and ran up to the concierge's desk, flashing his badge.

"Penthouse, officer," said the concierge, motioning to the bank of elevators.

The ride to the thirtieth floor seemed interminable. When the doors opened, Joplin found himself in an entry hall and hurried forward, dreading what he might find. A uniform came up to him and put his hands up, cautioning him not to come any further.

"I'm with the ME's office," Joplin said, holding up his badge.

"But we didn't call you," the officer said, looking puzzled. "The victim is still alive. We just sent him to Grady."

"Who was it, for God's sake?" Joplin asked, afraid to know the answer.

"It was Wesley Benning, Hollis," said Tom Halloran, coming into the entry hall. He looked about ten years older than the last time Joplin had seen him. "Not me, but I appreciate the concern."

"Are you okay?"

The attorney gave a weak smile. "I'll live," he said. "Unfortunately, I don't think Wesley will make it."

"How about Mrs. Benning?"

"She went with him in the ambulance."

"Can you tell me what happened?"

Halloran glanced briefly at the uniforms, then nodded. Joplin understood that he was going to get an abbreviated version of what the attorney might tell him later. He listened as Halloran talked about a meeting concerning the upcoming lawsuit that had suddenly gone south, resulting in Wesley Benning, who had been drinking, pulling a gun on him. Claudia Benning had intervened, thinking she could get him to give her the weapon. Instead, Wesley had shot himself in the head. Halloran had performed CPR while she called 911. Claudia had verified his recitation of events when the police arrived as the EMTs were loading Benning onto a gurney.

"We're waiting on a detective squad to get here now," he added.

As if on cue, there was a commotion in the entry hall as the elevator doors opened and a uniform rushed over. Joplin was relieved to see Ike Simmons and Ricky Knox.

Simmons spotted him and walked through to the living room. "We got the call about ten minutes after we'd left Ridgeview," he said. "Got here as fast as we could. I heard a little bit about what happened on the way. Halloran okay?"

"Physically. But I think he'd be a lot better if I could get him out of here. The first on scene took his and Mrs. Benning's statements, and you know where he lives."

Simmons nodded, then looked over at Halloran. "I'll need to come by your house a little later, Tom. But we can find out what we need to know here and at the hospital first."

"Thanks, Ike. I'll be there."

"Jesus! I forgot to call Maggie and let her know you were okay!" Joplin said as they got into the elevator.

"I called her before you got here. There were three or four calls from both of you when I was finally able to get to my phone. How did you know I'd be here anyway?"

"I didn't. Just a good guess," he said, then told Halloran about Libba's cell phone and what was on it. "When Maggie told me you'd just gotten back from Brunswick and had a stop to make, I figured you might be playing detective again." He looked sideways at Halloran, but the attorney didn't respond. The elevator doors opened into the lobby, and Joplin went over and said something to the concierge.

"I told him we're leaving your car here for a while," he said, coming back to Halloran. I'll call Ike from my car and ask him to get one of the uniforms to drop it off at your house."

"You do this for all your friends, Hollis?"

"I'm just glad I didn't have to save your ass again this time, Tom."

This time Halloran gave a real smile. "Me, too, Hollis. Save yours again, I mean."

———

Maggie welcomed them with open arms, big glasses of Jameson and Glenlivit, respectively, and a resounding lecture for Halloran. As they sat around the kitchen table, they filled her in on everything that had gone on that day, at which point she launched into lecture 2.0, this time with dire warnings of what she would do if he ever acted "so stupidly" again. Halloran took it meekly, aware that he might have gotten himself killed, if not for Claudia Benning, and feeling not a little guilt over what Wesley Benning had done.

"I was so wrong about everything," he said, as Maggie handed him a second Scotch. "It never occurred to me that this was something Wesley did without Claudia's knowing. If anything, I thought they might have collaborated with Carson Landers, as well as Joseph Feeney."

"Carson Landers?" Joplin said sharply. "The lawyer Carrie and I met at Houston's? What in the world made you suspect him to be involved?"

Halloran grimaced and took a sip of his drink. "He's been dogging me a little ever since Arliss' will went into probate. I felt as if he blamed me for it. As if he thought I should have prevented Arliss from cutting him out as trustee for the bequest to Emory. And then when we saw him and his son at Houston's that night, and he said his son was going to UGA instead of Emory, his alma mater, it crossed my mind that maybe Carson was in some financial trouble. That he might even have embezzled money from clients—maybe Emory, too—and was counting on the money he'd make as trustee to settle some accounts."

"Sons don't always do what their fathers want them to, Tom," said Maggie. "I hope you remember that when Tommy gets a little older."

"I'm sure you'll remind me, sweetie."

The doorbell rang before the retort could form on her lips. Maggie went to answer it, then ushered Ike Simmons into the kitchen. She sat and listened as they told Ike the same details they'd just finished telling her. Ike took notes, then offered his own information on the trip to Ridgeview.

"The psychiatrist totally stonewalled any interview with him, so we'd need to get a court order. But I'm not sure if it's even necessary, after what happened. He also said that Chandler hasn't left the premises since he voluntarily checked himself in in May. He gave up his cell phone then, and he hasn't had any visitors. I doubt if he even knows Libba is dead, much less anything about it."

"I may need to see him anyway," said Halloran. "I think I can get Libba's holographic will vacated, on the grounds that it was coerced, and no one outside the family needs to know that Chandler was her father. But as her closest biological relation, he has a right to know what's happened."

"Let me know if you decide to do that, okay?" said Simmons. "I'm still not sure how all this is going to shake out."

After telling Halloran a uniform would be there with his car within the hour, he and Joplin left. Despite how drained he felt, Halloran decided he needed to go to the hospital to touch base with Julie and, possibly, Claudia Benning. He had no idea what he would—or could—say to them, but he needed to make the effort. Even as he went over the terrible events of the afternoon with Simmons and Joplin and Maggie, his mind kept trying to figure out what he should have done, instead of confronting the Bennings. He'd told himself a dozen times that he'd been trying to protect Arliss Woodridge's family, but whatever his intentions had been, his actions had resulted in disaster. For Julie and Claudia Benning and, especially, for Wesley.

Half an hour later, they had taken Maggie's car and dropped the kids off at her parents' house. Once at Grady, it took a few phone calls to get permission for them to go up to the ICU waiting room. It was empty when they arrived, but a few minutes later, Julie, her face ravaged by tears, came out to see them. There was no hesitation as she reached out to hug both Hallorans, then began to sob again.

"Julie, I can't even begin to tell you how responsible I feel about what happened," Halloran began,

"No, Tom, I can't let you say that," she said fiercely, standing back and wiping her eyes with a wad of tissues. "My mother's been saying the same thing about herself, and I can't say she's entirely wrong about that. She's been the driving force behind all the animosity aimed at Libba since my grandfather met her, as well as the lawsuit. And it pushed my father to the brink. But what he did, including trying to kill himself, is his responsibility. Not yours, not even my mother's."

"Whatever you might say about her, Julie, she kept him from using the gun on me," said Halloran. "Try to remember that. In that moment, she had a choice, and she made the right one."

"Thank you for that. It might get me through this night. We just made the decision to… take Dad off life support. I need to get back in there."

"We'll be here," said Maggie, hugging her again.

Halloran did the same, and they watched as Julie Benning straightened her shoulders and walked back into the ICU to watch her father die.

———

The funeral for Wesley Benning was held the following Monday. It was a small, private affair, only a little larger than Libba's and by invitation only. Halloran was both surprised and touched that he and Maggie were included. Claudia even came up to him and hugged him, but seemed too overwhelmed to say anything. Despite everything she'd gone through, her face seemed almost peaceful, as if she'd finally let go of a terrible burden. One that might have been of her own making, but at least she'd put it down. Julie, he knew, was still just numb; it would take a long time for her to come to terms with her father's death, even though she had far fewer things to regret than her mother. Knowing she was in no shape to deal with Connie Sue's funeral, Halloran had arranged to reschedule it and assured her that he and Maggie would represent her at the ceremony.

Three days later, Halloran drove out to Ridgeview Institute. He had an order signed by the probate judge allowing him to see Chandler Woodridge, but he hoped he wouldn't have to use it. A meeting had been scheduled with Dr. Walter Langford, Chandler's psychiatrist, during which Halloran hoped to persuade the doctor that what he had to discuss with Chandler would be in his best interests, both legally and therapeutically.

Halloran turned off South Cobb Drive and drove onto the institute's property. He decided to take a quick tour that encompassed well-kept lawns, something called the Serenity Garden, and side streets that branched off into trails, a large swimming pool, tennis courts, and outside eating areas. All in all, it looked more like an aging resort than a facility that treated mental illnesses and all forms of substance abuse. He parked in front of the Admissions building, a contemporary, high-roofed, taupe-colored affair that Hollis Joplin would have hated. An elephant statue to the left of the walkway welcomed him. Inside was an enormous open area with orange walls and woodwork, furnished with orange furniture. Halloran wondered who had decided that orange was soothing to people in varying degrees of mental and pharmaceutical chaos.

He announced himself to one of two women who sat behind a long, low admissions desk. After waiting fifteen minutes, a tall man with hunched shoulders and gray glasses opened a door to the right and ushered him into a conference room down the hall.

"I'm Dr. Langford," he said, not offering his hand.

"Tom Halloran," he responded, offering his, which was taken reluctantly.

"As I told you over the phone, Mr. Halloran, I can't allow Mr. Woodridge's fragile mental state to be jeopardized. I agreed to see you because you have a court order, but our attorney has filed an injunction request, and I expect to hear from him within the hour."

"I understand your need to protect your patient, Doctor, and I don't want to jeopardize his recovery. But I think if you'll listen to what I have to say, you'll realize that my meeting with him could very well *help* him to recover."

Dr. Langford looked profoundly unmoved. "I doubt it," he said, "but I'm willing to listen."

Halloran took a deep breath, then began a narrative that began thirty years ago and moved into the recent past. Six months prior, to be exact. What he told the psychiatrist caused his eyes to widen as the expressions on his face reflected disbelief, disgust, and, finally, pity.

"You have proof of this?" he asked at last. "The news has been full of the family lawsuit, as well as Mrs. Woodridge's death. Mr. Benning's, too," he added. "All of which Chandler knows nothing about. He hasn't been able to earn any visiting privileges or even TV or newspaper privileges since he got here because of his unwillingness to work on his recovery. And even if he had, there's been nothing in the news about his...relationship to Libba Woodridge."

"I have proof of the facts in this case, to answer your question, and although I believe Chandler knows nothing about the most recent events you just mentioned, I'm convinced he *does* know Libba Cates Woodridge was his biological daughter. That knowledge, along with his father's death, is what caused his drug relapse and mental breakdown. And it may very well be what's keeping him from trying to get better. Sooner or later, he'll have to be released. Probably because his insurance company will deny further treatment. I think you'll have to agree that confronting Chandler with what I suspect happened, in a controlled, therapeutic environment, would be far better for him than his having to deal with it on his own. I would want you to sit in on my meeting with him, of course."

Dr. Langford seemed lost in thought for several minutes, then abruptly stood up. "I'm going to allow you to see him," he said. "But if I feel at any time that my patient is unable to handle what you say to him, I'll terminate the visit. Agreed?"

"Agreed," said Halloran.

He followed the psychiatrist into another conference room. At the time Arliss' will had been probated and Halloran had gathered the family together, Chandler Woodridge had been in the grip of his latest drug relapse, so he'd never actually met him. Halloran had seen pictures of him, but the man who sat at the end of the table looked nothing like them. He was still handsome, with the blond hair and blue eyes so prominent in the Woodridge family. But he'd put on a considerable amount of weight, probably due to antidepressants, as well as the fact that he wasn't using cocaine anymore. His face also had a haunted quality to it that didn't show in photographs. Or maybe it hadn't been there in the past.

Dr. Langford introduced him, then they each took a seat on either side of Chandler. He looked warily at Halloran, almost as if he expected a physical blow from him. Whatever he expected, it wasn't what Halloran delivered, and as the minutes went by and Halloran told the same story of love and abandonment, pain inflicted and received, and, most of all, guilt, that he'd told the psychiatrist a little while before, Chandler Woodridge's defenses fell away like ice falling from tree branches during a spring thaw.

Forty minutes later, Halloran walked out of the conference room. Chandler had gripped his hand before he got up from the table, his head still bowed, then Dr. Langford had nodded at Halloran, signaling that he could take care of things from then on. Suddenly aware of the time, he looked at his watch and realized he had just enough time to get to Grady before rush hour began.

CHAPTER FIFTY-FIVE

Hollis Joplin pressed his morphine-on-demand button and waited for the blessed relief that would flood through his pain-wracked body.

"Enjoy it while you can," said Carrie, sitting on the chair next to his bed. "They'll begin cutting back by the end of today."

"I know," he said, letting a resigned sigh escape. "Dr. Mallory already told me that this morning." The colostomy reversal surgery had just been done the previous morning, but they'd already hauled him out of bed twice that day, with threats of returning after dinner. "I don't understand. After my last surgery, back in May, I didn't get out of bed for days, and the morphine flowed like honey."

"You almost died from peritonitis, Hollis, and you were in a coma for ten days, remember? Plus, they had to take out a good bit of your intestines and then create a stoma for the colostomy. This was a far less invasive procedure, even though Dr. Mallory couldn't do it laparoscopically. But the good news is that it was very successful. You'll probably be able to have a bowel movement by tomorrow."

Joplin closed his eyes and sighed again. "I wish I had a girlfriend who wasn't a doctor and would just hold my hand and tell me everything is going to be alright. Could we please not talk about bowel movements right now?"

"Of course," said Carrie, patting his hand. "And everything *is* going to be alright."

Joplin was spared from responding by a knock at the door.

"Come in," said Carrie.

Tom Halloran entered the room carrying a plant with a yellow bow tied around it. "Am I interrupting anything?" he asked.

"Not a bit," Carrie said, jumping up from her seat. "Sit here, Tom. I think Hollis needs a break from me, and I need to go make some phone calls."

"Are you sure? I don't want to run you out of here."

"She's sure," said Joplin. "I'm being cranky."

Carrie smiled and leaned down to kiss his forehead. "I'll be back soon."

"I brought you a plant," Halloran said awkwardly, then deposited it on a table opposite the bed.

"Thanks. What kind is it?

Halloran looked blank, then read something that was on a plastic holder nestled in the leaves. "It's a spathiphyllum lily, whatever the hell that is. Maggie's the one who knows about plants."

"Is it poisonous to cats?"

"I have no idea, although I doubt anything could poison a cat who eats fried chicken and tacos. Maggie likes Quincy, but I think she's a little relieved that Carrie is living with you and can take care of him. How's that going by the way? I hear you guys are moving to a loft up the street."

"First of next month," said Joplin.

"Are you sure you'll be up to going through a move by then?"

"Not much to it, really. Carrie's already arranged to have all her stuff packed up, moved, and unpacked. A Goodwill truck is set to pick up mine. But I do get to take most of my clothes and Quincy, of course."

Halloran nodded solemnly and sat down. "Have you heard that Jonathan Demarest has been released?" he asked.

"Simmons called this morning. His lawyer's been raising a ruckus since Feeney was killed, and Wesley Benning's death seemed to tie things up with a pretty ribbon. The FBI agents still think he might have been involved in the serial killings in some way—or at least known what was going on—but there's not enough evidence to support that, so the charges have been dropped."

"I went to see Chandler Woodridge today," said Halloran.

"No kidding! The psychiatrist actually let you see him?"

"Yes, after I told him what I was going to say to Chandler and why I thought it might help him."

"And did it?"

"Yes, I think it did, although he was pretty devastated about Libba's death. Wesley's, too. And he still had a lot of guilt about Belinda Feeney, Libba's birth mother. He never knew she was pregnant, even though I suspect she tried to get in touch with him. But that was during a time that both of them were heavy users, and Chandler was in and out of rehab."

"You said 'still had a lot of guilt.' Do you mean he knew Libba was his daughter before today?"

Halloran nodded. "He admitted it to me, when I said I believed Joseph Feeney had gone to him first with Libba's birth certificate. Before he approached Wesley Benning."

"But how did you know?"

"I kept going over the sequence of events. Feeney got hold of the adoption records around the time Arliss and Libba got engaged, then managed to get his landscape company hired to take care of the house on Blackland when they got married. I think he took a while to find out as much as he could about them and the entire Woodridge family. He made it a point to show up at the house to check on things and probably got to know Rosa. Or maybe he would ask Jorge questions about what they heard or saw when they worked there. Just gossip, I imagine he framed it. Anyway, after a few months, he decided to play his ace in the hole. He didn't know Chandler had gone through his trust fund and was being supported by Arliss, who kept tight control over him. I think Feeney approached Chandler, thinking he could easily blackmail him or sell the proof of his paternity to hang over his father's head. Instead, Chandler was horrified. He'd been sober and clean for several months at the time, and all he could think about was that his father had married his own granddaughter. *His* biological daughter."

"Yeah, I can see where that might have messed with his mind," Joplin said.

"Yes, but it was what happened next that *really* messed with his mind."

"He told his father."

Halloran nodded grimly. "He told me that Arliss couldn't talk after he finished telling him. Didn't respond when he begged him to forgive him. Wouldn't let him near him when he tried to reach out to him. He said his father just got up and walked to the door and left. The next morning, he found out that Arliss had suffered a massive heart attack and died."

Neither one of them said anything for a long time. Joplin pushed his morphine button, not caring whether it would shorten the time he'd be allowed to keep it. He realized the irony, given what he was sure had happened next in Chandler's pitiful story. "So Chandler blamed himself and went on his biggest binge ever. I'm surprised he didn't just try to kill himself."

"He did," said Halloran. "He took an overdose of Xanax. A friend found him and called 911, and he was taken to Emory. Julie was called, and she got him admitted again to Ridgeview, once they determined that the insurance policy Arliss had provided would pay for an extended stay. And he's been there ever since."

"Jesus," said Joplin. "Does Julie know that's what caused her grandfather's heart attack?"

"No, and I doubt it would make any difference."

"What do you mean?"

"Julie knows that I intend to get the court to throw out Libba's holographic will. In my opinion, it was made under duress and because of Wesley Benning's coercion. She's okay with that, but she wants to restructure the money left to her by Arliss. And by Libba's original will. Essentially, she wants to pay off her parents' debts and draw up trust funds for both her mother and her uncle, for which I'll be trustee. She'll also provide generous annuities for her great-aunts. She wants an end to all the conflict and strife in her family over money. And I think she'll not only understand why Chandler went to his father, but agree with his reasons, even though the outcome was tragic."

"You're a better man than I am, Tom," said Joplin, shaking his head.

Halloran smiled. "What makes you say that?"

"I guess I've just been exposed to more of the underbelly of society than you have. Where you see some kind of Greek tragedy, I see an addict who abandoned a woman he got pregnant and a daughter he probably never wanted to know. I see another addict who let her children almost starve because of her habit and then left them motherless and vulnerable. Then there's the beauty queen wannabe who adopted a little girl to exploit and ignored another abandoned child. Not to mention a seventy-five-year old man who married a woman young enough to be his granddaughter, even if he didn't know she actually *was* his granddaughter. And don't forget the son-in-law who conspired with the half-brother, who was also a serial killer, to blackmail and extort the young, trophy wife. And who's to say Chandler talked to his father because he wanted to warn him that he was in an incestuous relationship? Maybe Chandler was engaging in a little blackmail himself."

Halloran looked surprised at first, then amused. "Is that what you're gut's telling you, Hollis?"

"My gut is telling me that if I hear any more about the Woodridge family, I'll need a lot more morphine."

Luckily, the door opened, and Sarah Petersen burst in, holding a vase of flowers and what looked to be some kind of photo album. Carrie followed her in, a big grin on her face.

"I didn't forget, Hollis," his boss said, coming over to his bed. She set the vase of flowers on the table that held the others and maneuvered Halloran out of the way. "I promised Hollis I would show this to him once the Woodridge case was closed. Have you ever been to a Gay Pride parade?"

For once, Tom Halloran seemed to be speechless. Joplin chuckled, then allowed himself to drift off as Sarah began to flip through the pages of her album.

ACKNOWLEDGEMENTS

First and foremost, I'd like to thank my manuscript readers, whose brutal honesty and much-appreciated support have helped to make this a better book: Sue Crawford, Tom and Nicole Armentrout, Bill Donovan, and Kristina Doss. I couldn't have done it without you. I also hope you'll stay with me for the next installment in the Joplin/Halloran series, *The Devil's Bidding*.

The many book clubs who read *Enough Rope* and invited me to be their guest author both encouraged me to keep writing and impressed me with their keen insights and suggestions for other books. The food and wine were always great, too.

My sister, Terry Leite Chandler, gave me a suggestion for a plotline for Carrie which I couldn't use in *Enough Rope*. I hope she likes what I did with it in this book.

Thanks to John Martucci of Martucci Design for creating the fantastic book cover. I think Jonathan Demarest would approve.

Once again, Morgana Gallaway has done a fabulous job in creating the print and Kindle versions of this book. Thanks for putting up with my nit-picking ways.

Melle NeSmith, the coroner for Davis County in Georgia, let me pester him about the coroner system as well as what might have happened if he'd come across Connie Sue Cates' body.

Finally, my heartfelt gratitude to those of you reading this book. If you enjoyed it, I hope you'll tell your friends and consider writing a review on Amazon. I'd also love to hear from you, and I promise to respond to any questions, suggestions, or constructive criticism. You can contact me at **www.pldoss.com**.

Please read on for an excerpt from the next Joplin/Halloran Mystery by P. L. Doss

THE DEVIL'S BIDDING

PROLOGUE

Cautiously, the cat crept out from under the bed. It had been a long time since the frightening sounds that had caused her to hide had stopped, but she was still wary. It was dark now, the pale light from the street showing only shadows, but that was no problem for her. She padded out into the hall, head turning, eyes darting, but saw no one. The kitchen was also dark, but she saw a shape on the floor, and, as she got closer, breathed in a scent that was familiar and comforting.

The cat began to head-bump the figure, but there was no response. No petting of her head or tickling behind her ear. She tried again, and when nothing happened, moved on to the utility room where her litter box and food were kept. There was only dry food for her, a disappointment, but she was hungry and ate most of it.

After using the litter box, she returned to the figure on the floor. More head-butting still brought no response, so she curled up and put her head on her owner's back, then closed her eyes. The usual warmth she expected wasn't there, but it didn't occur to her to wonder why.

CHAPTER ONE

The first thing Hollis Joplin did when he got to the Milton County Medical Examiner's Office that morning, after Sherika had handed him a manila envelope she said Fed Ex had delivered, was head to the break room for coffee. He'd shared a cup with Carrie earlier, but it hadn't been quite enough caffeine after a late, somewhat booze-filled Friday evening at Davio's. Carrie had then gone back to bed. As an assistant ME, she had weekend duty just once a month, but Joplin worked rotating shifts with the other death investigators, and he was on for Saturday.

Making a mental note to turn down a second one of Gerry's potent dirty Martinis next time, he shoved the envelope under his arm and grabbed a mug from the counter. He filled it from the large urn next to the microwave, hoping Sarah Petersen, his boss, had been the one to make the coffee that morning. She never seemed to make it either too weak or too strong, which was yet another reason she was held in high esteem by all the investigators. The pathologists, too, for that matter. Since becoming Chief Investigator well over a year ago, she'd turned the unit into a well-oiled machine, leading by example whenever possible. Which meant getting to the office before anyone else and making sure she knew what the people under her needed to do their jobs.

Like decent coffee.

Joplin had been summoned to a vehicular homicide on 400 before he left the condominium he shared with Carrie, so it was after nine-thirty by the time he got to his cubicle. He'd intended to get started on his report of the scene, but decided to open the envelope first. Setting his mug on the desk, he sat down and slit the flap with a pen knife he kept in a side drawer. Inside were several eight-by-ten photographs.

The first picture was of a front door, black, with two potted plants on either side. The next showed a narrow entry hall that held only a rug and a chest of some kind, with a still-life painting of some pears over it. The third picture was of a kitchen. The warm yellow walls held a pot rack and several prints of various herbs; stainless appliances and gray granite countertops made a nice contrast to them. Joplin was beginning to wonder if some realtor had heard that he and Carrie thinking of buying a house after their upcoming wedding, when he was stopped short by the next photo.

It was of a woman lying face-down on the kitchen floor. Her head was turned to the side, but her long brown hair covered her face. She was wearing jeans and a black, fitted jacket, but her feet were bare. Joplin moved quickly to the next photo, which showed the woman from a different angle. Whoever had taken it had stood or knelt near her head this time. Two more photos were close-ups of the woman's hands, which were on either side of her, palms down, as if she'd fallen and had tried to get up. There was a wide silver ring on the middle finger of her right hand and a diamond solitaire ring on the third finger of her left hand. The nails were pink and looked professionally manicured.

He was certain she was dead.

Sarah Petersen looked up from her computer to see Hollis Joplin standing in the doorway. His large head, thick blond hair looking a little unkempt, was cocked to one side, and his green eyes were definitely blood-shot.

"Can I talk to you?"

"Sure. What's up?"

He placed some photos on her desk and nodded toward them. "I'd like you to take a look at these."

She gave him a quick glance, eyebrows raised, then picked them up.

Shuffling through them, Sarah frowned when she got to the fifth picture. "You take these?" she asked, looking up at him.

"No. According to Sherika, FedEx delivered them. I've never seen them before. But my name is on the envelope."

"Obviously, it's a crime scene, even though there aren't any labels or case numbers on the backs of the photos. The question is: whose? You didn't take these, but somebody did."

"Right. I kept the envelope they came in, but it didn't tell me much. It was labeled 'Overnight Delivery', sent on November 8, 2013, but the ink on the sender's label was smeared, making it illegible."

"You think that might have been deliberate?"

"Sure seems like it."

The phone on Petersen's desk rang, cutting off further speculation. She was silent as she listened, but grabbed a pen and wrote something down. "We'll get on it," she said, then clicked off and handed Joplin the page from her note pad. "We'll have to figure this out later, Hollis. There's a body at that address that's more important right now. Why don't you leave these with me," she added, gesturing toward the photos.

"Fine with me. Maybe Sherika knows a little more about who sent them."

"If she doesn't, nobody does," Petersen said. Their receptionist had her finger on every pulse in the ME's office.

The living ones, anyway.

The address was in Brookhaven, which straddled both Dekalb and Milton counties. More specifically, it was in Historic Brookhaven, on West Brookhaven Drive. Joplin, an architecture buff, knew that Salson Stovall, along with Solomon Goodwin, had been responsible for much of the development there, inspiring wealthy Atlantans to build summer homes in the area in the late nineteenth century, much like their Buckhead neighbors.

But it wasn't an actual neighborhood until 1911, when several investors bought a tract of land they named "Brookhaven Estates" and hired Herbert Barker, a New Jersey golf pro, to design a golf course for it. The area then became the first community in Georgia to be created around a golf course.

Something that couldn't be said about Ansley and Druid Hills, which seemed to please the Historic Brookhavenites, from what Joplin could tell. And they totally separated themselves from the newly-created city of Brookhaven, which included North Brookhaven and Town Brookhaven, and was in less-wealthy Dekalb County.

He turned left off Peachtree, onto Peachtree-Dunwoody, then took Winall Down over to West Brookhaven Drive. The trees in the beautifully-kept yards that surrounded the Capital City Club were still ablaze with color, due to an extended Indian summer that year. Joplin turned left and drove slowly, looking for 1452. It was directly across from the clubhouse, but he was disappointed to see that it obviously wasn't one of the houses built by Hal Hentz or Neel Reid or even Preston Stevens, who had designed the clubhouse; he was pretty familiar with the styles of the houses they'd created. But it wasn't new, by any means; probably built in the early teens of the twentieth century, Joplin decided. Unfortunately, whatever style it had started out with, it hadn't retained it, and seemed to be comprised of a series of lateral additions made over the years.

Sarah had told him that the body wasn't actually in the house itself. It was in a carriage house at the back of the property. Joplin drove down the driveway to the right of the house and parked behind a gray Nissan sedan that he knew belonged to Ike Simmons, a senior detective with the Atlanta Homicide Unit. They had been partners for seven years before he'd left to join the Milton County ME's office. They'd also been best friends. Still were, for that matter.

He grabbed his bag and got out of the car, then walked around the other cars, which included an APD car and a blue Audi, to reach the front door of the carriage house. As it came into view, he began to walk more slowly, then stopped altogether. The door was black, with two potted plants on either side. To anyone else, this would have seemed like mere coincidence, but Hollis Joplin had an eidetic memory, and his mind retained images of anything he'd ever seen, often in three dimensions. It helped him in his work as the "eyes and ears" of the forensic pathologists who would perform autopsies on the bodies he saw at deaths scenes. But it had wreaked havoc on his ability to sleep at night since his teenage years, as well as on his relationships.

So Joplin knew exactly what he would find behind the black door with the plants on either side.